TALES OF HORROR

TALES OF HORROR

Terrifying Stories to Keep You Awake Past Midnight

EDITED AND WITH AN INTRODUCTION BY

BILL BOWERS

LYONS
PRESS

Essex, Connecticut

An imprint of Globe Pequot, the trade division of The Rowman & Littlefield Publishing Group, Inc.
4501 Forbes Blvd., Ste. 200
Lanham, MD 20706
www.rowman.com
Distributed by NATIONAL BOOK NETWORK

British Library Cataloguing in Publication Information available

Library of Congress Cataloging-in-Publication Data
Names: Bowers, Bill, 1957- editor.
Title: Tales of horror : terrifying stories to keep you awake past midnight / edited and with an introduction by Bill Bowers.
Description: Essex, Connecticut : Lyons Press, 2024. | Summary: "A classic collection of horror tales by masters of the genre!"-- Provided by publisher.
Identifiers: LCCN 2023042905 (print) | LCCN 2023042906 (ebook) | ISBN 9781493077502 (trade paperback) | ISBN 9781493077519 (epub)
Subjects: LCSH: Horror tales. | LCGFT: Short stories. | Horror fiction.
Classification: LCC PN6071.H727 T35 2024 (print) | LCC PN6071.H727 (ebook) | DDC 808.83/8738--dc23/eng/20230919
LC record available at https://lccn.loc.gov/2023042905
LC ebook record available at https://lccn.loc.gov/2023042906

For Eileen (1959–2023), without whom none of this would have been possible.

CONTENTS

CONTENTS

CONTENTS

Acknowledgments

No book is ever the work of a single person, no matter whose name appears on the cover. This volume is no exception. My heartfelt thanks:

To Eileen (1959–2023).

To Mom and Dad, who encouraged my love of reading.

To Gene Brissie, editorial director at Lyons Press, who saw the possibilities.

To former colleagues, friends, and fellow authors and editors Tom McCarthy and Jay Cassell, who encouraged a neophyte and helped him succeed.

And last but not least to Nick Lyons, founder of Lyons Press, who mentored me and changed my life.

INTRODUCTION

. . . beings more awful than the delirium of nightmare could ever have conceived.
—From "The Horror-Horn" by E. F. Benson

I'VE LOVED READING HORROR STORIES (AND GHOST STORIES AND MYS-teries) since childhood. At one point I borrowed *The Complete Works of Poe* from our hometown public library. My mother found this a bit unsettling. "But Poe's stories are so gruesome!" she told my father, the English teacher.

"Darling," he said calmly. "You're right, but I can think of worse things he could be doing than reading the works of a renowned author and pillar of American Romanticism."

So naturally I was thrilled when Lyons Press green-lit the book you're holding now. Here I've tried to assemble a collection of both classic stories that deserve to be celebrated again and others that are little known but deserve recognition from modern readers.

Some of the stories here have practically defined the horror genre, such as "The Monkey's Paw" by W. W. Jacobs, one of the most frequently anthologized English-language stories of all time. For the same reason, I've included not one but two stories by the aforementioned Edgar Allan Poe: "The Facts in the Case of M. Valdemar" and "The Cask of Amontillado."

This volume includes some rarely seen and anthologized stories, though these are no less worthy for having been so overlooked.

But I've also included some unexpected but certainly worthy tales, including "The Story of the Brazilian Cat" and "The Ring of Thoth" by Sir Arthur Conan Doyle. Doyle, of course, is best known for creating Sherlock Holmes, the world's most celebrated fictional detective and the star of countless films and television shows. But Sherlock's celebrity has overshadowed his creator's other works. Similarly, we have "The Wife of the Kenite" by Agatha Christie. Her novels and stories featuring Hercule Poirot and Miss Jane Marple are among the best-known murder mysteries in the world. (She's the best-selling fiction author of all time. Her novels have sold two *billion* copies.) This was Dame Agatha's very first published story, appearing years before her more famous works.

In the same vein is "The Most Dangerous Game" by Richard Connell, who wrote many stories, novels, and screenplays, though this may be his best-known work. Some readers may feel this is not exactly a "horror story," but I beg to differ: consider the utterly evil, racist mind of the villain of the piece.

I did find earlier English translations of the French body parts stories "The Flayed Hand" by Guy de Maupassant and "The Mummy's Foot" by Théophile Gautier—but in my opinion these left much to be desired. In fairness to the original (now anonymous) translators, translating anything from one language to another—while attempting to retain as much of the imagery and "sound" of the original as possible—is extremely challenging. But Gautier's story proved especially so. He was a masterful poet as well as a prose author, and his story has a hauntingly lyrical, poetic quality in French that is exceedingly difficult (for me, at least) to render in English. Here's hoping my effort in this regard will be deemed adequate and will not have M. Gautier spinning in his grave.

I've decided to present "The Canal" by Everil Worrell as it originally appeared in *Weird Tales* in 1927. The version seen here retains the author's original language, themes, conclusion, and length.

Readers today will likely notice spellings, phraseology, and punctuation in some of these stories that seem odd, even jarring, to modern eyes. But this is to be expected—language is a living, breathing entity, constantly evolving and changing. So I've kept the stories here as they were originally published.

It's my hope that you will enjoy perusing these ghastly but fascinating tales as much as I have enjoyed collecting them and that they will provide you with many hours of enjoyable reading.

The hour grows late. Did you hear that strange noise just now, out in the darkness?

Bill Bowers
Somewhere in rural New England

The Damned Thing

By Ambrose Bierce

I

ONE DOES NOT ALWAYS EAT WHAT IS ON THE TABLE

By the light of a tallow candle, which had been placed on one end of a rough table, a man was reading something written in a book. It was an old account book, greatly worn; and the writing was not, apparently, very legible, for the man sometimes held the page close to the flame of the candle to get a stronger light upon it. The shadow of the book would then throw into obscurity a half of the room, darkening a number of faces and figures; for besides the reader, eight other men were present. Seven of them sat against the rough log walls, silent and motionless, and, the room being small, not very far from the table. By extending an arm any one of them could have touched the eighth man, who lay on the table, face upward, partly covered by a sheet, his arms at his sides. He was dead.

The man with the book was not reading aloud, and no one spoke; all seemed to be waiting for something to occur; the dead man only was without expectation. From the blank darkness outside came in, through the aperture that served for a window, all the ever unfamiliar noises of night in the wilderness—the long, nameless note of a distant coyote; the stilly pulsing thrill of tireless insects in trees; strange cries of night birds, so different from those of the birds of day; the drone of great blundering beetles, and all that mysterious chorus of small sounds that seem always to have been but half heard when they have suddenly ceased, as if conscious of an indiscretion. But nothing of all this was noted in that company; its members were not overmuch addicted to idle interest in matters of no practical importance; that was obvious in every line of their rugged faces—obvious even in the dim light of the single candle. They were evidently men of the vicinity—farmers and woodsmen.

The person reading was a trifle different; one would have said of him that he was of the world, worldly, albeit there was that in his attire which attested a certain fellowship with the organisms of his environment. His coat would hardly have passed muster in San Francisco: his footgear was not of urban origin, and the hat that lay by him on the floor (he was the only one uncovered) was such that if one had considered it as an article of mere personal adornment he would have missed its meaning. In countenance the man was rather prepossessing, with just a hint of sternness; though that he may have assumed or cultivated, as appropriate to one in authority. For he was a coroner. It was by virtue of his office that he had possession of the book in which he was reading; it had been found among the dead man's effects—in his cabin, where the inquest was now taking place.

When the coroner had finished reading he put the book into his breast pocket. At that moment the door was pushed open and a young man entered. He, clearly, was not of mountain birth and breeding: he was clad as those who dwell in cities. His clothing was dusty, however, as from travel. He had, in fact, been riding hard to attend the inquest.

The coroner nodded; no one else greeted him.

"We have waited for you," said the coroner. "It is necessary to have done with this business to-night."

The young man smiled. "I am sorry to have kept you," he said. "I went away, not to evade your summons, but to post to my newspaper an account of what I suppose I am called back to relate."

The coroner smiled.

"The account that you posted to your newspaper," he said, "differs probably from that which you will give here under oath."

"That," replied the other, rather hotly and with a visible flush, "is as you choose. I used manifold paper and have a copy of what I sent. It was not written as news, for it is incredible, but as fiction. It may go as a part of my testimony under oath."

"But you say it is incredible."

"That is nothing to you, sir, if I also swear that it is true."

The coroner was apparently not greatly affected by the young man's manifest resentment. He was silent for some moments, his eyes upon the floor. The men about the sides of the cabin talked in whispers, but seldom withdrew their gaze from the face of the corpse. Presently the coroner lifted his eyes and said: "We will resume the inquest."

The men removed their hats. The witness was sworn.

"What is your name?" the coroner asked.

"William Harker."

"Age?"

"Twenty-seven."

"You knew the deceased, Hugh Morgan?"

"Yes."

"You were with him when he died?"

"Near him."

"How did that happen—your presence, I mean?"

"I was visiting him at this place to shoot and fish. A part of my purpose, however, was to study him, and his odd, solitary way of life. He seemed a good model for a character in fiction. I sometimes write stories."

"I sometimes read them."

"Thank you."

"Stories in general—not yours."

Some of the jurors laughed. Against a sombre background humor shows high lights. Soldiers in the intervals of battle laugh easily, and a jest in the death chamber conquers by surprise.

"Relate the circumstances of this man's death," said the coroner. "You may use any notes or memoranda that you please."

The witness understood. Pulling a manuscript from his breast pocket he held it near the candle, and turning the leaves until he found the passage that he wanted, began to read.

I

II
WHAT MAY HAPPEN IN A FIELD OF WILD OATS

" . . . The sun had hardly risen when we left the house. We were looking for quail, each with a shotgun, but we had only one dog. Morgan said that our best ground was beyond a certain ridge that he pointed out, and we crossed it by a trail through the *chaparral*. On the other side was comparatively level ground, thickly covered with wild oats. As we emerged from the *chaparral*, Morgan was but a few yards in advance. Suddenly, we heard, at a little distance to our right, and partly in front, a noise as of some animal thrashing about in the bushes, which we could see were violently agitated.

"'We've started a deer,' I said. 'I wish we had brought a rifle.'

"Morgan, who had stopped and was intently watching the agitated *chaparral*, said nothing, but had cocked both barrels of his gun, and was holding it in readiness to aim. I thought him a trifle excited, which surprised me, for he had a reputation for exceptional coolness, even in moments of sudden and imminent peril.

"'O, come!' I said. 'You are not going to fill up a deer with quail-shot, are you?'

"Still he did not reply; but, catching a sight of his face as he turned it slightly toward me, I was struck by the pallor of it. Then I understood that we had serious business on hand, and my first conjecture was that we had 'jumped' a grizzly. I advanced to Morgan's side, cocking my piece as I moved.

"The bushes were now quiet, and the sounds had ceased, but Morgan was as attentive to the place as before.

"'What is it? What the devil is it?' I asked.

"'That Damned Thing!' he replied, without turning his head. His voice was husky and unnatural. He trembled visibly.

"I was about to speak further, when I observed the wild oats near the place of the disturbance moving in the most inexplicable way. I can hardly describe it. It seemed as if stirred by a streak of wind, which not only bent it, but pressed it down—crushed it so that it did not rise, and this movement was slowly prolonging itself directly toward us.

4

"Nothing that I had ever seen had affected me so strangely as this unfamiliar and unaccountable phenomenon, yet I am unable to recall any sense of fear. I remember—and tell it here because, singularly enough, I recollected it then—that once, in looking carelessly out of an open window, I momentarily mistook a small tree close at hand for one of a group of larger trees at a little distance away. It looked the same size as the others, but, being more distinctly and sharply defined in mass and detail, seemed out of harmony with them. It was a mere falsification of the law of aerial perspective, but it startled, almost terrified me. We so rely upon the orderly operation of familiar natural laws that any seeming suspension of them is noted as a menace to our safety, a warning of unthinkable calamity. So now the apparently causeless movement of the herbage, and the slow, undeviating approach of the line of disturbance were distinctly disquieting. My companion appeared actually frightened, and I could hardly credit my senses when I saw him suddenly throw his gun to his shoulders and fire both barrels at the agitated grass! Before the smoke of the discharge had cleared away I heard a loud savage cry—a scream like that of a wild animal—and, flinging his gun upon the ground, Morgan sprang away and ran swiftly from the spot. At the same instant I was thrown violently to the ground by the impact of something unseen in the smoke—some soft, heavy substance that seemed thrown against me with great force.

"Before I could get upon my feet and recover my gun, which seemed to have been struck from my hands, I heard Morgan crying out as if in mortal agony, and mingling with his cries were such hoarse savage sounds as one hears from fighting dogs. Inexpressibly terrified, I struggled to my feet and looked in the direction of Morgan's retreat; and may heaven in mercy spare me from another sight like that! At a distance of less than thirty yards was my friend, down upon one knee, his head thrown back at a frightful angle, hatless, his long hair in disorder and his whole body in violent movement from side to side, backward and forward. His right arm was lifted and seemed to lack the hand—at least, I could see none. The other arm was invisible. At times, as my memory now reports this extraordinary scene, I could discern but a part of his body; it was as if he had been partly blotted out—I can not otherwise express it—then a shifting of his position would bring it all into view again.

"All this must have occurred within a few seconds, yet in that time Morgan assumed all the postures of a determined wrestler vanquished by superior weight and strength. I saw nothing but him, and him not always distinctly. During the entire incident his shouts and curses were heard, as if through an enveloping uproar of such sounds of rage and fury as I had never heard from the throat of man or brute!

"For a moment only I stood irresolute, then, throwing down my gun, I ran forward to my friend's assistance. I had a vague belief that he was suffering from a fit or some form of convulsion. Before I could reach his side he was down and quiet. All sounds had ceased, but, with a feeling of such terror as even these awful events had not inspired, I now saw the same mysterious movement of the wild oats prolonging itself from the trampled area about the prostrate man toward the edge of a wood. It was only when it had reached the wood that I was able to withdraw my eyes and look at my companion. He was dead."

III

A Man Though Naked May Be in Rags

The coroner rose from his seat and stood beside the dead man. Lifting an edge of the sheet he pulled it away, exposing the entire body, altogether naked and showing in the candle light a clay-like yellow. It had, however, broad maculations of bluish-black, obviously caused by extravasated blood from contusions. The chest and sides looked as if they had been beaten with a bludgeon. There were dreadful lacerations; the skin was torn in strips and shreds.

The coroner moved round to the end of the table and undid a silk handkerchief, which had been passed under the chin and knotted on the top of the head. When the handkerchief was drawn away it exposed what had been the throat. Some of the jurors who had risen to get a better view repented their curiosity, and turned away their faces. Witness Harker went to the open window and leaned out across the sill, faint and sick. Dropping the handkerchief upon the dead man's neck, the coroner stepped to an angle of the room, and from a pile of clothing produced one garment after another, each of which he held up a moment for inspection. All were torn, and stiff with blood. The jurors did not make a closer inspection. They seemed rather uninterested. They had, in truth, seen all this before; the only thing that was new to them being Harker's testimony.

"Gentlemen," the coroner said, "we have no more evidence, I think. Your duty has been already explained to you; if there is nothing you wish to ask you may go outside and consider your verdict."

The foreman rose—a tall, bearded man of sixty, coarsely clad.

"I should like to ask one question, Mr. Coroner," he said. "What asylum did this yer last witness escape from?"

"Mr. Harker," said the coroner, gravely and tranquilly, "from what asylum did you last escape?"

Harker flushed crimson again, but said nothing, and the seven jurors rose and solemnly filed out of the cabin.

"If you have done insulting me, sir," said Harker, as soon as he and the officer were left alone with the dead man, "I suppose I am at liberty to go?"

"Yes."

Harker started to leave, but paused, with his hand on the door latch. The habit of his profession was strong in him—stronger than his sense of personal dignity. He turned about and said:

"The book that you have there—I recognize it as Morgan's diary. You seemed greatly interested in it; you read in it while I was testifying. May I see it? The public would like—"

"The book will cut no figure in this matter," replied the official, slipping it into his coat pocket; "all the entries in it were made before the writer's death."

As Harker passed out of the house the jury reentered and stood about the table on which the now covered corpse showed under the sheet with sharp definition. The foreman seated himself near the candle, produced from his breast pocket a pencil and scrap of paper, and wrote rather laboriously the following verdict, which with various degrees of effort all signed:

"We, the jury, do find that the remains come to their death at the hands of a mountain lion, but some of us thinks, all the same, they had fits."

IV

An Explanation from the Tomb

In the diary of the late Hugh Morgan are certain interesting entries having, possibly, a scientific value as suggestions. At the inquest upon his body the book was not put in evidence; possibly the coroner thought it not worth while to confuse the jury. The date of the first of the entries mentioned cannot be ascertained; the upper part of the leaf is torn away; the part of the entry remaining is as follows:

" . . . would run in a half circle, keeping his head turned always toward the centre and again he would stand still, barking furiously. At last he ran away into the brush as fast as he could go. I thought at first that he had gone mad, but on returning to the house found no other alteration in his manner than what was obviously due to fear of punishment.

"Can a dog see with his nose? Do odors impress some olfactory centre with images of the thing emitting them? . . .

"Sept. 2.—Looking at the stars last night as they rose above the crest of the ridge east of the house, I observed them successively disappear—from left to right. Each was eclipsed but an instant, and only a few at the same time, but along the entire length of the ridge all that were within a degree or two of the crest were blotted out. It was as if something had passed along between me and them; but I could not see it, and the stars were not thick enough to define its outline. Ugh! I don't like this. . . . "

Several weeks' entries are missing, three leaves being torn from the book.

"Sept. 27.—It has been about here again—I find evidences of its presence every day. I watched again all of last night in the same cover, gun in hand, double-charged with buckshot. In the morning the fresh footprints were there, as before. Yet I would have sworn that I did not sleep—indeed, I hardly sleep at all. It is terrible, insupportable! If these amazing experiences are real I shall go mad; if they are fanciful I am mad already.

"Oct. 3.—I shall not go—it shall not drive me away. No, this is *my* house, my land. God hates a coward. . . .

"Oct. 5.—I can stand it no longer; I have invited Harker to pass a few weeks with me—he has a level head. I can judge from his manner if he thinks me mad.

"Oct. 7.—I have the solution of the problem; it came to me last night—suddenly, as by revelation. How simple—how terribly simple!

"There are sounds that we cannot hear. At either end of the scale are notes that stir no chord of that imperfect instrument, the human ear. They are too high or too grave. I have observed a flock of blackbirds occupying an entire treetop—the tops of several trees—and all in full song. Suddenly—in a moment—at absolutely the same instant—all spring into the air and fly away. How? They could not all see one another—whole treetops intervened. At no point could a leader have been visible to all. There must have been a signal of warning or command, high and shrill above the din, but by me unheard. I have observed, too, the same simultaneous flight when all were silent, among not only blackbirds, but other birds—quail, for example, widely separated by bushes—even on opposite sides of a hill.

"It is known to seamen that a school of whales basking or sporting on the surface of the ocean, miles apart, with the convexity of the earth between them, will sometimes dive at the same instant—all gone out of sight in a moment. The signal has been sounded—too grave for the ear of the sailor at the masthead and his comrades on the deck—who nevertheless feel its vibrations in the ship as the stones of a cathedral are stirred by the bass of the organ.

"As with sounds, so with colors. At each end of the solar spectrum the chemist can detect the presence of what are known as 'actinic' rays. They represent colors—integral colors in the composition of light—which we are unable to discern. The human eye is an imperfect instrument; its range is but a few octaves of the real 'chromatic scale.' I am not mad; there are colors that we can not see.

"And, God help me! the Damned Thing is of such a color!"

The Mummy's Foot

By Théophile Gautier

A new translation from the French by Bill Bowers.

I had sauntered idly into the shop of one of those dealers in old curiosities—"bric-à-brac" as they say in that Parisian *argot* that's so completely unintelligible elsewhere in France.

You have no doubt often browsed through the windows of some of these shops, which have become so numerous since it became so fashionable to buy antique furniture, that the humblest stockbroker feels obliged to have a room furnished in medieval style.

There's always something that belongs alike to the shop of the dealer in old ironwork, the upholsterer's warehouse, the alchemist's laboratory, and the painter's studio; in all these mysterious recesses, where only a discreet half-light filters through the shutters, the most obviously antique thing is the dust; the spider webs are more genuine than the laces, and the old pear-wood furniture is more modern than the mahogany that arrived from America just yesterday.

My bric-à-brac dealer's shop was a veritable Capernaum; all centuries and all countries seemed to have met there; an Etruscan terra cotta lamp stood upon a Boulle cabinet, with ebony panels decorated with simple filaments of inlaid copper; a duchess daybed from the reign of

Louis XV stretched her graceful feet nonchalantly under a massive Louis XIII table with heavy spirals of oaken legs, and carvings of intermingled flowers and chimeras.

The belted cuirass of a damasked suit of armor from Milan gleamed in a corner. The shelves and floor were littered with biscuit porcelain cupids and nymphs, Chinese porcelain figurines, conical vases of celadon crackled green enamel, cups from Saxony and old Sèvres weighed down the shelves and the nooks.

The denticulated shelves of sideboards held huge gleaming Japanese plaques, with red and blue designs outlined in gold, alongside the enamels of Bernard Palissy, with snakes, frogs, and lizards in relief.

From bursting cabinets tumbled cascades of silvery, gleaming China silk, the shimmering brocade sparkling like luminous beads in an oblique sunbeam; while portraits from every epoch smiled through their yellowed varnish from frames more or less tarnished.

The dealer followed me carefully through the twisting passageways winding among the piles of furniture, warding off with his hands the perilous swing of my coattail, examining my elbows with the disquieting attention of an antiques dealer or a money lender.

He was an odd figure—this dealer; an immense skull, as polished as a knee, was surrounded by a scant aureole of white hair, which, by contrast, emphasized the salmon-colored tint of his complexion, and gave the wrong impression of patriarchal benevolence, corrected, however, by the gleaming of two small, yellow eyes, which shifted in their orbits like two *Louis d'or* gold coins floating in quicksilver.

The curve of his nose had an aquiline silhouette, which recalled the Oriental or Jewish type. His hands, long, slender, with prominent veins and sinews protruding like violin strings, with nails like the claws on a bat's membranous wings moved with a senile trembling painful to behold, but those nervously quivering hands became firmer than pincers of steel, or a lobster's claws, when they picked up any precious object, an onyx cup, a Venetian glass, or a platter of Bohemian crystal. This weird old rascal had such a profoundly cabalistic air that, from mere appearance, he would have been burned at the stake three centuries ago.

"Will you not buy something from me today, sir? Here is a Malayan kris, with a blade that undulates like a flame; look at these grooves for the blood to drip from, these reversed serrated teeth to tear out the entrails as the dagger is withdrawn; it is a fine example of a savage weapon, and will look great in your trophy collection; this two-handed sword is very beautiful—it is the work of Josepe de la Hera; and this small sword with its carved guard—what superb workmanship!"

"No, I have enough weapons and instruments of carnage; I should like to have a figurine, any sort of object that can be used for a paperweight; for I can't bear those shoddy, cheap bronzes the stationery shops sell, which you invariably find on everybody's desk."

The old gnome, rummaging through his ancient wares, displayed for me some antique, or so-called antique, bronzes, fragments of malachite, little Hindu and Chinese idols, jade figures of ugly, fat little men, incarnations of Brahma and Vishnu, marvelously suitable for the purpose—scarcely divine—of holding papers and letters in place.

I was hesitating between a porcelain dragon covered with constellations of warts, its jaws embellished with teeth and tusks, and a hideous little Mexican fetish, representing realistically the god Vitziliputzli, when I spotted a charming foot, which at first I took for a fragment of some antique Venus.

It had that beautiful tawny reddish tint that gives Florentine bronzes their warm and lively appearance, so much better than the verdigris tones of ordinary bronzes, which might be taken readily for statues in a state of putrefaction; a satiny luster shivered over its rounded forms, polished by the amorous kisses of twenty centuries; for it must have been a Corinthian god, a work of the finest period, perhaps cast by Lysippos himself.

"Let me see that foot," I said to the merchant, who looked at me sideways with a crafty expression as he handed me the object so I could examine it at leisure.

I was surprised at how light it was. It was not a metal foot but really a foot of flesh, an embalmed foot, a mummy's foot; on close examination, you could distinguish the grain of the skin, and the almost imperceptible imprint of the weave of the wrappings. The toes were fine, delicate, ending in perfect nails, pure and transparent as agate; the big toe, slightly separate from the others in the antique manner was in pleasing contrast to the position of the other toes, and gave a suggestion of the freedom and lightness of a bird's foot. The sole, faintly streaked with almost invisible lines, showed that it had never touched the ground, or come in contact with anything but the finest mats woven from the rushes of the Nile, and the softest rugs of panther skin.

"Haha! You want the foot of the Princess Hermonthis," said the dealer with a strange, mocking laugh, staring at me with his owlish eyes. "Hahaha, for a paperweight! What an original idea! An artist's idea! If anyone had told the old pharaoh that his beloved daughter's foot would be used for a paperweight, he would have been mighty surprised, especially while he was having a mountain of hollow granite built in which to place her triple coffin, painted and gilded, covered with hieroglyphics and beautiful pictures of the judgment of souls," said the weird little dealer, in low tones, as though he were talking to himself.

"How much will you charge me for this piece of a mummy?"

"Ha! As much as I can get; for it is a superb piece; if I had the other foot, you couldn't have it for less than five hundred francs—the daughter of a Pharaoh! There's nothing more rare."

"It's certainly unusual; but still, how much do you want for it? First, I'll tell you one thing, namely that I have only five gold pieces. I will buy anything that costs that much, but nothing more expensive. You can search my pockets and my desk drawers, but you won't find one miserable five-franc piece more."

"Five gold coins for the foot of the Princess Hermonthis! It is very little, too little, in fact, for an authentic foot," said the dealer, shaking his head and rolling his eyes with a peculiar spinning motion. "Very well, take it and I'll throw in the outer covering," he said, rolling it in a shred of old damask—"very beautiful, genuine damask, which has never been re-dyed; it is strong, yet soft," he muttered, caressing the frayed tissue, typical for his habit of praising an article of so little value that he thought it was good for nothing but to give away.

He dropped the gold pieces into a medieval-looking pouch hanging from his belt, and repeated:

"The foot of Princess Hermonthis—to be used for a paperweight!"

Then, fastening his glimmering pupils on me, he said, his voice strident like the wailing of a cat that has just swallowed a bone:

"Old Pharaoh will not be pleased; he loved his daughter—that dear man."

"You speak of him as though you knew him; no matter how old you might be, you don't date back to the pyramids of Egypt," I answered laughingly from the shop's threshold.

I returned home, thrilled with my purchase.

To make use of it at once, I set the foot of the divine Princess Hermonthis on a stack of papers—sketches of verses, undecipherable mosaics of crossed-out words, unfinished articles, forgotten letters posted in the desk drawer, a mistake often made by absent-minded people; the effect was pleasing, bizarre, and romantic.

Very satisfied with this decoration, I went down into the street, and walked along with all the self-importance and pride suitable for a man who has the inexpressible advantage over all the passersby he elbows, of possessing a piece of the Princess Hermonthis, daughter of Pharaoh.

I found supremely ridiculous people who, unlike me, did not possess such a notably Egyptian paperweight, and it seemed to me the proper business of a sensible man to have a mummy's foot on his desk.

Happily, meeting several friends distracted me from my raptures over my recent acquisition. I went to dinner with them, for it would have been hard for me to dine alone.

When I returned that evening, my brain somewhat muddled by the effects of a few glasses of wine, the vague whiff of oriental perfume tickled delicately at my olfactory nerves. The heat of the room had warmed the natron, the bitumen, and the myrrh in which the priests who embalmed the dead had bathed the body of the Princess; it was a delicate yet penetrating perfume, which four thousand years had not been able to dissipate.

The dream of Egypt was eternity; its odors have the solidity of granite, and last as long.

I soon drank full gulps from the black cup of sleep; for an hour or two all remained dark; Oblivion and the void submerged me in their dark waves.

Even so my intellectual darkness cleared up, dreams began to brush me lightly in their silent flights.

The eyes of my soul opened, and I saw my room for what it really was. I might have believed I was awake, but a vague perception told me that I was asleep, and that something bizarre was about to happen.

The odor of myrrh had increased in intensity, and I felt a slight headache, which I quite reasonably attributed to the several glasses of Champagne that we had drunk to unknown gods, and to our future success.

I looked around my room with a feeling of expectation that nothing justified. Every piece of furniture was in its usual place; the lamp was burning on the nightstand, softly blurred by the milky whiteness of its ground crystal globe; the watercolors glowed beneath their Bohemian glass; the curtains drooped heavily; everything seemed sleepy and tranquil.

Still, after a few moments this calm interior seemed troubled, the woodwork creaked furtively, the ash-covered log suddenly spurted out a blue flame, and the plaques on their hooks seemed like metal eyes, watching, like me, for what was about to happen.

By chance my eyes fell on the table where I had placed the foot of the Princess Hermonthis.

Instead of remaining immobile, as suited a foot that has been embalmed for four thousand years, it was moving about, agitated, twitching and jumping over the papers like a frightened frog; you'd have thought it was in contact with a battery; I could distinctly hear the quick tapping of the little heel, hard as a gazelle's hoof.

I was quite unhappy with my acquisition, since I like sedentary paperweights and find it unnatural to see feet moving around without legs, and I was starting to feel something strongly resembling fear.

Suddenly I saw the fold of one of my curtains stirring, and heard a stomping sound like someone hopping around on one foot. I must admit I was feeling hot and cold by turns, that I felt a mysterious breeze blowing down my back, and that my hair stood on end suddenly, forcing my nightcap to move sideways.

The curtains parted, and I saw stepping out the strangest figure anyone could possibly imagine.

It was a young girl, her skin the color of dark café au lait like Amani the *bayadère*, of a perfect beauty of the purest Egyptian type. She had slanting, almond-shaped eyes, with eyebrows so black that they appeared blue; her nose was beautifully formed, almost Grecian in its delicacy; she might have been taken for a Corinthian bronze statue, but her prominent cheekbones and full, African lips indicated without a doubt the hiero-glyphic people from the banks of the Nile.

Her thin, spindly arms, like those of very young girls, were encircled with metal rings and bracelets of glass beads; her hair was twisted into little cords; at her breast hung a green Egyptian faience idol, whose whip with seven lashes identified her as Isis, guide of souls. A golden ornament gleamed on her forehead, and slight traces of rouge were visible on the coppery tint of her cheeks.

As for her costume, it was very strange.

Imagine a loincloth of bandages decorated with red and black hieroglyphs, heavy with bitumen, and apparently belonging to a newly unwrapped mummy.

In one of those leaps of fancy so common in dreams, I could hear the hoarse, rough voice of the bric-à-brac dealer reciting in a monotonous refrain the words he'd kept repeating enigmatically in his shop.

"Old Pharaoh will not be pleased—he loved his daughter very much—that dear man."

Particularly strange, and hardly reassuring, was that the apparition had only one foot—the other had been broken off at the ankle.

She approached the table, where the mummy's foot was fidgeting and jumping about with redoubled energy. She leaned against the edge, and I saw a tear sprout and bead up in her eyes.

Although she did not speak, I completely understood her thoughts. She was looking at the foot, for it was certainly her own, with an expression of coquettish sadness and infinite grace, which was extremely charming; but the foot was jumping and running about as if pushed by steel springs.

Two or three times she stretched out her hand to seize it, but did not succeed.

Then began between the Princess Hermonthis and her foot, which seemed gifted with an individuality of its own, a bizarre dialogue, in ancient Coptic, such as would have been spoken some thirty centuries ago among the sphinxes of the Land of Ser; fortunately, that night I knew Coptic perfectly.

The Princess Hermonthis said in a tone of voice as sweet and vibrant as a little crystal bell:

"Well, my dear little foot, you always flee from me, yet I took the best of care of you; I bathed you with perfumed water, in a basin of alabaster; I rubbed your heel with pumice stone soaked with oil of palm; your nails were trimmed with golden scissors, and polished with a hippopotamus tooth; I carefully selected for you painted and embroidered *tebtebti* sandals with upturned toes, which were the envy of all the young girls of Egypt; on your big toe, you wore rings representing sacred scarabs, and you supported one of the lightest bodies that a lazy foot could desire."

The foot answered in a sulking, sorrowful voice:

"You know well that I no longer belong to myself. I have been bought and paid for; the old merchant knew exactly what he was doing. He bears a grudge because you refused to marry him. This is a trick he has played on you. The Arab who forced open your royal tomb, in the subterranean pits of the necropolis of Thebes, was sent by him. He wanted to prevent you from attending the reunion of the shades, in the cities of the underworld. Do you have five pieces of gold to buy me back?"

"Alas, no! My jewels, my rings, my purses of gold and of silver, all have been stolen from me," answered the Princess Hermonthis with a sigh.

"Princess!" I then cried out, "I have never unjustly kept anyone's foot; even though you don't have the five gold coins it cost me, I will graciously return it to you; I would be in despair, were I the cause of the lameness of so charming a person as the Princess Hermonthis."

I delivered this discourse in the courtly manner of a troubadour, which must have surprised the beautiful Egyptian.

She turned toward me with an expression of recognition, and her eyes gleamed with bluish lights.

She took her foot, which this time let her, and, like a woman about to put on her laced boot, she adjusted it to her leg with great dexterity.

This operation completed, she took a few steps around the room, as if to reassure herself that she really was no longer lame.

"Ah, how happy my father will be, he who was so saddened because of my mutilation—he who, from the day of my birth, set a whole nation to work to dig me a tomb so deep that he could preserve me intact until that supreme last day, when souls must be weighed on the scales of Amenti! Come with me to my father; he will receive you gladly, for you have given me back my foot."

I found this proposition entirely natural. I decked myself out in a dressing-gown with huge, flamboyant sleeves, which gave me an extremely Pharaohesque appearance; I hurriedly put on a pair of Turkish slippers, and told the Princess Hermonthis that I was ready to follow her.

Before setting out, Hermonthis detached from her necklace the little green image and placed it on the papers scattered around the table.

"It is only fair," she said with a smile, "that I replace your paperweight."

She gave me her hand, which was soft and cool as the skin of a snake, and we departed.

For a time we sped as fast as an arrow through a grayish and fluid expanse, in which barely indistinguishable silhouettes flashed by us, on the right and left.

For an instant we saw nothing but sea and sky.

A few minutes later, towering obelisks pointed upward, and pylons, ramps with sphinxes on either side, were etched against the horizon.

We had arrived.

The princess led me before a mountain of pink granite in which there was an opening so low and narrow that, had it not been marked by two small pillars covered with strange carvings, it would have been difficult to distinguish from the fissures in the rock.

Hermonthis lighted a torch and led the way.

There were corridors hewn through the living rock. The walls, covered with panels of hieroglyphics and allegorical processions, must have been the work of thousands of hands for thousands of years; the corridors, of interminable length, ended in square rooms, in the middle of which pits had been dug, down which we descended by means of crampons or spiral staircases. These pits led us into other rooms, from which opened out other corridors strangely decorated with sparrow-hawks, serpents coiled in circles, the symbolic ankhs, shepherd's crooks, and river barges, prodigious works which no living eye could ever see, interminable legends in granite that only the dead had time to read throughout eternity.

At last we reached a hall so vast, so enormous, so immeasurable, that its limits could not be discerned. As far as the eye could see stretched rows of gigantic columns, between which sparkled livid stars of yellow light. These glittering points of light revealed incalculable depths beyond.

The Princess Hermonthis, still holding my hand, graciously greeted the mummies of her acquaintance.

My eyes gradually became accustomed to the shadowy twilight, and I began to distinguish the objects around me.

I saw, seated upon their thrones, the kings of the subterranean races. They were dignified old personages, or dried up, shriveled, wrinkled like parchment, and blackened with naphtha and bitumen. On their heads they wore crowns of gold, and their breastplates and gorgets gleamed with precious stones; their eyes were fixed like those of the sphinx, and their long beards were whitened by the snows of centuries. Behind them stood their embalmed subjects, in the rigid and constrained postures of Egyptian art, preserving eternally the attitudes prescribed by the hieratic code. Behind the subjects, their cats, ibises, and crocodiles, rendered even more monstrous by their wrappings, meowed, beat their wings, and grimaced.

All the Pharaohs were there: Cheops, Khafre, Psamtik, Sesostri, Amenhotep, all the dark-skinned rulers of the country of the pyramids and the royal tombs; on a still higher platform sat enthroned the kings Chronos, and Xixouthros, from the time of the Flood, and Tubal-Cain, who preceded it.

The beard of King Ziusudra had grown so long that it had already wound itself seven times around the granite table he leaned against dreamily, as though asleep.

Farther in the distance, through the dimness, across the mists of eternities, I beheld vaguely the seventy-two pre-Adamite kings, with their seventy-two peoples, vanished forever.

The Princess Hermonthis, after allowing me a few minutes to enjoy this dizzying spectacle, presented me to Pharaoh, her father, who nodded to me in a most majestic manner.

"I have found my foot! I have found my foot!" cried the Princess, clapping her little hands, with every indication of uncontrollable joy. "It was this gentleman who returned it to me."

The races of Kheme, the races of Nahasi, all the races, black, bronze, and copper-colored, repeated in a chorus:

"The Princess Hermonthis has found her foot."

Ziusudra himself was deeply affected.

He raised his heavy eyelids, ran his fingers through his moustache, and regarded me, his glance charged with the centuries.

"By Oms, the dog of Hell, and by Tmei, daughter of the Sun and of Truth, here is a brave and worthy young man," said Pharaoh, extending toward me his scepter, which terminated in a lotus flower. "What do you desire for your reward?"

Strengthened with the audacity that dreams give, when nothing seems impossible, I asked him for the hand of Hermonthis. Her hand for her foot seemed to me an antithetical recompense, in sufficiently good taste.

Pharaoh opened his glassy eyes wide, surprised at my joke, as well as my request.

"What country are you from, and how old are you?"

"I am French, and I am twenty-seven years old, venerable Pharaoh."

"Twenty-seven years! And he wishes to marry the Princess Hermonthis, who is thirty centuries old!" all the thrones, and all the circles of nations cried out at once.

Only Hermonthis did not seem to think my request improper.

"If you were even two thousand years old," continued the old king, "I would gladly bestow upon you the Princess; but the disproportion is too great; besides, our daughters must have husbands who will last, and you no longer know how to preserve yourselves. Of the last who were brought here, barely fifteen centuries ago, are nothing but a pinch of ashes. Look! My flesh is as hard as basalt, my bones are bars of steel. I shall be present on the last day of the world, with the body and features I had when alive. My daughter Hermonthis will last longer than a bronze statue. But by then the wind will have dispersed the last grain of your dust, and Isis herself, who knew how to recover the fragments of Osiris, would not be able to recompose your being. See how vigorous I still am, and how powerful is the strength of my arm," said he, shaking my hand in the English manner, so that my rings cut into my fingers.

He squeezed my hand so hard that I woke up, and discovered my friend Alfred, who was pulling on my arm and shaking me to make me get up.

"Listen here, sleepyhead! Do I have to drag you into the middle of the street and set off fireworks next to your ear to wake you up? It is afternoon. Don't you remember you promised to get me so we could see Manuel Aguado's Spanish paintings?"

"My God! I forgot all about it," I answered, dressing hurriedly. "We can go right now—I have the invitation here on my table." I went to get it; imagine my astonishment when I saw, not the mummy's foot I had bought the previous evening, but the little green image the Princess Hermonthis had left in its place!

3

The Pool of the Stone God

By Abraham Merritt

THIS IS PROFESSOR JAMES MARSTON'S STORY. A SCORE OF LEARNED
bodies have courteously heard him tell it, and then among themselves
have lamented that so brilliant a man should have such an obsession.
Professor Marston told it to me in San Francisco, just before he started
to find the island that holds his pool of the stone god and—the wings
that guard it. He seemed to me very sane. It is true that the equipment
of his expedition was unusual, and not the least curious part of it are the
suits of fine chain mail and masks and gauntlets with which each man of
the party is provided.

The five of us, said Professor Marston, sat side by side on the beach.
There was Wilkinson the first officer, Bates and Cassidy the two seamen,
Waters the pearler and myself. We had all been on our way to New
Guinea, I to study the fossils for the Smithsonian. The *Moranus* had
struck the hidden reef the night before and had sunk swiftly. We were
then, roughly, about five hundred miles northeast of the Guinea coast.
The five of us had managed to drop a lifeboat and get away. The boat was
well stocked with water and provisions. Whether the rest of the crew had
escaped we did not know. We had sighted the island at dawn and had
made for her. The lifeboat was drawn safely up on the sands.

"We'd better explore a bit, anyway," said Waters. "This may be a perfect place for us to wait rescue. At least until the typhoon season is over.

We've our pistols. Let's start by following this brook to its source, look over the place and then decide what we'll do."

The trees began to thin out. We saw ahead an open space. We reached it and stopped in sheer amazement. The clearing was perfectly square and about five hundred feet wide. The trees stopped abruptly at its edges as though held back by something unseen.

But it was not this singular impression that held us. At the far end of the square were a dozen stone huts clustered about one slightly larger. They reminded me powerfully of those prehistoric structures you see in parts of England and France. I approach now the most singular thing about this whole singular and sinister place. In the center of the space was a pool walled about with huge blocks of cut stone. At the side of the pool rose a great stone figure, carved in the semblance of a man with outstretched hands. It was at least twenty feet high and was extremely well executed. At the distance the statue seemed nude and yet it had a peculiar effect of drapery about it. As we drew nearer we saw that it was covered from ankles to neck with the most extraordinary carved wings. They looked exactly like bat wings when they were folded.

There was something extremely disquieting about this figure. The face was inexpressibly ugly and malignant. The eyes, Mongol-shaped, slanted evil. It was not from the face, though, that this feeling seemed to emanate. It was from the body covered with wings—and especially from the wings. They were part of the idol and yet they gave one the idea that they were clinging to it.

Cassidy, a big brute of a man, swaggered up to the idol and laid his hand on it. He drew it away quickly, his face white, his mouth twitching. I followed him and conquering my unscientific repugnance, examined the stone. It, like the huts and in fact the whole place, was clearly the work of that forgotten race whose monuments are scattered over the Southern Pacific. The carving of the wings was wonderful. They were batlike, as I have said, folded and each ended in a little ring of conventionalized feathers. They ranged in size from four to ten inches. I ran my fingers over one. Never have I felt the equal of the nausea that sent me to my knees before the idol. The wing had felt like smooth, cold stone, but I had the sensation of having touched back of the stone some monstrous obscene creature of a lower world. The sensation came of course, I reasoned, only from the temperature and texture of the stone—and yet this did not really satisfy me.

Dusk was soon due. We decided to return to the beach and examine the clearing further on the morrow. I desired greatly to explore the stone huts.

We started back through the forest. We walked some distance and then night fell. We lost the brook. After a half hour's wandering we heard it again. We started for it. The trees began to thin out and we thought we were approaching the beach. Then Waters clutched my arm. I stopped. Directly in front of us was the open space with the stone god leering under the moon and the green water shining at his feet!

We had made a circle. Bates and Wilkinson were exhausted. Cassidy swore that devils or no devils he was going to camp that night beside the pool!

The moon was very bright. And it was so very quiet. My scientific curiosity got the better of me and I thought I would examine the huts. I left Bates on guard and walked over to the largest. There was only one room and the moonlight shining through the chinks in the wall illuminated it clearly. At the back were two small basins set in the stone. I looked in one and saw a faint reddish gleam reflected from a number of globular objects. I drew a half dozen of them out. They were pearls, very wonderful pearls of a peculiarly rosy hue. I ran toward the door to call Bates—and stopped!

My eyes had been drawn to the stone idol. Was it an effect of the moonlight or did it move? No, it was the wings! They stood out from the stone and waved—they waved, I say, from the ankles to the neck of that monstrous statue.

Bates had seen them, too. He was standing with his pistol raised. Then there was a shot. And after that the air was filled with a rushing sound like that of a thousand fans. I saw the wings loose themselves from the stone god and sweep down in a cloud upon the four men. Another cloud raced up from the pool and joined them. I could not move. The wings circled swiftly around and about the four. All were now on their feet and I never saw such horror as was in their faces.

Then the wings closed in. They clung to my companions as they had clung to the stone.

I fell back into the hut. I lay there through the night insane with terror. Many times I heard the fan-like rushing about the enclosure, but nothing entered my hut. Dawn came, and silence, and I dragged myself to the door. There stood the stone god with the wings carved upon him as we had seen him ten hours before!

I ran over to the four lying on the grass. I thought that perhaps I had had a nightmare. But they were dead. That was not the worst of it. Each man was shrunken to his bones! They looked like collapsed white balloons. There was not a drop of blood in them. They were nothing but bones wrapped around in thin skin!

Mastering myself, I went close to the idol. There was something different about it. It seemed larger—as though, the thought went through my mind, as though it had eaten. Then I saw that it was covered with tiny drops of blood that had dropped from the ends of the wings that clothed it!

I do not remember what happened afterward. I awoke on the pearling schooner *Luana* which had picked me up, crazed with thirst as they supposed in the boat of the *Moranus*.

4

At Abdul Ali's Grave

By E. F. Benson

LUXOR, AS MOST OF THOSE WHO HAVE BEEN THERE WILL ALLOW, IS A place of notable charm, and boasts many attractions for the traveller, chief among which he will reckon an excellent hotel containing a billiard-room, a garden fit for the gods to sit in, any quantity of visitors, at least a weekly dance on board a tourist steamer, quail shooting, a climate as of Avilion, and a number of stupendously ancient monuments for those archeologically inclined. But to certain others, few indeed in number, but almost fanatically convinced of their own orthodoxy, the charm of Luxor, like some sleeping beauty, only wakes when these things cease, when the hotel has grown empty and the billiard-marker "has gone for a long rest" to Cairo, when the decimated quail and the decimating tourist have fled northwards, and the Theban plain, Dana to a tropical sun, is a gridiron across which no man would willingly make a journey by day, not even if Queen Hatasoo herself should signify that she would give him audience on the terraces of Deir-el-Bahari.

A suspicion however that the fanatic few were right, for in other respects they were men of estimable opinions, induced me to examine their convictions for myself, and thus it came about that two years ago, certain days toward the beginning of June saw me still there, a confirmed convert.

Much tobacco and the length of summer days had assisted us to the analysis of the charm of which summer in the south is possessed, and Weston—one of the earliest of the elect—and myself had discussed it at some length, and though we reserved as the principal ingredient a nameless something which baffled the chemist, and must be felt to be understood, we were easily able to detect certain other drugs of sight and sound, which we were agreed contributed to the whole. A few of them are here subjoined.

The waking in the warm darkness just before dawn to find that the desire for stopping in bed fails with the awakening.

The silent start across the Nile in the still air with our horses, who, like us, stand and sniff at the incredible sweetness of the coming morning without apparently finding it less wonderful in repetition.

The moment infinitesimal in duration but infinite in sensation, just before the sun rises, when the grey shrouded river is struck suddenly out of darkness, and becomes a sheet of green bronze.

The rose flush, rapid as a change of colour in some chemical combination, which shoots across the sky from east to west, followed immediately by the sunlight which catches the peaks of the western hills, and flows down like some luminous liquid.

The stir and whisper which goes through the world: a breeze springs up; a lark soars and sings; the boatman shouts "Yallah, Yallah"; the horses toss their heads.

The subsequent ride.

The subsequent breakfast on our return.

The subsequent absence of anything to do.

At sunset the ride into the desert thick with the scent of warm barren sand, which smells like nothing else in the world, for it smells of nothing at all.

The blaze of the tropical night.

Camel's milk.

Converse with the fellahin, who are the most charming and least accountable people on the face of the earth except when tourists are about, and when in consequence there is no thought but backsheesh.

Lastly, and with this we are concerned, the possibility of odd experiences.

The beginning of the things which make this tale occurred four days ago, when Abdul Mi, the oldest man in the village, died suddenly, full of days and riches. Both, some thought, had probably been somewhat exaggerated, but his relations affirmed without variation that he had as many years as he had English pounds, and that each was a hundred. The apt roundness of these numbers was incontestable, the thing was too neat not to be true, and before he had been dead for twenty-four hours it was a matter of orthodoxy. But with regard to his relations, that which turned their bereavement, which must soon have occurred, into a source of blank dismay instead of pious resignation, was that not one of these English pounds, not even their less satisfactory equivalent in notes, which, out of the tourist season, are looked upon at Luxor as a not very dependable variety of Philosopher's stone, though certainly capable of producing gold under favourable circumstances, could be found. Abdul Ali with his hundred years was dead, his century of sovereigns—they might as well have been an annuity—were dead with him, and his son Mohamed, who had previously enjoyed a sort of brevet rank in anticipation of the event, was considered to be throwing far more dust in the air than the genuine affection even of a chief mourner wholly justified.

Abdul, it is to be feared, was not a man of stereotyped respectability; though full of years and riches, he enjoyed no great reputation for honour. He drank wine whenever he could get it, he ate food during the days of Ramadan, scornful of the fact, when his appetite desired it, he was supposed to have the evil eye, and in his last moments he was attended by the notorious Achmet, who is well known here to be practised in Black Magic, and has been suspected of the much meaner crime of robbing the bodies of those lately dead. For in Egypt, while to despoil the bodies of ancient kings and priests is a privilege for which advanced and learned societies vie with each other, to rob the corpses of your contemporaries is considered the deed of a dog.

Mohamed, who soon exchanged the throwing of dust in the air for the more natural mode of expressing chagrin, which is to gnaw the nails, told us in confidence that he suspected Achmet of having ascertained the secret of where his father's money was, but it appeared that Achmet had as blank a face as anybody when his patient, who was striving to make some communication to him, went out into the great silence, and the suspicion that he knew where the money was gave way, in the minds, of those who were competent to form an estimate of his character, to a but dubious regret that he had just failed to learn that very important fact.

So Abdul died and was buried, and we all went to the funeral feast, at which we ate more roast meat than one naturally cares about at five in the afternoon on a June day, in consequence of which Weston and I, not requiring dinner, stopped at home after our return from the ride into the desert, and talked to Mohamed, Abdul's son, and Hussein, Abdul's youngest grandson, a boy of about twenty, who is also our valet, cook and housemaid, and they together woefully narrated of the money that had been and was not, and told us scandalous tales about Achmet concerning his weakness for cemeteries. They drank coffee and smoked, for though Hussein was our servant, we had been that day the guests of his father, and shortly after they had gone, up came Machmout.

Machmout, who says he thinks he is twelve, but does not know for certain, is kitchen-maid, groom and gardener, and has to an extraordinary degree some occult power resembling clairvoyance. Weston, who is a member of the Society for Psychical Research, and the tragedy of whose life has been the detection of the fraudulent medium Mrs. Blunt, says that it is all thought-reading, and has made notes of many of Machmout's performances, which may subsequently turn out to be of interest. Thought-reading, however, does not seem to me to fully explain the experience which followed Abdul's funeral, and with Machmout I have to put it down to White Magic, which should be a very inclusive term, or to Pure Coincidence, which is even more inclusive, and will cover all the inexplicable phenomena of the world, taken singly. Machmout's method of unloosing the forces of White Magic is simple, being the ink-mirror known by name to many, and it is as follows.

A little black ink is poured into the palm of Machmout's hand, or, as ink has been at a premium lately owing to the last post-boat from Cairo which contained stationery for us having stuck on a sand-bank, a small piece of black American cloth about an inch in diameter is found to be a perfect substitute. Upon this he gazes. After five or ten minutes his shrewd monkey-like expression is struck from his face, his eyes, wide open, remain fixed on the cloth, a complete rigidity sets in over his muscles, and he tells us of the curious things he sees. In whatever position he is, in that position he remains without the deflection of a hair's breadth until the ink is washed off or the cloth removed. Then he looks up and says "Khalás," which means, "It is finished."

We only engaged Machmout's services as second general domestic a fortnight ago, but the first evening he was with us he came upstairs when he had finished his work, and said, "I will show you White Magic; give me ink," and proceeded to describe the front hall of our house in London, saying that there were two horses at the door, and that a man and woman soon came out, gave the horses each a piece of bread and mounted. The thing was so probable that by the next mail I wrote asking my mother to write down exactly what she was doing and where at half-past five (English time) on the evening of June 12. At the corresponding time in Egypt Machmout was describing speaking to us of a "sitt" (lady) having tea in a room which he described with some minuteness, and I am waiting anxiously for her letter. The explanation which Weston gives us of all these phenomena is that a certain picture of people I know is present in my mind, though I may not be aware of it,—present to my subliminal self, I think, he says,—and that I give an unspoken suggestion to the hypnotised Machmout. My explanation is that there isn't any explanation, for no suggestion on my part would make my brother go out and ride at the moment when Machmout says he is so doing (if indeed we find that Machmout's visions are chronologically correct). Consequently I prefer the open mind and am prepared to believe anything. Weston, however, does not speak quite so calmly or scientifically about Machmout's last performance, and since it took place he has almost entirely ceased to urge me to become a member of the Society for Psychical Research, in order that I may no longer be hidebound by vain superstitions.

Machmout will not exercise these powers if his own folk are present, for he says that when he is in this state, if a man who knew Black Magic was in the room, or knew that he was practising White Magic, he could get the spirit who presides over the Black Magic to kill the spirit of White Magic, for the Black Magic is the more potent, and the two are foes. And as the spirit of White Magic is on occasions a powerful friend—he had before now befriended Machmout in a manner which I consider incredible—Machmout is very desirous that he should abide long with him. But Englishmen it appears do not know the Black Magic, so with us he is safe. The spirit of Black Magic, to speak to whom it is death, Machmout saw once "between heaven and earth, and night and day," so he phrases it, on the Karnak road. He may be known, he told us, by the fact that he is of paler skin than his people, that he has two long teeth, one in each corner of his mouth, and that his eyes, which are white all over, are as big as the eyes of a horse.

Machmout squatted himself comfortably in the corner, and I gave him the piece of black American cloth. As some minutes must elapse before he gets into the hypnotic state in which the visions begin, I strolled out on to the balcony for coolness. It was the hottest night we had yet had, and though the sun had set three hours, the thermometer still registered close on 100°. Above, the sky seemed veiled with grey, where it should have been dark velvety blue, and a fitful puffing wind from the south threatened three days of the sandy intolerable khamseen. A little way up the street to the left was a small café in front of which were glowing and waning little glowworm specks of light from the water pipes of Arabs sitting out there in the dark. From inside came the click of brass castanets in the hands of some dancing-girl, sounding sharp and precise against the wailing bagpipe music of the strings and pipes which accompany these movements which Arabs love and Europeans think so unpleasing. Eastwards the sky was paler and luminous, for the moon was imminently rising, and even as I looked the red rim of the enormous disc cut the line of the desert, and on the instant, with a curious aptness, one of the Arabs outside the café broke out into that wonderful chant—

"I cannot sleep for longing for thee, O full moon.

Far is thy throne over Mecca, slip down, O beloved, to me."

Immediately afterwards I heard the piping monotone of Machmout's voice begin, and in a moment or two I went inside.

We have found that the experiments gave the quickest result by contact, a fact which confirmed Weston in his explanation of them by thought transference of some elaborate kind, which I confess I cannot understand. He was writing at a table in the window when I came in, but looked up.

"Take his hand," he said; "at present he is quite incoherent."

"Do you explain that?" I asked.

"It is closely analogous, so Myers thinks, to talking in sleep. He has been saying something about a tomb. Do make a suggestion, and see if he gives it right. He is remarkably sensitive, and he responds quicker to you than to me. Probably Abdul's funeral suggested the tomb!"

A sudden thought struck me.

"Hush!" I said, "I want to listen."

Machmout's head was thrown a little back, and he held the hand in which was the piece of cloth rather above his face. As usual he was talking very slowly, and in a high staccato voice, absolutely unlike his usual tones.

"On one side of the grave," he pipes, "is a tamarisk tree, and the green beetles make fantasia about it. On the other side is a mud wall. There are many other graves about, but they are all asleep. This is the grave, because it is awake, and it moist and not sandy."

"I thought so," said Weston. "It is Abdul's grave he is talking about."

"There is a red moon sitting on the desert," continued Machmout, "and it is now. There is the puffing of khamseen, and much dust coming. The moon is red with dust, and because it is low."

"Still sensitive to external conditions," said Weston. "That is rather curious. Pinch him, will you?"

I pinched Machmout; he did not pay the slightest attention.

"In the last house of the street, and in the doorway stands a man. Ah! ah!" cried the boy, suddenly, "it is the Black Magic he knows. Don't let him come. He is going out of the house," he shrieked, "he is coming—no, he is going the other way towards the moon and the grave. He has the Black Magic with him, which can raise the dead, and he has a murdering knife, and a spade. I cannot see his face, for the Black Magic is between it and my eyes."

Weston had got up, and, like me, was hanging on Machmout's words.

"We will go there," he said. "Here is an opportunity of testing it. Listen a moment."

"He is walking, walking, walking," piped Machmout, "still walking to the moon and the grave. The moon sits no longer on the desert, but has sprung up a little way."

I pointed out of the window.

"That at any rate is true," I said.

Weston took the cloth out of Machmout's hand, and the piping ceased. In a moment he stretched himself, and rubbed his eyes.

"Khalás," he said.

"Yes, it is Khalás."

"Did I tell you of the sitt in England?" he asked.

"Yes, oh, yes," I answered; "thank you, little Machmout. The White Magic was very good to-night. Get you to bed."

Machmout trotted obediently out of the room, and Weston closed the door after him.

"We must be quick," he said. "It is worth while going and giving the thing a chance, though I wish he had seen something less gruesome. The odd thing is that he was not at the funeral, and yet he describes the grave accurately. What do you make of it?"

"I make that the White Magic has shown Machmout that somebody with Black Magic is going to Abdul's grave, perhaps to rob it," I answered resolutely.

"What are we to do when we get there?" asked Weston.

"See the Black Magic at work. Personally I am in a blue funk. So are you."

"There is no such thing as Black Magic," said Weston. "Ah, I have it. Give me that orange."

Weston rapidly skinned it, and cut from the rind two circles as big as a five shilling piece, and two long, white fangs of skin. The first he fixed in his eyes, the two latter in the corners of his mouth.

"The spirit of Black Magic?" I asked.

"The same."

He took up a long black burnous and wrapped it round him. Even in the bright lamp light, the spirit of Black Magic was a sufficiently terrific personage.

"I don't believe in Black Magic," he said, "but others do. If it is necessary to put a stop to—to anything that is going on, we will hoist the man on his own petard. Come along. Whom do you suspect it is—I mean, of course, who was the person you were thinking of when your thoughts were transferred to Machmout."

"What Machmout said," I answered, "suggested Achmet to me."

Weston indulged in a laugh of scientific incredulity, and we set off.

The moon, as the boy had told us, was just clear of the horizon, and as it rose higher, its colour at first red and sombre, like the blaze of some distant conflagration, paled to a tawny yellow. The hot wind from the south, blowing no longer fitfully but with a steadily increasing violence, was thick with sand, and of an incredibly scorching heat, and the tops of the palm trees in the garden of the deserted hotel on the right were lashing themselves to and fro with a harsh rattle of dry leaves. The cemetery lay on the outskirts of the village, and, as long as our way lay between the mud walls of the huddling street, the wind came to us only as the heat from behind closed furnace doors. Every now and then with a whisper and whistle rising into a great buffeting flap, a sudden whirlwind of dust would scour some twenty yards along the road, and then break like a shore-quenched wave against one or other of the mud walls or throw itself heavily against a house and fall in a shower of sand. But once free of obstructions we were opposed to the full heat and blast of the wind which blew full in our teeth. It was the first summer khamseen of the year, and for the moment I wished I had gone north with the tourist and the quail and the billiard marker, for khamseen fetches the marrow out of the bones, and turns the body to blotting paper.

We passed no one in the street, and the only sound we heard, except the wind, was the howling of moonstruck dogs.

The cemetery is surrounded by a tall mud-built wall, and sheltering for a few moments under this we discussed our movements. The row of tamarisks close to which the tomb lay went down the centre of the graveyard, and by skirting the wall outside and climbing softly over where they approached it, the fury of the wind might help us to get near the grave without being seen, if anyone happened to be there. We had just decided on this, and were moving on to put the scheme into execution, when the wind dropped for a moment, and in the silence we could hear the chump of the spade being driven into the earth, and what gave me a sudden thrill of intimate horror, the cry of the carrion-feeding hawk from the dusky sky just overhead.

Two minutes later we were creeping up in the shade of the tamarisks, to where Abdul had been buried. The great green beetles which live on the trees were flying about blindly, and once or twice one dashed into my face with a whirr of mail-clad wings. When we were within some twenty yards of the grave we stopped for a moment, and, looking cautiously out from our shelter of tamarisks, saw the figure of a man already waist deep in the earth, digging out the newly turned grave. Weston, who was standing behind me, had adjusted the characteristics of the spirit of Black Magic so as to be ready for emergencies, and turning round suddenly, and finding myself unawares face to face with that realistic impersonation, though my nerves are not precariously strong, I could have found it within me to shriek aloud. But that unsympathetic man of iron only shook with suppressed laughter, and, holding the eyes in his hand, motioned me forward again without speaking to where the trees grew thicker. There we stood not a dozen yards away from the grave.

We waited, I suppose, for some ten minutes, while the man, whom we saw to be Achmet, toiled on at his impious task. He was entirely naked, and his brown skin glistened with the dews of exertion in the moonlight. At times he chattered in a cold uncanny manner to himself, and once or twice he stopped for breath. Then he began scraping the earth away with his hands, and soon afterwards searched in his clothes, which were lying near, for a piece of rope, with which he stepped into the grave, and in a moment reappeared again with both ends in his hands. Then, standing astride the grave, he pulled strongly, and one end of the coffin appeared above the ground. He chipped a piece of the lid away to make sure that he had the right end, and then, setting it upright, wrenched off the top with his knife, and there faced us, leaning against the coffin lid, the small shrivelled figure of the dead Abdul, swathed like a baby in white.

I was just about to motion the spirit of Black Magic to make his appearance, when Machmout's words came into my head: "He had with him the Black Magic which can raise the dead," and sudden overwhelming curiosity, which froze disgust and horror into chill unfeeling things, came over me.

"Wait," I whispered to Weston, "he will use the Black Magic."

Again the wind dropped for a moment, and again, in the silence that came with it, I heard the chiding of the hawk overhead, this time nearer, and thought I heard more birds than one.

Achmet meantime had taken the covering from off the face, and had undone the swathing band, which at the moment after death is bound round the chin to close the jaw, and in Arab burial is always left there, and from where we stood I could see that the jaw dropped when the bandage was untied, as if, though the wind blew towards us with a ghastly scent of mortality on it, the muscles were not even now set, though the man had been dead sixty hours. But still a rank and burning curiosity to see what this unclean ghoul would do next stifled all other feelings in my mind. He seemed not to notice, or, at any rate, to disregard that mouth gaping awry, and moved about nimbly in the moonlight.

He took from a pocket of his clothes, which were lying near, two small black objects, which now are safely embedded in the mud at the bottom of the Nile, and rubbed them briskly together.

By degrees they grew luminous with a sickly yellow pallor of light, and from his hands went up a wavy, phosphorescent flame. One of these cubes he placed in the open mouth of the corpse, the other in his own, and, taking the dead man closely in his arms as though he would indeed dance with death, he breathed long breaths from his mouth into that dead cavern which was pressed to his. Suddenly he started back with a quick-drawn breath of wonder and perhaps of horror, and stood for a space as if irresolute, for the cube which the dead man held instead of lying loosely in the jaw was pressed tight between clenched teeth. After a moment of irresolution he stepped back quickly to his clothes again, and took up from near them the knife with which he had stripped off the coffin lid, and holding this in one hand behind his back, with the other he took out the cube from the dead man's mouth, though with a visible exhibition of force, and spoke.

"Abdul," he said, "I am your friend, and I swear I will give your money to Mohamed, if you will tell me where it is."

Certain I am that the lips of the dead moved, and the eyelids fluttered for a moment like the wings of a wounded bird, but at that sight the horror so grew on me that I was physically incapable of stifling the cry that rose to my lips, and Achmet turned round. Next moment the complete spirit of Black Magic glided out of the shade of the trees, and stood before him. The wretched man stood for a moment without stirring, then, turning with shaking knees to flee, he stepped back and fell into the grave he had just opened.

Weston turned on me angrily, dropping the eyes and the teeth of the Afrit.

"You spoiled it all," he cried. "It would perhaps have been the most interesting . . ." and his eye lighted on the dead Abdul, who peered open-eyed from the coffin, then swayed, tottered, and fell forward, face downwards on the ground close to him. For one moment he lay there, and then the body rolled slowly on to its back without visible cause of movement, and lay staring into the sky. The face was covered with dust, but with the dust was mingled fresh blood. A nail had caught the cloth that wound him, underneath which, as usual, were the clothes in which he had died, for the Arabs do not wash their dead, and it had torn a great rent through them all, leaving the right shoulder bare.

Weston strove to speak once, but failed. Then:

"I will go and inform the police," he said, "if you will stop here, and see that Achmet does not get out."

But this I altogether refused to do, and, after covering the body with the coffin to protect it from the hawks, we secured Achmet's arms with the rope he had already used that night, and took him off to Luxor.

Next morning Mohamed came to see us.

"I thought Achmet knew where the money was," he said exultantly. "Where was it?"

"In a little purse tied round the shoulder. The dog had already begun stripping it. See"—and he brought it out of his pocket—"it is all there in those English notes, five pounds each, and there are twenty of them."

Our conclusion was slightly different, for even Weston will allow that Achmet hoped to learn from dead lips the secret of the treasure, and then to kill the man anew and bury him. But that is pure conjecture.

The only other point of interest lies in the two black cubes which we picked up, and found to be graven with curious characters. These I put one evening into Machmout's hand, when he was exhibiting to us his curious powers of "thought transference." The effect was that he screamed aloud, crying out that the Black Magic had come, and though I did not feel certain about that, I thought they would be safer in mid-Nile. Weston grumbled a little, and said that he had wanted to take them to the British Museum, but that I feel sure was an afterthought.

The Secret of the Growing Gold

By Bram Stoker

WHEN MARGARET DELANDRE WENT TO LIVE AT BRENT'S ROCK THE whole neighbourhood awoke to the pleasure of an entirely new scandal. Scandals in connection with either the Delandre family or the Brents of Brent's Rock were not few; and if the secret history of the county had been written in full both names would have been found well represented. It is true that the status of each was so different that they might have belonged to different continents—or to different worlds for the matter of that—for hitherto their orbits had never crossed. The Brents were accorded by the whole section of the country a unique social dominance, and had ever held themselves as high above the yeoman class to which Margaret Delandre belonged, as a blue-blooded Spanish hidalgo out-tops his peasant tenantry.

The Delandres had an ancient record and were proud of it in their way as the Brents were of theirs. But the family had never risen above yeomanry; and although they had been once well-to-do in the good old times of foreign wars and protection, their fortunes had withered under the scorching of the free trade sun and the "piping times of peace." They had, as the elder members used to assert, "stuck to the land," with the result that they had taken root in it, body and soul. In fact, they, having chosen the life of vegetables, had flourished as vegetation does—blossomed and thrived in the good season and suffered in the bad. Their holding, Dander's Croft, seemed to have been worked out, and to be typical of the family which had inhabited it. The latter had declined generation after generation, sending out now and again some abortive shoot of unsatisfied energy in the shape of a soldier or sailor, who had worked his way to the minor grades of the services and had there stopped, cut short either from unheeding gallantry in action or from that destroying cause to men without breeding or youthful care—the recognition of a position above them which they feel unfitted to fill. So, little by little, the family dropped lower and lower, the men brooding and dissatisfied, and drinking themselves into the grave, the women drudging at home, or marrying beneath them—or worse. In process of time all disappeared, leaving only two in the Croft, Wykham Delandre and his sister Margaret. The man and woman seemed to have inherited in masculine and feminine form respectively the evil tendency of their race, sharing in common the principles, though manifesting them in different ways, of sullen passion, voluptuousness and recklessness.

The history of the Brents had been something similar, but showing the causes of decadence in their aristocratic and not their plebeian forms. They, too, had sent their shoots to the wars; but their positions had been different and they had often attained honour—for without flaw they were gallant, and brave deeds were done by them before the selfish dissipation which marked them had sapped their vigour.

The present head of the family—if family it could now be called when one remained of the direct line—was Geoffrey Brent. He was almost a type of worn out race, manifesting in some ways its most brilliant qualities, and in others its utter degradation. He might be fairly compared with some of those antique Italian nobles whom the painters have preserved to us with their courage, their unscrupulousness, their refinement of lust and cruelty—the voluptuary actual with the fiend potential. He was certainly handsome, with that dark, aquiline, commanding beauty which women so generally recognise as dominant. With men he was distant and cold; but such a bearing never deters womankind. The inscrutable laws of sex have so arranged that even a timid woman is not afraid of a fierce and haughty man. And so it was that there was hardly a woman of any kind or degree, who lived within view of Brent's Rock, who did not cherish some form of secret admiration for the handsome wastrel. The category was a wide one, for Brent's Rock rose up steeply from the midst of a level region and for a circuit of a hundred miles it lay on the horizon, with its high old towers and steep roofs cutting the level edge of wood and hamlet, and far-scattered mansions.

So long as Geoffrey Brent confined his dissipations to London and Paris and Vienna—anywhere out of sight and sound of his home—opinion was silent. It is easy to listen to far off echoes unmoved, and we can treat them with disbelief, or scorn, or disdain, or whatever attitude of coldness may suit our purpose. But when the scandal came close home it was another matter; and the feelings of independence and integrity which is in people of every community which is not utterly spoiled, asserted itself and demanded that condemnation should be expressed. Still there was a certain reticence in all, and no more notice was taken of the existing facts than was absolutely necessary. Margaret Delandre bore herself so fearlessly and so openly—she accepted her position as the justified companion of Geoffrey Brent so naturally that people came to believe that she was secretly married to him, and therefore thought it wiser to hold their tongues lest time should justify her and also make her an active enemy.

The one person who, by his interference, could have settled all doubts was debarred by circumstances from interfering in the matter. Wykham Delandre had quarrelled with his sister—or perhaps it was that she had quarrelled with him—and they were on terms not merely of armed neutrality but of bitter hatred. The quarrel had been antecedent to Margaret going to Brent's Rock. She and Wykham had almost come to blows. There had certainly been threats on one side and on the other; and in the end Wykham, overcome with passion, had ordered his sister to leave his house. She had risen straightway, and, without waiting to pack up even her own personal belongings, had walked out of the house. On the threshold she had paused for a moment to hurl a bitter threat at Wykham that he would rue in shame and despair to the last hour of his life his act of that day. Some weeks had since passed; and it was understood in the neighbourhood that Margaret had gone to London, when she suddenly appeared driving out with Geoffrey Brent, and the entire neighbourhood knew before nightfall that she had taken up her abode at the Rock. It was no subject of surprise that Brent had come back unexpectedly, for such was his usual custom. Even his own servants never knew when to expect him, for there was a private door, of which he alone had the key, by which he sometimes entered without anyone in the house being aware of his coming. This was his usual method of appearing after a long absence.

Wykham Delandre was furious at the news. He vowed vengeance— and to keep his mind level with his passion drank deeper than ever. He tried several times to see his sister, but she contemptuously refused to meet him. He tried to have an interview with Brent and was refused by him also. Then he tried to stop him in the road, but without avail, for Geoffrey was not a man to be stopped against his will. Several actual encounters took place between the two men, and many more were threatened and avoided. At last Wykham Delandre settled down to a morose, vengeful acceptance of the situation.

Neither Margaret nor Geoffrey was of a pacific temperament, and it was not long before there began to be quarrels between them. One thing would lead to another, and wine flowed freely at Brent's Rock. Now and again the quarrels would assume a bitter aspect, and threats would be exchanged in uncompromising language that fairly awed the listening servants. But such quarrels generally ended where domestic altercations do, in reconciliation, and in a mutual respect for the fighting qualities proportionate to their manifestation. Fighting for its own sake is found by a certain class of persons, all the world over, to be a matter of absorbing interest, and there is no reason to believe that domestic conditions minimise its potency. Geoffrey and Margaret made occasional absences from Brent's Rock, and on each of these occasions Wykham Delandre also absented himself; but as he generally heard of the absence too late to be of any service, he returned home each time in a more bitter and discontented frame of mind than before.

At last there came a time when the absence from Brent's Rock became longer than before. Only a few days earlier there had been a quarrel, exceeding in bitterness anything which had gone before; but this, too, had been made up, and a trip on the Continent had been mentioned before the servants. After a few days Wykham Delandre also went away, and it was some weeks before he returned. It was noticed that he was full of some new importance—satisfaction, exaltation—they hardly knew how to call it. He went straightway to Brent's Rock, and demanded to see Geoffrey Brent, and on being told that he had not yet returned, said, with a grim decision which the servants noted:

"I shall come again. My news is solid—it can wait!" and turned away. Week after week went by, and month after month; and then there came a rumour, certified later on, that an accident had occurred in the Zermatt valley. Whilst crossing a dangerous pass the carriage containing an English lady and the driver had fallen over a precipice, the gentleman of the party, Mr. Geoffrey Brent, having been fortunately saved as he had been walking up the hill to ease the horses. He gave information, and search was made. The broken rail, the excoriated roadway, the marks where the horses had struggled on the decline before finally pitching over into the torrent—all told the sad tale. It was a wet season, and there had been much snow in the winter, so that the river was swollen beyond its usual volume, and the eddies of the stream were packed with ice. All search was made, and finally the wreck of the carriage and the body of one horse were found in an eddy of the river. Later on the body of the driver was found on the sandy, torrent-swept waste near Täsch; but the body of the lady, like that of the other horse, had quite disappeared, and was—what was left of it by that time—whirling amongst the eddies of the Rhone on its way down to the Lake of Geneva.

Wykham Delandre made all the enquiries possible, but could not find any trace of the missing woman. He found, however, in the books of the various hotels the name of "Mr. and Mrs. Geoffrey Brent." And he had a stone erected at Zermatt to his sister's memory, under her married name, and a tablet put up in the church at Bretten, the parish in which both Brent's Rock and Dander's Croft were situated.

There was a lapse of nearly a year, after the excitement of the matter had worn away, and the whole neighbourhood had gone on its accustomed way. Brent was still absent, and Delandre more drunken, more morose, and more revengeful than before.

Then there was a new excitement. Brent's Rock was being made ready for a new mistress. It was officially announced by Geoffrey himself in a letter to the Vicar, that he had been married some months before to an Italian lady, and that they were then on their way home. Then a small army of workmen invaded the house; and hammer and plane sounded, and a general air of size and paint pervaded the atmosphere. One wing of the old house, the south, was entirely re-done; and then the great body of the workmen departed, leaving only materials for the doing of the old hall when Geoffrey Brent should have returned, for he had directed that the decoration was only to be done under his own eyes. He had brought with him accurate drawings of a hall in the house of his bride's father, for he wished to reproduce for her the place to which she had been accustomed. As the moulding had all to be re-done, some scaffolding poles and boards were brought in and laid on one side of the great hall, and also a great wooden tank or box for mixing the lime, which was laid in bags beside it.

When the new mistress of Brent's Rock arrived the bells of the church rang out, and there was a general jubilation. She was a beautiful creature, full of the poetry and fire and passion of the South; and the few English words which she had learned were spoken in such a sweet and pretty broken way that she won the hearts of the people almost as much by the music of her voice as by the melting beauty of her dark eyes.

Geoffrey Brent seemed more happy than he had ever before appeared; but there was a dark, anxious look on his face that was new to those who knew him of old, and he started at times as though at some noise that was unheard by others.

And so months passed and the whisper grew that at last Brent's Rock was to have an heir. Geoffrey was very tender to his wife, and the new bond between them seemed to soften him. He took more interest in his tenants and their needs than he had ever done; and works of charity on his part as well as on his sweet young wife's were not lacking. He seemed to have set all his hopes on the child that was coming, and as he looked deeper into the future the dark shadow that had come over his face seemed to die gradually away.

All the time Wykham Delandre nursed his revenge. Deep in his heart had grown up a purpose of vengeance which only waited an opportunity to crystallise and take a definite shape. His vague idea was somehow centred in the wife of Brent, for he knew that he could strike him best through those he loved, and the coming time seemed to hold in its womb the opportunity for which he longed. One night he sat alone in the living-room of his house. It had once been a handsome room in its way, but time and neglect had done their work and it was now little better than a ruin, without dignity or picturesqueness of any kind. He had been drinking heavily for some time and was more than half stupefied. He thought he heard a noise as of someone at the door and looked up. Then he called half savagely to come in; but there was no response. With a muttered blasphemy he renewed his potations. Presently he forgot all around him, sank into a daze, but suddenly awoke to see standing before him someone or something like a battered, ghostly edition of his sister. For a few moments there came upon him a sort of fear. The woman before him, with distorted features and burning eyes seemed hardly human, and the only thing that seemed a reality of his sister, as she had been, was her wealth of golden hair, and this was now streaked with grey. She eyed her brother with a long, cold stare; and he, too, as he looked and began to realise the actuality of her presence, found the hatred of her which he had had, once again surging up in his heart. All the brooding passion of the past year seemed to find a voice at once as he asked her:

"Why are you here? You're dead and buried."

"I am here, Wykham Delandre, for no love of you, but because I hate another even more than I do you!" A great passion blazed in her eyes.

"Him?" he asked, in so fierce a whisper that even the woman was for an instant startled till she regained her calm.

"Yes, him!" she answered. "But make no mistake, my revenge is my own; and I merely use you to help me to it." Wykham asked suddenly:

"Did he marry you?"

The woman's distorted face broadened out in a ghastly attempt at a smile. It was a hideous mockery, for the broken features and seamed scars took strange shapes and strange colours, and queer lines of white showed out as the straining muscles pressed on the old cicatrices.

"So you would like to know! It would please your pride to feel that your sister was truly married! Well, you shall not know. That was my revenge on you, and I do not mean to change it by a hair's breadth. I have come here tonight simply to let you know that I am alive, so that if any violence be done me where I am going there may be a witness."

"Where are you going?" demanded her brother.

"That is my affair! and I have not the least intention of letting you know!" Wykham stood up, but the drink was on him and he reeled and fell. As he lay on the floor he announced his intention of following his sister; and with an outburst of splenetic humour told her that he would follow her through the darkness by the light of her hair, and of her beauty. At this she turned on him, and said that there were others beside him that would rue her hair and her beauty too. "As he will," she hissed; "for the hair remains though the beauty be gone. When he withdrew the lynch-pin and sent us over the precipice into the torrent, he had little thought of my beauty. Perhaps his beauty would be scarred like mine were he whirled, as I was, among the rocks of the Visp, and frozen on the ice pack in the drift of the river. But let him beware! His time is coming!" and with a fierce gesture she flung open the door and passed out into the night.

Later on that night, Mrs. Brent, who was but half-asleep, became suddenly awake and spoke to her husband:

"Geoffrey, was not that the click of a lock somewhere below our window?"

But Geoffrey—though she thought that he, too, had started at the noise—seemed sound asleep, and breathed heavily. Again Mrs. Brent dozed; but this time awoke to the fact that her husband had arisen and was partially dressed. He was deadly pale, and when the light of the lamp which he had in his hand fell on his face, she was frightened at the look in his eyes.

"What is it, Geoffrey? What dost thou?" she asked.

"Hush! little one," he answered, in a strange, hoarse voice. "Go to sleep. I am restless, and wish to finish some work I left undone."

"Bring it here, my husband," she said; "I am lonely and I fear when thou art away."

For reply he merely kissed her and went out, closing the door behind him. She lay awake for awhile, and then nature asserted itself, and she slept.

Suddenly she started broad awake with the memory in her ears of a smothered cry from somewhere not far off. She jumped up and ran to the door and listened, but there was no sound. She grew alarmed for her husband, and called out: "Geoffrey! Geoffrey!"

After a few moments the door of the great hall opened, and Geoffrey appeared at it, but without his lamp.

"Hush!" he said, in a sort of whisper, and his voice was harsh and stern. "Hush! Get to bed! I am working, and must not be disturbed. Go to sleep, and do not wake the house!"

With a chill in her heart—for the harshness of her husband's voice was new to her—she crept back to bed and lay there trembling, too frightened to cry, and listened to every sound. There was a long pause of silence, and then the sound of some iron implement striking muffled blows! Then there came a clang of a heavy stone falling, followed by a muffled curse. Then a dragging sound, and then more noise of stone on stone. She lay all the while in an agony of fear, and her heart beat dreadfully. She heard a curious sort of scraping sound; and then there was silence. Presently the door opened gently, and Geoffrey appeared. His wife pretended to be asleep; but through her eyelashes she saw him wash from his hands something white that looked like lime.

In the morning he made no allusion to the previous night, and she was afraid to ask any question.

From that day there seemed some shadow over Geoffrey Brent. He neither ate nor slept as he had been accustomed, and his former habit of turning suddenly as though someone were speaking from behind him revived. The old hall seemed to have some kind of fascination for him. He used to go there many times in the day, but grew impatient if anyone, even his wife, entered it. When the builder's foreman came to inquire about continuing his work Geoffrey was out driving; the man went into the hall, and when Geoffrey returned the servant told him of his arrival and where he was. With a frightful oath he pushed the servant aside and hurried up to the old hall. The workman met him almost at the door; and as Geoffrey burst into the room he ran against him. The man apologised:

"Beg pardon, sir, but I was just going out to make some enquiries. I directed twelve sacks of lime to be sent here, but I see there are only ten."

"Damn the ten sacks and the twelve too!" was the ungracious and incomprehensible rejoinder.

The workman looked surprised, and tried to turn the conversation.

"I see, sir, there is a little matter which our people must have done; but the governor will of course see it set right at his own cost."

"What do you mean?"

"That 'ere 'arth-stone, sir: Some idiot must have put a scaffold pole on it and cracked it right down the middle, and it's thick enough you'd think to stand hanythink." Geoffrey was silent for quite a minute, and then said in a constrained voice and with much gentler manner:

"Tell your people that I am not going on with the work in the hall at present. I want to leave it as it is for a while longer."

"All right sir. I'll send up a few of our chaps to take away these poles and lime bags and tidy the place up a bit."

"No! No!" said Geoffrey, "leave them where they are. I shall send and tell you when you are to get on with the work." So the foreman went away, and his comment to his master was:

"I'd send in the bill, sir, for the work already done. 'Pears to me that money's a little shaky in that quarter."

Once or twice Delandre tried to stop Brent on the road, and, at last, finding that he could not attain his object rode after the carriage, calling out:

"What has become of my sister, your wife?" Geoffrey lashed his horses into a gallop, and the other, seeing from his white face and from his wife's collapse almost into a faint that his object was attained, rode away with a scowl and a laugh.

That night when Geoffrey went into the hall he passed over to the great fireplace, and all at once started back with a smothered cry. Then with an effort he pulled himself together and went away, returning with a light. He bent down over the broken hearth-stone to see if the moonlight falling through the storied window had in any way deceived him. Then with a groan of anguish he sank to his knees.

There, sure enough, through the crack in the broken stone were protruding a multitude of threads of golden hair just tinged with grey!

He was disturbed by a noise at the door, and looking round, saw his wife standing in the doorway. In the desperation of the moment he took action to prevent discovery, and lighting a match at the lamp, stooped down and burned away the hair that rose through the broken stone. Then rising nonchalantly as he could, he pretended surprise at seeing his wife beside him.

For the next week he lived in an agony; for, whether by accident or design, he could not find himself alone in the hall for any length of time. At each visit the hair had grown afresh through the crack, and he had to watch it carefully lest his terrible secret should be discovered. He tried to find a receptacle for the body of the murdered woman outside the house, but someone always interrupted him; and once, when he was coming out of the private doorway, he was met by his wife, who began to question him about it, and manifested surprise that she should not have before noticed the key which he now reluctantly showed her. Geoffrey dearly and passionately loved his wife, so that any possibility of her discovering his dread secrets, or even of doubting him, filled him with anguish; and after a couple of days had passed, he could not help coming to the conclusion that, at least, she suspected something.

That very evening she came into the hall after her drive and found him there sitting moodily by the deserted fireplace. She spoke to him directly.

"Geoffrey, I have been spoken to by that fellow Delandre, and he says horrible things. He tells to me that a week ago his sister returned to his house, the wreck and ruin of her former self, with only her golden hair as of old, and announced some fell intention. He asked me where she is— and oh, Geoffrey, she is dead, she is dead! So how can she have returned? Oh! I am in dread, and I know not where to turn!"

For answer, Geoffrey burst into a torrent of blasphemy which made her shudder. He cursed Delandre and his sister and all their kind, and in especial he hurled curse after curse on her golden hair.

"Oh, hush! hush!" she said, and was then silent, for she feared her husband when she saw the evil effect of his humour. Geoffrey in the torrent of his anger stood up and moved away from the hearth; but suddenly stopped as he saw a new look of terror in his wife's eyes. He followed their glance, and then he too, shuddered—for there on the broken hearth-stone lay a golden streak as the point of the hair rose though the crack.

"Look, look!" she shrieked. "Is it some ghost of the dead! Come away—come away!" and seizing her husband by the wrist with the frenzy of madness, she pulled him from the room.

That night she was in a raging fever. The doctor of the district attended her at once, and special aid was telegraphed for to London. Geoffrey was in despair, and in his anguish at the danger of his young wife almost forgot his own crime and its consequences. In the evening the doctor had to leave to attend to others; but he left Geoffrey in charge of his wife. His last words were:

"Remember, you must humour her till I come in the morning, or till some other doctor has her case in hand. What you have to dread is another attack of emotion. See that she is kept warm. Nothing more can be done."

Late in the evening, when the rest of the household had retired, Geoffrey's wife got up from her bed and called to her husband.

"Come!" she said. "Come to the old hall! I know where the gold comes from! I want to see it grow!"

Geoffrey would fain have stopped her, but he feared for her life or reason on the one hand, and lest in a paroxysm she should shriek out her terrible suspicion, and seeing that it was useless to try to prevent her, wrapped a warm rug around her and went with her to the old hall. When they entered, she turned and shut the door and locked it.

"We want no strangers amongst us three tonight!" she whispered with a wan smile.

"We three! nay we are but two," said Geoffrey with a shudder; he feared to say more.

"Sit here," said his wife as she put out the light. "Sit here by the hearth and watch the gold growing. The silver moonlight is jealous! See, it steals along the floor towards the gold—our gold!" Geoffrey looked with growing horror, and saw that during the hours that had passed the golden hair had protruded further through the broken hearth-stone. He tried to hide it by placing his feet over the broken place; and his wife, drawing her chair beside him, leant over and laid her head on his shoulder.

"Now do not stir, dear," she said; "let us sit still and watch. We shall find the secret of the growing gold!" He passed his arm round her and sat silent; and as the moonlight stole along the floor she sank to sleep.

He feared to wake her; and so sat silent and miserable as the hours stole away.

Before his horror-struck eyes the golden-hair from the broken stone grew and grew; and as it increased, so his heart got colder and colder, till at last he had not power to stir, and sat with eyes full of terror watching his doom.

In the morning when the London doctor came, neither Geoffrey nor his wife could be found. Search was made in all the rooms, but without avail. As a last resource the great door of the old hall was broken open, and those who entered saw a grim and sorry sight.

There by the deserted hearth Geoffrey Brent and his young wife sat cold and white and dead. Her face was peaceful, and her eyes were closed in sleep; but his face was a sight that made all who saw it shudder, for there was on it a look of unutterable horror. The eyes were open and stared glassily at his feet, which were twined with tresses of golden hair, streaked with grey, which came through the broken hearth-stone.

6

His Unconquerable Enemy

By W. C. Morrow

I WAS SUMMONED FROM CALCUTTA TO THE HEART OF INDIA TO PER-
form a difficult surgical operation on one of the women of a great rajah's
household. I found the rajah a man of a noble character, but possessed,
as I afterwards discovered, of a sense of cruelty purely Oriental and in
contrast to the indolence of his disposition. He was so grateful for the
success that attended my mission that he urged me to remain a guest at
the palace as long as it might please me to stay, and I thankfully accepted
the invitation.

One of the male servants early attracted my notice for his marvellous capacity of malice. His name was Neranya, and I am certain that
there must have been a large proportion of Malay blood in his veins, for,
unlike the Indians (from whom he differed also in complexion), he was
extremely alert, active, nervous, and sensitive. A redeeming circumstance
was his love for his master. Once his violent temper led him to the com-
mission of an atrocious crime,—the fatal stabbing of a dwarf. In punishment for this the rajah ordered that Neranya's right arm (the offending
one) be severed from his body. The sentence was executed in a bungling
fashion by a stupid fellow armed with an axe, and I, being a surgeon, was
compelled, in order to save Neranya's life, to perform an amputation of
the stump, leaving not a vestige of the limb remaining.

After this he developed an augmented fiendishness. His love for the
rajah was changed to hate, and in his mad anger he flung discretion to the

winds. Driven once to frenzy by the rajah's scornful treatment, he sprang upon the rajah with a knife, but, fortunately, was seized and disarmed. To his unspeakable dismay the rajah sentenced him for this offence to suffer amputation of the remaining arm. It was done as in the former instance. This had the effect of putting a temporary curb on Neranya's spirit, or, rather, of changing the outward manifestations of his diabolism. Being armless, he was at first largely at the mercy of those who ministered to his needs,—a duty which I undertook to see was properly discharged, for I felt an interest in this strangely distorted nature. His sense of help-lessness, combined with a damnable scheme for revenge which he had secretly formed, caused Neranya to change his fierce, impetuous, and unruly conduct into a smooth, quiet, insinuating bearing, which he car-ried so artfully as to deceive those with whom he was brought in contact, including the rajah himself.

Neranya, being exceedingly quick, intelligent, and dexterous, and having an unconquerable will, turned his attention to the cultivating of an enlarged usefulness of his legs, feet, and toes, with so excellent effect that in time he was able to perform wonderful feats with those members. Thus his capability, especially for destructive mischief, was considerably restored.

One morning the rajah's only son, a young man of an uncommonly amiable and noble disposition, was found dead in bed. His murder was a most atrocious one, his body being mutilated in a shocking manner, but in my eyes the most significant of all the mutilations was the entire removal and disappearance of the young prince's arms.

The death of the young man nearly brought the rajah to the grave. It was not, therefore, until I had nursed him back to health that I began a systematic inquiry into the murder. I said nothing of my own discoveries and conclusions until after the rajah and his officers had failed and my work had been done; then I submitted to him a written report, making a close analysis of all the circumstances and closing by charging the crime to Neranya. The rajah, convinced by my proof and argument, at once ordered Neranya to be put to death, this to be accomplished slowly and with frightful tortures. The sentence was so cruel and revolting that it filled me with horror, and I implored that the wretch be shot. Finally, through a sense of gratitude to me, the rajah relaxed. When Neranya was charged with the crime he denied it, of course, but, seeing that the rajah was convinced, he threw aside all restraint, and, dancing, laughing, and shrieking in the most horrible manner, confessed his guilt, gloated over it, and reviled the rajah to his teeth,—this, knowing that some fearful death awaited him.

The rajah decided upon the details of the matter that night, and in the morning he informed me of his decision. It was that Neranya's life should be spared, but that both of his legs should be broken with hammers, and that then I should amputate the limbs at the trunk! Appended to this horrible sentence was a provision that the maimed wretch should be kept and tortured at regular intervals by such means as afterwards might be devised.

Sickened to the heart by the awful duty set out for me, I nevertheless performed it with success, and I care to say nothing more about that part of the tragedy. Neranya escaped death very narrowly and was a long time in recovering his wonted vitality. During all these weeks the rajah neither saw him nor made inquiries concerning him, but when, as in duty bound, I made official report that the man had recovered his strength, the rajah's eyes brightened, and he emerged with deadly activity from the stupor into which he so long had been plunged.

The rajah's palace was a noble structure, but it is necessary here to describe only the grand hall. It was an immense chamber, with a floor of polished, inlaid stone and a lofty, arched ceiling. A soft light stole into it through stained glass set in the roof and in high windows on one side. In the middle of the room was a rich fountain, which threw up a tall, slender column of water, with smaller and shorter jets grouped around it. Across one end of the hall, half-way to the ceiling, was a balcony, which communicated with the upper story of a wing, and from which a flight of stone stairs descended to the floor of the hall. During the hot summers this room was delightfully cool; it was the rajah's favorite lounging-place, and when the nights were hot he had his cot taken thither, and there he slept.

This hall was chosen for Neranya's permanent prison; here was he to stay so long as he might live, with never a glimpse of the shining world or the glorious heavens. To one of his nervous, discontented nature such confinement was worse than death. At the rajah's order there was constructed for him a small pen of open iron-work, circular, and about four feet in diameter, elevated on four slender iron posts, ten feet above the floor, and placed between the balcony and the fountain. Such was Neranya's prison. The pen was about four feet in depth, and the pen-top was left open for the convenience of the servants whose duty it should be to care for him. These precautions for his safe confinement were taken at my suggestion, for, although the man was now deprived of all four of his limbs, I still feared that he might develop some extraordinary, unheard-of power for mischief. It was provided that the attendants should reach his cage by means of a movable ladder.

All these arrangements having been made and Neranya hoisted into his cage, the rajah emerged upon the balcony to see him for the first time since the last amputation. Neranya had been lying panting and helpless on the floor of his cage, but when his quick ear caught the sound of the rajah's footfall he squirmed about until he had brought the back of his head against the railing, elevating his eyes above his chest, and enabling him to peer through the open-work of the cage. Thus the two deadly enemies faced each other. The rajah's stern face paled at sight of the hideous, shapeless thing which met his gaze; but he soon recovered, and the old hard, cruel, sinister look returned. Neranya's black hair and beard had grown long, and they added to the natural ferocity of his aspect. His eyes blazed upon the rajah with a terrible light, his lips parted, and he gasped for breath; his face was ashen with rage and despair, and his thin, distended nostrils quivered.

The rajah folded his arms and gazed down from the balcony upon the frightful wreck that he had made. Oh, the dreadful pathos of that picture; the inhumanity of it; the deep and dismal tragedy of it! Who might look into the wild, despairing heart of the prisoner and see and understand the frightful turmoil there; the surging, choking passion; unbridled but impotent ferocity; frantic thirst for a vengeance that should be deeper than hell! Neranya gazed, his shapeless body heaving, his eyes aflame; and then, in a strong, clear voice, which rang throughout the great hall, with rapid speech he hurled at the rajah the most insulting defiance, the most awful curses. He cursed the womb that had conceived him, the food that should nourish him, the wealth that had brought him power; cursed him in the name of Buddha and all the wise men; cursed by the sun, the moon, and the stars; by the continents, mountains, oceans, and rivers; by all things living; cursed his head, his heart, his entrails; cursed in a whirlwind of unmentionable words; heaped unimaginable insults and contumely upon him; called him a knave, a beast, a fool, a liar, an infamous and unspeakable coward.

The rajah heard it all calmly, without the movement of a muscle, without the slightest change of countenance; and when the poor wretch had exhausted his strength and fallen helpless and silent to the floor, the rajah, with a grim, cold smile, turned and strode away.

The days passed. The rajah, not deterred by Neranya's curses often heaped upon him, spent even more time than formerly in the great hall, and slept there oftener at night; and finally Neranya wearied of cursing and defying him, and fell into a sullen silence. The man was a study for me, and I observed every change in his fleeting moods. Generally his condition was that of miserable despair, which he attempted bravely to conceal. Even the boon of suicide had been denied him, for when he would wriggle into an erect position the rail of his pen was a foot above his head, so that he could not clamber over and break his skull on the stone floor beneath; and when he had tried to starve himself the attendants forced food down his throat; so that he abandoned such attempts. At times his eyes would blaze and his breath would come in gasps, for imaginary vengeance was working within him; but steadily he became quieter and more tractable, and was pleasant and responsive when I would converse with him. Whatever might have been the tortures which the rajah had decided on, none as yet had been ordered; and although Neranya knew that they were in contemplation, he never referred to them or complained of his lot.

The awful climax of this situation was reached one night, and even after this lapse of years I cannot approach its description without a shudder.

It was a hot night, and the rajah had gone to sleep in the great hall, lying on a high cot placed on the main floor just underneath the edge of the balcony. I had been unable to sleep in my own apartment, and so

I had stolen into the great hall through the heavily curtained entrance at the end farthest from the balcony. As I entered I heard a peculiar, soft sound above the patter of the fountain. Neranya's cage was partly concealed from my view by the spraying water, but I suspected that the unusual sound came from him. Stealing a little to one side, and crouching against the dark hangings of the wall, I could see him in the faint light which dimly illuminated the hall, and then I discovered that my surmise was correct—Neranya was quietly at work. Curious to learn more, and knowing that only mischief could have been inspiring him, I sank into a thick robe on the floor and watched him.

To my great astonishment Neranya was tearing off with his teeth the bag which served as his outer garment. He did it cautiously, casting sharp glances frequently at the rajah, who, sleeping soundly on his cot below, breathed heavily. After starting a strip with his teeth, Neranya, by the same means, would attach it to the railing of his cage and then wriggle away, much after the manner of a caterpillar's crawling, and this would cause the strip to be torn out the full length of his garment. He repeated this operation with incredible patience and skill until his entire garment had been torn into strips. Two or three of these he tied end to end with his teeth, lips, and tongue, tightening the knots by placing one end of the strip under his body and drawing the other taut with his teeth. In this way he made a line several feet long, one end of which he made fast to the rail with his mouth. It then began to dawn upon me that he was going to make an insane attempt—impossible of achievement without hands, feet, arms, or legs—to escape from his cage! For what purpose? The rajah was asleep in the hall—ah! I caught my breath. Oh, the desperate, insane thirst for revenge which could have unhinged so clear and firm a mind! Even though he should accomplish the impossible feat of climbing over the railing of his cage that he might fall to the floor below (for how could he slide down the rope?), he would be in all probability killed or stunned; and even if he should escape these dangers it would be impossible for him to clamber upon the cot without rousing the rajah, and impossible even though the rajah were dead! Amazed at the man's daring, and convinced that his sufferings and brooding had destroyed his reason, nevertheless I watched him with breathless interest.

With other strips tied together he made a short swing across one side of his cage. He caught the long line in his teeth at a point not far from the rail; then, wriggling with great effort to an upright position, his back braced against the rail, he put his chin over the swing and worked toward one end. He tightened the grasp of his chin on the swing, and with tremendous exertion, working the lower end of his spine against the railing, he began gradually to ascend the side of his cage. The labor was so great that he was compelled to pause at intervals, and his breathing was hard and painful; and even while thus resting he was in a position of terrible strain, and his pushing against the swing caused it to press hard against his windpipe and nearly strangle him.

After amazing effort he had elevated the lower end of his body until it protruded above the railing, the top of which was now across the lower end of his abdomen. Gradually he worked his body over, going backward, until there was sufficient excess of weight on the outer side of the rail; and then, with a quick lurch, he raised his head and shoulders and swung into a horizontal position on top of the rail. Of course, he would have fallen to the floor below had it not been for the line which he held in his teeth. With so great nicety had he estimated the distance between his mouth and the point where the rope was fastened to the rail, that the line tightened and checked him just as he reached the horizontal position on the rail. If one had told me beforehand that such a feat as I had just seen this man accomplish was possible, I should have thought him a fool.

Neranya was now balanced on his stomach across the top of the rail, and he eased his position by bending his spine and hanging down on either side as much as possible. Having rested thus for some minutes, he began cautiously to slide off backward, slowly paying out the line through his teeth, finding almost a fatal difficulty in passing the knots. Now, it is quite possible that the line would have escaped altogether from his teeth laterally when he would slightly relax his hold to let it slip, had it not been for a very ingenious plan to which he had resorted. This consisted in his having made a turn of the line around his neck before he attached the swing, thus securing a threefold control of the line,—one by his teeth, another by friction against his neck, and a third by his ability to compress it between his cheek and shoulder. It was quite evident now that the minutest details of a most elaborate plan had been carefully worked out by him before beginning the task, and that possibly weeks of difficult theoretical study had been consumed in the mental preparation. As I observed him I was reminded of certain hitherto unaccountable things which he had been doing for some weeks past—going through certain hitherto inexplicable motions, undoubtedly for the purpose of training his muscles for the immeasurably arduous labor which he was now performing.

A stupendous and seemingly impossible part of his task had been accomplished. Could he reach the floor in safety? Gradually he worked himself backward over the rail, in imminent danger of falling; but his nerve never wavered, and I could see a wonderful light in his eyes. With something of a lurch, his body fell against the outer side of the railing, to which he was hanging by his chin, the line still held firmly in his teeth. Slowly he slipped his chin from the rail, and then hung suspended by the line in his teeth. By almost imperceptible degrees, with infinite caution, he descended the line, and, finally, his unwieldy body rolled upon the floor, safe and unhurt!

What miracle would this superhuman monster next accomplish? I was quick and strong, and was ready and able to intercept any dangerous act; but not until danger appeared would I interfere with this extraordinary scene.

I must confess to astonishment upon having observed that Neranya, instead of proceeding directly toward the sleeping rajah, took quite another direction. Then it was only escape, after all, that the wretch contemplated, and not the murder of the rajah. But how could he escape? The only possible way to reach the outer air without great risk was by ascending the stairs to the balcony and leaving by the corridor which opened upon it, and thus fall into the hands of some British soldiers quartered thereabout, who might conceive the idea of hiding him; but surely it was impossible for Neranya to ascend that long flight of stairs! Nevertheless, he made directly for them, his method of progression this: He lay upon his back, with the lower end of his body toward the stairs; then bowed his spine upward, thus drawing his head and shoulders a little forward; straightened, and then pushed the lower end of his body forward a space equal to that through which he had drawn his head; repeating this again and again, each time, while bending his spine, preventing his head from slipping by pressing it against the floor. His progress was laborious and slow, but sensible; and, finally, he arrived at the foot of the stairs.

It was manifest that his insane purpose was to ascend them. The desire for freedom must have been strong within him! Wriggling to an upright position against the newel-post, he looked up at the great height which he had to climb and sighed; but there was no dimming of the light in his eyes. How could he accomplish the impossible task?

His solution of the problem was very simple, though daring and perilous as all the rest. While leaning against the newel-post he let himself fall diagonally upon the bottom step, where he lay partly hanging over, but safe, on his side. Turning upon his back, he wriggled forward along the step to the rail and raised himself to an upright position against it as he had against the newel-post, fell as before, and landed on the second step. In this manner, with inconceivable labor, he accomplished the ascent of the entire flight of stairs.

It being apparent to me that the rajah was not the object of Neranya's movements, the anxiety which I had felt on that account was now entirely dissipated. The things which already he had accomplished were entirely beyond the nimblest imagination. The sympathy which I had always felt for the wretched man was now greatly quickened; and as infinitesimally small as I knew his chances for escape to be, I nevertheless hoped that he would succeed. Any assistance from me, however, was out of the question; and it never should be known that I had witnessed the escape.

Neranya was now upon the balcony, and I could dimly see him wriggling along toward the door which led out upon the balcony. Finally he stopped and wriggled to an upright position against the rail, which had wide openings between the balusters. His back was toward me, but he slowly turned and faced me and the hall. At that great distance I could not distinguish his features, but the slowness with which he had worked, even before he had fully accomplished the ascent of the stairs, was evidence all too eloquent of his extreme exhaustion. Nothing but a most desperate resolution could have sustained him thus far, but he had drawn upon the last remnant of his strength. He looked around the hall with a sweeping glance, and then down upon the rajah, who was sleeping immediately beneath him, over twenty feet below. He looked long and earnestly, sinking lower, and lower, and lower upon the rail. Suddenly, to my inconceivable astonishment and dismay, he toppled through and shot downward from his lofty height! I held my breath, expecting to see him crushed upon the stone floor beneath; but instead of that he fell full upon the rajah's breast, driving him through the cot to the floor. I sprang forward with a loud cry for help, and was instantly at the scene of the catastrophe. With indescribable horror I saw that Neranya's teeth were buried in the rajah's throat! I tore the wretch away, but the blood was pouring from the rajah's arteries, his chest was crushed in, and he was gasping in the agony of death. People came running in, terrified. I turned to Neranya. He lay upon his back, his face hideously smeared with blood. Murder, and not escape, had been his intentions from the beginning; and he had employed the only method by which there was ever a possibility of accomplishing it. I knelt beside him, and saw that he too was dying; his back had been broken by the fall. He smiled sweetly into my face, and a triumphant look of accomplished revenge sat upon his face even in death.

The Story of the Brazilian Cat

By Arthur Conan Doyle

IT IS HARD LUCK ON A YOUNG FELLOW TO HAVE EXPENSIVE TASTES, great expectations, aristocratic connections, but no actual money in his pocket, and no profession by which he may earn any. The fact was that my father, a good, sanguine, easy-going man, had such confidence in the wealth and benevolence of his bachelor elder brother, Lord Southerton, that he took it for granted that I, his only son, would never be called upon to earn a living for myself. He imagined that if there were not a vacancy for me on the great Southerton Estates, at least there would be found some post in that diplomatic service which still remains the special preserve of our privileged classes. He died too early to realize how false his calculations had been. Neither my uncle nor the State took the slightest notice of me, or showed any interest in my career. An occasional brace of pheasants, or basket of hares, was all that ever reached me to remind me that I was heir to Otwell House and one of the richest estates in the country. In the meantime, I found myself a bachelor and man about town, living in a suite of apartments in Grosvenor Mansions, with no occupation save that of pigeon-shooting and polo-playing at Hurlingham. Month by month I realized that it was more and more difficult to get the brokers to renew my bills, or to cash any further post-obits upon an unentailed property. Ruin lay right across my path, and every day I saw it clearer, nearer, and more absolutely unavoidable.

What made me feel my own poverty the more was that, apart from the great wealth of Lord Southerton, all my other relations were fairly well-to-do. The nearest of these was Everard King, my father's nephew and my own first cousin, who had spent an adventurous life in Brazil, and had now returned to this country to settle down on his fortune. We never knew how he made his money, but he appeared to have plenty of it, for he bought the estate of Greylands, near Clipton-on-the-Marsh, in Suffolk. For the first year of his residence in England he took no more notice of me than my miserly uncle; but at last one summer morning, to my very great relief and joy, I received a letter asking me to come down that very day and spend a short visit at Greylands Court. I was expecting a rather long visit to Bankruptcy Court at the time, and this interruption seemed almost providential. If I could only get on terms with this unknown relative of mine, I might pull through yet. For the family credit he could not let me go entirely to the wall. I ordered my valet to pack my valise, and I set off the same evening for Clipton-on-the-Marsh.

After changing at Ipswich, a little local train deposited me at a small, deserted station lying amidst a rolling grassy country, with a sluggish and winding river curving in and out amidst the valleys, between high, silted banks, which showed that we were within reach of the tide. No carriage was awaiting me (I found afterwards that my telegram had been delayed), so I hired a dogcart at the local inn. The driver, an excellent fellow, was full of my relative's praises, and I learned from him that Mr. Everard King was already a name to conjure with in that part of the county. He had entertained the school-children, he had thrown his grounds open to visitors, he had subscribed to charities—in short, his benevolence had been so universal that my driver could only account for it on the supposition that he had parliamentary ambitions.

My attention was drawn away from my driver's panegyric by the appearance of a very beautiful bird which settled on a telegraph-post beside the road. At first I thought that it was a jay, but it was larger, with a brighter plumage. The driver accounted for its presence at once by saying that it belonged to the very man whom we were about to visit. It seems that the acclimatization of foreign creatures was one of his hobbies, and that he had brought with him from Brazil a number of birds and beasts which he was endeavouring to rear in England. When once we had passed the gates of Greylands Park we had ample evidence of this taste of his. Some small spotted deer, a curious wild pig known, I believe, as a peccary, a gorgeously feathered oriole, some sort of armadillo, and a singular lumbering in-toed beast like a very fat badger, were among the creatures which I observed as we drove along the winding avenue.

Mr. Everard King, my unknown cousin, was standing in person upon the steps of his house, for he had seen us in the distance, and guessed that it was I. His appearance was very homely and benevolent, short and stout, forty-five years old, perhaps, with a round, good-humoured face, burned brown with the tropical sun, and shot with a thousand wrinkles. He wore white linen clothes, in true planter style, with a cigar between his lips, and a large Panama hat upon the back of his head. It was such a figure as one associates with a verandahed bungalow, and it looked curiously out of place in front of this broad, stone English mansion, with its solid wings and its Palladio pillars before the doorway.

"My dear!" he cried, glancing over his shoulder; "my dear, here is our guest! Welcome, welcome to Greylands! I am delighted to make your acquaintance, Cousin Marshall, and I take it as a great compliment that you should honour this sleepy little country place with your presence."

Nothing could be more hearty than his manner, and he set me at my ease in an instant. But it needed all his cordiality to atone for the frigidity and even rudeness of his wife, a tall, haggard woman, who came forward at his summons. She was, I believe, of Brazilian extraction, though she spoke excellent English, and I excused her manners on the score of her ignorance of our customs. She did not attempt to conceal, however, either then or afterwards, that I was no very welcome visitor at Greylands Court. Her actual words were, as a rule, courteous, but she was the possessor of a pair of particularly expressive dark eyes, and I read in them very clearly from the first that she heartily wished me back in London once more.

However, my debts were too pressing and my designs upon my wealthy relative were too vital for me to allow them to be upset by the ill-temper of his wife, so I disregarded her coldness and reciprocated the extreme cordiality of his welcome. No pains had been spared by him to make me comfortable. My room was a charming one. He implored me to tell him anything which could add to my happiness. It was on the tip of my tongue to inform him that a blank cheque would materially help towards that end, but I felt that it might be premature in the present state of our acquaintance. The dinner was excellent, and as we sat together afterwards over his Havanas and coffee, which later he told me was specially prepared upon his own plantation, it seemed to me that all my driver's eulogies were justified, and that I had never met a more large-hearted and hospitable man.

But, in spite of his cheery good nature, he was a man with a strong will and a fiery temper of his own. Of this I had an example upon the following morning. The curious aversion which Mrs. Everard King had conceived towards me was so strong, that her manner at breakfast was almost offensive. But her meaning became unmistakable when her husband had quitted the room.

"The best train in the day is at twelve-fifteen," said she.

"But I was not thinking of going today," I answered, frankly—perhaps even defiantly, for I was determined not to be driven out by this woman.

"Oh, if it rests with you—" said she, and stopped with a most insolent expression in her eyes.

"I am sure," I answered, "that Mr. Everard King would tell me if I were outstaying my welcome."

"What's this? What's this?" said a voice, and there he was in the room. He had overheard my last words, and a glance at our faces had told him the rest. In an instant his chubby, cheery face set into an expression of absolute ferocity.

"Might I trouble you to walk outside, Marshall?" said he. (I may mention that my own name is Marshall King.)

He closed the door behind me, and then, for an instant, I heard him talking in a low voice of concentrated passion to his wife. This gross breach of hospitality had evidently hit upon his tenderest point. I am no eavesdropper, so I walked out on to the lawn. Presently I heard a hurried step behind me, and there was the lady, her face pale with excitement, and her eyes red with tears.

"My husband has asked me to apologize to you, Mr. Marshall King," said she, standing with downcast eyes before me.

"Please do not say another word, Mrs. King."

Her dark eyes suddenly blazed out at me.

"You fool!" she hissed, with frantic vehemence, and turning on her heel swept back to the house.

The insult was so outrageous, so insufferable, that I could only stand staring after her in bewilderment. I was still there when my host joined me. He was his cheery, chubby self once more.

"I hope that my wife has apologized for her foolish remarks," said he.

"Oh, yes—yes, certainly!"

He put his hand through my arm and walked with me up and down the lawn.

"You must not take it seriously," said he. "It would grieve me inexpressibly if you curtailed your visit by one hour. The fact is—there is no reason why there should be any concealment between relatives—that my poor dear wife is incredibly jealous. She hates that anyone—male or female—should for an instant come between us. Her ideal is a desert island and an eternal tete-a-tete. That gives you the clue to her actions, which are, I confess, upon this particular point, not very far removed from mania. Tell me that you will think no more of it."

"No, no; certainly not."

"Then light this cigar and come round with me and see my little menagerie."

The whole afternoon was occupied by this inspection, which included all the birds, beasts, and even reptiles which he had imported. Some were free, some in cages, a few actually in the house. He spoke with enthusiasm of his successes and his failures, his births and his deaths, and he would cry out in his delight, like a schoolboy, when, as we walked, some gaudy bird would flutter up from the grass, or some curious beast slink into the cover. Finally he led me down a corridor which extended from one wing of the house. At the end of this there was a heavy door with a sliding shutter in it, and beside it there projected from the wall an iron handle attached to a wheel and a drum. A line of stout bars extended across the passage.

"I am about to show you the jewel of my collection," said he. "There is only one other specimen in Europe, now that the Rotterdam cub is dead. It is a Brazilian cat."

"But how does that differ from any other cat?"

"You will soon see that," said he, laughing. "Will you kindly draw that shutter and look through?"

I did so, and found that I was gazing into a large, empty room, with stone flags, and small, barred windows upon the farther wall. In the centre of this room, lying in the middle of a golden patch of sunlight, there was stretched a huge creature, as large as a tiger, but as black and sleek as ebony. It was simply a very enormous and very well-kept black cat, and it cuddled up and basked in that yellow pool of light exactly as a cat would do. It was so graceful, so sinewy, and so gently and smoothly diabolical, that I could not take my eyes from the opening.

"Isn't he splendid?" said my host, enthusiastically.

"Glorious! I never saw such a noble creature."

"Some people call it a black puma, but really it is not a puma at all. That fellow is nearly eleven feet from tail to tip. Four years ago he was a little ball of black fluff, with two yellow eyes staring out of it. He was sold me as a new-born cub up in the wild country at the head-waters of the Rio Negro. They speared his mother to death after she had killed a dozen of them."

"They are ferocious, then?"

"The most absolutely treacherous and bloodthirsty creatures upon earth. You talk about a Brazilian cat to an up-country Indian, and see him get the jumps. They prefer humans to game. This fellow has never tasted living blood yet, but when he does he will be a terror. At present he won't stand anyone but me in his den. Even Baldwin, the groom, dare not go near him. As to me, I am his mother and father in one."

As he spoke he suddenly, to my astonishment, opened the door and slipped in, closing it instantly behind him. At the sound of his voice the huge, lithe creature rose, yawned and rubbed its round, black head affectionately against his side, while he patted and fondled it.

"Now, Tommy, into your cage!" said he.

The monstrous cat walked over to one side of the room and coiled itself up under a grating. Everard King came out, and taking the iron handle which I have mentioned, he began to turn it. As he did so the line of bars in the corridor began to pass through a slot in the wall and closed up the front of this grating, so as to make an effective cage. When it was in position he opened the door once more and invited me into the room, which was heavy with the pungent, musty smell peculiar to the great carnivora.

"That's how we work it," said he. "We give him the run of the room for exercise, and then at night we put him in his cage. You can let him out by turning the handle from the passage, or you can, as you have seen, coop him up in the same way. No, no, you should not do that!"

I had put my hand between the bars to pat the glossy, heaving flank. He pulled it back, with a serious face.

"I assure you that he is not safe. Don't imagine that because I can take liberties with him anyone else can. He is very exclusive in his friends—aren't you, Tommy? Ah, he hears his lunch coming to him! Don't you, boy?"

A step sounded in the stone-flagged passage, and the creature had sprung to his feet, and was pacing up and down the narrow cage, his yellow eyes gleaming, and his scarlet tongue rippling and quivering over the white line of his jagged teeth. A groom entered with a coarse joint upon a tray, and thrust it through the bars to him. He pounced lightly upon it, carried it off to the corner, and there, holding it between his paws, tore and wrenched at it, raising his bloody muzzle every now and then to look at us. It was a malignant and yet fascinating sight.

"You can't wonder that I am fond of him, can you?" said my host, as we left the room, "especially when you consider that I have had the rearing of him. It was no joke bringing him over from the centre of South America; but here he is safe and sound—and, as I have said, far the most perfect specimen in Europe. The people at the Zoo are dying to have him, but I really can't part with him. Now, I think that I have inflicted my hobby upon you long enough, so we cannot do better than follow Tommy's example, and go to our lunch."

My South American relative was so engrossed by his grounds and their curious occupants, that I hardly gave him credit at first for having any interests outside them. That he had some, and pressing ones, was soon borne in upon me by the number of telegrams which he received. They arrived at all hours, and were always opened by him with the utmost eagerness and anxiety upon his face. Sometimes I imagined that it must be the Turf, and sometimes the Stock Exchange, but certainly he had some very urgent business going forwards which was not transacted upon the Downs of Suffolk. During the six days of my visit he had never fewer than three or four telegrams a day, and sometimes as many as seven or eight.

I had occupied these six days so well, that by the end of them I had succeeded in getting upon the most cordial terms with my cousin. Every night we had sat up late in the billiard-room, he telling me the most extraordinary stories of his adventures in America—stories so desperate and reckless, that I could hardly associate them with the brown little, chubby man before me. In return, I ventured upon some of my own reminiscences of London life, which interested him so much, that he vowed he would come up to Grosvenor Mansions and stay with me. He was anxious to see the faster side of city life, and certainly, though I say it, he could not have chosen a more competent guide. It was not until the last day of my visit that I ventured to approach that which was on my mind. I told him frankly about my pecuniary difficulties and my impending ruin, and I asked his advice—though I hoped for something more solid. He listened attentively, puffing hard at his cigar.

"But surely," said he, "you are the heir of our relative, Lord Southerton?"

"I have every reason to believe so, but he would never make me any allowance."

"No, no, I have heard of his miserly ways. My poor Marshall, your position has been a very hard one. By the way, have you heard any news of Lord Southerton's health lately?"

"He has always been in a critical condition ever since my childhood."

"Exactly—a creaking hinge, if ever there was one. Your inheritance may be a long way off. Dear me, how awkwardly situated you are!"

"I had some hopes, sir, that you, knowing all the facts, might be inclined to advance——"

"Don't say another word, my dear boy," he cried, with the utmost cordiality; "we shall talk it over tonight, and I give you my word that whatever is in my power shall be done."

I was not sorry that my visit was drawing to a close, for it is unpleasant to feel that there is one person in the house who eagerly desires your departure. Mrs. King's sallow face and forbidding eyes had become more and more hateful to me. She was no longer actively rude—her fear of her husband prevented her—but she pushed her insane jealousy to the extent of ignoring me, never addressing me, and in every way making my stay at Greylands as uncomfortable as she could. So offensive was her manner during that last day, that I should certainly have left had it not been for that interview with my host in the evening which would, I hoped, retrieve my broken fortunes.

It was very late when it occurred, for my relative, who had been receiving even more telegrams than usual during the day, went off to his study after dinner, and only emerged when the household had retired to bed. I heard him go round locking the doors, as custom was of a night, and finally he joined me in the billiard-room. His stout figure was wrapped in a dressing-gown, and he wore a pair of red Turkish slippers without any heels. Settling down into an arm-chair, he brewed himself a glass of grog, in which I could not help noticing that the whisky considerably predominated over the water.

"My word!" said he, "what a night!"

It was, indeed. The wind was howling and screaming round the house, and the latticed windows rattled and shook as if they were coming in. The glow of the yellow lamps and the flavour of our cigars seemed the brighter and more fragrant for the contrast.

"Now, my boy," said my host, "we have the house and the night to ourselves. Let me have an idea of how your affairs stand, and I will see what can be done to set them in order. I wish to hear every detail."

Thus encouraged, I entered into a long exposition, in which all my tradesmen and creditors from my landlord to my valet, figured in turn. I had notes in my pocket-book, and I marshalled my facts, and gave, I flatter myself, a very businesslike statement of my own unbusinesslike ways and lamentable position. I was depressed, however, to notice that my companion's eyes were vacant and his attention elsewhere. When he did occasionally throw out a remark it was so entirely perfunctory and pointless, that I was sure he had not in the least followed my remarks. Every now and then he roused himself and put on some show of interest, asking me to repeat or to explain more fully, but it was always to sink once more into the same brown study. At last he rose and threw the end of his cigar into the grate.

"I'll tell you what, my boy," said he. "I never had a head for figures, so you will excuse me. You must jot it all down upon paper, and let me have a note of the amount. I'll understand it when I see it in black and white."

The proposal was encouraging. I promised to do so.

"And now it's time we were in bed. By Jove, there's one o'clock striking in the hall."

The tingling of the chiming clock broke through the deep roar of the gale. The wind was sweeping past with the rush of a great river.

"I must see my cat before I go to bed," said my host. "A high wind excites him. Will you come?"

"Certainly," said I.

"Then tread softly and don't speak, for everyone is asleep."

We passed quietly down the lamp-lit Persian-rugged hall, and through the door at the farther end. All was dark in the stone corridor, but a stable lantern hung on a hook, and my host took it down and lit it. There was no grating visible in the passage, so I knew that the beast was in its cage.

"Come in!" said my relative, and opened the door.

A deep growling as we entered showed that the storm had really excited the creature. In the flickering light of the lantern, we saw it, a huge black mass coiled in the corner of its den and throwing a squat, uncouth shadow upon the whitewashed wall. Its tail switched angrily among the straw.

"Poor Tommy is not in the best of tempers," said Everard King, holding up the lantern and looking in at him. "What a black devil he looks, doesn't he? I must give him a little supper to put him in a better humour. Would you mind holding the lantern for a moment?"

I took it from his hand and he stepped to the door.

"His larder is just outside here," said he. "You will excuse me for an instant won't you?" He passed out, and the door shut with a sharp metallic click behind him.

That hard crisp sound made my heart stand still. A sudden wave of terror passed over me. A vague perception of some monstrous treachery turned me cold. I sprang to the door, but there was no handle upon the inner side.

"Here!" I cried. "Let me out!"

"All right! Don't make a row!" said my host from the passage. "You've got the light all right."

"Yes, but I don't care about being locked in alone like this."

"Don't you?" I heard his hearty, chuckling laugh. "You won't be alone long."

"Let me out, sir!" I repeated angrily. "I tell you I don't allow practical jokes of this sort."

"Practical is the word," said he, with another hateful chuckle. And then suddenly I heard, amidst the roar of the storm, the creak and whine of the winch-handle turning and the rattle of the grating as it passed through the slot. Great God, he was letting loose the Brazilian cat!

In the light of the lantern I saw the bars sliding slowly before me. Already there was an opening a foot wide at the farther end. With a scream I seized the last bar with my hands and pulled with the strength of a madman. I was a madman with rage and horror. For a minute or more I held the thing motionless. I knew that he was straining with all his force upon the handle, and that the leverage was sure to overcome me. I gave inch by inch, my feet sliding along the stones, and all the time I begged and prayed this inhuman monster to save me from this horrible death. I conjured him by his kinship. I reminded him that I was his guest; I begged to know what harm I had ever done him. His only answers were the tugs and jerks upon the handle, each of which, in spite of all my struggles, pulled another bar through the opening. Clinging and clutching, I was dragged across the whole front of the cage, until at last, with aching wrists and lacerated fingers, I gave up the hopeless struggle. The grating clanged back as I released it, and an instant later I heard the shuffle of the Turkish slippers in the passage, and the slam of the distant door. Then everything was silent.

The creature had never moved during this time. He lay still in the corner, and his tail had ceased switching. This apparition of a man adhering to his bars and dragged screaming across him had apparently filled him with amazement. I saw his great eyes staring steadily at me. I had dropped the lantern when I seized the bars, but it still burned upon the floor, and I made a movement to grasp it, with some idea that its light might protect me. But the instant I moved, the beast gave a deep and menacing growl. I stopped and stood still, quivering with fear in every limb. The cat (if one may call so fearful a creature by so homely a name) was not more than ten feet from me. The eyes glimmered like two disks of phosphorus in the darkness. They appalled and yet fascinated me. I could not take my own eyes from them. Nature plays strange tricks with us at such moments of intensity, and those glimmering lights waxed and waned with a steady rise and fall. Sometimes they seemed to be tiny points of extreme brilliancy—little electric sparks in the black obscurity—then they would widen and widen until all that corner of the room was filled with their shifting and sinister light. And then suddenly they went out altogether.

The beast had closed its eyes. I do not know whether there may be any truth in the old idea of the dominance of the human gaze, or whether the huge cat was simply drowsy, but the fact remains that, far from showing any symptom of attacking me, it simply rested its sleek, black head upon its huge forepaws and seemed to sleep. I stood, fearing to move lest I should rouse it into malignant life once more. But at least I was able to think clearly now that the baleful eyes were off me. Here I was shut up for the night with the ferocious beast. My own instincts, to say nothing of the words of the plausible villain who laid this trap for me, warned me that the animal was as savage as its master. How could I stave it off until morning? The door was hopeless, and so were the narrow, barred windows. There was no shelter anywhere in the bare, stone-flagged room. To cry for assistance was absurd. I knew that this den was an outhouse, and that the corridor which connected it with the house was at least a hundred feet long. Besides, with the gale thundering outside, my cries were not likely to be heard. I had only my own courage and my own wits to trust to.

And then, with a fresh wave of horror, my eyes fell upon the lantern. The candle had burned low, and was already beginning to gutter. In ten minutes it would be out. I had only ten minutes then in which to do something, for I felt that if I were once left in the dark with that fearful beast I should be incapable of action. The very thought of it paralysed me. I cast my despairing eyes round this chamber of death, and they rested upon one spot which seemed to promise I will not say safety, but less immediate and imminent danger than the open floor.

I have said that the cage had a top as well as a front, and this top was left standing when the front was wound through the slot in the wall. It consisted of bars at a few inches' interval, with stout wire netting between, and it rested upon a strong stanchion at each end. It stood now as a great barred canopy over the crouching figure in the corner. The space between this iron shelf and the roof may have been from two or three feet. If I could only get up there, squeezed in between bars and ceiling, I should have only one vulnerable side. I should be safe from below, from behind, and from each side. Only on the open face of it could I be attacked. There, it is true, I had no protection whatever; but at least, I should be out of the brute's path when he began to pace about his den. He would have to come out of his way to reach me. It was now or never, for if once the light were out it would be impossible. With a gulp in my throat I sprang up, seized the iron edge of the top, and swung myself panting on to it. I writhed in face downwards, and found myself looking straight into the terrible eyes and yawning jaws of the cat. Its fetid breath came up into my face like the steam from some foul pot.

It appeared, however, to be rather curious than angry. With a sleek ripple of its long, black back it rose, stretched itself, and then rearing itself on its hind legs, with one forepaw against the wall, it raised the other, and drew its claws across the wire meshes beneath me. One sharp, white hook tore through my trousers—for I may mention that I was still in evening dress—and dug a furrow in my knee. It was not meant as an attack, but rather as an experiment, for upon my giving a sharp cry of pain he dropped down again, and springing lightly into the room, he began walking swiftly round it, looking up every now and again in my direction. For my part I shuffled backwards until I lay with my back against the wall, screwing myself into the smallest space possible. The farther I got the more difficult it was for him to attack me.

He seemed more excited now that he had begun to move about, and he ran swiftly and noiselessly round and round the den, passing continually underneath the iron couch upon which I lay. It was wonderful to see so great a bulk passing like a shadow, with hardly the softest thudding of velvety pads. The candle was burning low—so low that I could hardly see the creature. And then, with a last flare and splutter it went out altogether. I was alone with the cat in the dark!

It helps one to face a danger when one knows that one has done all that possibly can be done. There is nothing for it then but to quietly await the result. In this case, there was no chance of safety anywhere except the precise spot where I was. I stretched myself out, therefore, and lay silently, almost breathlessly, hoping that the beast might forget my presence if I did nothing to remind him. I reckoned that it must already be two o'clock. At four it would be full dawn. I had not more than two hours to wait for daylight.

Outside, the storm was still raging, and the rain lashed continually against the little windows. Inside, the poisonous and fetid air was overpowering. I could neither hear nor see the cat. I tried to think about other things—but only one had power enough to draw my mind from my terrible position. That was the contemplation of my cousin's villainy, his unparalleled hypocrisy, his malignant hatred of me. Beneath that cheerful face there lurked the spirit of a medieval assassin. And as I thought of it I saw more clearly how cunningly the thing had been arranged. He had apparently gone to bed with the others. No doubt he had his witness to prove it. Then, unknown to them, he had slipped down, had lured me into his den and abandoned me. His story would be so simple. He had left me to finish my cigar in the billiard-room. I had gone down on my own account to have a last look at the cat. I had entered the room without observing that the cage was opened, and I had been caught. How could such a crime be brought home to him? Suspicion, perhaps—but proof, never!

How slowly those dreadful two hours went by! Once I heard a low, rasping sound, which I took to be the creature licking its own fur. Several times those greenish eyes gleamed at me through the darkness, but never in a fixed stare, and my hopes grew stronger that my presence had been forgotten or ignored. At last the least faint glimmer of light came through the windows—I first dimly saw them as two grey squares upon the black wall, then grey turned to white, and I could see my terrible companion once more. And he, alas, could see me!

It was evident to me at once that he was in a much more dangerous and aggressive mood than when I had seen him last. The cold of the morning had irritated him, and he was hungry as well. With a continual growl he paced swiftly up and down the side of the room which was farthest from my refuge, his whiskers bristling angrily, and his tail switching and lashing. As he turned at the corners his savage eyes always looked upwards at me with a dreadful menace. I knew then that he meant to kill me. Yet I found myself even at that moment admiring the sinuous grace of the devilish thing, its long, undulating, rippling movements, the gloss of its beautiful flanks, the vivid, palpitating scarlet of the glistening tongue which hung from the jet-black muzzle. And all the time that deep, threatening growl was rising and rising in an unbroken crescendo. I knew that the crisis was at hand.

It was a miserable hour to meet such a death—so cold, so comfortless, shivering in my light dress clothes upon this gridiron of torment upon which I was stretched. I tried to brace myself to it, to raise my soul above it, and at the same time, with the lucidity which comes to a perfectly desperate man, I cast round for some possible means of escape. One thing was clear to me. If that front of the cage was only back in its position once more, I could find a sure refuge behind it. Could I possibly pull it back? I hardly dared to move for fear of bringing the creature upon me. Slowly, very slowly, I put my hand forward until it grasped the edge of the front, the final bar which protruded through the wall. To my surprise it came quite easily to my jerk. Of course the difficulty of drawing it out arose from the fact that I was clinging to it. I pulled again, and three inches of it came through. It ran apparently on wheels. I pulled again . . . and then the cat sprang!

It was so quick, so sudden, that I never saw it happen. I simply heard the savage snarl, and in an instant afterwards the blazing yellow eyes, the flattened black head with its red tongue and flashing teeth, were within reach of me. The impact of the creature shook the bars upon which I lay, until I thought (as far as I could think of anything at such a moment) that they were coming down. The cat swayed there for an instant, the head and front paws quite close to me, the hind paws clawing to find a grip upon the edge of the grating. I heard the claws rasping as they clung to the wire-netting, and the breath of the beast made me sick. But its bound had been miscalculated. It could not retain its position. Slowly, grinning with rage, and scratching madly at the bars, it swung backwards and dropped heavily upon the floor. With a growl it instantly faced round to me and crouched for another spring.

I knew that the next few moments would decide my fate. The creature had learned by experience. It would not miscalculate again. I must act promptly, fearlessly, if I were to have a chance for life. In an instant I had formed my plan. Pulling off my dress-coat, I threw it down over the head of the beast. At the same moment I dropped over the edge, seized the end of the front grating, and pulled it frantically out of the wall.

It came more easily than I could have expected. I rushed across the room, bearing it with me; but, as I rushed, the accident of my position put me upon the outer side. Had it been the other way, I might have come off scathless. As it was, there was a moment's pause as I stopped it and tried to pass in through the opening which I had left. That moment was enough to give time to the creature to toss off the coat with which I had blinded him and to spring upon me. I hurled myself through the gap and pulled the rails to behind me, but he seized my leg before I could entirely withdraw it. One stroke of that huge paw tore off my calf as a shaving of wood curls off before a plane. The next moment, bleeding and fainting, I was lying among the foul straw with a line of friendly bars between me and the creature which ramped so frantically against them.

Too wounded to move, and too faint to be conscious of fear, I could only lie, more dead than alive, and watch it. It pressed its broad, black chest against the bars and angled for me with its crooked paws as I have seen a kitten do before a mouse-trap. It ripped my clothes, but, stretch as it would, it could not quite reach me. I have heard of the curious numbing effect produced by wounds from the great carnivora, and now I was destined to experience it, for I had lost all sense of personality, and was as interested in the cat's failure or success as if it were some game which I was watching. And then gradually my mind drifted away into strange vague dreams, always with that black face and red tongue coming back into them, and so I lost myself in the nirvana of delirium, the blessed relief of those who are too sorely tried.

Tracing the course of events afterwards, I conclude that I must have been insensible for about two hours. What roused me to consciousness once more was that sharp metallic click which had been the precursor of my terrible experience. It was the shooting back of the spring lock. Then, before my senses were clear enough to entirely apprehend what they saw, I was aware of the round, benevolent face of my cousin peering in through the open door. What he saw evidently amazed him. There was the cat crouching on the floor. I was stretched upon my back in my shirt-sleeves within the cage, my trousers torn to ribbons and a great pool of blood all round me. I can see his amazed face now, with the morning sunlight upon it. He peered at me, and peered again. Then he closed the door behind him, and advanced to the cage to see if I were really dead.

I cannot undertake to say what happened. I was not in a fit state to witness or to chronicle such events. I can only say that I was suddenly conscious that his face was away from me—that he was looking towards the animal.

"Good old Tommy!" he cried. "Good old Tommy!"

Then he came near the bars, with his back still towards me.

"Down, you stupid beast!" he roared. "Down, sir! Don't you know your master?"

Suddenly even in my bemuddled brain a remembrance came of those words of his when he had said that the taste of blood would turn the cat into a fiend. My blood had done it, but he was to pay the price.

"Get away!" he screamed. "Get away, you devil! Baldwin! Baldwin! Oh, my God!"

And then I heard him fall, and rise, and fall again, with a sound like the ripping of sacking. His screams grew fainter until they were lost in the worrying snarl. And then, after I thought that he was dead, I saw, as in a nightmare, a blinded, tattered, blood-soaked figure running wildly round the room—and that was the last glimpse which I had of him before I fainted once again.

I was many months in my recovery—in fact, I cannot say that I have ever recovered, for to the end of my days I shall carry a stick as a sign of my night with the Brazilian cat. Baldwin, the groom, and the other servants could not tell what had occurred, when, drawn by the death-cries of their master, they found me behind the bars, and his remains—or what they afterwards discovered to be his remains—in the clutch of the creature which he had reared. They stalled him off with hot irons, and afterwards shot him through the loophole of the door before they could finally extricate me. I was carried to my bedroom, and there, under the roof of my would-be murderer, I remained between life and death for several weeks. They had sent for a surgeon from Clipton and a nurse from London, and in a month I was able to be carried to the station, and so conveyed back once more to Grosvenor Mansions.

I have one remembrance of that illness, which might have been part of the ever-changing panorama conjured up by a delirious brain were it not so definitely fixed in my memory. One night, when the nurse was absent, the door of my chamber opened, and a tall woman in blackest mourning slipped into the room. She came across to me, and as she bent her sallow face I saw by the faint gleam of the night-light that it was the Brazilian woman whom my cousin had married. She stared intently into my face, and her expression was more kindly than I had ever seen it.

"Are you conscious?" she asked.

I feebly nodded—for I was still very weak.

"Well; then, I only wished to say to you that you have yourself to blame. Did I not do all I could for you? From the beginning I tried to drive you from the house. By every means, short of betraying my husband, I tried to save you from him. I knew that he had a reason for bringing you here. I knew that he would never let you get away again. No one knew him as I knew him, who had suffered from him so often. I did not dare to tell you all this. He would have killed me. But I did my best for you. As things have turned out, you have been the best friend that I have ever had. You have set me free, and I fancied that nothing but death would do that. I am sorry if you are hurt, but I cannot reproach myself. I told you that you were a fool—and a fool you have been." She crept out of the room, the bitter, singular woman, and I was never destined to see her again. With what remained from her husband's property she went back to her native land, and I have heard that she afterwards took the veil at Pernambuco.

It was not until I had been back in London for some time that the doctors pronounced me to be well enough to do business. It was not a very welcome permission to me, for I feared that it would be the signal for an inrush of creditors; but it was Summers, my lawyer, who first took advantage of it.

"I am very glad to see that your lordship is so much better," said he. "I have been waiting a long time to offer my congratulations."

"What do you mean, Summers? This is no time for joking."

"I mean what I say," he answered. "You have been Lord Southerton for the last six weeks, but we feared that it would retard your recovery if you were to learn it."

Lord Southerton! One of the richest peers in England! I could not believe my ears. And then suddenly I thought of the time which had elapsed, and how it coincided with my injuries.

"Then Lord Southerton must have died about the same time that I was hurt?"

"His death occurred upon that very day." Summers looked hard at me as I spoke, and I am convinced—for he was a very shrewd fellow—that he had guessed the true state of the case. He paused for a moment as if awaiting a confidence from me, but I could not see what was to be gained by exposing such a family scandal.

"Yes, a very curious coincidence," he continued, with the same knowing look. "Of course, you are aware that your cousin Everard King was the next heir to the estates. Now, if it had been you instead of him who had been torn to pieces by this tiger, or whatever it was, then of course he would have been Lord Southerton at the present moment."

"No doubt," said I.

"And he took such an interest in it," said Summers. "I happen to know that the late Lord Southerton's valet was in his pay, and that he used to have telegrams from him every few hours to tell him how he was getting on. That would be about the time when you were down there. Was it not strange that he should wish to be so well informed, since he knew that he was not the direct heir?"

"Very strange," said I. "And now, Summers, if you will bring me my bills and a new cheque-book, we will begin to get things into order."

The Wife of the Kenite

By Agatha Christie

HERR SCHAEFER REMOVED HIS HAT AND WIPED HIS PERSPIRING BROW. He was hot. He was hungry and thirsty—especially the latter. But, above all, he was anxious. Before him stretched the yellow expanse of the veldt. Behind him, the line of the horizon was broken by the "dumps" of the outlying portion of the Reef. And from far away, in the direction of Johannesburg, came a sound like distant thunder. But it was not thunder, as Herr Schaefer knew only too well. It was monotonous and regular, and represented the triumph of law and order over the forces of Revolution.

Incidentally, it was having a most wearing effect on the nerves of Herr Schaefer. The position in which he found himself was an unpleasant one. The swift efficient proclamation of martial law, followed by the dramatic arrival of Smuts with the tyres of his car shot flat, had had the effect of completely disorganising the carefully laid plans of Schaefer and his friends, and Schaefer himself had narrowly escaped being laid by the heels. For the moment he was at large, but the present was uncomfortable, and the future too problematical to be pleasant.

In good, sound German, Herr Schaefer cursed the country, the climate, the Rand and all workers thereon, and most especially his late employers, the Reds. As a paid agitator, he had done his work with true German efficiency, but his military upbringing, and his years of service with the German Army in Belgium, led him to admire the forcefulness of Smuts, and to despise unfeignedly the untrained rabble, devoid of discipline, which had crumbled to pieces at the first real test.

"They are scum," said Herr Schaefer, gloomily, moistening his cracked lips. "Swine! No drilling. No order. No discipline. Ragged commandos riding loose about the veldt! Ah! If they had but one Prussian drill sergeant!"

Involuntarily his back straightened. For a year he had been endeavouring to cultivate a slouch which, together with a ragged beard, might make his apparent dealing in such innocent vegetable produce as cabbages, cauliflowers, and potatoes less open to doubt. A momentary shiver went down his spine as he reflected that certain papers might even now be in the hands of the military—papers whereon the word "cabbage" stood opposite "dynamite," and potatoes were labelled "detonators."

The sun was nearing the horizon. Soon the cool of the evening would set in. If he could only reach a friendly farm (there were one or two hereabouts, he knew), he would find shelter for the night, and explicit directions that might set him on the road to freedom on the morrow.

Suddenly his eyes narrowed appreciatively upon a point to his extreme left.

"Mealies!" said Herr Schaefer. "Where there are mealies there is a farm not far off."

His reasoning proved correct. A rough track led through the cultivated belt of land. He came first to a cluster of kraals, avoided them dextrously (since he had no wish to be seen if the farm should not prove to be one of those he sought), and skirting a slight rise, came suddenly upon the farm itself. It was the usual low building, with a corrugated roof, and a stoep running round two sides of it.

The sun was setting now, a red, angry blur on the horizon, and a woman was standing in the open doorway, looking out into the falling dusk. Herr Schaefer pulled his hat well over his eyes and came up the steps.

"Is this by any chance the farm of Mr. Henshel?" he asked.

The woman nodded without speaking, staring at him with wide blue eyes. Schaefer drew a deep breath of relief, and looked back at her with a measure of appreciation. He admired the Dutch, wide-bosomed type such as this. A grand creature, with her full breast and her wide hips; not young, nearer forty than thirty, fair hair just touched with grey parted simply in the middle of her wide forehead, something grand and forceful about her, like a patriarch's wife of old.

"A fine mother of sons," thought Herr Schaefer appreciatively. "Also, let us hope, a good cook!"

His requirements of women were primitive and simple.

"Mr. Henshel expects me, I think," said the German, and added in a slightly lower tone: "I am interested in potatoes."

She gave the expected reply.

"We, too, are cultivators of vegetables." She spoke the words correctly, but with a strong accent. Her English was evidently not her strong point and Schaefer put her down as belonging to one of those Dutch Nationalist families who forbid their children to use the interloper's tongue. With a big, work-stained hand, she pointed behind him.

"You come from Jo'burg—yes?"

He nodded.

"Things are finished there. I escaped by the skin of my teeth. Then I lost myself on the veldt. It is pure chance that I found my way here."

The Dutch woman shook her head. A strange ecstatic smile irradiated her broad features.

"There is no chance—only God. Enter, then."

Approving her sentiments, for Herr Schaefer liked a woman to be religious, he crossed the threshold. She drew back to let him pass, the smile still lingering on her face, and just for a moment the thought that there was something here he did not quite understand flashed across Herr Schaefer's mind. He dismissed the idea as of little importance.

The house was built, like most, in the form of an H. The inner hall, from which rooms opened out all round, was pleasantly cool. The table was spread in preparation for a meal. The woman showed him to a bedroom, and on his return to the hall, when he had removed the boots from his aching feet, he found Henshel awaiting him. An Englishman, this, with a mean, vacuous face, a little rat of a fellow drunk with catchwords and phrases. It was amongst such as he that most of Schaefer's work had lain, and he knew the type well. Abuse of capitalists, of the "rich who

batten on the poor," the iniquities of the Chamber of Mines, the heroic
endurance of the miners—these were the topics on which Henshel expatiated, Schaefer nodding wearily with his mind fixed solely on food and
drink.

At last the woman appeared, bearing a steaming tureen of soup. They
sat down together and fell to. It was good soup. Henshel continued to
talk; his wife was silent. Schaefer contented himself with monosyllables
and appropriate grunts. When Mrs. Henshel left the room to bring in
the next course, he said appreciatively: "Your wife is a good cook. You are
lucky. Not all Dutch women cook well."

Henshel stared at him.

"My wife is not Dutch."

Schaefer looked his astonishment, but the shortness of Henshel's
tone, and some unacknowledged uneasiness in himself forbade him asking further. It was odd, though. He had been so sure that she was Dutch.

After the meal, he sat on the stoep in the cool dusk smoking. Somewhere in the house behind him a door banged. It was followed by the
noise of a horse's hoofs. Vaguely uneasy, he sat forward listening as they
grew fainter in the distance, then started violently to find Mrs. Henshel
standing at his elbow with a steaming cup of coffee. She set it down on
a little table beside him.

"My husband has ridden over to Cloete's—to make the arrangements for getting you away in the morning," she explained.

"Oh! I see."

Curious, how his uneasiness persisted.

"When will he be back?"

"Some time after midnight."

His uneasiness was not allayed. Yet what was it that he feared?
Surely not that Henshel would give him up to the police? No, the man
was sincere enough—a red-hot Revolutionist. The fact of the matter was
that he, Conrad Schaefer, had got nerves! A German soldier (Schaefer
unconsciously always thought of himself as a soldier) had no business
with nerves. He took up the cup beside him and drank it down, making
a grimace as he did so. What filthy stuff this Boer coffee always was!
Roasted acorns! He was sure of it—roasted acorns!

He put the cup down again, and as he did so, a deep sigh came from the woman standing by his side. He had almost forgotten her presence.

"Will you not sit down?" he asked, making no motion, however, to rise from his own seat.

She shook her head.

"I have to clear away, and wash the dishes, and make my house straight."

Schaefer nodded an approving head.

"The children are already in bed, I suppose," he said genially.

There was a pause before she answered.

"I have no children."

Schaefer was surprised. From the first moment he saw her he had definitely associated her with motherhood.

She took up the cup and walked to the entrance door with it. Then she spoke over her shoulder.

"I had one child. It died . . ."

"Ach! I am sorry," said Schaefer, kindly.

The woman did not answer. She stood there motionless. And suddenly Schaefer's uneasiness returned a hundred-fold. Only this time, he connected it definitely—not with the house, not with Henshel, but with this slow-moving, grandly fashioned woman—this wife of Henshel's who was neither English nor Dutch. His curiosity roused afresh, he asked her the question point blank. What nationality was she?

"Flemish."

She said the word abruptly, then passed into the house, leaving Herr Schaefer disturbed and upset.

Flemish! That was it, was it? Flemish! His mind flew swiftly to and fro, from the mud flats of Belgium to the sun-baked plateaus of South Africa. Flemish! He didn't like it. Both the French and the Belgians were so extraordinarily unreasonable! They couldn't forget.

His mind felt curiously confused. He yawned two or three times, wide, gaping yawns. He must get to bed and sleep—sleep—. Pah! How bitter that coffee had been—he could taste it still.

A light sprang up in the house. He got up and made his way to the door. His legs felt curiously unsteady. Inside, the big woman was sitting reading by the light of a small oil lamp. Herr Schaefer felt strangely reassured at the sight of the heavy volume on her knee. The Bible! He approved of women reading the Bible. He was a religious man himself, with a thorough belief in the German God, the God of the Old Testament, a God of blood and battles, of thunder and lightning, of material rewards and dire material vengeance, swift to anger and terrible in wrath.

He stumbled to a chair (what was the matter with his legs?); and in a thick, strange voice, suppressing another terrific yawn, he asked her what chapter she was reading.

Her blue eyes, under their level brows met his, something inscrutable in their depths. So might have looked a prophetess of Israel.

"The fourth chapter of Judges."

He nodded, yawning again. He must go to bed . . . but the effort to rise was too much for him . . . his eyelids closed . . .

"The fourth chapter of Judges." What was the fourth chapter of Judges? His uneasiness returned, swelled into terror. Something was wrong . . . Judges . . . Sleep overcame him. He went down into the depths—and horror went with him . . .

He awoke, dragging himself back to consciousness . . . Time had passed—much time, he felt certain of it. Where was he? He blinked up at the light—there were pains in his arms and legs . . . he felt sick . . . the taste of the coffee was still in his mouth . . . But what was this? He was lying on the floor, bound hand and foot with strips of towel, and standing over him was the sinister figure of the woman who was not Dutch. His wits came back to him in a flash of sheer desperate fear. He was in danger . . . great danger . . .

She marked the growth of consciousness in his eyes, and answered it as though he had actually spoken.

"Yes, I will tell you now. You remember passing through a place called Voogplaat, in Belgium?"

He recalled the name. Some twopenny-ha'penny village he had passed through with his regiment.

She nodded, and went on.

"You came to my door with some other soldiers. My man was away with the Belgian Army. My first man—not Henshel, I have only been married to him two years. The boy, my little one—he was only four years of age—ran out. He began to cry—what child would not? He feared the soldiers. You ordered him to stop. He could not. You seized a chopper—ah God!—and struck off his hand! You laughed, and said: 'That hand will never wield a weapon against Germany.'"

"It is not true," cried Schaefer, shrilly, "And even if it was—it was war!"

She paid no heed, but went on.

"I struck you in the face. What mother would not have done otherwise? You caught up the child . . . and dashed him against the wall . . ."

She stopped, her voice broken, her breast heaving . . .

Schaefer murmured feebly, abandoning the idea of denial.

"It was war . . . it was war . . ."

The sweat stood on his brow. He was alone with this woman, miles from help . . .

"I recognised you at once this afternoon in spite of your beard. You did not recognise me. You said it was chance led you here—but I knew it was God . . ."

Her bosom heaved, her eyes flashed with a fanatical light. Her God was Schaefer's God—a God of vengeance. She was uplifted by the strange, stern frenzy of a Priestess of old.

"He has delivered you into my hands."

Wild words poured from Schaefer, arguments, prayers, appeals for mercy, threats. And all left her untouched.

"God sent me another sign. When I opened the Bible tonight, I saw what He would have me do. Blessed above women shall Jael, the wife of Heber the Kenite, be . . ."

She stooped and took from the floor a hammer and some long, shining nails . . . A scream burst from Schaefer's throat. He remembered now the fourth chapter of Judges, that dramatic story of black inhospitality! Sisera fleeing from his enemies . . . a woman standing at the door of a tent . . . Jael, the wife of Heber the Kenite . . .

And sonorously, in her deep voice with the broad Flemish accent, her eyes shining as the Israelite woman's may have shone in bygone days, she spoke the words of triumph:

"This is the day in which the Lord hath delivered mine enemy into my hand . . ."

9

The Facts in the Case of M. Valdemar

By Edgar Allen Poe

OF COURSE I SHALL NOT PRETEND TO CONSIDER IT ANY MATTER FOR wonder, that the extraordinary case of M. Valdemar has excited discussion. It would have been a miracle had it not—especially under the circumstances. Through the desire of all parties concerned, to keep the affair from the public, at least for the present, or until we had farther opportunities for investigation—through our endeavors to effect this—a garbled or exaggerated account made its way into society, and became the source of many unpleasant misrepresentations, and, very naturally, of a great deal of disbelief.

It is now rendered necessary that I give the facts— as far as I comprehend them myself. They are, succinctly, these: My attention, for the last three years, had been repeatedly drawn to the subject of Mesmerism; and, about nine months ago it occurred to me, quite suddenly, that in the series of experiments made hitherto, there had been a very remarkable and most unaccountable omission:—no person had as yet been mesmerized in articulo mortis. It remained to be seen, first, whether, in such condition, there existed in the patient any susceptibility to the magnetic influence; secondly, whether, if any existed, it was impaired or increased by the condition; thirdly, to what extent, or for how long a period, the encroachments of Death might be arrested by the process. There were other points to be ascertained, but these most excited my curiosity—the last in especial, from the immensely important character of its consequences.

In looking around me for some subject by whose means I might test these particulars, I was brought to think of my friend, M. Ernest Valdemar, the well-known compiler of the "Bibliotheca Forensica," and author (under the nom de plume of Issachar Marx) of the Polish versions of "Wallenstein" and "Gargantua." M. Valdemar, who has resided principally at Harlaem, N.Y., since the year 1839, is (or was) particularly noticeable for the extreme spareness of his person—his lower limbs much resembling those of John Randolph; and, also, for the whiteness of his whiskers, in violent contrast to the blackness of his hair—the latter, in consequence, being very generally mistaken for a wig. His temperament was markedly nervous, and rendered him a good subject for mesmeric experiment. On two or three occasions I had put him to sleep with little difficulty, but was disappointed in other results which his peculiar constitution had naturally led me to anticipate. His will was at no period positively, or thoroughly, under my control, and in regard to clairvoyance, I could accomplish with him nothing to be relied upon. I always attributed my failure at these points to the disordered state of his health. For some months previous to my becoming acquainted with him, his physicians had declared him in a confirmed phthisis. It was his custom, indeed, to speak calmly of his approaching dissolution, as of a matter neither to be avoided nor regretted.

When the ideas to which I have alluded first occurred to me, it was of course very natural that I should think of M. Valdemar. I knew the steady philosophy of the man too well to apprehend any scruples from him; and he had no relatives in America who would be likely to interfere. I spoke to him frankly upon the subject; and, to my surprise, his interest seemed vividly excited. I say to my surprise, for, although he had always yielded his person freely to my experiments, he had never before given me any tokens of sympathy with what I did. His disease was if that character which would admit of exact calculation in respect to the epoch of its termination in death; and it was finally arranged between us that he would send for me about twenty-four hours before the period announced by his physicians as that of his decease.

It is now rather more than seven months since I received, from M. Valdemar himself, the subjoined note:

My DEAR P—,

You may as well come now. D—and F—are agreed that I cannot hold out beyond to-morrow midnight; and I think they have hit the time very nearly.

VALDEMAR

I received this note within half an hour after it was written, and in fifteen minutes more I was in the dying man's chamber. I had not seen him for ten days, and was appalled by the fearful alteration which the brief interval had wrought in him. His face wore a leaden hue; the eyes were utterly lustreless; and the emaciation was so extreme that the skin had been broken through by the cheek-bones. His expectoration was excessive. The pulse was barely perceptible. He retained, nevertheless, in a very remarkable manner, both his mental power and a certain degree of physical strength. He spoke with distinctness—took some palliative medicines without aid—and, when I entered the room, was occupied in penciling memoranda in a pocket-book. He was propped up in the bed by pillows. Doctors D—and F—were in attendance.

After pressing Valdemar's hand, I took these gentlemen aside, and obtained from them a minute account of the patient's condition. The left lung had been for eighteen months in a semi-osseous or cartilaginous state, and was, of course, entirely useless for all purposes of vitality. The right, in its upper portion, was also partially, if not thoroughly, ossified, while the lower region was merely a mass of purulent tubercles, running one into another. Several extensive perforations existed; and, at one point, permanent adhesion to the ribs had taken place. These appearances in the right lobe were of comparatively recent date. The ossification had proceeded with very unusual rapidity; no sign of it had been discovered a month before, and the adhesion had only been observed during the three previous days. Independently of the phthisis, the patient was suspected of aneurism of the aorta; but on this point the osseous symptoms rendered an exact diagnosis impossible. It was the opinion of both physicians that M. Valdemar would die about midnight on the morrow (Sunday). It was then seven o'clock on Saturday evening.

On quitting the invalid's bed-side to hold conversation with myself, Doctors D—and F—had bidden him a final farewell. It had not been their intention to return; but, at my request, they agreed to look in upon the patient about ten the next night.

When they had gone, I spoke freely with M. Valdemar on the subject of his approaching dissolution, as well as, more particularly, of the experiment proposed. He still professed himself quite willing and even anxious to have it made, and urged me to commence it at once. A male and a female nurse were in attendance; but I did not feel myself altogether at liberty to engage in a task of this character with no more reliable witnesses than these people, in case of sudden accident, might prove. I therefore postponed operations until about eight the next night, when the arrival of a medical student with whom I had some acquaintance, (Mr. Theodore L—l), relieved me from farther embarrassment. It had been my design, originally, to wait for the physicians; but I was induced to proceed, first, by the urgent entreaties of M. Valdemar, and secondly, by my conviction that I had not a moment to lose, as he was evidently sinking fast.

Mr. L—l was so kind as to accede to my desire that he would take notes of all that occurred, and it is from his memoranda that what I now have to relate is, for the most part, either condensed or copied verbatim.

It wanted about five minutes of eight when, taking the patient's hand, I begged him to state, as distinctly as he could, to Mr. L—l, whether he (M. Valdemar) was entirely willing that I should make the experiment of mesmerizing him in his then condition.

He replied feebly, yet quite audibly, "Yes, I wish to be. I fear you have mesmerized"—adding immediately afterwards, "deferred it too long."

While he spoke thus, I commenced the passes which I had already found most effectual in subduing him. He was evidently influenced with the first lateral stroke of my hand across his forehead; but although I exerted all my powers, no farther perceptible effect was induced until some minutes after ten o'clock, when Doctors D—and F—called, according to appointment. I explained to them, in a few words, what I designed, and as they opposed no objection, saying that the patient was already in the death agony, I proceeded without hesitation—exchanging, however, the lateral passes for downward ones, and directing my gaze entirely into the right eye of the sufferer.

By this time his pulse was imperceptible and his breathing was stertorous, and at intervals of half a minute.

This condition was nearly unaltered for a quarter of an hour. At the expiration of this period, however, a natural although a very deep sigh escaped the bosom of the dying man, and the stertorous breathing ceased—that is to say, its stertorousness was no longer apparent; the intervals were undiminished. The patient's extremities were of an icy coldness.

At five minutes before eleven I perceived unequivocal signs of the mesmeric influence. The glassy roll of the eye was changed for that expression of uneasy inward examination which is never seen except in cases of sleep-waking, and which it is quite impossible to mistake. With a few rapid lateral passes I made the lids quiver, as in incipient sleep, and with a few more I closed them altogether. I was not satisfied, however, with this, but continued the manipulations vigorously, and with the fullest exertion of the will, until I had completely stiffened the limbs of the slumberer, after placing them in a seemingly easy position. The legs were at full length; the arms were nearly so, and reposed on the bed at a moderate distance from the loin. The head was very slightly elevated.

When I had accomplished this, it was fully midnight, and I requested the gentlemen present to examine M. Valdemar's condition. After a few experiments, they admitted him to be an unusually perfect state of mesmeric trance. The curiosity of both the physicians was greatly excited. Dr. D—resolved at once to remain with the patient all night, while Dr. F—took leave with a promise to return at daybreak. Mr. L—l and the nurses remained.

We left M. Valdemar entirely undisturbed until about three o'clock in the morning, when I approached him and found him in precisely the same condition as when Dr. F—went away—that is to say, he lay in the same position; the pulse was imperceptible; the breathing was gentle (scarcely noticeable, unless through the application of a mirror to the lips); the eyes were closed naturally; and the limbs were as rigid and as cold as marble. Still, the general appearance was certainly not that of death.

As I approached M. Valdemar I made a kind of half effort to influence his right arm into pursuit of my own, as I passed the latter gently to and fro above his person. In such experiments with this patient I had never perfectly succeeded before, and assuredly I had little thought of succeeding now; but to my astonishment, his arm very readily, although feebly, followed every direction I assigned it with mine. I determined to hazard a few words of conversation.

"M. Valdemar," I said, "are you asleep?" He made no answer, but I perceived a tremor about the lips, and was thus induced to repeat the question, again and again. At its third repetition, his whole frame was agitated by a very slight shivering; the eyelids unclosed themselves so far as to display a white line of the ball; the lips moved sluggishly, and from between them, in a barely audible whisper, issued the words:

"Yes;—asleep now. Do not wake me!—let me die so!"

I here felt the limbs and found them as rigid as ever. The right arm, as before, obeyed the direction of my hand. I questioned the sleep-waker again:

"Do you still feel pain in the breast, M. Valdemar?"

The answer now was immediate, but even less audible than before: "No pain—I am dying."

I did not think it advisable to disturb him farther just then, and nothing more was said or done until the arrival of Dr. F—, who came a little before sunrise, and expressed unbounded astonishment at finding the patient still alive. After feeling the pulse and applying a mirror to the lips, he requested me to speak to the sleep-waker again. I did so, saying:

"M. Valdemar, do you still sleep?"

As before, some minutes elapsed ere a reply was made; and during the interval the dying man seemed to be collecting his energies to speak. At my fourth repetition of the question, he said very faintly, almost inaudibly: "Yes; still asleep—dying."

It was now the opinion, or rather the wish, of the physicians, that M. Valdemar should be suffered to remain undisturbed in his present apparently tranquil condition, until death should supervene—and this, it was generally agreed, must now take place within a few minutes. I concluded, however, to speak to him once more, and merely repeated my previous question.

While I spoke, there came a marked change over the countenance of the sleep-waker. The eyes rolled themselves slowly open, the pupils disappearing upwardly; the skin generally assumed a cadaverous hue, resembling not so much parchment as white paper; and the circular hectic spots which, hitherto, had been strongly defined in the centre of each cheek, went out at once. I use this expression, because the suddenness of their departure put me in mind of nothing so much as the extinguishment of a candle by a puff of the breath. The upper lip, at the same time, writhed itself away from the teeth, which it had previously covered completely; while the lower jaw fell with an audible jerk, leaving the mouth widely extended, and disclosing in full view the swollen and blackened tongue. I presume that no member of the party then present had been unaccustomed to death-bed horrors; but so hideous beyond conception was the appearance of M. Valdemar at this moment, that there was a general shrinking back from the region of the bed.

I now feel that I have reached a point of this narrative at which every reader will be startled into positive disbelief. It is my business, however, simply to proceed.

There was no longer the faintest sign of vitality in M. Valdemar; and concluding him to be dead, we were consigning him to the charge of the nurses, when a strong vibratory motion was observable in the tongue. This continued for perhaps a minute. At the expiration of this period, there issued from the distended and motionless jaws a voice—such as it would be madness in me to attempt describing. There are, indeed, two or three epithets which might be considered as applicable to it in part; I might say, for example, that the sound was harsh, and broken and hollow; but the hideous whole is indescribable, for the simple reason that no similar sounds have ever jarred upon the ear of humanity. There were two particulars, nevertheless, which I thought then, and still think, might fairly be stated as characteristic of the intonation—as well adapted to convey some idea of its unearthly peculiarity. In the first place, the voice seemed to reach our ears—at least mine—from a vast distance, or from some deep cavern within the earth. In the second place, it impressed me (I fear, indeed, that it will be impossible to make myself comprehended) as gelatinous or glutinous matters impress the sense of touch.

I have spoken both of "sound" and of "voice." I mean to say that the sound was one of distinct—of even wonderfully, thrillingly distinct—syllabification. M. Valdemar spoke—obviously in reply to the question I had propounded to him a few minutes before. I had asked him, it will be remembered, if he still slept. He now said:

"Yes;—no;—I have been sleeping—and now—now—I am dead."

No person present even affected to deny, or attempted to repress, the unutterable, shuddering horror which these few words, thus uttered, were so well calculated to convey. Mr. L—l (the student) swooned. The nurses immediately left the chamber, and could not be induced to return. My own impressions I would not pretend to render intelligible to the reader. For nearly an hour, we busied ourselves, silently—without the utterance of a word—in endeavors to revive Mr. L—l. When he came to himself, we addressed ourselves again to an investigation of M. Valdemar's condition.

It remained in all respects as I have last described it, with the exception that the mirror no longer afforded evidence of respiration. An attempt to draw blood from the arm failed. I should mention, too, that this limb was no farther subject to my will. I endeavored in vain to make it follow the direction of my hand. The only real indication, indeed, of the mesmeric influence, was now found in the vibratory movement of the tongue, whenever I addressed M. Valdemar a question. He seemed to be making an effort to reply, but had no longer sufficient volition. To queries put to him by any other person than myself he seemed utterly insensible—although I endeavored to place each member of the company in mesmeric rapport with him. I believe that I have now related all that is necessary to an understanding of the sleep-waker's state at this epoch. Other nurses were procured; and at ten o'clock I left the house in company with the two physicians and Mr. L—l.

In the afternoon we all called again to see the patient. His condition remained precisely the same. We had now some discussion as to the propriety and feasibility of awakening him; but we had little difficulty in agreeing that no good purpose would be served by so doing. It was evident that, so far, death (or what is usually termed death) had been arrested by the mesmeric process. It seemed clear to us all that to awaken M. Valdemar would be merely to insure his instant, or at least his speedy dissolution.

From this period until the close of last week—an interval of nearly seven months—we continued to make daily calls at M. Valdemar's house, accompanied, now and then, by medical and other friends. All this time the sleeper-waker remained exactly as I have last described him. The nurses' attentions were continual.

It was on Friday last that we finally resolved to make the experiment of awakening or attempting to awaken him; and it is the (perhaps) unfortunate result of this latter experiment which has given rise to so much discussion in private circles—to so much of what I cannot help thinking unwarranted popular feeling.

For the purpose of relieving M. Valdemar from the mesmeric trance, I made use of the customary passes. These, for a time, were unsuccessful. The first indication of revival was afforded by a partial descent of the iris. It was observed, as especially remarkable, that this lowering of the pupil was accompanied by the profuse out-flowing of a yellowish ichor (from beneath the lids) of a pungent and highly offensive odor.

It was now suggested that I should attempt to influence the patient's arm, as heretofore. I made the attempt and failed. Dr. F—then intimated a desire to have me put a question. I did so, as follows:

"M. Valdemar, can you explain to us what are your feelings or wishes now?"

There was an instant return of the hectic circles on the cheeks; the tongue quivered, or rather rolled violently in the mouth (although the jaws and lips remained rigid as before); and at length the same hideous voice which I have already described, broke forth:

"For God's sake!—quick!—quick!—put me to sleep—or, quick!—waken me!—quick!—I say to you that I am dead!"

I was thoroughly unnerved, and for an instant remained undecided what to do. At first I made an endeavor to re-compose the patient; but, failing in this through total abeyance of the will, I retraced my steps and as earnestly struggled to awaken him. In this attempt I soon saw that I should be successful—or at least I soon fancied that my success would be complete—and I am sure that all in the room were prepared to see the patient awaken.

For what really occurred, however, it is quite impossible that any human being could have been prepared.

As I rapidly made the mesmeric passes, amid ejaculations of "dead! dead!" absolutely bursting from the tongue and not from the lips of the sufferer, his whole frame at once—within the space of a single minute, or even less, shrunk—crumbled—absolutely rotted away beneath my hands. Upon the bed, before that whole company, there lay a nearly liquid mass of loathsome—of detestable putridity.

10

The Horror-Horn

By E. F. Benson

For the past ten days Alhubel had basked in the radiant mid-winter weather proper to its eminence of over 6,000 feet. From rising to setting the sun (so surprising to those who have hitherto associated it with a pale, tepid plate indistinctly shining through the murky air of England) had blazed its way across the sparkling blue, and every night the serene and windless frost had made the stars sparkle like illuminated diamond dust. Sufficient snow had fallen before Christmas to content the skiers, and the big rink, sprinkled every evening, had given the skaters each morning a fresh surface on which to perform their slippery antics. Bridge and dancing served to while away the greater part of the night, and to me, now for the first time tasting the joys of a winter in the Engadine, it seemed that a new heaven and a new earth had been lighted, warmed, and refrigerated for the special benefit of those who like myself had been wise enough to save up their days of holiday for the winter.

But a break came in these ideal conditions: one afternoon the sun grew vapour-veiled and up the valley from the north-west a wind frozen with miles of travel over ice-bound hill-sides began scouting through the calm halls of the heavens. Soon it grew dusted with snow, first in small flakes driven almost horizontally before its congealing breath and then in larger tufts as of swansdown. And though all day for a fortnight before the fate of nations and life and death had seemed to me of far less importance than to get certain tracings of the skate-blades on the ice of proper shape and size, it now seemed that the one paramount consideration was to hurry back to the hotel for shelter: it was wiser to leave rocking-turns alone than to be frozen in their quest.

I had come out here with my cousin, Professor Ingram, the celebrated physiologist and Alpine climber. During the serenity of the last fortnight he had made a couple of notable winter ascents, but this morning his weather-wisdom had mistrusted the signs of the heavens, and instead of attempting the ascent of the Piz Passug he had waited to see whether his misgivings justified themselves. So there he sat now in the hall of the admirable hotel with his feet on the hot-water pipes and the latest delivery of the English post in his hands. This contained a pamphlet concerning the result of the Mount Everest expedition, of which he had just finished the perusal when I entered.

"A very interesting report," he said, passing it to me, "and they certainly deserve to succeed next year. But who can tell, what that final six thousand feet may entail? Six thousand feet more when you have already accomplished twenty-three thousand does not seem much, but at present no one knows whether the human frame can stand exertion at such a height. It may affect not the lungs and heart only, but possibly the brain. Delirious hallucinations may occur. In fact, if I did not know better, I should have said that one such hallucination had occurred to the climbers already."

"And what was that?" I asked.

"You will find that they thought they came across the tracks of some naked human foot at a great altitude. That looks at first sight like an hallucination. What more natural than that a brain excited and exhilarated by the extreme height should have interpreted certain marks in the snow as the footprints of a human being? Every bodily organ at these altitudes is exerting itself to the utmost to do its work, and the brain seizes on those marks in the snow and says 'Yes, I'm all right, I'm doing my job, and I perceive marks in the snow which I affirm are human footprints.' You know, even at this altitude, how restless and eager the brain is, how vividly, as you told me, you dream at night. Multiply that stimulus and that consequent eagerness and restlessness by three, and how natural that the brain should harbour illusions! What after all is the delirium which often accompanies high fever but the effort of the brain to do its work under the pressure of feverish conditions? It is so eager to continue perceiving that it perceives things which have no existence!"

"And yet you don't think that these naked human footprints were illusions," said I. "You told me you would have thought so, if you had not known better."

He shifted in his chair and looked out of the window a moment. The air was thick now with the density of the big snow-flakes that were driven along by the squealing north-west gale.

"Quite so," he said. "In all probability the human footprints were real human footprints. I expect that they were the footprints, anyhow, of a being more nearly a man than anything else. My reason for saying so is that I know such beings exist. I have even seen quite near at hand—and I assure you I did not wish to be nearer in spite of my intense curiosity—the creature, shall we say, which would make such footprints. And if the snow was not so dense, I could show you the place where I saw him."

He pointed straight out of the window, where across the valley lies the huge tower of the Ungeheuerhorn with the carved pinnacle of rock at the top like some gigantic rhinoceros-horn. On one side only, as I knew, was the mountain practicable, and that for none but the finest climbers; on the other three a succession of ledges and precipices rendered it unscalable. Two thousand feet of sheer rock form the tower; below are five hundred feet of fallen boulders, up to the edge of which grow dense woods of larch and pine.

"Upon the Ungeheuerhorn?" I asked.

"Yes. Up till twenty years ago it had never been ascended, and I, like several others, spent a lot of time in trying to find a route up it. My guide and I sometimes spent three nights together at the hut beside the Blumen glacier, prowling round it, and it was by luck really that we found the route, for the mountain looks even more impracticable from the far side than it does from this. But one day we found a long, transverse fissure in the side which led to a negotiable ledge; then there came a slanting ice couloir which you could not see till you got to the foot of it. However, I need not go into that."

The big room where we sat was filling up with cheerful groups driven indoors by this sudden gale and snowfall, and the cackle of merry tongues grew loud. The band, too, that invariable appanage of tea-time at Swiss resorts, had begun to tune up for the usual potpourri from the works of Puccini. Next moment the sugary, sentimental melodies began.

"Strange contrast!" said Ingram. "Here are we sitting warm and cosy, our ears pleasantly tickled with these little baby tunes and outside is the great storm growing more violent every moment, and swirling round the austere cliffs of the Ungeheuerhorn: the Horror-Horn, as indeed it was to me."

"I want to hear all about it," I said. "Every detail: make a short story long, if it's short. I want to know why it's *your* Horror-horn?"

"Well, Chanton and I (he was my guide) used to spend days prowling about the cliffs, making a little progress on one side and then being stopped, and gaining perhaps five hundred feet on another side and then being confronted by some insuperable obstacle, till the day when by luck we found the route. Chanton never liked the job, for some reason that I could not fathom. It was not because of the difficulty or danger of the climbing, for he was the most fearless man I have ever met when dealing with rocks and ice, but he was always insistent that we should get off the mountain and back to the Blumen hut before sunset. He was scarcely easy even when we had got back to shelter and locked and barred the door, and I well remember one night when, as we ate our supper, we heard some animal, a wolf probably, howling somewhere out in the night. A positive panic seized him, and I don't think he closed his eyes till morning. It struck me then that there might be some grisly legend about the mountain, connected possibly with its name, and next day I asked him why the peak was called the Horror-horn. He put the question off at first, and said that, like the Schreckhorn, its name was due to its precipices and falling stones; but when I pressed him further he acknowledged that there was a legend about it, which his father had told him. There were creatures, so it was supposed, that lived in its caves, things human in shape, and covered, except for the face and hands, with long black hair. They were dwarfs in size, four feet high or thereabouts, but of prodigious strength and agility, remnants of some wild primeval race. It seemed that they were still in an upward stage of evolution, or so I guessed, for the story ran that sometimes girls had been carried off by them, not as prey, and not for any such fate as for those captured by cannibals, but to be bred from. Young men also had been raped by them, to be mated with the females of their tribe. All this looked as if the creatures, as I said, were tending towards humanity. But naturally I did not believe a word of it, as applied to the conditions of the present day. Centuries ago, conceivably, there may have been such beings, and, with the extraordinary tenacity of tradition, the news of this had been handed down and was still current round the hearths of the peasants. As for their numbers, Chanton told me that three had been once seen together by a man who owing to his swiftness on skis had escaped to tell the tale. This man, he averred, was no other than his grandfather, who had been benighted one winter evening as he passed through the dense woods below the Ungeheuerhorn, and Chanton supposed that they had been driven down to these lower altitudes in search of food during severe winter weather, for otherwise the recorded sights of them had always taken place among the rocks of the peak itself. They had pursued his grandfather, then a young man, at an extraordinarily swift canter, running sometimes upright as men run, sometimes on all-fours in the manner of beasts, and their howls were just such as that we had heard that night in the Blumen hut. Such at any rate was the story Chanton told me, and, like you, I regarded it as the very moonshine of superstition. But the very next day I had reason to reconsider my judgment about it.

"It was on that day that after a week of exploration we hit on the only route at present known to the top of our peak. We started as soon as there was light enough to climb by, for, as you may guess, on very difficult rocks it is impossible to climb by lantern or moonlight. We hit on the long fissure I have spoken of, we explored the ledge which from below seemed to end in nothingness, and with an hour's step-cutting ascended the couloir which led upwards from it. From there onwards it was a rock-climb, certainly of considerable difficulty, but with no heart-breaking discoveries ahead, and it was about nine in the morning that we stood on the top. We did not wait there long, for that side of the mountain is raked by falling stones loosened, when the sun grows hot, from the ice that holds them, and we made haste to pass the ledge where the falls are most frequent. After that there was the long fissure to descend, a matter of no great difficulty, and we were at the end of our work by midday, both of us, as you may imagine, in the state of the highest elation.

"A long and tiresome scramble among the huge boulders at the foot of the cliff then lay before us. Here the hill-side is very porous and great caves extend far into the mountain. We had unroped at the base of the fissure, and were picking our way as seemed good to either of us among these fallen rocks, many of them bigger than an ordinary house, when, on coming round the corner of one of these, I saw that which made it clear that the stories Chanton had told me were no figment of traditional superstition.

"Not twenty yards in front of me lay one of the beings of which he had spoken. There it sprawled naked and basking on its back with face turned up to the sun, which its narrow eyes regarded unwinking. In form it was completely human, but the growth of hair that covered limbs and trunk alike almost completely hid the sun-tanned skin beneath. But its face, save for the down on its cheeks and chin, was hairless, and I looked on a countenance the sensual and malevolent bestiality of which froze me with horror. Had the creature been an animal, one would have felt scarcely a shudder at the gross animalism of it; the horror lay in the fact that it was a man. There lay by it a couple of gnawed bones, and, its meal finished, it was lazily licking its protuberant lips, from which came a purring murmur of content. With one hand it scratched the thick hair on its belly, in the other it held one of these bones, which presently split in half beneath the pressure of its finger and thumb. But my horror was not based on the information of what happened to those men whom these creatures caught, it was due only to my proximity to a thing so human and so infernal. The peak, of which the ascent had a moment ago filled us with such elated satisfaction, became to me an Ungeheuerhorn indeed, for it was the home of beings more awful than the delirium of nightmare could ever have conceived.

"Chanton was a dozen paces behind me, and with a backward wave of my hand I caused him to halt. Then withdrawing myself with infinite precaution, so as not to attract the gaze of that basking creature, I slipped back round the rock, whispered to him what I had seen, and with blanched faces we made a long detour, peering round every corner, and crouching low, not knowing that at any step we might not come upon another of these beings, or that from the mouth of one of these caves in the mountain-side there might not appear another of those hairless and dreadful faces, with perhaps this time the breasts and insignia of womanhood. That would have been the worst of all.

"Luck favoured us, for we made our way among the boulders and shifting stones, the rattle of which might at any moment have betrayed us, without a repetition of my experience, and once among the trees we ran as if the Furies themselves were in pursuit. Well now did I understand, though I dare say I cannot convey, the qualms of Chanton's mind when he spoke to me of these creatures. Their very humanity was what made them so terrible, the fact that they were of the same race as ourselves, but of a type so abysmally degraded that the most brutal and inhuman of men would have seemed angelic in comparison."

The music of the small band was over before he had finished the narrative, and the chattering groups round the tea-table had dispersed. He paused a moment.

"There was a horror of the spirit," he said, "which I experienced then, from which, I verily believe, I have never entirely recovered. I saw then how terrible a living thing could be, and how terrible, in consequence, was life itself. In us all I suppose lurks some inherited germ of that ineffable bestiality, and who knows whether, sterile as it has apparently become in the course of centuries, it might not fructify again. When I saw that creature sun itself, I looked into the abyss out of which we have crawled. And these creatures are trying to crawl out of it now, if they exist any longer. Certainly for the last twenty years there has been no record of their being seen, until we come to this story of the footprint seen by the climbers on Everest. If that is authentic, if the party did not mistake the footprint of some bear, or what not, for a human tread, it seems as if still this bestranded remnant of mankind is in existence."

Now, Ingram had told his story well; but sitting in this warm and civilised room, the horror which he had clearly felt had not communicated itself to me in any very vivid manner. Intellectually, I agreed, I could appreciate his horror, but certainly my spirit felt no shudder of interior comprehension.

"But it is odd," I said, "that your keen interest in physiology did not disperse your qualms. You were looking, so I take it, at some form of man more remote probably than the earliest human remains. Did not something inside you say 'This is of absorbing significance'?"

He shook his head.

"No: I only wanted to get away," said he. "It was not, as I have told you, the terror of what, according to Chanton's story, might await us if we were captured; it was sheer horror at the creature itself. I quaked at it."

The snowstorm and the gale increased in violence that night, and I slept uneasily, plucked again and again from slumber by the fierce battling of the wind that shook my windows as if with an imperious demand for admittance. It came in billowy gusts, with strange noises intermingled with it as for a moment it abated, with flutings and moanings that rose to shrieks as the fury of it returned. These noises, no doubt, mingled themselves with my drowsed and sleepy consciousness, and once I tore myself out of nightmare, imagining that the creatures of the Horror-horn had gained footing on my balcony and were rattling at the window-bolts. But before morning the gale had died away, and I awoke to see the snow falling dense and fast in a windless air. For three days it continued, without intermission, and with its cessation there came a frost such as I have never felt before. Fifty degrees were registered one night, and more the next, and what the cold must have been on the cliffs of the Ungeheuer-horn I cannot imagine. Sufficient, so I thought, to have made an end altogether of its secret inhabitants: my cousin, on that day twenty years ago, had missed an opportunity for study which would probably never fall again either to him or another.

I received one morning a letter from a friend saying that he had arrived at the neighbouring winter resort of St. Luigi, and proposing that I should come over for a morning's skating and lunch afterwards. The place was not more than a couple of miles off, if one took the path over the low, pine-clad foot-hills above which lay the steep woods below the first rocky slopes of the Ungeheuerhorn; and accordingly, with a knapsack containing skates on my back, I went on skis over the wooded slopes and down by an easy descent again on to St. Luigi. The day was overcast, clouds entirely obscured the higher peaks though the sun was visible, pale and unluminous, through the mists. But as the morning went on, it gained the upper hand, and I slid down into St. Luigi beneath a sparkling firmament. We skated and lunched, and then, since it looked as if thick weather was coming up again, I set out early about three o'clock for my return journey.

Hardly had I got into the woods when the clouds gathered thick above, and streamers and skeins of them began to descend among the pines through which my path threaded its way. In ten minutes more their opacity had so increased that I could hardly see a couple of yards in front of me. Very soon I became aware that I must have got off the path, for snow-cowled shrubs lay directly in my way, and, casting back to find it again, I got altogether confused as to direction. But, though progress was difficult, I knew I had only to keep on the ascent, and presently I should come to the brow of these low foot-hills, and descend into the open valley where Alhubel stood. So on I went, stumbling and sliding over obstacles, and unable, owing to the thickness of the snow, to take off my skis, for I should have sunk over the knees at each step. Still the ascent continued, and looking at my watch I saw that I had already been near an hour on my way from St. Luigi, a period more than sufficient to complete my whole journey. But still I stuck to my idea that though I had certainly strayed far from my proper route a few minutes more must surely see me over the top of the upward way, and I should find the ground declining into the next valley. About now, too, I noticed that the mists were growing suffused with rose-colour, and, though the inference was that it must be close on sunset, there was consolation in the fact that they were there and might lift at any moment and disclose to me my whereabouts. But the fact that night would soon be on me made it needful to bar my mind against that despair of loneliness which so eats out the heart of a man who is lost in woods or on mountain-side, that, though still there is plenty of vigour in his limbs, his nervous force is sapped, and he can do no more than lie down and abandon himself to whatever fate may await him. . . . And then I heard that which made the thought of loneliness seem bliss indeed, for there was a worse fate than loneliness. What I heard resembled the howl of a wolf, and it came from not far in front of me where the ridge—was it a ridge?—still rose higher in vestment of pines.

From behind me came a sudden puff of wind, which shook the frozen snow from the drooping pine-branches, and swept away the mists as a broom sweeps the dust from the floor. Radiant above me were the unclouded skies, already charged with the red of the sunset, and in front I saw that I had come to the very edge of the wood through which I had wandered so long. But it was no valley into which I had penetrated, for there right ahead of me rose the steep slope of boulders and rocks soaring upwards to the foot of the Ungeheuerhorn. What, then, was that cry of a wolf which had made my heart stand still?

I saw, not twenty yards from me was a fallen tree, and leaning against the trunk of it was one of the denizens of the Horror-Horn, and it was a woman. She was enveloped in a thick growth of hair grey and tufted, and from her head it streamed down over her shoulders and her bosom, from which hung withered and pendulous breasts. And looking on her face I comprehended not with my mind alone, but with a shudder of my spirit, what Ingram had felt. Never had nightmare fashioned so terrible a countenance; the beauty of sun and stars and of the beasts of the field and the kindly race of men could not atone for so hellish an incarnation of the spirit of life. A fathomless bestiality modelled the slavering mouth and the narrow eyes; I looked into the abyss itself and knew that out of that abyss on the edge of which I leaned the generations of men had climbed. What if that ledge crumbled in front of me and pitched me headlong into its nethermost depths? . . .

In one hand she held by the horns a chamois that kicked and struggled. A blow from its hindleg caught her withered thigh, and with a grunt of anger she seized the leg in her other hand, and, as a man may pull from its sheath a stem of meadow-grass, she plucked it off the body, leaving the torn skin hanging round the gaping wound. Then putting the red, bleeding member to her mouth she sucked at it as a child sucks a stick of sweetmeat. Through flesh and gristle her short, brown teeth penetrated, and she licked her lips with a sound of purring. Then dropping the leg by her side, she looked again at the body of the prey now quivering in its death-convulsion, and with finger and thumb gouged out one of its eyes. She snapped her teeth on it, and it cracked like a soft-shelled nut.

It must have been but a few seconds that I stood watching her, in some indescribable catalepsy of terror, while through my brain there pealed the panic-command of my mind to my stricken limbs "Begone, begone, while there is time." Then, recovering the power of my joints and muscles, I tried to slip behind a tree and hide myself from this apparition. But the woman—shall I say?—must have caught my stir of movement, for she raised her eyes from her living feast and saw me. She craned forward her neck, she dropped her prey, and half rising began to move towards me. As she did this, she opened her mouth, and gave forth a howl such as I had heard a moment before. It was answered by another, but faintly and distantly.

Sliding and slipping, with the toes of my skis tripping in the obstacles below the snow, I plunged forward down the hill between the pine-trunks. The low sun already sinking behind some rampart of mountain in the west reddened the snow and the pines with its ultimate rays. My knapsack with the skates in it swung to and fro on my back, one ski-stick had already been twitched out of my hand by a fallen branch of pine, but not a second's pause could I allow myself to recover it. I gave no glance behind, and I knew not at what pace my pursuer was on my track, or indeed whether any pursued at all, for my whole mind and energy, now working at full power again under the stress of my panic, was devoted to getting away down the hill and out of the wood as swiftly as my limbs could bear me. For a little while I heard nothing but the hissing snow of my headlong passage, and the rustle of the covered undergrowth beneath my feet, and then, from close at hand behind me, once more the wolf-howl sounded and I heard the plunging of footsteps other than my own.

The strap of my knapsack had shifted, and as my skates swung to and fro on my back it chafed and pressed on my throat, hindering free passage of air, of which, God knew, my labouring lungs were in dire need, and without pausing I slipped it free from my neck, and held it in the hand from which my ski-stick had been jerked. I seemed to go a little more easily for this adjustment, and now, not so far distant, I could see below me the path from which I had strayed. If only I could reach that, the smoother going would surely enable me to out-distance my pursuer, who even on the rougher ground was but slowly overhauling me, and at the sight of that riband stretching unimpeded downhill, a ray of hope pierced the black panic of my soul. With that came the desire, keen and insistent, to see who or what it was that was on my tracks, and I spared a backward glance. It was she, the hag whom I had seen at her gruesome meal; her long grey hair flew out behind her, her mouth chattered and gibbered, her fingers made grabbing movements, as if already they closed on me.

But the path was now at hand, and the nearness of it I suppose made me incautious. A hump of snow-covered bush lay in my path, and, thinking I could jump over it, I tripped and fell, smothering myself in snow. I heard a maniac noise, half scream, half laugh, from close behind, and before I could recover myself the grabbing fingers were at my neck, as if a steel vice had closed there. But my right hand in which I held my knapsack of skates was free, and with a blind back-handed movement I whirled it behind me at the full length of its strap, and knew that my desperate blow had found its billet somewhere. Even before I could look round I felt the grip on my neck relax, and something subsided into the very bush which had entangled me. I recovered my feet and turned.

There she lay, twitching and quivering. The heel of one of my skates piercing the thin alpaca of the knapsack had hit her full on the temple, from which the blood was pouring, but a hundred yards away I could see another such figure coming downwards on my tracks, leaping and bounding. At that panic rose again within me, and I sped off down the white smooth path that led to the lights of the village already beckoning. Never once did I pause in my headlong going: there was no safety until I was back among the haunts of men. I flung myself against the door of the hotel, and screamed for admittance, though I had but to turn the handle and enter; and once more as when Ingram had told his tale, there was the sound of the band, and the chatter of voices, and there, too, was he himself, who looked up and then rose swiftly to his feet as I made my clattering entrance.

"I have seen them too," I cried. "Look at my knapsack. Is there not blood on it? It is the blood of one of them, a woman, a hag, who tore off the leg of a chamois as I looked, and pursued me through the accursed wood. I——"

Whether it was I who spun round, or the room which seemed to spin round me, I knew not, but I heard myself falling, collapsed on the floor, and the next time that I was conscious at all I was in bed. There was Ingram there, who told me that I was quite safe, and another man, a stranger, who pricked my arm with the nozzle of a syringe, and reassured me. . . .

A day or two later I gave a coherent account of my adventure, and three or four men, armed with guns, went over my traces. They found the bush in which I had stumbled, with a pool of blood which had soaked into the snow, and, still following my ski-tracks, they came on the body of a chamois, from which had been torn one of its hindlegs and one eye-socket was empty. That is all the corroboration of my story that I can give the reader, and for myself I imagine that the creature which pursued me was either not killed by my blow or that her fellows removed her body. . . . Anyhow, it is open to the incredulous to prowl about the caves of the Ungeheuerhorn, and see if anything occurs that may convince them.

The Spider

By Hanns Heinz Ewers

WHEN THE STUDENT OF MEDICINE, RICHARD BRACQUEMONT, DECIDED to move into room #7 of the small Hotel Stevens, Rue Alfred Stevens (Paris 6), three persons had already hanged themselves from the cross-bar of the window in that room on three successive Fridays.

The first was a Swiss traveling salesman. They found his corpse on Saturday evening. The doctor determined that the death must have occurred between five and six o'clock on Friday afternoon. The corpse hung on a strong hook that had been driven into the window's cross-bar to serve as a hanger for articles of clothing. The window was closed, and the dead man had used the curtain cord as a noose. Since the window was very low, he hung with his knees practically touching the floor—a sign of the great discipline the suicide must have exercised in carrying out his design. Later, it was learned that he was a married man, a father. He had been a man of a continually happy disposition; a man who had achieved a secure place in life. There was not one written word to be found that would have shed light on his suicide . . . not even a will.

Furthermore, none of his acquaintances could recall hearing anything at all from him that would have permitted anyone to predict his end.

The second case was not much different. The artist, Karl Krause, a high wire cyclist in the nearby Medrano Circus, moved into room #7 two days later. When he did not show up at Friday's performance, the director sent an employee to the hotel. There, he found Krause in the unlocked room hanging from the window cross-bar in circumstances exactly like those of the previous suicide. This death was as perplexing as the first. Krause was popular. He earned a very high salary, and had appeared to enjoy life at its fullest. Once again, there was no suicide note; no sinister hints. Krause's sole survivor was his mother to whom the son had regularly sent 300 marks on the first of the month.

For Madame Dubonnet, the owner of the small, cheap guesthouse whose clientele was composed almost completely of employees in a nearby Montmartre vaudeville theater, this second curious death in the same room had very unpleasant consequences. Already several of her guests had moved out, and other regular clients had not come back. She appealed for help to her personal friend, the inspector of police of the ninth precinct, who assured her that he would do everything in his power to help her. He pushed zealously ahead not only with the investigation into the grounds for the suicides of the two guests, but he also placed an officer in the mysterious room.

This man, Charles-Maria Chaumié, actually volunteered for the task. Chaumié was an old "Marsouin," a marine sergeant with eleven years of service, who had lain so many nights at posts in Tonkin and Annam, and had greeted so many stealthily creeping river pirates with a shot from his rifle that he seemed ideally suited to encounter the "ghost" that everyone on Rue Alfred Stevens was talking about.

From then on, each morning and each evening, Chaumié paid a brief visit to the police station to make his report, which, for the first few days, consisted only of his statement that he had not noticed anything unusual. On Wednesday evening, however, he hinted that he had found a clue.

Pressed to say more, he asked to be allowed more time before making any comment, since he was not sure that what he had discovered had any relationship to the two deaths, and he was afraid he might say something that would make him look foolish.

On Thursday, his behavior seemed a bit uncertain, but his mood was noticeably more serious. Still, he had nothing to report. On Friday morning, he came in very excited and spoke, half humorously, half seriously, of the strangely attractive power that his window had. He would not elaborate this notion and said that, in any case, it had nothing to do with the suicides; and that it would be ridiculous of him to say any more. When, on that same Friday, he failed to make his regular evening report, someone went to his room and found him hanging from the cross-bar of the window.

All the circumstances, down to the minutest detail, were the same here as in the previous cases. Chaumié's legs dragged along the ground. The curtain cord had been used for a noose. The window was closed, the door to the room had not been locked and death had occurred at six o'clock. The dead man's mouth was wide open, and his tongue protruded from it.

Chaumié's death, the third in as many weeks in room #7, had the following consequences: all the guests, with the exception of a German high-school teacher in room #16, moved out. The teacher took advantage of the occasion to have his rent reduced by a third. The next day, Mary Garden, the famous Opéra Comique singer, drove up to the Hotel Stevens and paid two hundred francs for the red curtain cord, saying it would bring her luck. The story, small consolation for Madame Dubonnet, got into the papers.

If these events had occurred in summer, in July or August, Madame Dubonnet would have secured three times that price for her cord, but as it was in the middle of a troubled year, with elections, disorders in the Balkans, bank crashes in New York, the visit of the King and Queen of England, the result was that the affaire Rue Alfred Stevens was talked of less than it deserved to be. As for the newspaper accounts, they were brief, being essentially the police reports word for word.

These reports were all that Richard Bracquemont, the medical student, knew of the matter.

There was one detail about which he knew nothing because neither the police inspector nor any of the eyewitnesses had mentioned it to the press. It was only later, after what happened to the medical student, that anyone remembered that when the police removed Sergeant Charles-Maria Chaumié's body from the window cross-bar a large black spider crawled from the dead man's open mouth. A hotel porter flicked it away, exclaiming, "Ugh, another of those damned creatures."

When in later investigations which concerned themselves mostly with Bracquemont the servant was interrogated, he said that he had seen a similar spider crawling on the Swiss traveling salesman's shoulder when his body was removed from the window cross-bar. But Richard Bracquemont knew nothing of all this.

It was more than two weeks after the last suicide that Bracquemont moved into the room. It was a Sunday. Bracquemont conscientiously recorded everything that happened to him in his journal. That journal now follows.

***

Monday, February 28

I moved in yesterday evening. I unpacked my two wicker suitcases and straightened the room a little. Then I went to bed. I slept so soundly that it was nine o'clock the next morning before a knock at my door woke me. It was my hostess, bringing me breakfast herself. One could read her concern for me in the eggs, the bacon and the superb café au lait she brought me. I washed and dressed, then smoked a pipe as I watched the servant make up the room.

So, here I am. I know well that the situation may prove dangerous, but I think I may just be the one to solve the problem. If, once upon a time, Paris was worth a mass (conquest comes at a dearer rate these days), it is well worth risking my life *pour un si bel enjeu*. I have at least one chance to win, and I mean to risk it.

As it is, I'm not the only one who has had this notion. Twenty-seven people have tried for access to the room. Some went to the police, some went directly to the hotel owner. There were even three women among the candidates. There was plenty of competition. No doubt the others are poor devils like me.

And yet, it was I who was chosen. Why? Because I was the only one who hinted that I had some plan—or the semblance of a plan. Naturally, I was bluffing.

These journal entries are intended for the police. I must say that it amuses me to tell those gentlemen how neatly I fooled them. If the Inspector has any sense, he'll say, "Hm. This Bracquemont is just the man we need." In any case, it doesn't matter what he'll say. The point is I'm here now, and I take it as a good sign that I've begun my task by bamboozling the police. I had gone first to Madame Dubonnet, and it was she who sent me to the police. They put me off for a whole week—as they put off my rivals as well. Most of them gave up in disgust, having something better to do than hang around the musty squad room. The Inspector was beginning to get irritated at my tenacity. At last, he told me I was wasting my time. That the police had no use for bungling amateurs. "Ah, if only you had a plan. Then . . ."

On the spot, I announced that I had such a plan, though naturally I had no such thing. Still, I hinted that my plan was brilliant, but dangerous, that it might lead to the same end as that which had overtaken the police officer, Chaumié. Still, I promised to describe it to him if he would give me his word that he would personally put it into effect. He made excuses, claiming he was too busy but when he asked me to give him at least a hint of my plan, I saw that I had piqued his interest.

I rattled off some nonsense made up of whole cloth. God alone knows where it all came from.

I told him that six o'clock of a Friday is an occult hour. It is the last hour of the Jewish week; the hour when Christ disappeared from his tomb and descended into hell. That he would do well to remember that the three suicides had taken place at approximately that hour. That was all I could tell him just then, I said, but I pointed him to The Revelations of St. John.

The Inspector assumed the look of a man who understood all that I had been saying, then he asked me to come back that evening.

I returned, precisely on time, and noted a copy of the New Testament on the Inspector's desk. I had, in the meantime, been at the Revelations myself without however having understood a syllable. Perhaps the Inspector was cleverer than I. Very politely-nay- deferentially, he let me know that, despite my extremely vague intimations, he believed he grasped my line of thought and was ready to expedite my plan in every way.

And here, I must acknowledge that he has indeed been tremendously helpful. It was he who made the arrangement with the owner that I was to have anything I needed so long as I stayed in the room. The Inspector gave me a pistol and a police whistle, and he ordered the officers on the beat to pass through the Rue Alfred Stevens as often as possible, and to watch my window for any signal. Most important of all, he had a desk telephone installed which connects directly with the police station. Since the station is only four minutes away, I see no reason to be afraid.

Wednesday, March 1
Nothing has happened. Not yesterday. Not today.

Madame Dubonnet brought a new curtain cord from another room—the rooms are mostly empty, of course. Madame Dubonnet takes every opportunity to visit me, and each time she brings something with her. I have asked her to tell me again everything that happened here, but I have learned nothing new. She has her own opinion of the suicides. Her view is that the music hall artist, Krause, killed himself because of an unhappy love affair. During the last year that Krause lived in the hotel, a young woman had made frequent visits to him. These visits had stopped, just before his death. As for the Swiss gentleman, Madame Dubonnet confessed herself baffled. On the other hand, the death of the policeman was easy to explain. He had killed himself just to annoy her.

These are sad enough explanations, to be sure, but I let her babble on to take the edge off my boredom.

Thursday, March 3
Still nothing. The Inspector calls twice a day. Each time, I tell him that all is well. Apparently, these words do not reassure him.

I have taken out my medical books and I study, so that my self-imposed confinement will have some purpose.

Friday, March 4
I ate uncommonly well at noon. The landlady brought me half a bottle of champagne. It seemed a meal for a condemned man. Madame Dubonnet looked at me as if I were already three-quarters dead. As she was leaving, she begged me tearfully to come with her, fearing no doubt that I would hang myself "just to annoy her."

I studied the curtain cord once again. Would I hang myself with it? Certainly, I felt little desire to do so. The cord is stiff and rough—not the sort of cord one makes a noose of. One would need to be truly determined before one could imitate the others.

I am seated now at my table. At my left, the telephone. At my right, the revolver. I'm not frightened; but I am curious.

Six o'clock, the same evening

Nothing has happened. I was about to add, "Unfortunately." The fatal hour has come—and has gone, like any six o'clock on any evening. I won't hide the fact that I occasionally felt a certain impulse to go to the window, but for a quite different reason than one might imagine.

The Inspector called me at least ten times between five and six o'clock. He was as impatient as I was. Madame Dubonnet, on the other hand, is happy. A week has passed without someone in #7 hanging himself. Marvelous.

Monday, March 7

I have a growing conviction that I will learn nothing; that the previous suicides are related to the circumstances surrounding the lives of the three men. I have asked the Inspector to investigate the cases further, convinced that someone will find their motivations. As for me, I hope to stay here as long as possible. I may not conquer Paris here, but I live very well and I'm fattening up nicely. I'm also studying hard, and I am making real progress. There is another reason, too, that keeps me here.

Wednesday, March 9

So! I have taken one step more. Clarimonda.

I haven't yet said anything about Clarimonda. It is she who is my "third" reason for staying here. She is also the reason I was tempted to go to the window during the "fateful" hour last Friday. But of course, not to hang myself.

Clarimonda. Why do I call her that? I have no idea what her name is, but it ought to be Clarimonda. When finally I ask her name, I'm sure it will turn out to be Clarimonda.

I noticed her almost at once . . . in the very first days. She lives across the narrow street; and her window looks right into mine. She sits there, behind her curtains.

I ought to say that she noticed me before I saw her; and that she was obviously interested in me. And no wonder. The whole neighborhood knows I am here, and why. Madame Dubonnet has seen to that.

I am not of a particularly amorous disposition. In fact, my relations with women have been rather meager. When one comes from Verdun to Paris to study medicine, and has hardly money enough for three meals a day, one has something else to think about besides love. I am then not very experienced with women, and I may have begun my adventure with her stupidly. Never mind. It's exciting just the same.

At first, the idea of establishing some relationship with her simply did not occur to me. It was only that, since I was here to make observations, and, since there was nothing in the room to observe, I thought I might as well observe my neighbor—openly, professionally. Anyhow, one can't sit all day long just reading.

Clarimonda, I have concluded, lives alone in the small flat across the way. The flat has three windows, but she sits only before the window that looks into mine. She sits there, spinning on an old-fashioned spindle, such as my grandmother inherited from a great aunt. I had no idea anyone still used such spindles. Clarimonda's spindle is a lovely object. It appears to be made of ivory; and the thread she spins is of an exceptional fineness. She works all day behind her curtains, and stops spinning only as the sun goes down. Since darkness comes abruptly here in this narrow street and in this season of fogs, Clarimonda disappears from her place at five o'clock each evening.

I have never seen a light in her flat.

What does Clarimonda look like? I'm not quite sure. Her hair is black and wavy; her face pale. Her nose is short and finely shaped with delicate nostrils that seem to quiver. Her lips, too, are pale: and when she smiles, it seems that her small teeth are as keen as those of some beast of prey. Her eyelashes are long and dark; and her huge dark eyes have an intense glow. I guess all these details more than I know them. It is hard to see clearly through the curtains.

Something else: she always wears a black dress embroidered with a lilac motif; and black gloves, no doubt to protect her hands from the effects of her work. It is a curious sight: her delicate hands moving perpetually, swiftly grasping the thread, pulling it, releasing it, taking it up again; as if one were watching the indefatigable motions of an insect.

Our relationship? For the moment, still very superficial, though it feels deeper. It began with a sudden exchange of glances in which each of us noted the other. I must have pleased her, because one day she studied me a while longer, then smiled tentatively. Naturally, I smiled back. In this fashion, two days went by, each of us smiling more frequently with the passage of time. Yet something kept me from greeting her directly.

Until today. This afternoon, I did it. And Clarimonda returned my greeting. It was done subtly enough, to be sure, but I saw her nod.

Thursday, March 10

Yesterday, I sat for a long time over my books, though I can't truthfully say that I studied much. I built castles in the air and dreamed of Clarimonda.

I slept fitfully.

This morning, when I approached my window, Clarimonda was already in her place. I waved, and she nodded back. She laughed and studied me for a long time.

I tried to read, but I felt much too uneasy. Instead, I sat down at my window and gazed at Clarimonda. She too had laid her work aside. Her hands were folded in her lap. I drew my curtain wider with the window cord, so that I might see better. At the same moment, Clarimonda did the same with the curtains at her window. We exchanged smiles.

We must have spent a full hour gazing at each other.

Finally, she took up her spinning.

Saturday, March 12

The days pass. I eat and drink. I sit at the desk. I light my pipe; I look down at my book but I don't read a word, though I try again and again. Then I go to the window where I wave to Clarimonda. She nods. We smile. We stare at each other for hours.

Yesterday afternoon, at six o'clock, I grew anxious. The twilight came early, bringing with it something like anguish. I sat at my desk. I waited until I was invaded by an irresistible need to go to the window—not to hang myself, but just to see Clarimonda. I sprang up and stood beside the curtain where it seemed to me I had never been able to see so clearly, though it was already dark. Clarimonda was spinning, but her eyes looked into mine. I felt myself strangely contented even as I experienced a light sensation of fear.

The telephone rang. It was the Inspector tearing me out of my trance with his idiotic questions. I was furious.

This morning, the Inspector and Madame Dubonnet visited me. She is enchanted with how things are going. I have now lived for two weeks in room #7. The Inspector, however, does not feel he is getting results. I hinted mysteriously that I was on the trail of something most unusual. The jackass took me at my word and fulfilled my dearest wish. I've been allowed to stay in the room for another week. God knows it isn't Madame Dubonnet's cooking or wine-cellar that keeps me here. How quickly one can be sated with such things. No. I want to stay because of the window Madame Dubonnet fears and hates. That beloved window that shows me Clarimonda. I have stared out of my window, trying to discover whether she ever leaves her room, but I've never seen her set foot on the street.

As for me, I have a large, comfortable armchair and a green shade over the lamp whose glow envelopes me in warmth. The Inspector has left me with a huge packet of fine tobacco—and yet I cannot work. I read two or three pages only to discover that I haven't understood a word. My eyes see the letters, but my brain refuses to make any sense of them. Absurd. As if my brain were posted: "No Trespassing." It is as if there were no room in my head for any other thought than the one: Clarimonda. I push my books away; I lean back deeply into my chair. I dream.

Sunday, March 13

This morning I watched a tiny drama while the servant was tidying my room. I was strolling in the corridor when I paused before a small window in which a large garden spider had her web. Madame Dubonnet will not have it removed because she believes spiders bring luck, and she's had enough misfortunes in her house lately. Today, I saw a much smaller spider, a male, moving across the strong threads towards the middle of the web, but when his movements alerted the female, he drew back shyly to the edge of the web from which he made a second attempt to cross it. Finally, the female in the middle appeared attentive to his wooing, and stopped moving. The male tugged at a strand gently, then more strongly till the whole web shook. The female stayed motionless. The male moved quickly forward and the female received him quietly, calmly, giving herself over completely to his embraces. For a long minute, they hung together motionless at the center of the huge web.

Then I saw the male slowly extricating himself, one leg over the other. It was as if he wanted tactfully to leave his companion alone in the dream of love, but as he started away, the female, overwhelmed by a wild life, was after him, hunting him ruthlessly. The male let himself drop from a thread; the female followed, and for a while the lovers hung there, imitating a piece of art. Then they fell to the window-sill where the male, summoning all his strength, tried again to escape. Too late. The female already had him in her powerful grip, and was carrying him back to the center of the web. There, the place that had just served as the couch for their lascivious embraces took on quite another aspect. The lover wriggled, trying to escape from the female's wild embrace, but she was too much for him. It was not long before she had wrapped him completely in her thread, and he was helpless. Then she dug her sharp pincers into his body, and sucked full draughts of her young lover's blood. Finally, she detached herself from the pitiful and unrecognizable shell of his body and threw it out of her web.

So that is what love is like among these creatures. Well for me that I am not a spider.

Monday, March 14
I don't look at my books any longer. I spend my days at the window. When it is dark, Clarimonda is no longer there, but if I close my eyes, I continue to see her.

This journal has become something other than I intended. I've spoken about Madame Dubonnet, about the Inspector; about spiders and about Clarimonda. But I've said nothing about the discoveries I undertook to make. It can't be helped.

Tuesday, March 15

We have invented a strange game, Clarimonda and I. We play it all day long. I greet her; then she greets me. Then I tap my fingers on the windowpanes. The moment she sees me doing that, she too begins tapping. I wave to her; she waves back. I move my lips as if speaking to her; she does the same. I run my hand through my sleep-disheveled hair and instantly her hand is at her forehead. It is a child's game, and we both laugh over it. Actually, she doesn't laugh. She only smiles a gently contained smile. And I smile back in the same way.

The game is not as trivial as it seems. It's not as if we were grossly imitating each other—that would weary us both. Rather, we are communicating with each other. Sometimes, telepathically, it would seem, since Clarimonda follows my movements instantaneously almost before she has had time to see them. I find myself inventing new movements, or new combinations of movements, but each time she repeats them with disconcerting speed. Sometimes. I change the order of the movements to surprise her, making whole series of gestures as rapidly as possible; or I leave out some motions and weave in others, the way children play "Simon Says." What is amazing is that Clarimonda never once makes a mistake, no matter how quickly I change gestures.

That's how I spend my days . . . but never for a moment do I feel that I'm killing time. It seems, on the contrary, that never in my life have I been better occupied.

Wednesday. March 16

Isn't it strange that it hasn't occurred to me to put my relationship with Clarimonda on a more serious basis than these endless games. Last night, I thought about this . . . I can, of course, put on my hat and coat, walk down two flights of stairs, take five steps across the street and mount two flights to her door which is marked with a small sign that says "Clarimonda." Clarimonda what? I don't know. Something. Then I can knock and . . .

Up to this point I imagine everything very clearly, but I cannot see what should happen next. I know that the door opens. But then I stand before it, looking into a dark void. Clarimonda doesn't come. Nothing comes. Nothing is there, only the black, impenetrable dark.

Sometimes, it seems to me that there can be no other Clarimonda but the one I see in the window; the one who plays gesture-games with me. I cannot imagine a Clarimonda wearing a hat, or a dress other than her black dress with the lilac motif. Nor can I imagine a Clarimonda without black gloves. The very notion that I might encounter Clarimonda somewhere in the streets or in a restaurant eating, drinking or chatting is so improbable that it makes me laugh.

Sometimes I ask myself whether I love her. It's impossible to say, since I have never loved before. However, if the feeling that I have for Clarimonda is really love, then love is something entirely different from anything I have seen among my friends or read about in novels. It is hard for me to be sure of my feelings and harder still to think of anything that doesn't relate to Clarimonda or, what is more important, to our game. Undeniably, it is our game that concerns me. Nothing else—and this is what I understand least of all.

There is no doubt that I am drawn to Clarimonda, but with this attraction there is mingled another feeling, fear. No. That's not it either. Say rather a vague apprehension in the presence of the unknown. And this anxiety has a strangely voluptuous quality so that I am at the same time drawn to her even as I am repelled by her. It is as if I were moving in giant circles around her, sometimes coming close, sometimes retreating . . . back and forth, back and forth. Once, I am sure of it, it will happen, and I will join her.

Clarimonda sits at her window and spins her slender, eternally fine thread, making a strange cloth whose purpose I do not understand. I am amazed that she is able to keep from tangling her delicate thread. Hers is surely a remarkable design, containing mythical beasts and strange masks.

Thursday, March 17

I am curiously excited. I don't talk to people any more. I barely say "hello" to Madame Dubonnet or to the servant. I hardly give myself time to eat.

All I can do is sit at the window and play the game with Clarimonda. It is an enthralling game. Overwhelming.

I have the feeling something will happen tomorrow.

Friday, March 18
Yes. Yes. Something will happen today. I tell myself—as loudly as I can—that that's why I am here. And yet, horribly enough, I am afraid. And in the fear that the same thing is going to happen to me as happened to my predecessors, there is strangely mingled another fear: a terror of Clarimonda. And I cannot separate the two fears.

I am frightened. I want to scream.

Six o'clock, evening
I have my hat and coat on. Just a couple of words.

At five o'clock, I was at the end of my strength. I'm perfectly aware now that there is a relationship between my despair and the "sixth hour" that was so significant in the previous weeks. I no longer laugh at the trick I played the Inspector.

I was sitting at the window, trying with all my might to stay in my chair, but the window kept drawing me. I had to resume the game with Clarimonda. And yet, the window horrified me. I saw the others hanging there: the Swiss traveling salesman, fat, with a thick neck and a grey stubbly beard; the thin artist; and the powerful police sergeant. I saw them, one after the other, hanging from the same hook, their mouths open, their tongues sticking out. And then, I saw myself among them.

Oh, this unspeakable fear. It was clear to me that it was provoked as much by Clarimonda as by the cross-bar and the horrible hook. May she pardon me . . . but it is the truth. In my terror, I keep seeing the three men hanging there, their legs dragging on the floor.

And yet, the fact is I had not felt the slightest desire to hang myself; nor was I afraid that I would want to do so. No, it was the window I feared; and Clarimonda. I was sure that something horrid was going to happen. Then I was overwhelmed by the need to go to the window—to stand before it. I had to . . .

The telephone rang. I picked up the receiver and before I could hear a word, I screamed, "Come. Come at once."

It was as if my shrill cry had in that instant dissipated the shadows from my soul. I grew calm. I wiped the sweat from my forehead. I drank a glass of water. Then I considered what I should say to the Inspector when he arrived. Finally, I went to the window. I waved and smiled. And Clarimonda too waved and smiled.

Five minutes later, the Inspector was here. I told him that I was getting to the bottom of the matter, but I begged him not to question me just then. That very soon I would be in a position to make important revelations. Strangely enough, though I was lying to him, I myself had the feeling that I was telling the truth. Even now, against my will, I have that same conviction.

The Inspector could not help noticing my agitated state of mind, especially since I apologized for my anguished cry over the telephone. Naturally, I tried to explain it to him, and yet I could not find a single reason to give for it. He said affectionately that there was no need ever to apologize to him; that he was always at my disposal; that that was his duty. It was better that he should come a dozen times to no effect rather than fail to be here when he was needed. He invited me to go out with him for the evening. It would be a distraction for me. It would do me good not to be alone for a while. I accepted the invitation though I was very reluctant to leave the room.

Saturday, March 19
We went to the Gaieté Rochechouart, La Cigale, and La Lune Rousse. The Inspector was right: It was good for me to get out and breathe the fresh air. At first, I had an uncomfortable feeling, as if I were doing something wrong; as if I were a deserter who had turned his back on the flag. But that soon went away. We drank a lot, laughed and chatted. This morning, when I went to my window, Clarimonda gave me what I thought was a look of reproach, though I may only have imagined it. How could she have known that I had gone out last night? In any case, the look lasted only for an instant, then she smiled again.

We played the game all day long.

Sunday, March 20
Only one thing to record: we played the game.

Monday, March 21
We played the game—all day long.

Tuesday, March 22
Yes, the game. We played it again. And nothing else. Nothing at all.

Sometimes I wonder what is happening to me? What is it I want? Where is all this leading? I know the answer: there is nothing else I want except what is happening. It is what I want . . . what I long for. This only.

Clarimonda and I have spoken with each other in the course of the last few days, but very briefly; scarcely a word. Sometimes we moved our lips, but more often we just looked at each other with deep understanding.

I was right about Clarimonda's reproachful look because I went out with the Inspector last Friday. I asked her to forgive me. I said it was stupid of me, and spiteful to have gone. She forgave me, and I promised never to leave the window again. We kissed, pressing our lips against each of our windowpanes.

Wednesday, March 23
I know now that I love Clarimonda. That she has entered into the very fiber of my being. It may be that the loves of other men are different. But does there exist one head, one ear, one hand that is exactly like hundreds of millions of others? There are always differences, and it must be so with love. My love is strange, I know that, but is it any the less lovely because of that? Besides, my love makes me happy.

If only I were not so frightened. Sometimes my terror slumbers and I forget it for a few moments, then it wakes and does not leave me. The fear is like a poor mouse trying to escape the grip of a powerful serpent. Just wait a bit, poor sad terror. Very soon, the serpent love will devour you.

Thursday, March 24
I have made a discovery: I don't play with Clarimonda. She plays with me.

Last night, thinking as always about our game, I wrote down five new and intricate gesture patterns with which I intended to surprise Clarimonda today. I gave each gesture a number. Then I practiced the series, so I could do the motions as quickly as possible, forwards or backwards. Or sometimes only the even-numbered ones, sometimes the odd. Or the first and the last of the five patterns. It was tiring work, but it made me happy and seemed to bring Clarimonda closer to me. I practiced for hours until I got all the motions down pat, like clockwork.

This morning, I went to the window. Clarimonda and I greeted each other, then our game began. Back and forth! It was incredible how quickly she understood what was to be done; how she kept pace with me.

There was a knock at the door. It was the servant bringing me my shoes. I took them. On my way back to the window, my eye chanced to fall on the slip of paper on which I had noted my gesture patterns. It was then that I understood: in the game just finished, I had not made use of a single one of my patterns.

I reeled back and had to hold on to the chair to keep from falling. It was unbelievable. I read the paper again—and again. It was still true: I had gone through a long series of gestures at the window, and not one of the patterns had been mine.

I had the feeling, once more, that I was standing before Clarimonda's wide open door, through which, though I stared, I could see nothing but a dark void. I knew, too, that if I chose to turn from that door now, I might be saved; and that I still had the power to leave. And yet, I did not leave—because I felt myself at the very edge of the mystery: as if I were holding the secret in my hands.

"Paris! You will conquer Paris," I thought. And in that instant, Paris was more powerful than Clarimonda.

I don't think about that any more. Now, I feel only love. Love, and a delicious terror.

Still, the moment itself endowed me with strength. I read my notes again, engraving the gestures on my mind. Then I went back to the window only to become aware that there was not one of my patterns that I wanted to use. Standing there, it occurred to me to rub the side of my nose; instead I found myself pressing my lips to the windowpane. I tried to drum with my fingers on the window sill; instead, I brushed my fingers through my hair. And so I understood that it was not that Clarimonda did what I did. Rather, my gestures followed her lead and with such lightning rapidity that we seemed to be moving simultaneously. I, who had been so proud because I thought I had been influencing her, I was in fact being influenced by her. Her influence . . . so gentle . . . so delightful.

I have tried another experiment. I clenched my hands and put them in my pockets firmly intending not to move them one bit. Clarimonda raised her hand and, smiling at me, made a scolding gesture with her finger. I did not budge, and yet I could feel how my right hand wished to leave my pocket. I shoved my fingers against the lining, but against my will, my hand left the pocket; my arm rose into the air. In my turn, I made a scolding gesture with my finger and smiled. It seemed to me that it was not I who was doing all this. It was a stranger whom I was watching. But, of course, I was mistaken. It was I making the gesture, and the person watching me was the stranger; that very same stranger who, not long ago, was so sure that he was on the edge of a great discovery. In any case, it was not I.

Of what use to me is this discovery? I am here to do Clarimonda's will. Clarimonda, whom I love with an anguished heart.

Friday, March 25

I have cut the telephone cord. I have no wish to be continually disturbed by the idiotic Inspector just as the mysterious hour arrives.

God. Why did I write that? Not a word of it is true. It is as if someone else were directing my pen.

But I want to . . . want to . . . to write the truth here . . . though it is costing me great effort. But I want to . . . once more . . . do what I want.

I have cut the telephone cord . . . ah . . .

Because I had to . . . there it is. Had to . . .

We stood at our windows this morning and played the game, which is now different from what it was yesterday. Clarimonda makes a movement and I resist it for as long as I can. Then I give in and do what she wants without further struggle. I can hardly express what a joy it is to be so conquered; to surrender entirely to her will.

We played. All at once, she stood up and walked back into her room, where I could not see her; she was so engulfed by the dark. Then she came back with a desk telephone, like mine, in her hands. She smiled and set the telephone on the window sill, after which she took a knife and cut the cord. Then I carried my telephone to the window where I cut the cord. After that, I returned my phone to its place.

That's how it happened . . .

I sit at my desk where I have been drinking tea the servant brought me. He has come for the empty teapot, and I ask him for the time, since my watch isn't running properly. He says it is five fifteen. Five fifteen . . .

I know that if I look out of my window, Clarimonda will be there making a gesture that I will have to imitate. I will look just the same. Clarimonda is there, smiling. If only I could turn my eyes away from hers.

Now she parts the curtain. She takes the cord. It is red, just like the cord in my window. She ties a noose and hangs the cord on the hook in the window cross-bar.

She sits down and smiles.

No. Fear is no longer what I feel. Rather, it is a sort of oppressive terror which I would not want to avoid for anything in the world. Its grip is irresistible, profoundly cruel, and voluptuous in its attraction.

I could go to the window, and do what she wants me to do, but I wait. I struggle. I resist though I feel a mounting fascination that becomes more intense each minute.

Here I am once more. Rashly, I went to the window where I did what Clarimonda wanted. I took the cord, tied a noose, and hung it on the hook . . .

Now, I want to see nothing else—except to stare at this paper. Because if I look, I know what she will do . . . now . . . at the sixth hour of the last day of the week. If I see her, I will have to do what she wants. Have to . . .

I won't see her . . .

I laugh. Loudly. No. I'm not laughing. Something is laughing in me, and I know why. It is because of my . . . I won't . . .

I won't, and yet I know very well that I have to . . . have to look at her. I must . . . must . . . and then . . . all that follows.

11

If I still wait, it is only to prolong this exquisite torture. Yes, that's it. This breathless anguish is my supreme delight. I write quickly, quickly . . . just so I can continue to sit here; so I can attenuate these seconds of pain.

Again, terror. Again. I know that I will look toward her. That I will stand up. That I will hang myself.

That doesn't frighten me. That is beautiful . . . even precious.

There is something else. What will happen afterwards? I don't know, but since my torment is so delicious. I feel . . . feel that something horrible must follow.

Think . . . think . . . Write something. Anything at all . . . to keep from looking toward her . . .

My name . . . Richard Bracquemont. Richard Bracquemont . . . Richard Bracquemont . . . Richard . . .

I can't . . . go on. I must . . . no . . . no . . . must look at her . . . Richard Bracquemont . . . no . . . no more . . . Richard . . . Richard Bracque— . . .

***

The inspector of the ninth precinct, after repeated and vain efforts to telephone Richard, arrived at the Hotel Stevens at 6:05. He found the body of the student Richard Bracquemont hanging from the cross-bar of the window in room #7, in the same position as each of his three predecessors.

The expression on the student's face, however, was different, reflecting an appalling fear. Bracquemont's eyes were wide open and bulging from their sockets. His lips were drawn into a rictus, and his jaws were clamped together. A huge black spider whose body was dotted with purple spots lay crushed and nearly bitten in two between his teeth.

On the table, there lay the student's journal. The inspector read it and went immediately to investigate the house across the street. What he learned was that the second floor of that building had not been lived in for many months.

The Man of Science

By Jerome K. Jerome

I MET A MAN IN THE STRAND ONE DAY THAT I KNEW VERY WELL, AS I thought, though I had not seen him for years. We walked together to Charing Cross, and there we shook hands and parted. Next morning, I spoke of this meeting to a mutual friend, and then I learnt, for the first time, that the man had died six months before.

The natural inference was that I had mistaken one man for another, an error that, not having a good memory for faces, I frequently fall into. What was remarkable about the matter, however, was that throughout our walk I had conversed with the man under the impression that he was that other dead man, and, whether by coincidence or not, his replies had never once suggested to me my mistake.

As soon as I finished, Jephson, who had been listening very thoughtfully, asked me if I believed in spiritualism "to its fullest extent."

"That is rather a large question," I answered. "What do you mean by 'spiritualism to its fullest extent'?"

"Well, do you believe that the spirits of the dead have not only the power of revisiting this earth at their will, but that, when here, they have the power of action, or rather, of exciting to action? Let me put a definite case. A spiritualist friend of mine, a sensible and by no means imaginative man, once told me that a table, through the medium of which the spirit of a friend had been in the habit of communicating with him, came slowly across the room towards him, of its own accord, one night as he sat alone, and pinioned him against the wall. Now can any of you believe that, or can't you?"

"I could," Brown took it upon himself to reply; "but, before doing so, I should wish for an introduction to the friend who told you the story. Speaking generally," he continued, "it seems to me that the difference between what we call the natural and the supernatural is merely the difference between frequency and rarity of occurrence. Having regard to the phenomena we are compelled to admit, I think it illogical to disbelieve anything we are unable to disprove."

"For my part," remarked MacShaughnassy, "I can believe in the ability of our spirit friends to give the quaint entertainments credited to them much easier than I can in their desire to do so."

"You mean," added Jephson, "that you cannot understand why a spirit, not compelled as we are by the exigencies of society, should care to spend its evenings carrying on a laboured and childish conversation with a room full of abnormally uninteresting people."

"That is precisely what I cannot understand," MacShaughnassy agreed.

"Nor I, either," said Jephson. "But I was thinking of something very different altogether. Suppose a man died with the dearest wish of his heart unfulfilled, do you believe that his spirit might have power to return to earth and complete the interrupted work?"

"Well," answered MacShaughnassy, "if one admits the possibility of spirits retaining any interest in the affairs of this world at all, it is certainly more reasonable to imagine them engaged upon a task such as you suggest, than to believe that they occupy themselves with the performance of mere drawing-room tricks. But what are you leading up to?"

"Why, to this," replied Jephson, seating himself straddle-legged across his chair, and leaning his arms upon the back. "I was told a story this morning at the hospital by an old French doctor. The actual facts are few and simple; all that is known can be read in the Paris police records of sixty-two years ago.

"The most important part of the case, however, is the part that is not known, and that never will be known.

"The story begins with a great wrong done by one man unto another man. What the wrong was I do not know. I am inclined to think, however, it was connected with a woman. I think that, because he who had been wronged hated him who had wronged him with a hate such as does not often burn in a man's brain, unless it be fanned by the memory of a woman's breath.

"Still that is only conjecture, and the point is immaterial. The man who had done the wrong fled, and the other man followed him. It became a point-to-point race, the first man having the advantage of a day's start. The course was the whole world, and the stakes were the first man's life.

"Travellers were few and far between in those days, and this made the trail easy to follow. The first man, never knowing how far or how near the other was behind him, and hoping now and again that he might have baffled him, would rest for a while. The second man, knowing always just how far the first one was before him, never paused, and thus each day the man who was spurred by Hate drew nearer to the man who was spurred by Fear.

"At this town the answer to the never-varied question would be:—

"'At seven o'clock last evening, M'sieur.'

"'Seven—ah; eighteen hours. Give me something to eat, quick, while the horses are being put to.'

"At the next the calculation would be sixteen hours.

"Passing a lonely chalet, Monsieur puts his head out of the window:—

"'How long since a carriage passed this way, with a tall, fair man inside?'

"'Such a one passed early this morning, M'sieur.'

"'Thanks, drive on, a hundred francs apiece if you are through the pass before daybreak.'

"'And what for dead horses, M'sieur?'

"'Twice their value when living.'

"One day the man who was ridden by Fear looked up, and saw before him the open door of a cathedral, and, passing in, knelt down and prayed. He prayed long and fervently, for men, when they are in sore straits, clutch eagerly at the straws of faith. He prayed that he might be forgiven his sin, and, more important still, that he might be pardoned the consequences of his sin, and be delivered from his adversary; and a few chairs from him, facing him, knelt his enemy, praying also.

"But the second man's prayer, being a thanksgiving merely, was short, so that when the first man raised his eyes, he saw the face of his enemy gazing at him across the chair-tops, with a mocking smile upon it.

"He made no attempt to rise, but remained kneeling, fascinated by the look of joy that shone out of the other man's eyes. And the other man moved the high-backed chairs one by one, and came towards him softly.

"Then, just as the man who had been wronged stood beside the man who had wronged him, full of gladness that his opportunity had come, there burst from the cathedral tower a sudden clash of bells, and the man, whose opportunity had come, broke his heart and fell back dead, with that mocking smile still playing round his mouth.

"And so he lay there.

"Then the man who had done the wrong rose up and passed out, praising God.

"What became of the body of the other man is not known. It was the body of a stranger who had died suddenly in the cathedral. There was none to identify it, none to claim it.

"Years passed away, and the survivor in the tragedy became a worthy and useful citizen, and a noted man of science.

"In his laboratory were many objects necessary to him in his researches, and, prominent among them, stood in a certain corner a human skeleton. It was a very old and much-mended skeleton, and one day the long-expected end arrived, and it tumbled to pieces.

"Thus it became necessary to purchase another.

"The man of science visited a dealer he well knew—a little parchment-faced old man who kept a dingy shop, where nothing was ever sold, within the shadow of the towers of Notre Dame.

"The little parchment-faced old man had just the very thing that Monsieur wanted—a singularly fine and well-proportioned 'study.' It should be sent round and set up in Monsieur's laboratory that very afternoon.

"The dealer was as good as his word. When Monsieur entered his laboratory that evening, the thing was in its place.

"Monsieur seated himself in his high-backed chair, and tried to collect his thoughts. But Monsieur's thoughts were unruly, and inclined to wander, and to wander always in one direction.

"Monsieur opened a large volume and commenced to read. He read of a man who had wronged another and fled from him, the other man following. Finding himself reading this, he closed the book angrily, and went and stood by the window and looked out. He saw before him the sun-pierced nave of a great cathedral, and on the stones lay a dead man with a mocking smile upon his face.

"Cursing himself for a fool, he turned away with a laugh. But his laugh was short-lived, for it seemed to him that something else in the room was laughing also. Struck suddenly still, with his feet glued to the ground, he stood listening for a while: then sought with starting eyes the corner from where the sound had seemed to come. But the white thing standing there was only grinning.

"Monsieur wiped the damp sweat from his head and hands, and stole out.

"For a couple of days he did not enter the room again. On the third, telling himself that his fears were those of a hysterical girl, he opened the door and went in. To shame himself, he took his lamp in his hand, and crossing over to the far corner where the skeleton stood, examined it. A set of bones bought for three hundred francs. Was he a child, to be scared by such a bogey!

"He held his lamp up in front of the thing's grinning head. The flame of the lamp flickered as though a faint breath had passed over it.

"The man explained this to himself by saying that the walls of the house were old and cracked, and that the wind might creep in anywhere. He repeated this explanation to himself as he recrossed the room, walking backwards, with his eyes fixed on the thing. When he reached his desk, he sat down and gripped the arms of his chair till his fingers turned white.

"He tried to work, but the empty sockets in that grinning head seemed to be drawing him towards them. He rose and battled with his inclination to fly screaming from the room. Glancing fearfully about him, his eye fell upon a high screen, standing before the door. He dragged it forward, and placed it between himself and the thing, so that he could not see it—nor it see him. Then he sat down again to his work. For a while he forced himself to look at the book in front of him, but at last, unable to control himself any longer, he suffered his eyes to follow their own bent.

"It may have been an hallucination. He may have accidentally placed the screen so as to favour such an illusion. But what he saw was a bony hand coming round the corner of the screen, and, with a cry, he fell to the floor in a swoon.

"The people of the house came running in, and lifting him up, carried him out, and laid him upon his bed. As soon as he recovered, his first question was, where had they found the thing—where was it when they entered the room? and when they told him they had seen it standing where it always stood, and had gone down into the room to look again, because of his frenzied entreaties, and returned trying to hide their smiles, he listened to their talk about overwork, and the necessity for change and rest, and said they might do with him as they would.

"So for many months the laboratory door remained locked. Then there came a chill autumn evening when the man of science opened it again, and closed it behind him.

"He lighted his lamp, and gathered his instruments and books around him, and sat down before them in his high-backed chair. And the old terror returned to him.

"But this time he meant to conquer himself. His nerves were stronger now, and his brain clearer; he would fight his unreasoning fear. He crossed to the door and locked himself in, and flung the key to the other end of the room, where it fell among jars and bottles with an echoing clatter.

"Later on, his old housekeeper, going her final round, tapped at his door and wished him good-night, as was her custom. She received no response, at first, and, growing nervous, tapped louder and called again; and at length an answering 'good-night' came back to her.

"She thought little about it at the time, but afterwards she remembered that the voice that had replied to her had been strangely grating and mechanical. Trying to describe it, she likened it to such a voice as she would imagine coming from a statue.

"Next morning his door remained still locked. It was no unusual thing for him to work all night and far into the next day, so no one thought to be surprised. When, however, evening came, and yet he did not appear, his servants gathered outside the room and whispered, remembering what had happened once before.

"They listened, but could hear no sound. They shook the door and called to him, then beat with their fists upon the wooden panels. But still no sound came from the room.

"Becoming alarmed, they decided to burst open the door, and, after many blows, it gave way, and they crowded in.

He sat bolt upright in his high-backed chair. They thought at first he had died in his sleep. But when they drew nearer and the light fell upon him, they saw the livid marks of bony fingers round his throat; and in his eyes there was a terror such as is not often seen in human eyes."

Brown was the first to break the silence that followed. He asked me if I had any brandy on board. He said he felt he should like just a nip of brandy before going to bed. That is one of the chief charms of Jephson's stories: they always make you feel you want a little brandy.

The Most Dangerous Game

By Richard Connell

"OFF THERE TO THE RIGHT—SOMEWHERE—IS A LARGE ISLAND," SAID Whitney. "It's rather a mystery—"

"What island is it?" Rainsford asked.

"The old charts call it 'Ship-Trap Island,'" Whitney replied. "A suggestive name, isn't it? Sailors have a curious dread of the place. I don't know why. Some superstition—"

"Can't see it," remarked Rainsford, trying to peer through the dank tropical night that was palpable as it pressed its thick warm blackness in upon the yacht.

"You've good eyes," said Whitney, with a laugh, "and I've seen you pick off a moose moving in the brown fall bush at four hundred yards, but even you can't see four miles or so through a moonless Caribbean night."

"Nor four yards," admitted Rainsford. "Ugh! It's like moist black velvet."

"It will be light enough in Rio," promised Whitney. "We should make it in a few days. I hope the jaguar guns have come from Purdey's. We should have some good hunting up the Amazon. Great sport, hunting."

"The best sport in the world," agreed Rainsford.

"For the hunter," amended Whitney. "Not for the jaguar."

"Don't talk rot, Whitney," said Rainsford. "You're a big-game hunter, not a philosopher. Who cares how a jaguar feels?"

"Perhaps the jaguar does," observed Whitney.

"Bah! They've no understanding."

"Even so, I rather think they understand one thing—fear. The fear of pain and the fear of death."

"Nonsense," laughed Rainsford. "This hot weather is making you soft, Whitney. Be a realist. The world is made up of two classes—the hunters and the huntees. Luckily, you and I are hunters. Do you think we've passed that island yet?"

"I can't tell in the dark. I hope so."

"Why?" asked Rainsford.

"The place has a reputation—a bad one."

"Cannibals?" suggested Rainsford.

"Hardly. Even cannibals wouldn't live in such a God-forsaken place. But it's gotten into sailor lore, somehow. Didn't you notice that the crew's nerves seemed a bit jumpy today?"

"They were a bit strange, now you mention it. Even Captain Nielsen—"

"Yes, even that tough-minded old Swede, who'd go up to the devil himself and ask him for a light. Those fishy blue eyes held a look I never saw there before. All I could get out of him was 'This place has an evil name among seafaring men, sir.' Then he said to me, very gravely, 'Don't you feel anything?'—as if the air about us was actually poisonous. Now, you mustn't laugh when I tell you this—I did feel something like a sudden chill.

"There was no breeze. The sea was as flat as a plate-glass window. We were drawing near the island then. What I felt was a—a mental chill; a sort of sudden dread."

"Pure imagination," said Rainsford. "One superstitious sailor can taint the whole ship's company with his fear."

"Maybe. But sometimes I think sailors have an extra sense that tells them when they are in danger. Sometimes I think evil is a tangible thing—with wave lengths, just as sound and light have. An evil place can, so to speak, broadcast vibrations of evil. Anyhow, I'm glad we're getting out of this zone. Well, I think I'll turn in now, Rainsford."

"I'm not sleepy," said Rainsford. "I'm going to smoke another pipe up on the afterdeck."

"Good night, then, Rainsford. See you at breakfast."

"Right. Good night, Whitney."

There was no sound in the night as Rainsford sat there but the muffled throb of the engine that drove the yacht swiftly through the darkness, and the swish and ripple of the wash of the propeller.

Rainsford, reclining in a steamer chair, indolently puffed on his favorite brier. The sensuous drowsiness of the night was on him. "It's so dark," he thought, "that I could sleep without closing my eyes; the night would be my eyelids—"

An abrupt sound startled him. Off to the right he heard it, and his ears, expert in such matters, could not be mistaken. Again he heard the sound, and again. Somewhere, off in the blackness, someone had fired a gun three times.

Rainsford sprang up and moved quickly to the rail, mystified. He strained his eyes in the direction from which the reports had come, but it was like trying to see through a blanket. He leaped upon the rail and balanced himself there, to get greater elevation; his pipe, striking a rope, was knocked from his mouth. He lunged for it; a short, hoarse cry came from his lips as he realized he had reached too far and had lost his balance. The cry was pinched off short as the blood-warm waters of the Caribbean Sea closed over his head.

He struggled up to the surface and tried to cry out, but the wash from the speeding yacht slapped him in the face and the salt water in his open mouth made him gag and strangle. Desperately he struck out with strong strokes after the receding lights of the yacht, but he stopped before he had swum fifty feet. A certain coolheadedness had come to him; it was not the first time he had been in a tight place. There was a chance that his cries could be heard by someone aboard the yacht, but that chance was slender and grew more slender as the yacht raced on. He wrestled himself out of his clothes and shouted with all his power. The lights of the yacht became faint and ever-vanishing fireflies; then they were blotted out entirely by the night.

Rainsford remembered the shots. They had come from the right, and doggedly he swam in that direction, swimming with slow, deliberate strokes, conserving his strength. For a seemingly endless time he fought

13

the sea. He began to count his strokes; he could do possibly a hundred more and then—

Rainsford heard a sound. It came out of the darkness, a high screaming sound, the sound of an animal in an extremity of anguish and terror.

He did not recognize the animal that made the sound; he did not try to; with fresh vitality he swam toward the sound. He heard it again; then it was cut short by another noise, crisp, staccato.

"Pistol shot," muttered Rainsford, swimming on.

Ten minutes of determined effort brought another sound to his ears—the most welcome he had ever heard—the muttering and growling of the sea breaking on a rocky shore. He was almost on the rocks before he saw them; on a night less calm he would have been shattered against them. With his remaining strength he dragged himself from the swirling waters. Jagged crags appeared to jut up into the opaqueness; he forced himself upward, hand over hand. Gasping, his hands raw, he reached a flat place at the top. Dense jungle came down to the very edge of the cliffs. What perils that tangle of trees and underbrush might hold for him did not concern Rainsford just then. All he knew was that he was safe from his enemy, the sea, and that utter weariness was on him. He flung himself down at the jungle edge and tumbled headlong into the deepest sleep of his life.

When he opened his eyes he knew from the position of the sun that it was late in the afternoon. Sleep had given him new vigor; a sharp hunger was picking at him. He looked about him, almost cheerfully.

"Where there are pistol shots, there are men. Where there are men, there is food," he thought. But what kind of men, he wondered, in so forbidding a place? An unbroken front of snarled and ragged jungle fringed the shore.

He saw no sign of a trail through the closely knit web of weeds and trees; it was easier to go along the shore, and Rainsford floundered along by the water. Not far from where he landed, he stopped.

Some wounded thing—by the evidence, a large animal—had thrashed about in the underbrush; the jungle weeds were crushed down and the moss was lacerated; one patch of weeds was stained crimson. A

148

small, glittering object not far away caught Rainsford's eye and he picked it up. It was an empty cartridge.

"A twenty-two," he remarked. "That's odd. It must have been a fairly large animal too. The hunter had his nerve with him to tackle it with a light gun. It's clear that the brute put up a fight. I suppose the first three shots I heard was when the hunter flushed his quarry and wounded it. The last shot was when he trailed it here and finished it."

He examined the ground closely and found what he had hoped to find—the print of hunting boots. They pointed along the cliff in the direction he had been going. Eagerly he hurried along, now slipping on a rotten log or a loose stone, but making headway; night was beginning to settle down on the island.

Bleak darkness was blacking out the sea and jungle when Rainsford sighted the lights. He came upon them as he turned a crook in the coast line; and his first thought was that he had come upon a village, for there were many lights. But as he forged along he saw to his great astonishment that all the lights were in one enormous building—a lofty structure with pointed towers plunging upward into the gloom. His eyes made out the shadowy outlines of a palatial chateau; it was set on a high bluff, and on three sides of it cliffs dived down to where the sea licked greedy lips in the shadows.

"Mirage," thought Rainsford. But it was no mirage, he found, when he opened the tall spiked iron gate. The stone steps were real enough; the massive door with a leering gargoyle for a knocker was real enough; yet above it all hung an air of unreality.

He lifted the knocker, and it creaked up stiffly, as if it had never before been used. He let it fall, and it startled him with its booming loudness. He thought he heard steps within; the door remained closed. Again Rainsford lifted the heavy knocker, and let it fall. The door opened then—opened as suddenly as if it were on a spring—and Rainsford stood blinking in the river of glaring gold light that poured out. The first thing Rainsford's eyes discerned was the largest man Rainsford had ever seen—a gigantic creature, solidly made and black bearded to the waist. In his hand the man held a long-barreled revolver, and he was pointing it straight at Rainsford's heart.

Out of the snarl of beard two small eyes regarded Rainsford.

"Don't be alarmed," said Rainsford, with a smile which he hoped was disarming. "I'm no robber. I fell off a yacht. My name is Sanger Rainsford of New York City."

The menacing look in the eyes did not change. The revolver pointed as rigidly as if the giant were a statue. He gave no sign that he understood Rainsford's words, or that he had even heard them. He was dressed in uniform—a black uniform trimmed with gray astrakhan.

"I'm Sanger Rainsford of New York," Rainsford began again. "I fell off a yacht. I am hungry."

The man's only answer was to raise with his thumb the hammer of his revolver. Then Rainsford saw the man's free hand go to his forehead in a military salute, and he saw him click his heels together and stand at attention. Another man was coming down the broad marble steps, an erect, slender man in evening clothes. He advanced to Rainsford and held out his hand.

In a cultivated voice marked by a slight accent that gave it added precision and deliberateness, he said, "It is a very great pleasure and honor to welcome Mr. Sanger Rainsford, the celebrated hunter, to my home."

Automatically Rainsford shook the man's hand.

"I've read your book about hunting snow leopards in Tibet, you see," explained the man. "I am General Zaroff."

Rainsford's first impression was that the man was singularly handsome; his second was that there was an original, almost bizarre quality about the general's face. He was a tall man past middle age, for his hair was a vivid white; but his thick eyebrows and pointed military mustache were as black as the night from which Rainsford had come. His eyes, too, were black and very bright. He had high cheekbones, a sharpcut nose, a spare, dark face—the face of a man used to giving orders, the face of an aristocrat. Turning to the giant in uniform, the general made a sign. The giant put away his pistol, saluted, withdrew.

"Ivan is an incredibly strong fellow," remarked the general, "but he has the misfortune to be deaf and dumb. A simple fellow, but, I'm afraid, like all his race, a bit of a savage."

"Is he Russian?"

"He is a Cossack," said the general, and his smile showed red lips and pointed teeth. "So am I."

"Come," he said, "we shouldn't be chatting here. We can talk later. Now you want clothes, food, rest. You shall have them. This is a most restful spot."

Ivan had reappeared, and the general spoke to him with lips that moved but gave forth no sound.

"Follow Ivan, if you please, Mr. Rainsford," said the general. "I was about to have my dinner when you came. I'll wait for you. You'll find that my clothes will fit you, I think."

It was to a huge, beam-ceilinged bedroom with a canopied bed big enough for six men that Rainsford followed the silent giant. Ivan laid out an evening suit, and Rainsford, as he put it on, noticed that it came from a London tailor who ordinarily cut and sewed for none below the rank of duke.

The dining room to which Ivan conducted him was in many ways remarkable. There was a medieval magnificence about it; it suggested a baronial hall of feudal times with its oaken panels, its high ceiling, its vast refectory tables where twoscore men could sit down to eat. About the hall were mounted heads of many animals—lions, tigers, elephants, moose, bears; larger or more perfect specimens Rainsford had never seen. At the great table the general was sitting, alone.

"You'll have a cocktail, Mr. Rainsford," he suggested. The cocktail was surpassingly good; and, Rainsford noted, the table appointments were of the finest—the linen, the crystal, the silver, the china.

They were eating borsch, the rich, red soup with whipped cream so dear to Russian palates. Half apologetically General Zaroff said, "We do our best to preserve the amenities of civilization here. Please forgive any lapses. We are well off the beaten track, you know. Do you think the champagne has suffered from its long ocean trip?"

"Not in the least," declared Rainsford. He was finding the general a most thoughtful and affable host, a true cosmopolite. But there was one small trait of the general's that made Rainsford uncomfortable. Whenever he looked up from his plate he found the general studying him, appraising him narrowly.

"Perhaps," said General Zaroff, "you were surprised that I recognized your name. You see, I read all books on hunting published in English, French, and Russian. I have but one passion in my life, Mr. Rainsford, and it is the hunt."

"You have some wonderful heads here," said Rainsford as he ate a particularly well-cooked filet mignon. "That Cape buffalo is the largest I ever saw."

"Oh, that fellow. Yes, he was a monster."

"Did he charge you?"

"Hurled me against a tree," said the general. "Fractured my skull. But I got the brute."

"I've always thought," said Rainsford, "that the Cape buffalo is the most dangerous of all big game."

For a moment the general did not reply; he was smiling his curious red-lipped smile. Then he said slowly, "No. You are wrong, sir. The Cape buffalo is not the most dangerous big game." He sipped his wine. "Here in my preserve on this island," he said in the same slow tone, "I hunt more dangerous game."

Rainsford expressed his surprise. "Is there big game on this island?"

The general nodded. "The biggest."

"Really?"

"Oh, it isn't here naturally, of course. I have to stock the island."

"What have you imported, general?" Rainsford asked. "Tigers?"

The general smiled. "No," he said. "Hunting tigers ceased to interest me some years ago. I exhausted their possibilities, you see. No thrill left in tigers, no real danger. I live for danger, Mr. Rainsford."

The general took from his pocket a gold cigarette case and offered his guest a long black cigarette with a silver tip; it was perfumed and gave off a smell like incense.

"We will have some capital hunting, you and I," said the general. "I shall be most glad to have your society."

"But what game—" began Rainsford.

"I'll tell you," said the general. "You will be amused, I know. I think I may say, in all modesty, that I have done a rare thing. I have invented a new sensation. May I pour you another glass of port?"

"Thank you, general."

The general filled both glasses, and said, "God makes some men poets. Some He makes kings, some beggars. Me He made a hunter. My hand was made for the trigger, my father said. He was a very rich man with a quarter of a million acres in the Crimea, and he was an ardent sportsman. When I was only five years old he gave me a little gun, specially made in Moscow for me, to shoot sparrows with. When I shot some of his prize turkeys with it, he did not punish me; he complimented me on my marksmanship. I killed my first bear in the Caucasus when I was ten. My whole life has been one prolonged hunt. I went into the army—it was expected of noblemen's sons—and for a time commanded a division of Cossack cavalry, but my real interest was always the hunt. I have hunted every kind of game in every land. It would be impossible for me to tell you how many animals I have killed."

The general puffed at his cigarette.

"After the debacle in Russia I left the country, for it was imprudent for an officer of the Czar to stay there. Many noble Russians lost everything. I, luckily, had invested heavily in American securities, so I shall never have to open a tearoom in Monte Carlo or drive a taxi in Paris. Naturally, I continued to hunt—grizzlies in your Rockies, crocodiles in the Ganges, rhinoceroses in East Africa. It was in Africa that the Cape buffalo hit me and laid me up for six months. As soon as I recovered I started for the Amazon to hunt jaguars, for I had heard they were unusually cunning. They weren't." The Cossack sighed. "They were no match at all for a hunter with his wits about him, and a high-powered rifle. I was bitterly disappointed. I was lying in my tent with a splitting headache one night when a terrible thought pushed its way into my mind. Hunting was beginning to bore me! And hunting, remember, had been my life. I have heard that in America businessmen often go to pieces when they give up the business that has been their life."

"Yes, that's so," said Rainsford.

The general smiled. "I had no wish to go to pieces," he said. "I must do something. Now, mine is an analytical mind, Mr. Rainsford. Doubtless that is why I enjoy the problems of the chase."

"No doubt, General Zaroff."

"So," continued the general, "I asked myself why the hunt no longer fascinated me. You are much younger than I am, Mr. Rainsford, and have not hunted as much, but you perhaps can guess the answer."

"What was it?"

"Simply this: hunting had ceased to be what you call 'a sporting proposition.' It had become too easy. I always got my quarry. Always. There is no greater bore than perfection."

The general lit a fresh cigarette.

"No animal had a chance with me any more. That is no boast; it is a mathematical certainty. The animal had nothing but his legs and his instinct. Instinct is no match for reason. When I thought of this it was a tragic moment for me, I can tell you."

Rainsford leaned across the table, absorbed in what his host was saying.

"It came to me as an inspiration what I must do," the general went on.

"And that was?"

The general smiled the quiet smile of one who has faced an obstacle and surmounted it with success. "I had to invent a new animal to hunt," he said.

"A new animal? You're joking."

"Not at all," said the general. "I never joke about hunting. I needed a new animal. I found one. So I bought this island, built this house, and here I do my hunting. The island is perfect for my purposes—there are jungles with a maze of traits in them, hills, swamps—"

"But the animal, General Zaroff?"

"Oh," said the general, "it supplies me with the most exciting hunting in the world. No other hunting compares with it for an instant. Every day I hunt, and I never grow bored now, for I have a quarry with which I can match my wits."

Rainsford's bewilderment showed in his face.

"I wanted the ideal animal to hunt," explained the general. "So I said, 'What are the attributes of an ideal quarry?' And the answer was, of course, 'It must have courage, cunning, and, above all, it must be able to reason.'"

"But no animal can reason," objected Rainsford.

"My dear fellow," said the general, "there is one that can."

"But you can't mean—" gasped Rainsford.

"And why not?"

"I can't believe you are serious, General Zaroff. This is a grisly joke."

"Why should I not be serious? I am speaking of hunting."

"Hunting? Great Guns, General Zaroff, what you speak of is murder."

The general laughed with entire good nature. He regarded Rainsford quizzically. "I refuse to believe that so modern and civilized a young man as you seem to be harbors romantic ideas about the value of human life. Surely your experiences in the war—"

"Did not make me condone cold-blooded murder," finished Rainsford stiffly.

Laughter shook the general. "How extraordinarily droll you are!" he said. "One does not expect nowadays to find a young man of the educated class, even in America, with such a naive, and, if I may say so, mid-Victorian point of view. It's like finding a snuffbox in a limousine. Ah, well, doubtless you had Puritan ancestors. So many Americans appear to have had. I'll wager you'll forget your notions when you go hunting with me. You've a genuine new thrill in store for you, Mr. Rainsford."

"Thank you, I'm a hunter, not a murderer."

"Dear me," said the general, quite unruffled, "again that unpleasant word. But I think I can show you that your scruples are quite ill founded."

"Yes?"

"Life is for the strong, to be lived by the strong, and, if needs be, taken by the strong. The weak of the world were put here to give the strong pleasure. I am strong. Why should I not use my gift? If I wish to hunt, why should I not? I hunt the scum of the earth: sailors from tramp ships—lascars, blacks, Chinese, whites, mongrels—a thoroughbred horse or hound is worth more than a score of them."

"But they are men," said Rainsford hotly.

"Precisely," said the general. "That is why I use them. It gives me pleasure. They can reason, after a fashion. So they are dangerous."

"But where do you get them?"

The general's left eyelid fluttered down in a wink. "This island is called Ship Trap," he answered. "Sometimes an angry god of the high seas sends them to me. Sometimes, when Providence is not so kind, I help Providence a bit. Come to the window with me."

Rainsford went to the window and looked out toward the sea.

"Watch! Out there!" exclaimed the general, pointing into the night. Rainsford's eyes saw only blackness, and then, as the general pressed a button, far out to sea Rainsford saw the flash of lights.

The general chuckled. "They indicate a channel," he said, "where there's none; giant rocks with razor edges crouch like a sea monster with wide-open jaws. They can crush a ship as easily as I crush this nut." He dropped a walnut on the hardwood floor and brought his heel grinding down on it. "Oh, yes," he said, casually, as if in answer to a question, "I have electricity. We try to be civilized here."

"Civilized? And you shoot down men?"

A trace of anger was in the general's black eyes, but it was there for but a second; and he said, in his most pleasant manner, "Dear me, what a righteous young man you are! I assure you I do not do the thing you suggest. That would be barbarous. I treat these visitors with every consideration. They get plenty of good food and exercise. They get into splendid physical condition. You shall see for yourself tomorrow."

"What do you mean?"

"We'll visit my training school," smiled the general. "It's in the cellar. I have about a dozen pupils down there now. They're from the Spanish bark San Lucar that had the bad luck to go on the rocks out there. A very inferior lot, I regret to say. Poor specimens and more accustomed to the deck than to the jungle." He raised his hand, and Ivan, who served as waiter, brought thick Turkish coffee. Rainsford, with an effort, held his tongue in check.

"It's a game, you see," pursued the general blandly. "I suggest to one of them that we go hunting. I give him a supply of food and an excellent hunting knife. I give him three hours' start. I am to follow, armed only with a pistol of the smallest caliber and range. If my quarry eludes me for three whole days, he wins the game. If I find him"—the general smiled—"he loses."

"Suppose he refuses to be hunted?"

"Oh," said the general, "I give him his option, of course. He need not play that game if he doesn't wish to. If he does not wish to hunt, I turn him over to Ivan. Ivan once had the honor of serving as official knouter to the Great White Czar, and he has his own ideas of sport. Invariably, Mr. Rainsford, invariably they choose the hunt."

"And if they win?"

The smile on the general's face widened. "To date I have not lost," he said. Then he added, hastily: "I don't wish you to think me a braggart, Mr. Rainsford. Many of them afford only the most elementary sort of problem. Occasionally I strike a tartar. One almost did win. I eventually had to use the dogs."

"The dogs?"

"This way, please. I'll show you."

The general steered Rainsford to a window. The lights from the windows sent a flickering illumination that made grotesque patterns on the courtyard below, and Rainsford could see moving about there a dozen or so huge black shapes; as they turned toward him, their eyes glittered greenly.

"A rather good lot, I think," observed the general. "They are let out at seven every night. If anyone should try to get into my house—or out of it—something extremely regrettable would occur to him." He hummed a snatch of song from the Folies Bergere.

"And now," said the general, "I want to show you my new collection of heads. Will you come with me to the library?"

"I hope," said Rainsford, "that you will excuse me tonight, General Zaroff. I'm really not feeling well."

"Ah, indeed?" the general inquired solicitously. "Well, I suppose that's only natural, after your long swim. You need a good, restful night's sleep. Tomorrow you'll feel like a new man, I'll wager. Then we'll hunt, eh? I've one rather promising prospect—" Rainsford was hurrying from the room.

"Sorry you can't go with me tonight," called the general. "I expect rather fair sport—a big, strong, black. He looks resourceful—Well, good night, Mr. Rainsford; I hope you have a good night's rest."

The bed was good, and the pajamas of the softest silk, and he was tired in every fiber of his being, but nevertheless Rainsford could not quiet his brain with the opiate of sleep. He lay, eyes wide open. Once he thought he heard stealthy steps in the corridor outside his room. He sought to throw open the door; it would not open. He went to the window and looked out. His room was high up in one of the towers. The lights of the chateau were out now, and it was dark and silent; but there was a fragment of sallow moon, and by its wan light he could see, dimly, the courtyard. There, weaving in and out in the pattern of shadow, were black, noiseless forms; the hounds heard him at the window and looked up, expectantly, with their green eyes. Rainsford went back to the bed and lay down. By many methods he tried to put himself to sleep. He had achieved a doze when, just as morning began to come, he heard, far off in the jungle, the faint report of a pistol.

General Zaroff did not appear until luncheon. He was dressed faultlessly in the tweeds of a country squire. He was solicitous about the state of Rainsford's health.

"As for me," sighed the general, "I do not feel so well. I am worried, Mr. Rainsford. Last night I detected traces of my old complaint."

To Rainsford's questioning glance the general said, "Ennui. Boredom."

Then, taking a second helping of crepes Suzette, the general explained: "The hunting was not good last night. The fellow lost his head. He made a straight trail that offered no problems at all. That's the trouble with these sailors; they have dull brains to begin with, and they do not know how to get about in the woods. They do excessively stupid and obvious things. It's most annoying. Will you have another glass of Chablis, Mr. Rainsford?"

"General," said Rainsford firmly, "I wish to leave this island at once."

The general raised his thickets of eyebrows; he seemed hurt. "But, my dear fellow," the general protested, "you've only just come. You've had no hunting—"

"I wish to go today," said Rainsford. He saw the dead black eyes of the general on him, studying him. General Zaroff's face suddenly brightened.

He filled Rainsford's glass with venerable Chablis from a dusty bottle.

"Tonight," said the general, "we will hunt—you and I."

Rainsford shook his head. "No, general," he said. "I will not hunt."

The general shrugged his shoulders and delicately ate a hothouse grape. "As you wish, my friend," he said. "The choice rests entirely with you. But may I not venture to suggest that you will find my idea of sport more diverting than Ivan's?"

He nodded toward the corner to where the giant stood, scowling, his thick arms crossed on his hogshead of chest.

"You don't mean—" cried Rainsford.

"My dear fellow," said the general, "have I not told you I always mean what I say about hunting? This is really an inspiration. I drink to a foeman worthy of my steel—at last." The general raised his glass, but Rainsford sat staring at him.

"You'll find this game worth playing," the general said enthusiastically. "Your brain against mine. Your woodcraft against mine. Your strength and stamina against mine. Outdoor chess! And the stake is not without value, eh?"

"And if I win—" began Rainsford huskily.

"I'll cheerfully acknowledge myself defeated if I do not find you by midnight of the third day," said General Zaroff. "My sloop will place you on the mainland near a town." The general read what Rainsford was thinking.

"Oh, you can trust me," said the Cossack. "I will give you my word as a gentleman and a sportsman. Of course you, in turn, must agree to say nothing of your visit here."

"I'll agree to nothing of the kind," said Rainsford.

"Oh," said the general, "in that case—But why discuss that now? Three days hence we can discuss it over a bottle of Veuve Clicquot, unless—"

The general sipped his wine.

Then a businesslike air animated him. "Ivan," he said to Rainsford, "will supply you with hunting clothes, food, a knife. I suggest you wear moccasins; they leave a poorer trail. I suggest, too, that you avoid the big swamp in the southeast corner of the island. We call it Death Swamp. There's quicksand there. One foolish fellow tried it. The deplorable part of it was that Lazarus followed him. You can imagine my feelings, Mr. Rainsford. I loved Lazarus; he was the finest hound in my pack. Well,

I must beg you to excuse me now. I always take a siesta after lunch. You'll hardly have time for a nap, I fear. You'll want to start, no doubt. I shall not follow till dusk. Hunting at night is so much more exciting than by day, don't you think? Au revoir, Mr. Rainsford, au revoir." General Zaroff, with a deep, courtly bow, strolled from the room.

From another door came Ivan. Under one arm he carried khaki hunting clothes, a haversack of food, a leather sheath containing a long-bladed hunting knife; his right hand rested on a cocked revolver thrust in the crimson sash about his waist.

Rainsford had fought his way through the bush for two hours. "I must keep my nerve. I must keep my nerve," he said through tight teeth.

He had not been entirely clearheaded when the chateau gates snapped shut behind him. His whole idea at first was to put distance between himself and General Zaroff; and, to this end, he had plunged along, spurred on by the sharp rowers of something very like panic. Now he had got a grip on himself, had stopped, and was taking stock of himself and the situation. He saw that straight flight was futile; inevitably it would bring him face to face with the sea. He was in a picture with a frame of water, and his operations, clearly, must take place within that frame.

"I'll give him a trail to follow," muttered Rainsford, and he struck off from the rude path he had been following into the trackless wilderness. He executed a series of intricate loops; he doubled on his trail again and again, recalling all the lore of the fox hunt, and all the dodges of the fox. Night found him leg-weary, with hands and face lashed by the branches, on a thickly wooded ridge. He knew it would be insane to blunder on through the dark, even if he had the strength. His need for rest was imperative and he thought, "I have played the fox, now I must play the cat of the fable." A big tree with a thick trunk and outspread branches was near by, and, taking care to leave not the slightest mark, he climbed up into the crotch, and, stretching out on one of the broad limbs, after a fashion, rested. Rest brought him new confidence and almost a feeling of security. Even so zealous a hunter as General Zaroff could not trace him there, he told himself; only the devil himself could follow that complicated trail through the jungle after dark. But perhaps the general was a devil—

An apprehensive night crawled slowly by like a wounded snake and sleep did not visit Rainsford, although the silence of a dead world was on the jungle. Toward morning when a dingy gray was varnishing the sky, the cry of some startled bird focused Rainsford's attention in that direction. Something was coming through the bush, coming slowly, carefully, coming by the same winding way Rainsford had come. He flattened himself down on the limb and, through a screen of leaves almost as thick as tapestry, he watched. . . . That which was approaching was a man.

It was General Zaroff. He made his way along with his eyes fixed in utmost concentration on the ground before him. He paused, almost beneath the tree, dropped to his knees and studied the ground. Rainsford's impulse was to hurl himself down like a panther, but he saw that the general's right hand held something metallic—a small automatic pistol.

The hunter shook his head several times, as if he were puzzled. Then he straightened up and took from his case one of his black cigarettes; its pungent incenselike smoke floated up to Rainsford's nostrils.

Rainsford held his breath. The general's eyes had left the ground and were traveling inch by inch up the tree. Rainsford froze there, every muscle tensed for a spring. But the sharp eyes of the hunter stopped before they reached the limb where Rainsford lay; a smile spread over his brown face. Very deliberately he blew a smoke ring into the air; then he turned his back on the tree and walked carelessly away, back along the trail he had come. The swish of the underbrush against his hunting boots grew fainter and fainter.

The pent-up air burst hotly from Rainsford's lungs. His first thought made him feel sick and numb. The general could follow a trail through the woods at night; he could follow an extremely difficult trail; he must have uncanny powers; only by the merest chance had the Cossack failed to see his quarry.

Rainsford's second thought was even more terrible. It sent a shudder of cold horror through his whole being. Why had the general smiled? Why had he turned back?

Rainsford did not want to believe what his reason told him was true, but the truth was as evident as the sun that had by now pushed through the morning mists. The general was playing with him! The general was saving him for another day's sport! The Cossack was the cat; he was the mouse. Then it was that Rainsford knew the full meaning of terror.

"I will not lose my nerve. I will not."

He slid down from the tree, and struck off again into the woods. His face was set and he forced the machinery of his mind to function. Three hundred yards from his hiding place he stopped where a huge dead tree leaned precariously on a smaller, living one. Throwing off his sack of food, Rainsford took his knife from its sheath and began to work with all his energy.

The job was finished at last, and he threw himself down behind a fallen log a hundred feet away. He did not have to wait long. The cat was coming again to play with the mouse.

Following the trail with the sureness of a bloodhound came General Zaroff. Nothing escaped those searching black eyes, no crushed blade of grass, no bent twig, no mark, no matter how faint, in the moss. So intent was the Cossack on his stalking that he was upon the thing Rainsford had made before he saw it. His foot touched the protruding bough that was the trigger. Even as he touched it, the general sensed his danger and leaped back with the agility of an ape. But he was not quite quick enough; the dead tree, delicately adjusted to rest on the cut living one, crashed down and struck the general a glancing blow on the shoulder as it fell; but for his alertness, he must have been smashed beneath it. He staggered, but he did not fall; nor did he drop his revolver. He stood there, rubbing his injured shoulder, and Rainsford, with fear again gripping his heart, heard the general's mocking laugh ring through the jungle.

"Rainsford," called the general, "if you are within sound of my voice, as I suppose you are, let me congratulate you. Not many men know how to make a Malay mancatcher. Luckily for me I, too, have hunted in Malacca. You are proving interesting, Mr. Rainsford. I am going now to have my wound dressed; it's only a slight one. But I shall be back. I shall be back."

When the general, nursing his bruised shoulder, had gone, Rainsford took up his flight again. It was flight now, a desperate, hopeless flight, that carried him on for some hours. Dusk came, then darkness, and still he pressed on. The ground grew softer under his moccasins; the vegetation grew ranker, denser; insects bit him savagely.

Then, as he stepped forward, his foot sank into the ooze. He tried to wrench it back, but the muck sucked viciously at his foot as if it were a giant leech. With a violent effort, he tore his feet loose. He knew where he was now. Death Swamp and its quicksand.

His hands were tightly closed as if his nerve were something tangible that someone in the darkness was trying to tear from his grip. The softness of the earth had given him an idea. He stepped back from the quicksand a dozen feet or so and, like some huge prehistoric beaver, he began to dig.

Rainsford had dug himself in in France when a second's delay meant death. That had been a placid pastime compared to his digging now. The pit grew deeper; when it was above his shoulders, he climbed out and from some hard saplings cut stakes and sharpened them to a fine point. These stakes he planted in the bottom of the pit with the points sticking up. With flying fingers he wove a rough carpet of weeds and branches and with it he covered the mouth of the pit. Then, wet with sweat and aching with tiredness, he crouched behind the stump of a lightning-charred tree.

He knew his pursuer was coming; he heard the padding sound of feet on the soft earth, and the night breeze brought him the perfume of the general's cigarette. It seemed to Rainsford that the general was coming with unusual swiftness; he was not feeling his way along, foot by foot. Rainsford, crouching there, could not see the general, nor could he see the pit. He lived a year in a minute. Then he felt an impulse to cry aloud with joy, for he heard the sharp crackle of the breaking branches as the cover of the pit gave way; he heard the sharp scream of pain as the pointed stakes found their mark. He leaped up from his place of concealment. Then he cowered back. Three feet from the pit a man was standing, with an electric torch in his hand.

"You've done well, Rainsford," the voice of the general called. "Your Burmese tiger pit has claimed one of my best dogs. Again you score. I think, Mr. Rainsford, I'll see what you can do against my whole pack. I'm going home for a rest now. Thank you for a most amusing evening."

At daybreak Rainsford, lying near the swamp, was awakened by a sound that made him know that he had new things to learn about fear. It was a distant sound, faint and wavering, but he knew it. It was the baying of a pack of hounds.

Rainsford knew he could do one of two things. He could stay where he was and wait. That was suicide. He could flee. That was postponing the inevitable. For a moment he stood there, thinking. An idea that held a wild chance came to him, and, tightening his belt, he headed away from the swamp.

The baying of the hounds drew nearer, then still nearer, nearer, ever nearer. On a ridge Rainsford climbed a tree. Down a watercourse, not a quarter of a mile away, he could see the bush moving. Straining his eyes, he saw the lean figure of General Zaroff; just ahead of him Rainsford made out another figure whose wide shoulders surged through the tall jungle weeds; it was the giant Ivan, and he seemed pulled forward by some unseen force; Rainsford knew that Ivan must be holding the pack in leash.

They would be on him any minute now. His mind worked frantically. He thought of a native trick he had learned in Uganda. He slid down the tree. He caught hold of a springy young sapling and to it he fastened his hunting knife, with the blade pointing down the trail; with a bit of wild grapevine he tied back the sapling. Then he ran for his life. The hounds raised their voices as they hit the fresh scent. Rainsford knew now how an animal at bay feels.

He had to stop to get his breath. The baying of the hounds stopped abruptly, and Rainsford's heart stopped too. They must have reached the knife.

He shinned excitedly up a tree and looked back. His pursuers had stopped. But the hope that was in Rainsford's brain when he climbed died, for he saw in the shallow valley that General Zaroff was still on his feet. But Ivan was not. The knife, driven by the recoil of the springing tree, had not wholly failed.

Rainsford had hardly tumbled to the ground when the pack took up the cry again.

"Nerve, nerve, nerve!" he panted, as he dashed along. A blue gap showed between the trees dead ahead. Ever nearer drew the hounds. Rainsford forced himself on toward that gap. He reached it. It was the shore of the sea. Across a cove he could see the gloomy gray stone of the chateau. Twenty feet below him the sea rumbled and hissed. Rainsford hesitated. He heard the hounds. Then he leaped far out into the sea. . . .

When the general and his pack reached the place by the sea, the Cossack stopped. For some minutes he stood regarding the blue-green expanse of water. He shrugged his shoulders. Then he sat down, took a drink of brandy from a silver flask, lit a cigarette, and hummed a bit from Madame Butterfly.

General Zaroff had an exceedingly good dinner in his great paneled dining hall that evening. With it he had a bottle of Pol Roger and half a bottle of Chambertin. Two slight annoyances kept him from perfect enjoyment. One was the thought that it would be difficult to replace Ivan; the other was that his quarry had escaped him; of course, the American hadn't played the game—so thought the general as he tasted his after-dinner liqueur. In his library he read, to soothe himself, from the works of Marcus Aurelius. At ten he went up to his bedroom. He was deliciously tired, he said to himself, as he locked himself in. There was a little moonlight, so, before turning on his light, he went to the window and looked down at the courtyard. He could see the great hounds, and he called, "Better luck another time," to them. Then he switched on the light.

A man, who had been hiding in the curtains of the bed, was standing there.

"Rainsford!" screamed the general. "How in God's name did you get here?"

"Swam," said Rainsford. "I found it quicker than walking through the jungle."

The general sucked in his breath and smiled. "I congratulate you," he said. "You have won the game."

Rainsford did not smile. "I am still a beast at bay," he said, in a low, hoarse voice. "Get ready, General Zaroff."

The general made one of his deepest bows. "I see," he said. "Splendid! One of us is to furnish a repast for the hounds. The other will sleep in this very excellent bed. On guard, Rainsford." . . .

He had never slept in a better bed, Rainsford decided.

In the Vault

By H. P. Lovecraft

THERE IS NOTHING MORE ABSURD, AS I VIEW IT, THAN THAT CONVEN-tional association of the homely and the wholesome which seems to per-vade the psychology of the multitude. Mention a bucolic Yankee setting, a bungling and thick-fibred village undertaker, and a careless mishap in a tomb, and no average reader can be brought to expect more than a hearty albeit grotesque phase of comedy. God knows, though, that the prosy tale which George Birch's death permits me to tell has in it aspects beside which some of our darkest tragedies are light.

Birch acquired a limitation and changed his business in 1881, yet never discussed the case when he could avoid it. Neither did his old physician Dr. Davis, who died years ago. It was generally stated that the affliction and shock were results of an unlucky slip whereby Birch had locked himself for nine hours in the receiving tomb of Peck Valley Cemetery, escaping only by crude and disastrous mechanical means; but while this much was undoubtedly true, there were other and blacker things which the man used to whisper to me in his drunken delirium toward the last. He confided in me because I was his doctor, and because he probably felt the need of confiding in someone else after Davis died. He was a bachelor, wholly without relatives.

Birch, before 1881, had been the village undertaker of Peck Valley; and was a very calloused and primitive specimen even as such specimens go. The practices I heard attributed to him would be unbelievable today, at least in a city; and even Peck Valley would have shuddered a bit had it known the easy ethics of its mortuary artist in such debatable matters as the ownership of costly "laying-out" apparel invisible beneath the casket's lid, and the degree of dignity to be maintained in posing and adapting the unseen members of lifeless tenants to containers not always calculated with sublimest accuracy. Most distinctly Birch was lax, insensitive, and professionally undesirable; yet I still think he was not an evil man. He was merely crass of fibre and function—thoughtless, careless, and liquor-ish, as his easily avoidable accident proves, and without that modicum of imagination which holds the average citizen within certain limits fixed by taste.

Just where to begin Birch's story I can hardly decide, since I am no practiced teller of tales. I suppose one should start in the cold December of 1880, when the ground froze and the cemetery delvers found they could dig no more graves till spring. Fortunately the village was small and the death rate low, so that it was possible to give all of Birch's inanimate charges a temporary haven in the single antiquated receiving tomb. The undertaker grew doubly lethargic in the bitter weather, and seemed to outdo even himself in carelessness. Never did he knock together flimsier and ungainlier caskets, or disregard more flagrantly the needs of the rusty lock on the tomb door which he slammed open and shut with such nonchalant abandon.

At last the spring thaw came, and graves were laboriously prepared for the nine silent harvests of the grim reaper which waited in the tomb. Birch, though dreading the bother of removal and interment, began his task of transference one disagreeable April morning, but ceased before noon because of a heavy rain that seemed to irritate his horse, after having laid but one mortal tenement to its permanent rest. That was Darius Peck, the nonagenarian, whose grave was not far from the tomb. Birch decided that he would begin the next day with little old Matthew Fenner, whose grave was also near by; but actually postponed the matter for three days, not getting to work till Good Friday, the 15th. Being without superstition, he did not heed the day at all; though ever afterward he refused to do anything of importance on that fateful sixth day of the week. Certainly, the events of that evening greatly changed George Birch.

On the afternoon of Friday, April 15th, then, Birch set out for the tomb with horse and wagon to transfer the body of Matthew Fenner. That he was not perfectly sober, he subsequently admitted; though he had not then taken to the wholesale drinking by which he later tried to forget certain things. He was just dizzy and careless enough to annoy his sensitive horse, which as he drew it viciously up at the tomb neighed and pawed and tossed its head, much as on that former occasion when the rain had vexed it. The day was clear, but a high wind had sprung up; and Birch was glad to get to shelter as he unlocked the iron door and entered the side-hill vault. Another might not have relished the damp, odorous chamber with the eight carelessly placed coffins; but Birch in those days was insensitive, and was concerned only in getting the right coffin for the right grave. He had not forgotten the criticism aroused when Hannah Bixby's relatives, wishing to transport her body to the cemetery in the city whither they had moved, found the casket of Judge Capwell beneath her headstone.

The light was dim, but Birch's sight was good, and he did not get Asaph Sawyer's coffin by mistake, although it was very similar. He had, indeed, made that coffin for Matthew Fenner; but had cast it aside at last as too awkward and flimsy, in a fit of curious sentimentality aroused by recalling how kindly and generous the little old man had been to him during his bankruptcy five years before. He gave old Matt the very best his skill could produce, but was thrifty enough to save the rejected specimen, and to use it when Asaph Sawyer died of a malignant fever. Sawyer was not a lovable man, and many stories were told of his almost inhuman vindictiveness and tenacious memory for wrongs real or fancied. To him Birch had felt no compunction in assigning the carelessly made coffin which he now pushed out of the way in his quest for the Fenner casket.

It was just as he had recognised old Matt's coffin that the door slammed to in the wind, leaving him in a dusk even deeper than before. The narrow transom admitted only the feeblest of rays, and the overhead ventilation funnel virtually none at all; so that he was reduced to a profane fumbling as he made his halting way among the long boxes toward the latch. In this funereal twilight he rattled the rusty handles, pushed at the iron panels, and wondered why the massive portal had grown so suddenly recalcitrant. In this twilight too, he began to realise the truth and to shout loudly as if his horse outside could do more than neigh an unsympathetic reply. For the long-neglected latch was obviously broken, leaving the careless undertaker trapped in the vault, a victim of his own oversight.

The thing must have happened at about three-thirty in the afternoon. Birch, being by temperament phlegmatic and practical, did not shout long; but proceeded to grope about for some tools which he recalled seeing in a corner of the tomb. It is doubtful whether he was touched at all by the horror and exquisite weirdness of his position, but the bald fact of imprisonment so far from the daily paths of men was enough to exasperate him thoroughly. His day's work was sadly interrupted, and unless chance presently brought some rambler hither, he might have to remain all night or longer. The pile of tools soon reached, and a hammer and chisel selected, Birch returned over the coffins to the door. The air had begun to be exceedingly unwholesome; but to this detail he paid no attention as he toiled, half by feeling, at the heavy and corroded metal of the latch. He would have given much for a lantern or bit of candle; but lacking these, bungled semi-sightlessly as best he might.

When he perceived that the latch was hopelessly unyielding, at least to such meagre tools and under such tenebrous conditions as these, Birch glanced about for other possible points of escape. The vault had been dug from a hillside, so that the narrow ventilation funnel in the top ran through several feet of earth, making this direction utterly useless to consider. Over the door, however, the high, slit-like transom in the brick facade gave promise of possible enlargement to a diligent worker; hence upon this his eyes long rested as he racked his brains for means to reach it. There was nothing like a ladder in the tomb, and the coffin niches on the sides and rear—which Birch seldom took the trouble to use—afforded no ascent to the space above the door. Only the coffins themselves remained as potential stepping-stones, and as he considered these he speculated on the best mode of transporting them. Three coffin-heights, he reckoned, would permit him to reach the transom; but he could do better with four. The boxes were fairly even, and could be piled up like blocks; so he began to compute how he might most stably use the eight to rear a scalable platform four deep. As he planned, he could not but wish that the units of his contemplated staircase had been more securely made. Whether he had imagination enough to wish they were empty, is strongly to be doubted.

Finally he decided to lay a base of three parallel with the wall, to place upon this two layers of two each, and upon these a single box to serve as the platform. This arrangement could be ascended with a minimum of awkwardness, and would furnish the desired height. Better still, though, he would utilise only two boxes of the base to support the superstructure, leaving one free to be piled on top in case the actual feat of escape required an even greater altitude. And so the prisoner toiled in the twilight, heaving the unresponsive remnants of mortality with little ceremony as his miniature Tower of Babel rose course by course. Several of the coffins began to split under the stress of handling, and he planned to save the stoutly built casket of little Matthew Fenner for the top, in order that his feet might have as certain a surface as possible. In the semi-gloom he trusted mostly to touch to select the right one, and indeed came upon it almost by accident, since it tumbled into his hands as if through some odd volition after he had unwittingly placed it beside another on the third layer.

The tower at length finished, and his aching arms rested by a pause during which he sat on the bottom step of his grim device, Birch cautiously ascended with his tools and stood abreast of the narrow transom. The borders of the space were entirely of brick, and there seemed little doubt but that he could shortly chisel away enough to allow his body to pass. As his hammer blows began to fall, the horse outside whinnied in a tone which may have been encouraging and to others may have been mocking. In either case it would have been appropriate; for the unexpected tenacity of the easy-looking brickwork was surely a sardonic commentary on the vanity of mortal hopes, and the source of a task whose performance deserved every possible stimulus.

Dusk fell and found Birch still toiling. He worked largely by feeling now, since newly gathered clouds hid the moon; and though progress was still slow, he felt heartened at the extent of his encroachments on the top and bottom of the aperture. He could, he was sure, get out by midnight—though it is characteristic of him that this thought was untinged with eerie implications. Undisturbed by oppressive reflections on the time, the place, and the company beneath his feet, he philosophically chipped away the stony brickwork; cursing when a fragment hit him in the face, and laughing when one struck the increasingly excited horse that pawed near the cypress tree. In time the hole grew so large that he ventured to try his body in it now and then, shifting about so that the coffins beneath him rocked and creaked. He would not, he found, have to pile another on his platform to make the proper height; for the hole was on exactly the right level to use as soon as its size might permit.

It must have been midnight at least when Birch decided he could get through the transom. Tired and perspiring despite many rests, he descended to the floor and sat a while on the bottom box to gather strength for the final wriggle and leap to the ground outside. The hungry horse was neighing repeatedly and almost uncannily, and he vaguely wished it would stop. He was curiously unelated over his impending escape, and almost dreaded the exertion, for his form had the indolent stoutness of early middle age. As he remounted the splitting coffins he felt his weight very poignantly; especially when, upon reaching the topmost one, he heard that aggravated crackle which bespeaks the wholesale rending of wood. He had, it seems, planned in vain when choosing the stoutest coffin for the platform; for no sooner was his full bulk again upon it than the rotting lid gave way, jouncing him two feet down on a surface which even he did not care to imagine. Maddened by the sound, or by the stench which billowed forth even to the open air, the waiting horse gave a scream that was too frantic for a neigh, and plunged madly off through the night, the wagon rattling crazily behind it.

Birch, in his ghastly situation, was now too low for an easy scramble out of the enlarged transom; but gathered his energies for a determined try. Clutching the edges of the aperture, he sought to pull himself up, when he noticed a queer retardation in the form of an apparent drag on both his ankles. In another moment he knew fear for the first time that night; for struggle as he would, he could not shake clear of the unknown grasp which held his feet in relentless captivity. Horrible pains, as of savage wounds, shot through his calves; and in his mind was a vortex of fright mixed with an unquenchable materialism that suggested splinters, loose nails, or some other attribute of a breaking wooden box. Perhaps he screamed. At any rate he kicked and squirmed frantically and automatically whilst his consciousness was almost eclipsed in a half-swoon.

Instinct guided him in his wriggle through the transom, and in the crawl which followed his jarring thud on the damp ground. He could not walk, it appeared, and the emerging moon must have witnessed a horrible sight as he dragged his bleeding ankles toward the cemetery lodge; his fingers clawing the black mould in brainless haste, and his body responding with that maddening slowness from which one suffers when chased by the phantoms of nightmare. There was evidently, however, no pursuer; for he was alone and alive when Armington, the lodge-keeper, answered his feeble clawing at the door.

Armington helped Birch to the outside of a spare bed and sent his little son Edwin for Dr. Davis. The afflicted man was fully conscious, but would say nothing of any consequence; merely muttering such things as "Oh, my ankles!," "Let go!," or "Shut in the tomb." Then the doctor came with his medicine-case and asked crisp questions, and removed the patient's outer clothing, shoes, and socks. The wounds—for both ankles were frightfully lacerated about the Achilles' tendons—seemed to puzzle the old physician greatly, and finally almost to frighten him. His questioning grew more than medically tense, and his hands shook as he dressed the mangled members; binding them as if he wished to get the wounds out of sight as quickly as possible.

For an impersonal doctor, Davis' ominous and awestruck cross-examination became very strange indeed as he sought to drain from the weakened undertaker every least detail of his horrible experience. He was oddly anxious to know if Birch were sure—absolutely sure—of the identity of that top coffin of the pile; how he had chosen it, how he had been certain of it as the Fenner coffin in the dusk, and how he had distinguished it from the inferior duplicate coffin of vicious Asaph Sawyer. Would the firm Fenner casket have caved in so readily? Davis, an old-time village practitioner, had of course seen both at the respective funerals, as indeed he had attended both Fenner and Sawyer in their last illnesses. He had even wondered, at Sawyer's funeral, how the vindictive farmer had managed to lie straight in a box so closely akin to that of the diminutive Fenner.

After a full two hours Dr. Davis left, urging Birch to insist at all times that his wounds were caused entirely by loose nails and splintering wood. What else, he added, could ever in any case be proved or believed? But it would be well to say as little as could be said, and to let no other doctor treat the wounds. Birch heeded this advice all the rest of his life till he told me his story; and when I saw the scars—ancient and whitened as they then were—I agreed that he was wise in so doing. He always remained lame, for the great tendons had been severed; but I think the greatest lameness was in his soul. His thinking processes, once so phlegmatic and logical, had become ineffaceably scarred; and it was pitiful to note his response to certain chance allusions such as "Friday," "Tomb," "Coffin," and words of less obvious concatenation. His frightened horse had gone home, but his frightened wits never quite did that. He changed his business, but something always preyed upon him. It may have been just fear, and it may have been fear mixed with a queer belated sort of remorse for bygone crudities. His drinking, of course, only aggravated what it was meant to alleviate.

When Dr. Davis left Birch that night he had taken a lantern and gone to the old receiving tomb. The moon was shining on the scattered brick fragments and marred facade, and the latch of the great door yielded readily to a touch from the outside. Steeled by old ordeals in dissecting rooms, the doctor entered and looked about, stifling the nausea of mind and body that everything in sight and smell induced. He cried aloud once, and a little later gave a gasp that was more terrible than a cry. Then he fled back to the lodge and broke all the rules of his calling by rousing and shaking his patient, and hurling at him a succession of shuddering whispers that seared into the bewildered ears like the hissing of vitriol.

"It was Asaph's coffin, Birch, just as I thought! I knew his teeth, with the front ones missing on the upper jaw—never, for God's sake, show those wounds! The body was pretty badly gone, but if ever I saw vindictiveness on any face—or former face . . . You know what a fiend he was for revenge—how he ruined old Raymond thirty years after their boundary suit, and how he stepped on the puppy that snapped at him a year ago last August . . . He was the devil incarnate, Birch, and I believe his eye-for-an-eye fury could beat old Father Death himself. God, what a rage! I'd hate to have it aimed at me!

"Why did you do it, Birch? He was a scoundrel, and I don't blame you for giving him a cast-aside coffin, but you always did go too damned far! Well enough to skimp on the thing some way, but you knew what a little man old Fenner was.

"I'll never get the picture out of my head as long as I live. You kicked hard, for Asaph's coffin was on the floor. His head was broken in, and everything was tumbled about. I've seen sights before, but there was one thing too much here. An eye for an eye! Great heavens, Birch, but you got what you deserved. The skull turned my stomach, but the other was worse—those ankles cut neatly off to fit Matt Fenner's cast-aside coffin!"

The Cask of Amontillado

By Edgar Allan Poe

THE THOUSAND INJURIES OF FORTUNATO I HAD BORNE AS I BEST COULD, but when he ventured upon insult I vowed revenge. You, who so well know the nature of my soul, will not suppose, however, that gave utterance to a threat. At length I would be avenged; this was a point definitely, settled—but the very definitiveness with which it was resolved precluded the idea of risk. I must not only punish but punish with impunity. A wrong is unredressed when retribution overtakes its redresser. It is equally unredressed when the avenger fails to make himself felt as such to him who has done the wrong.

It must be understood that neither by word nor deed had I given Fortunato cause to doubt my good will. I continued, as was my wont, to smile in his face, and he did not perceive that my smile *now* was at the thought of his immolation.

He had a weak point—this Fortunato—although in other regards he was a man to be respected and even feared. He prided himself on his connoisseurship in wine. Few Italians have the true virtuoso spirit. For the most part their enthusiasm is adopted to suit the time and opportunity, to practise imposture upon the British and Austrian millionaires. In painting and gemmary, Fortunato, like his countrymen, was a quack, but in the matter of old wines he was sincere. In this respect I did not differ from him materially;—I was skillful in the Italian vintages myself, and bought largely whenever I could.

It was about dusk, one evening during the supreme madness of the carnival season, that I encountered my friend. He accosted me with excessive warmth, for he had been drinking much. The man wore motley. He had on a tight-fitting parti-striped dress, and his head was surmounted by the conical cap and bells. I was so pleased to see him that I thought I should never have done wringing his hand.

I said to him—"My dear Fortunato, you are luckily met. How remarkably well you are looking to-day. But I have received a pipe of what passes for Amontillado, and I have my doubts."

"How?" said he. "Amontillado, A pipe? Impossible! And in the middle of the carnival!"

"I have my doubts," I replied; "and I was silly enough to pay the full Amontillado price without consulting you in the matter. You were not to be found, and I was fearful of losing a bargain."

"Amontillado!"

"I have my doubts."

"Amontillado!"

"And I must satisfy them."

"Amontillado!"

"As you are engaged, I am on my way to Luchresi. If any one has a critical turn it is he. He will tell me—"

"Luchresi cannot tell Amontillado from Sherry."

"And yet some fools will have it that his taste is a match for your own.

"Come, let us go."

"Whither?"

"To your vaults."

"My friend, no; I will not impose upon your good nature. I perceive you have an engagement. Luchresi—"

"I have no engagement;—come."

"My friend, no. It is not the engagement, but the severe cold with which I perceive you are afflicted. The vaults are insufferably damp. They are encrusted with nitre."

"Let us go, nevertheless. The cold is merely nothing. Amontillado! You have been imposed upon. And as for Luchresi, he cannot distinguish Sherry from Amontillado."

Thus speaking, Fortunato possessed himself of my arm; and putting on a mask of black silk and drawing a roquelaire closely about my person, I suffered him to hurry me to my palazzo.

There were no attendants at home; they had absconded to make merry in honour of the time. I had told them that I should not return until the morning, and had given them explicit orders not to stir from the house. These orders were sufficient, I well knew, to insure their immediate disappearance, one and all, as soon as my back was turned.

I took from their sconces two flambeaux, and giving one to Fortunato, bowed him through several suites of rooms to the archway that led into the vaults. I passed down a long and winding staircase, requesting him to be cautious as he followed. We came at length to the foot of the descent, and stood together upon the damp ground of the catacombs of the Montresors.

The gait of my friend was unsteady, and the bells upon his cap jingled as he strode.

"The pipe," he said.

"It is farther on," said I; "but observe the white web-work which gleams from these cavern walls."

He turned towards me, and looked into my eyes with two filmy orbs that distilled the rheum of intoxication.

"Nitre?" he asked, at length.

"Nitre," I replied. "How long have you had that cough?"

"Ugh! ugh! ugh!—ugh! ugh! ugh!—ugh! ugh! ugh!—ugh! ugh! ugh!—ugh! ugh! ugh!"

My poor friend found it impossible to reply for many minutes.

"It is nothing," he said, at last.

"Come," I said, with decision, "we will go back; your health is precious. You are rich, respected, admired, beloved; you are happy, as once I was. You are a man to be missed. For me it is no matter. We will go back; you will be ill, and I cannot be responsible. Besides, there is Luchresi—"

"Enough," he said; "the cough's a mere nothing; it will not kill me. I shall not die of a cough."

"True—true," I replied; "and, indeed, I had no intention of alarming you unnecessarily—but you should use all proper caution. A draught of this Medoc will defend us from the damps."

Here I knocked off the neck of a bottle which I drew from a long row of its fellows that lay upon the mould.

"Drink," I said, presenting him the wine.

He raised it to his lips with a leer. He paused and nodded to me familiarly, while his bells jingled.

"I drink," he said, "to the buried that repose around us."

"And I to your long life."

He again took my arm, and we proceeded.

"These vaults," he said, "are extensive."

"The Montresors," I replied, "were a great and numerous family."

"I forget your arms."

"A huge human foot d'or, in a field azure; the foot crushes a serpent rampant whose fangs are imbedded in the heel."

"And the motto?"

"Nemo me impune lacessit."

"Good!" he said.

The wine sparkled in his eyes and the bells jingled. My own fancy grew warm with the Medoc. We had passed through long walls of piled skeletons, with casks and puncheons intermingling, into the inmost recesses of the catacombs. I paused again, and this time I made bold to seize Fortunato by an arm above the elbow.

"The nitre!" I said; "see, it increases. It hangs like moss upon the vaults. We are below the river's bed. The drops of moisture trickle among the bones. Come, we will go back ere it is too late. Your cough—"

"It is nothing," he said; "let us go on. But first, another draught of the Medoc."

I broke and reached him a flagon of De Grave. He emptied it at a breath. His eyes flashed with a fierce light. He laughed and threw the bottle upwards with a gesticulation I did not understand.

I looked at him in surprise. He repeated the movement—a grotesque one.

"You do not comprehend?" he said.

"Not I," I replied.

"Then you are not of the brotherhood."

"How?"

"You are not of the masons."

"Yes, yes," I said; "yes, yes."

"You? Impossible! A mason?"

"A mason," I replied.

"A sign," he said, "a sign."

"It is this," I answered, producing from beneath the folds of my roquelaire a trowel.

"You jest," he exclaimed, recoiling a few paces. "But let us proceed to the Amontillado."

"Be it so," I said, replacing the tool beneath the cloak and again offering him my arm. He leaned upon it heavily. We continued our route in search of the Amontillado. We passed through a range of low arches, descended, passed on, and descending again, arrived at a deep crypt, in which the foulness of the air caused our flambeaux rather to glow than flame.

At the most remote end of the crypt there appeared another less spacious. Its walls had been lined with human remains, piled to the vault overhead, in the fashion of the great catacombs of Paris. Three sides of this interior crypt were still ornamented in this manner. From the fourth side the bones had been thrown down, and lay promiscuously upon the earth, forming at one point a mound of some size. Within the wall thus exposed by the displacing of the bones, we perceived a still interior crypt or recess, in depth about four feet, in width three, in height six or seven. It seemed to have been constructed for no especial use within itself, but formed merely the interval between two of the colossal supports of the roof of the catacombs, and was backed by one of their circumscribing walls of solid granite.

It was in vain that Fortunato, uplifting his dull torch, endeavoured to pry into the depth of the recess. Its termination the feeble light did not enable us to see.

"Proceed," I said; "herein is the Amontillado. As for Luchresi—"

"He is an ignoramus," interrupted my friend, as he stepped unsteadily forward, while I followed immediately at his heels. In an instant he had reached the extremity of the niche, and finding his progress arrested by the rock, stood stupidly bewildered. A moment more and I had fettered him to the granite. In its surface were two iron staples, distant from each other about two feet, horizontally. From one of these depended a short chain, from the other a padlock. Throwing the links about his waist, it was but the work of a few seconds to secure it. He was too much astounded to resist. Withdrawing the key I stepped back from the recess.

"Pass your hand," I said, "over the wall; you cannot help feeling the nitre. Indeed, it is very damp. Once more let me implore you to return. No? Then I must positively leave you. But I must first render you all the little attentions in my power."

"The Amontillado!" ejaculated my friend, not yet recovered from his astonishment.

"True," I replied; "the Amontillado."

As I said these words I busied myself among the pile of bones of which I have before spoken. Throwing them aside, I soon uncovered a quantity of building stone and mortar. With these materials and with the aid of my trowel, I began vigorously to wall up the entrance of the niche.

I had scarcely laid the first tier of the masonry when I discovered that the intoxication of Fortunato had in a great measure worn off. The earliest indication I had of this was a low moaning cry from the depth of the recess. It was not the cry of a drunken man. There was then a long and obstinate silence. I laid the second tier, and the third, and the fourth; and then I heard the furious vibrations of the chain. The noise lasted for several minutes, during which, that I might hearken to it with the more satisfaction, I ceased my labours and sat down upon the bones. When at last the clanking subsided, I resumed the trowel, and finished without interruption the fifth, the sixth, and the seventh tier. The wall was now nearly upon a level with my breast. I again paused, and holding the flambeaux over the mason-work, threw a few feeble rays upon the figure within.

A succession of loud and shrill screams, bursting suddenly from the throat of the chained form, seemed to thrust me violently back. For a brief moment I hesitated, I trembled. Unsheathing my rapier, I began to grope with it about the recess; but the thought of an instant reassured me. I placed my hand upon the solid fabric of the catacombs, and felt satisfied. I reapproached the wall; I replied to the yells of him who clamoured. I re-echoed, I aided, I surpassed them in volume and in strength. I did this, and the clamourer grew still.

It was now midnight, and my task was drawing to a close. I had completed the eighth, the ninth and the tenth tier. I had finished a portion of the last and the eleventh; there remained but a single stone to be fitted and plastered in. I struggled with its weight; I placed it partially in its destined position. But now there came from out the niche a low laugh that erected the hairs upon my head. It was succeeded by a sad voice, which I had difficulty in recognizing as that of the noble Fortunato. The voice said—

"Ha! ha! ha!—he! he! he!—a very good joke, indeed—an excellent jest. We will have many a rich laugh about it at the palazzo—he! he! he!—over our wine—he! he! he!"

"The Amontillado!" I said.

"He! he! he!—he! he! he!—yes, the Amontillado. But is it not getting late? Will not they be awaiting us at the palazzo, the Lady Fortunato and the rest? Let us be gone."

"Yes," I said, "let us be gone."

"For the love of God, Montresor!"

"Yes," I said, "for the love of God!"

But to these words I hearkened in vain for a reply. I grew impatient. I called aloud—

"Fortunato!"

No answer. I called again—

"Fortunato!"

No answer still. I thrust a torch through the remaining aperture and let it fall within. There came forth in return only a jingling of the bells. My heart grew sick; it was the dampness of the catacombs that made it so. I hastened to make an end of my labour. I forced the last stone into its position; I plastered it up. Against the new masonry I re-erected the old rampart of bones. For the half of a century no mortal has disturbed them. In pace requiescat!

The Flayed Hand

By Guy de Maupassant

A NEW TRANSLATION FROM THE FRENCH BY BILL BOWERS.

About eight months ago, one of my friends, Louis R., and I met up one evening with some of our old college friends. We drank punch and smoked, chatted about literature and art, and joked about various pranks we'd played, like any other group of young men. Suddenly the door burst open, and one guy who had been a good friend of mine since childhood burst in like a hurricane.

"Guess where I've just come from?" he shouted.

"I bet on the winning Mabille racehorse," said one of the guys.

"No," said another guy, "you're being silly; you just borrowed money after burying a rich uncle, or from pawning your watch."

"You're just now sobering up," shouted a third guy, "and, since you smelled the punch in Louis's room, you came up here to start drinking again."

"You're all wrong," he replied. "I'm from P., in Normandy, where I've spent the last eight days, and I've brought along a friend of mine, a well-known crook, whom I'm hoping to introduce to you."

With that he pulled from his pocket a flayed hand; this hand was frightful, black, dried out, and clenched. The muscles, of extraordinary strength, were bound inside and out by a strip of parchment-like skin.

The narrow yellow nails remained at the ends of the fingers. The thing smelled to high heaven.

"Just imagine," said my friend, "the other day they sold off the effects of an old sorcerer, recently deceased, well known all over the country. Every Saturday night he used to fly to witches' gatherings on a broomstick; he practiced both white and black magic, made cows give blue milk, and made them wear tails like one of Saint Anthony's companions. The old scoundrel always had a deep affection for this hand, which, he said, was that of a notorious criminal, tortured to death in 1736 for having thrown his wife headfirst into a well—for which I do not blame him—and then hanging in the belfry the priest who had married them. After this double crime he ran away, and, during his subsequent career, which was brief but full, he robbed twelve travelers, burned a score of monks out of their monastery, and made a nuns' convent into a seraglio."

"But what are you going to do with this horror?" we asked.

"Well, I'll use it for a handle on my doorbell pull to frighten away my creditors."

"My friend," said Henry Smith, a big, phlegmatic Englishman, "I believe that this hand is only some kind of Indian meat, preserved by some new process; I advise you to make bouillon of it."

"Don't go on like this," said a medical student cold-bloodedly. He was drunk, three sheets to the wind. "But if you follow my advice, Pierre, you will give this piece of human debris a Christian burial, before its owner comes to ask for it back. Then, too, this hand has acquired some bad habits—you know the old saying: 'Who has killed will kill.'"

"And who has drunk will drink," replied the host as he poured out a big glass of punch for the student, who emptied it in one gulp, then slid dead drunk under the table. His sudden exit from the company was greeted with a burst of laughter, and Pierre, raising his glass and saluting the hand, shouted:

"I drink to your master's next visit!"

Then we spoke of other things, and before long everyone headed home. About two o'clock the next day, as I was passing Pierre's door, I entered and found him reading and smoking.

"Well, how goes it?" said I.

"Very well," he responded.

"And your hand?"

"My hand? You must have seen it on the bell pull. I put it there when I returned home last night. But guess what? Some idiot, probably to play a stupid joke on me, came and rang my doorbell around midnight. I asked who was there, but no one replied, so I went back to bed and fell asleep."

At that moment the door opened, and Pierre's landlord, a fat and extremely rude man, entered without even greeting us.

"Sir," he said, "I'm asking you to immediately remove that carrion you have hung on your bell pull. If you don't I'm going to have to ask you to leave."

"Listen," responded Pierre, very gravely, "you're insulting a hand that does not deserve it. You should know that it belonged to a man of very high breeding."

The landlord turned on his heel and left without a word. Pierre followed him out, removed the hand, and tied it to the bell cord hanging in his alcove.

"That's better," he said. "This hand, like the 'Brother, everyone must die' of the Trappists, will make me think serious thoughts every night before I fall asleep."

After an hour I left him and returned home.

I slept badly that night. I was nervous, agitated; several times I awoke with a start. Once I even imagined that a man had broken into my room, and I jumped up and searched the closets and under the bed. Around six o'clock in the morning I was starting to doze off at last, when a violent pounding at my door made me leap out of bed. It was my friend Pierre's valet, barely dressed, pale and trembling.

"Ah, sir!" he shouted, sobbing, "my poor master. Someone has murdered him."

I dressed hurriedly and ran to Pierre's place. The house was full of people shouting and arguing, and everything was in a commotion. Everyone was talking at the same time, recounting and commenting on the occurrence in all sorts of ways. With great difficulty I reached the bedroom. The door was guarded, but I identified myself to the guy at the door, and he let me enter. Four police officers were standing in the center of the apartment, pencils in hand, examining every detail, conferring in low voices and writing from time to time in their notebooks.

Two doctors were talking by the bed, on which Pierre lay, unconscious. He was not dead, but his expression was frightful. His eyes were wide open, and his dilated pupils seemed to stare fixedly, with unspeakable terror, at something horrible and unknown. His hands were clenched tightly. His body, up to his chin, was covered with a quilt, which I lifted. On his neck were the marks of five fingers, which had embedded themselves deeply into the flesh. A few drops of blood spotted his shirt. At that moment one thing struck me. By chance I looked at the bell pull in his alcove. The flayed hand was no longer there. The doctors had doubtless removed it to avoid any questions from those entering the room where the injured man lay, because that hand was truly frightful. I did not ask what had become of it.

Here is a newspaper clipping from the next day about the crime, with all the details that the police were able to determine:

A terrible attempt was made yesterday on the life of young Pierre B., a law student from one of Normandy's best families. The young man had returned home about ten o'clock in the evening, and excused his valet, Bouvin, telling him that he was tired and was going to bed. About midnight, Bouvin was suddenly awakened by the furious ringing of his master's bell. Afraid, he lighted a lamp and waited. The bell was silent for about a minute, then rang again with such vehemence that the valet, lost in terror, fled from his room to awaken the concierge, who ran to summon the police. After about fifteen minutes, two policemen forced open the door. A horrible sight met their eyes. The furniture was overturned, giving evidence of a fearful struggle between the victim and his assailant. In the middle of the room, upon his back, his body rigid, with livid face and frightfully dilated eyes, lay, motionless, young Pierre B., bearing on his neck the deep impressions of five fingers. Dr. Bourdeau was called immediately, and his report says that the aggressor must have been possessed of prodigious strength and must have had an extraordinarily thin and sinewy hand, because the fingers had left in the victim's neck what looked like five bullet holes, which had penetrated from either side until they almost met in the middle. There is no clue to the motive of the crime or to its perpetrator. The investigation is ongoing.

The following appeared in the same newspaper the next day:

M. Pierre B., the victim of the frightful assault of which we published an account yesterday, has regained consciousness after two hours of the most assiduous care by Dr. Bourdeau. His life is not in danger, but it is strongly feared that he has lost his mind. No trace of his assailant has been found.

My poor friend was indeed crazy. For seven months, I went to visit him every day at the hospital where we had placed him, but he did not recover the light of reason. In his delirium, strange words escaped him, and, like all madmen, he had one fixed idea: He believed himself continually pursued by a specter. One day someone came to get me in a hurry, saying he had gotten worse, and when I arrived I found him in agony. For two hours he remained very calm, then, suddenly, rising from his bed in spite of our efforts, he shouted, waving his arms as if in the grip of the most awful terror: "Get it away! Get it away! It's strangling me! Help! Help!" Twice he ran around the room, screaming, then fell down face forward, dead.

Because he was an orphan, I had to take his body to the little village of P. in Normandy, where his parents were buried. It was the same village from which he had arrived the evening he found us drinking in Louis R.'s room, when he had showed us the flayed hand. His body was enclosed in a lead coffin, and four days later, I walked sadly with the elderly priest, who had first taught him, to the little cemetery where they had dug his grave. The weather was magnificent, and sunshine from a cloudless sky flooded the earth. The birds were singing from the blackberry bushes on the embankment, where we had gone many times when we were children to eat the berries. Again I imagined I could see Pierre and me sneaking along behind the hedgerow and slipping through the gap that we knew so well, down at the very end of the plot of land where they used to bury the poor people. And we would return home, our cheeks and lips black with the juice of the berries we had eaten. I looked at the blackberry bushes; they were covered with fruit; mechanically I picked some and brought them to my mouth. The priest had opened his breviary, and was muttering his prayers in a low voice. At the end of the walk I could hear the shovels of the gravediggers. All of a sudden they called out to us, the priest closed his book, and we went to see what they wanted. They had found a coffin. With one blow from a pickaxe, they had dislodged the lid, and we could see inside a skeleton of unusual stature, lying on its back, its hollow eyes seeming to threaten and defy us. I felt troubled, almost afraid, but did not know why.

"Hold on!" shouted one of the men, "Look! One of the rascal's hands has been severed at the wrist. Ah, here it is!" and he picked up from beside the body a huge withered hand, and held it out to us.

"See," said the other with a laugh, "look how he's glaring at you, as if he would go for your throat to make you give him back his hand."

"Come on, my friends," said the priest, "leave the dead in peace, and close up the coffin. We will dig another grave elsewhere for poor Pierre."

The next day everything was finished, and I returned to Paris, after leaving fifty francs with the old priest to say masses for the repose of the soul of him whose sepulcher we had disturbed.

In Amundsen's Tent

By John Martin Leahy

"INSIDE THE TENT, IN A LITTLE BAG, I LEFT A LETTER, ADDRESSED TO H.M. the King, giving information of what he [*sic*] had accomplished . . . Besides this letter, I wrote a short epistle to Captain Scott, who, I assumed, would be the first to find the tent." Captain Amundsen: *The South Pole*.

"We have just arrived at this tent, 2 miles from our camp, therefore about 1 1/2 miles from the pole. In the tent we find a record of five Norwegians having been here, as follows:

'Roald Amundsen

Olav Olavson Bjaaland

Hilmer Hanssen

Sverre H. Hassel

Oscar Wisting

10 Dec. 1911.'

"Left a note to say I had visited the tent with companions."

Captain Scott: his Last Journal

"Travelers," says Richard A. Proctor, "are sometimes said to tell marvelous stories; but it is a noteworthy fact that, in nine cases out of ten, the marvelous stories of travelers have been confirmed."

Certainly no traveler ever set down a more marvelous story than that of Robert Drumgold. This record I am at last giving to the world in 192—, with my humble apologies to the spirit of the hapless explorer for withholding it so long. But the truth is that Eastman, Dahlstrom, and I thought it the work of a mind deranged; little wonder, forsooth, if his mind had given way, what with the fearful sufferings which he had gone through and the horror of that fate which was closing in upon him.

What was it, that *thing* (if thing it was) which came to him, the sole survivor of the party which had reached the Southern Pole?

Yes, we thought that the mind of poor Robert Drumgold had given way, that the horror in Amundsen's tent and that thing which came to Drumgold there in his own—we thought all was madness only. Hence our suppression of this part of the Drumgold manuscript. We feared that the publication of so extraordinary a record might cast a cloud of doubt upon the real achievements of the Sutherland expedition.

But of late our ideas and beliefs have undergone a change that is nothing less than a metamorphosis. This metamorphosis, it is scarcely necessary to say, was due to the startling discoveries made in the region of the Southern Pole by the late Captain Stanley Livingstone, as confirmed and extended by the expedition conducted by Darwin Frontenac. Captain Livingstone, we now learn, kept his real discovery, what with the doubts and derision which met him on his return to the world, a secret from every living soul but two—Darwin Frontenac and Bond McQuestion. It is but now, on the return of Frontenac, that we learn how truly wonderful and amazing were those discoveries made by the ill-starred captain. And yet, despite the success of the Frontenac expedition, it must be admitted that the mystery down there in the Antarctic is enhanced rather than dissipated. Darwin Fontenac and his companions saw much; but we know that there are things and beings down there that they did not see. The Antarctic—or, rather, part of it—has thus suddenly become the most interesting and certainly the most fearful place upon this interesting and fearful globe of ours.

So another marvelous story told—or, rather, only partly told—by a traveler has been confirmed. And here are Eastman and I preparing to go once more to the Antarctic to confirm, as we hope, another story—one eery and fearful as any ever conceived by any romanticist.

And to think that it was ourselves; Eastman, Dahlstrom, and I, who made the discovery.

How vividly it all rises before me again—the white expanse, glaring, blinding in the untampered light of the Antarctic sun; the dogs straining in the harness, the cases on the sleds long and black like coffins; our sudden halt as Eastman fetched up in his tracks, pointed and said, "Hello! What's that?"

A half-mile or so off to the left, some object broke the blinding white of the plain.

"*Nunatak*, I suppose," was my answer.

"Looks to me like a cairn or a tent," Dahlstrom said.

"How on Earth," I queried, "could a tent have got down here in 87° 30' south? We are far from the route of either Amundsen or Scott."

"H'm," said Eastman, shoving his amber-colored glasses up onto his forehead that he might get a better look, "I wonder. Jupiter Ammon, Nels," he added, glancing at Dahlstrom, "I believe that you are right."

"It certainly," Dahlstrom nodded, "looks like a cairn or a tent to me. I don't think it's a *nunatak*."

"Well," said I, "it would not be difficult to put it to the proof."

"And that my hearties," exclaimed Eastman, "is just what we'll do! We'll soon see what it is—whether it is a cairn, a tent, or only a *nunatak*."

The next moment we were in motion, heading straight for that mysterious object there in the midst of the eternal desolation of snow and ice.

"Look there!" Eastman, who was leading the way, suddenly shouted. "See that? It *is* a tent!"

A few moments, and I saw that it was indeed so. But who had pitched it there? What were we to find within it?

I could never describe those thoughts and feelings which were ours as we approached that spot. The snow lay piled about the tent to a depth of four feet or more. Nearby a splintered ski protruded from the surface—and that was all.

And the stillness! The air, at the moment, was without the slightest movement. No sound but those made by our movements, and those of the dogs, and our own breathing, broke that awful silence of death.

"Poor devils!" said Eastman at last. "One thing, they certainly pitched their tent well."

The tent was supported by a single pole, set in the middle. To this pole three guy-lines were fastened, one of them as taut as the day its stake had been driven into the surface. But this was not all; a half-dozen lines, or more, were attached to the sides of the tent. There it stood, and had stood for we knew not how long, bidding defiance to the fierce winds of that terrible region.

Dahlstrom and I got each a spade and began to remove the snow. The entrance we found unfastened but completely blocked by a couple of provision-cases (empty) and a piece of canvas.

"How on Earth," I exclaimed, "did those things get into that position?"

"The wind," said Dahlstrom. "And, if the entrance had not been blocked, there wouldn't have been any tent here now; the wind would have split and destroyed it long ago."

"H'm," mused Eastman. "The wind did it, Nels—blocked the place like that? I wonder."

The next moment we had cleared the entrance. I thrust my head through the opening. Strangely enough, very little snow had drifted in. The tent was of a dark green color, a circumstance which rendered the light within somewhat weird and ghastly—or perhaps my imagination contributed not a little to that effect.

"What do you see, Bill?" asked Eastman. "What's inside?"

My answer was a cry, and the next instant I had sprung back from the entrance.

"What is it, Bill?" Eastman exclaimed. "Great heaven, what is it, man?"

"A head!" I told him.

"A head?"

"A human head!"

He and Dahlstrom stooped and peered in.

"What is the meaning of this?" Eastman cried. "A severed human head!"

Dahlstrom dashed a mittened hand across his eyes.

"Are we dreaming?" he exclaimed.

"'Tis no dream, Nels," returned our leader. "I wish to heaven it was. A head! A human head!"

"Is there nothing more?" I asked.

"Nothing. No body, not even a stripped bone—only that severed head. Could the dogs . . . ?"

"Yes?" queried Dahlstrom.

"Could the dogs have done this?"

"Dogs!" Dahlstrom said. "This is not the work of dogs."

We entered and stood looking down upon that grisly remnant of mortality.

"It wasn't dogs," said Dahlstrom.

"Not dogs?" Eastman queried. "What other explanation is there? Except—cannibalism."

Cannibalism! A shudder went through my heart. I may as well say at once, however, that our discovery of a good supply of pemmican and biscuit on the sled, at that moment completely hidden by the snow, was to show us that that fearful explanation was not the true one. The dogs! That was it, that was the explanation—even though what the victim himself had set down told us a very different story. Yes, the explorer had been set upon by his dogs and devoured. But there were things that militated against that theory. Why had the animals left that head—in the frozen eyes (they were blue eyes) and upon the frozen features of which was a look of horror that sends a shudder through my very soul even now? Why, the head did not have even the mark of a single fang, though it appeared to have been *chewed* from the trunk. Dahlstrom, however, was of the opinion that it had been *hacked* off.

And there, in the man's story, in the story of Robert Drumgold, we found another mystery—a mystery as insoluble (if it was true) as the presence here of his severed head. There the story was, scrawled in lead pencil across the pages of his journal. But what were we to make of a record—the concluding pages of it, that is—so strange and so dreadful?

But enough of this, of what we thought and of what we wondered. The journal itself lies before me, and I now proceed to set down the story of Robert Drumgold in his own words. Not a word, not a comma shall be deleted, inserted or changed.

Let it begin with his entry for January the 3rd, at the end of which day the little party was only fifteen miles (geographical) from the Pole.

Here it is:

JAN. 3.—Lat. of our camp 89° 45' 10." Only fifteen miles more, and the Pole is ours—unless Amundsen or Scott has beaten us to it, or both. But it will be ours just the same, even though the glory of discovery is found to be another's. What shall we find there?

All are in fine spirits. Even the dogs seem to know that this is the consummation of some great achievement. And a thing that is a mystery to us is the interest they have shown this day in the region before us. Did we halt, there they were gazing and gazing straight south and sometimes sniffing and sniffing. What does it mean?

Yes, in fine spirits all—dogs as well as we three men. Everything is auspicious. The weather for the last three days has been simply glorious. Not once, in this time, has the temperature been below minus 5. As I write this, the thermometer shows one degree above. The blue of the sky is like that of which painters dream, and, in that blue, tower cloud-formations, violet-tinged in the shadows, that are beautiful beyond all description. If it were possible to forget the fact that nothing stands between ourselves and a horrible death save the meager supply of food on the sleds, one could think he was in some fairyland—a glorious fairyland of white and blue and violet.

A fairyland? Why has that thought so often occurred to me? Why have I so often likened this desolate, terrible region to fairyland? Terrible? Yes, to human beings it is terrible—frightful beyond all words. But, though so unutterably terrible to men, it may not be so in reality. After all, are all things, even of this Earth of ours, to say nothing of the universe, made for man—this being (a godlike spirit in the body of a quasi-ape) who, set in the midst of wonders, leers and slavers in madness and hate and wallows in the muck of a thousand lusts? May there not be other beings—yes, even on this very Earth of ours—more wonderful— yes, and more terrible too—than he?

Heaven knows, more than once, in this desolation of snow and ice, have I seemed to feel their presence in the air about us—nameless entities, disembodied, *watching* things.

Little wonder, forsooth, that I have again and again thought of these strange words of one of America's greatest scientists, Alexander Winchell:

"Nor is incorporated rational existence conditioned on warm blood, nor on any temperature which does not change the forms of matter of which the organism may be composed. There may be intelligences corporealized after some concept not involving the processes of ingestion, assimilation and reproduction. Such bodies would not require daily food and warmth. They might be lost in the abysses of the ocean, or laid upon a stormy cliff through the tempests of an arctic winter, or plunged in a volcano for a hundred years, and yet retain consciousness and thought."

All this Winchell tells us is conceivable, and he adds:

"Bodies are merely the local fitting of intelligence to particular modification of universal matter and force."

And these entities, nameless things whose presence I seem to feel at times—are they benignant beings or things more fearful than even the madness of the human brain ever has fashioned?

But, then, I must stop this. If Sutherland or Travers were to read what I have set down here, he, *they* would think that I was losing my senses or would declare me already insane. And yet, as there is a heaven above us, it seems that I do actually believe that this frightful place knows the presence of beings other than ourselves and our dogs—things which we can not see but which are watching us.

Enough of this.

Only fifteen miles from the Pole. Now for a sleep and on to our goal in the morning. Morning! There is no morning here, but day unending. The sun now rides as high at midnight as he does at midday. Of course, there is a change in his altitude, but it is so slight as to be imperceptible without an instrument.

But the Pole! Tomorrow the Pole! What will we find there? Only an unbroken expanse of White, or . . . ?

JAN. 4.—The mystery and horror of this day—oh, how could I ever set that down? Sometimes, so fearful were those hours through which we have just passed, I even find myself wondering if it wasn't all only a dream. A dream! I would to heaven that it had been a dream! As for the end—there, there. I must keep such thoughts out of my head.

Got under way at an early hour. Weather more wondrous than ever. Sky an azure that would have sent a painter into ecstasies. Cloud-formations indescribably beautiful and grand. The going, however, was pretty difficult. The place a great plain stretching away with a monotonous uniformity of surface as far as the eye could reach. A plain never trod by human foot before? At length, when our dead reckoning showed that we were drawing near to the Pole, we had the answer to that. Then it was that the keen eyes of Travers detected some object rising above the blinding white of the snow.

On the instant Sutherland had thrust his amber glasses up onto his forehead and had his binoculars to his eyes.

"Cairn!" he exclaimed, and his voice sounded hollow and very strange. "A cairn or a—*tent*. Boys, they have beaten us to the Pole!"

He handed the glasses to Travers and leaned, as though a sudden weariness had settled upon him, against the provision-cases on his sled.

"Forestalled!" said he. "Forestalled!"

I felt very sorry for our leader in those, his moments of terrible disappointment, but for the life of me I did not know what to say. And so I said nothing.

At that moment a cloud concealed the sun; and the place where we stood was suddenly involved in a gloom that was deep and awful. So sudden and pronounced, indeed, was the change that we gazed about us with curious and wondering looks. Far off to the right and to the left, the plain blazed white and blinding. Soon, however, the last gleam of sunshine had vanished from off it. I raised my look up to the heavens. Here and there edges of cloud were touched as though with the light of wrathful golden fire. Even then, however, that light was fading. A few minutes, and the last angry gleam of the sun had vanished. The gloom seemed to deepen about us every moment. A curious haze was concealing the blue expanse of the sky overhead. There was not the slightest movement in the gloomy and weird atmosphere. The silence was heavy, awful, the silence of the abode of utter desolation and of death.

"What on Earth are we in for now?" said Travers.

Sutherland moved from his sled and stood gazing about into the eerie gloom.

"Queer change, this!" said he. "It would have delighted the heart of Doré."

"It means a blizzard, most likely," I observed. "Hadn't we better make camp before it strikes us? No telling what a blizzard may be like in this awful spot."

"Blizzard?" said Sutherland. "I don't think it means a blizzard, Bob. No telling, though. Mighty queer change, certainly. And how different the place looks now, in this strange gloom! It is surely weird and terrible—that is, it certainly *looks* weird and terrible."

He turned his look to Travers.

"Well, Bill," he asked, "what did you make of it?"

He waved a hand in the direction of that mysterious object the sight of which had so suddenly brought us to a halt. I say in the direction of the object, for the thing itself was no longer to be seen.

"I believe it is a tent," Travers told him.

"Well," said our leader, "we can soon find out what it is—cairn or tent, for one or the other it must certainly be."

The next instant the heavy, awful silence was broken by the sharp crack of his whip. "Mush on, you poor brutes!" he cried. "On we go to see what is over there. Here we are at the South Pole. Let us see who has beaten us to it."

But the dogs didn't want to go on, which did not surprise me at all, because, for some time now, they had been showing signs of some strange, inexplicable uneasiness. What had got into the creatures, anyway? For a time we puzzled over it; then we knew, though the explanation was still an utter mystery to us. They were afraid. Afraid? An inadequate word, indeed. It was fear, stark, terrible, that had entered the poor brutes. But whence had come this inexplicable fear? That also we soon knew. The thing they feared, whatever it was, was in that very direction in which we were headed!

A cairn, a tent? What did this thing mean?

"What on Earth is the matter with the critters?" exclaimed Travers. "Can it be that . . . ?"

"It's for us to find out what it means," said Sutherland.

Again we got in motion. The place was still involved in that strange, weird gloom. The silence was still that awful silence of desolation and of death.

Slowly but steadily we moved forward, urging on the reluctant, fearful animals with our whips.

At last Sutherland, who was leading, cried out that he saw it. He halted, peering forward into the gloom, and we urged our teams up alongside his.

"It must be a tent," he said.

And a tent we found it to be—a small one supported by a single bamboo and well guyed in all directions. Made of drab-colored gabardine. To the top of the tentpole another had been lashed. From this, motionless in the still air, hung the remains of a small Norwegian flag and, underneath it, a pennant with the word "Fram" upon it. Amundsen's tent!

What should we find inside it? And what was the meaning of that— the strange way it bulged out on one side?

The entrance was securely laced. The tent, it was certain, had been here for a year, all through the long Antarctic night; and yet, to our astonishment, but little snow was piled up about it, and most of this was drift. The explanation of this must, I suppose, be that, before the air currents have reached the Pole, almost all the snow has been deposited from them.

For some minutes we just stood there, and many, and some of them dreadful enough, were the thoughts that came and went. Through the long Antarctic night! What strange things this tent could tell us had it been vouchsafed the power of words! But strange things it might tell us, nevertheless. For what was that inside, making the tent bulge out in so unaccountable a manner? I moved forward to feel of it there with my mittened hand, but, for some reason that I can not explain, I of a sudden drew back. At that instant one of the dogs whined—the sound so strange and the terror of the animal so unmistakable that I shuddered and felt a chill pass through my heart. Others of the dogs began to whine in that mysterious manner, and all shrank back cowering from the tent.

"What does it mean?" said Travers, his voice sunk almost to a whisper. "Look at them. It is as though they are imploring us to keep away."

"To keep away," echoed Sutherland, his look leaving the dogs and fixing itself once more on the tent.

"Their senses," said Travers, "are keener than ours. They already know what we can't know until we see it."

"See it!" Sutherland exclaimed. "I wonder. Boys, what are we going to see when we look into that tent? Poor fellows! They reached the Pole. But did they ever leave it? Are we going to find them in there dead?"

"Dead?" said Travers with a sudden start. "The dogs would never act that way if 'twas only a corpse inside. And, besides, if that theory was true, wouldn't the sleds be here to tell the story? Yet look around. The level uniformity of the place shows that no sled lies buried here."

"That is true," said our leader. "What *can* it mean? What *could* make the tent bulge out like that? Well, here is the mystery before us, and all we have to do is unlace the entrance and look inside to solve it."

He stepped to the entrance, followed by Travers and me, and began to unlace it. At that instant an icy current of air struck the place and the pennant above our heads flapped with a dull and ominous sound. One of the dogs, too, thrust his muzzle skyward, and a deep and long-drawn howl, sad, terrible as that of a lost soul, arose. And whilst the mournful, savage sound yet filled the air, a strange thing happened:

Through a sudden rent in that gloomy curtain of cloud, the sun sent a golden, awful light down upon the spot where we stood. It was but a shaft of light, only three or four hundred feet wide, though miles in length, and there we stood in the very middle of it, the plain on each side involved in that weird gloom, now denser and more eery than ever in contrast to that sword of golden fire which thus so suddenly had been flung down across the snow.

"Queer place this!" said Travers. "Just like a beam lying across a stage in a theater."

Travers' simile was a most apposite one, more so than he perhaps ever dreamed himself. That place was a stage, our light the wrathful fire of the Antarctic sun, ourselves the actors in a scene stranger than any ever beheld in the mimic world.

For some moments, so strange was it all, we stood there looking about us in wonder and perhaps each one of us in not a little secret awe.

"Queer place, all right!" said Sutherland. "But . . ."

He laughed a hollow, sardonic laugh. Up above, the pennant flapped and flapped again, the sound of it hollow and ghostly. Again rose the long-drawn, mournful, fiercely sad howl of the wolf-dog.

"But," added our leader, "we don't want to be imagining things, you know."

"Of course not," said Travers.

"Of course not," I echoed.

A little space, and the entrance was open and Sutherland had thrust head and shoulders through it.

I don't know how long it was that he stood there like that. Perhaps it was only a few seconds, but to Travers and me it seemed rather long.

"What is it?" Travers exclaimed at last. "What do you see?"

The answer was a scream—oh, the horror of that sound I can never forget!—and Sutherland came staggering back and, I believe, would have fallen had we not sprung and caught him.

"What is it?" cried Travers. "In God's name, Sutherland, what did you see?"

Sutherland beat the side of his head with his hand, and his look was wild and horrible·.

"What is it?" I exclaimed. "What did you see in there?"

"I can't tell you—I can't! Oh, oh, I wish that I had never seen it! Don't look! Boys, don't look into that tent—unless you are prepared to welcome madness, or worse."

"What gibberish is this?" Travers demanded, gazing at our leader in utter astonishment. "Come, come, man! Buck up. Get a grip on yourself. Let's have an end to this nonsense. Why should the sight of a dead man, or dead men, affect you in this mad fashion?"

"Dead men?"

Sutherland laughed, the sound wild, maniacal.

"Dead men? If 'twas only that! Is this the South Pole? Is this Earth, or are we in a nightmare on some other planet?"

"For heaven's sake," cried Travers, "come out of it! What's got into you? Don't let your nerves go like this."

"A dead man?" queried our leader, peering into the face of Travers. "You think I saw a dead man? I wish it was only a dead man. Thank God, you two didn't look!"

On the instant Travers had turned.

"Well," said he, "I am going to look!"

But Sutherland cried out, screamed, sprang after him and tried to drag him back.

"It would mean horror and perhaps madness!" cried Sutherland. "Look at me. Do you want to be like me?"

"No!" Travers returned. "But I am going to see what is in that tent."

He struggled to break free, but Sutherland clung to him in a frenzy of madness.

"Help me, Bob!" Sutherland cried. "Hold him back, or we'll all go insane."

But I did not help him to hold Travers back, for, of course, 'twas my belief that Sutherland himself was insane. Nor did Sutherland hold Travers. With a sudden wrench, Travers was free. The next instant he had thrust head and shoulders through the entrance of the tent.

Sutherland groaned and watched him with eyes full of unutterable horror.

I moved toward the entrance, but Sutherland flung himself at me with such violence that I was sent over into the snow. I sprang to my feet full of anger and amazement.

"What the hell," I cried, "is the matter with you, anyway? Have you gone crazy?"

The answer was a groan, horrible beyond all words of man, but that sound did not come from Sutherland. I turned. Travers was staggering away from the entrance, a hand pressed over his face, sounds that I could never describe breaking from deep in his throat. Sutherland, as the man came staggering up to him, thrust forth an arm and touched Travers lightly on the shoulder. The effect was instantaneous and frightful. Travers sprang aside as though a serpent had struck at him, screamed and screamed yet again.

"There, there!" said Sutherland gently. "I told you not to do it. I tried to make you understand, but—but you thought that I was mad."

"It can't belong to Earth!" moaned Travers.

"No," said Sutherland. "That horror was never born on this planet of ours. And the inhabitants of Earth, though they do not know it, can thank God Almighty for that."

"But it is *here*!" Travers exclaimed. "How did it come to this awful place? And where did it come from?"

"Well," consoled Sutherland, "it is dead—it must be dead."

"Dead? How do we know that it is dead? And don't forget this: it didn't come here alone!"

Sutherland started. At that moment the sunlight vanished, and everything was once more involved in gloom.

"What do you mean?" Sutherland asked. "Not alone? How do you know that it did not come alone?"

"Why, it is there *inside* the tent; but the entrance was laced—from the *outside*!"

"Fool, fool that I am!" cried Sutherland a little fiercely. "Why didn't I think of that? Not alone! Of course it was not alone!"

He gazed about into the gloom, and I knew the nameless fear and horror that chilled him to the very heart, for they chilled me to my own.

Of a sudden arose again that mournful, savage howl of the wolf-dog. We three men started as though 'twas the voice of some ghoul from hell's most dreadful corner.

"Shut up, you brute!" gritted Travers. "Shut up, or I'll brain you!"

Whether it was Travers' threat or not, I do not know; but that howl sank, ceased almost on the instant. Again the silence of desolation of death lay upon the spot. But above the tent the pennant stirred and rustled, the sound of it, I thought, like the slithering of some repulsive serpent.

"What did you see in there?" I asked them.

"Bob—Bob," said Sutherland, "don't ask us that."

"The thing itself," said I, turning, "can't be any worse that this mystery and nightmare of imagination."

But the two of them threw themselves before me and barred my way. "No!" said Sutherland firmly. "You must not look into that tent, Bob. You must not see that—that—I don't know what to call it. Trust us; believe us, Bob! 'Tis for your sake that we say that you must not do it. We, Travers and I, can never be the same men again—the brains, the *souls* of us can never be what they were before *we saw that!*"

"Very well," I acquiesced. "I can't help saying, though, that the whole thing seems to me like the dream of a madman."

"That," said Sutherland, "is a small matter indeed. Insane? Believe that it is the dream of a madman. Believe that we are insane. Believe that you are insane yourself. Believe anything that you like. Only *don't look!*"

"Very well," I told them. "I won't look. I give in. You two have made a coward of me."

"A coward?" said Sutherland. "Don't talk nonsense, Bob. There are some things that a man should never know; there are some things that a man should never see; that horror there in Amundsen's tent is—*both!*"

"But you said that it is dead."

Travers groaned. Sutherland laughed a little wildly.

"Trust us," said the latter; "believe us, Bob. 'Tis for your sake, not for our own. For that is too late now. We have seen it, and you have not."

For some minutes we stood there by that tent; in that weird gloom, then turned to leave the cursed spot. I said that undoubtedly Amundsen had left some records inside, that possibly Scott, too, had reached the Pole and visited the tent, and that we ought to secure any such mementos. Sutherland and Travers nodded, but each declared that he would not put his head through that entrance again for all the wealth of Ormus and of Ind—or words to that effect. We must, they said, get away from the awful place—get back to the world of men with our fearful message.

"You won't tell me what you saw," I said, "and yet you want to get back so that you can tell it to the world."

"We aren't going to tell the world what we saw," answered Sutherland. "In the first place, we couldn't and in the second place, if we could, not a living soul would believe us. But we can warn people, for that thing in there did not come alone. Where is the other one—or the others?"

"Dead, too, let us hope!" I exclaimed.

"Amen!" said Sutherland. "But maybe, as Bill says, it isn't dead. Probably . . ."

Sutherland paused and a wild indescribable look came into his eyes.

"Maybe it—*can't die!*"

"Probably," said I nonchalantly, yet with secret disgust and with poignant sorrow.

What was the use? What good would it do to try to reason with a couple of madmen? Yes, we must get away from this spot, or they would have me insane, too. And the long road back? Could we ever make it now? And what had they seen? What unimaginable horror was there behind that thin wall of gabardine? Well, whatever it was, it was real. Of that I could not entertain the slightest doubt. Real? Real enough to wreck, virtually instantaneously, the strong brains of two strong men. But—but were my poor companions really mad, after all?

"Or maybe," Sutherland was saying, "the other one, or the others, went back to Venus or Mars or Sirius or Algol, or hell itself, or wherever they came from, to get more of their kind. If that is so, heaven have pity on poor humanity! *And*, if it or they are still here on Earth, then sooner or later—it may be a dozen years, it may be a century—but sooner or later the world will know it, know it to its woe and to its horror. For they, if living, or if gone for others, will come again."

"I was thinking . . . ," began Travers, his eyes fixed on the tent.

"Yes?" Sutherland queried.

"That," Travers told him, "it might be a good plan to empty the rifle into that thing. Maybe it isn't dead; maybe it can't die—maybe it only *changes*. Probably it is just hibernating, so, to speak."

"If so," I laughed, "it will probably hibernate till doomsday."

But neither one of my companions laughed.

"Or," said Travers, "it may be a demon, a ghost materialized. I can't say incarnated."

"A ghost materialized!" I exclaimed. "Well, may not every man or woman be just that? Heaven knows, many a one acts like a demon or a fiend incarnate."

"They may be," nodded Sutherland. "But that hypothesis doesn't help us any here."

"I may help things some," said Travers, starting toward his sled.

A moment or two, and he had got out the rifle.

"I thought," said he, "that nothing could ever take me back to that entrance. But the hope that I may . . ."

Sutherland groaned.

"It isn't Earthly, Bill," he said hoarsely. "It's a nightmare. I think we had better go now."

Travers was going—straight toward the tent.

"Come back, Bill!" groaned Sutherland. "Come back! Let us go while we can."

But Travers did not come back.

Slowly he moved forward, rifle thrust out before him, finger on the trigger. He reached the tent, hesitated a moment, then thrust the rifle-barrel through. As fast as he could work trigger and lever, he emptied the weapon into the tent into that horror inside it.

He whirled and came back as though in fear the tent was about to spew forth behind him all the legions of foulest hell.

What was that? The blood seemed to freeze in my veins and heart as there arose from out the tent a sound—a sound low and throbbing—a sound that no man ever had heard on Earth—one that I hope no man will ever hear again.

A panic, a madness seized upon us, upon men and dogs alike, and away we fled from that cursed place.

The sound ceased. But again we heard it. It was more fearful, more unearthly, soul-maddening, hellish than before.

"Look!" cried Sutherland. "Oh, my God, *look at that!*"

The tent was barely visible now. A moment or two, and the curtain of gloom would conceal it. At first I could not imagine what had made Sutherland cry out like that. Then I saw it, in that very moment before the gloom hid it from view. The tent was *moving!* It swayed, jerked like some shapeless monster in the throes of death, like some nameless thing seen in the horror of nightmare or limned on the brain of utter madness itself.

And that is what happened there; that is what we saw. I have set it down at some length and to the best of my ability under the truly awful circumstances in which I am placed. In these hastily scrawled pages is recorded an experience that, I believe, is not surpassed by the wildest to be found in the pages of the most imaginative romanticist. Whether the record is destined ever to reach the world, ever to be scanned by the eye of another—only the future can answer that.

I will try to hope for the best. I can not blink the fact, however, that things are pretty bad for us. It is not only this sinister, nameless mystery from which we are fleeing—though heaven knows that is horrible enough—but it is the *minds* of my companions. And, added to that, is the fear for my own. But there, I must get myself in hand. After all, as Sutherland said, I didn't see it. I must not give way. We must somehow get our story to the world, though we may have for our reward only the mockery of the world's unbelief, its scoffing—the world, against which is now moving, gathering, a menace more dreadful than any that ever moved in the fevered brain of any prophet of woe and blood and disaster.

We are a dozen miles or so from the Pole now. In that mad dash away from that tent of horror, lost our bearings and for a time, I fear, went panicky. The strange, eery gloom denser than ever. Then came a fall of fine snow-crystals, which rendered things worse than ever. Just when about to give up in despair, chanced upon one of our beacons. This gave us our bearings, and we pressed on to this spot.

Travers has just thrust his head into the tent to tell us that he is sure he saw something moving! This must be looked into.

If Robert Drumgold could only have left as full a record of those days which followed as he had of that fearful 4th of January! No man can ever know what the three explorers went through in their struggle to escape that doom from which there was no escape, a doom the mystery and horror of which perhaps surpass in gruesomeness what the most dreadful Gothic imagination ever conceived in its utterest abandonment to delirium and madness.

JAN. 5.—Travers had seen something, for we, the three of us, saw it again today. Was it that horror, that thing not of Earth, which they saw in Amundsen's tent? We don't know what it is. All we know is that it is something that moves. God have pity on us all—and on every man and woman and child on Earth if this thing is what we fear!

6th.—Made 25 mi. today. But that must have been imagination. Effect on dogs most terrible. Poo. brutes! It is as horrible to them as it is to us. Sometimes I think even more. Why is it following us?

7th.—Two of dogs gone this morning. One or another of us on guard all "night." Nothing seen, not a sound heard, but the animals have vanished. Did they desert us? We say that is what happened, but each man of us knows that none of us believes it. Made 18 mi. Fear that Travers is going mad.

8th.—Travers gone! He took the watch last night at 12, relieving Sutherland. That was the last seen of Travers—the last that we shall ever see. No tracks—not a sign in the snow. Travers, poor Travers, gone! Who will be the next?

JAN. 9.—*Saw it again!* Why does it let us see it like this—sometimes? Is it that horror in Amundsen's tent? Sutherland declares that it is not— that it is something even more hellish. But then S. is mad now—mad— mad—mad. If I wasn't sane, I could think that it all was only imagination. *But I saw it!*

JAN. 11.—Think it is the 11th but not sure. I can no longer be sure of anything—save that I am alone and that it is watching me. It is always watching. And some time it will come and get me—as it got Travers and Sutherland and half of the dogs.

Yes, today must be the 11th. For it was yesterday—surely it was only yesterday—that it took Sutherland. I didn't see it take him, for a fog had come up, and Sutherland—he would go on in the fog—was so slow in following that the vapor hid him from view. At last when he didn't come, I went back. But S. was gone—man, dogs, sled, everything was gone. Poor Sutherland! But then he was mad. Probably that was why it took him. Has it spared me because I am yet sane? S. had the rifle. Always he clung to that rifle—as though a bullet could save him from what we saw! My only weapon is an ax. But what good is an ax?

JAN. 13.—Maybe it is the 14th. I don't know. What does it matter? Saw it *three* times today. Each time it was closer. Dogs still now. That sound again. But I dare not look out. The ax.

Hours later. Can't write any more.

Silence. Voices—I seem to hear voices. But that sound again.

Coming nearer. At entrance now—now . . .

For the Blood Is the Life

By F. Marion Crawford

WE HAD DINED AT SUNSET ON THE BROAD ROOF OF THE OLD TOWER, because it was cooler there during the great heat of summer. Besides, the little kitchen was built at one corner of the great square platform, which made it more convenient than if the dishes had to be carried down the steep stone steps, broken in places and everywhere worn with age. The tower was one of those built all down the west coast of Calabria by the Emperor Charles V early in the sixteenth century, to keep off the Barbary pirates, when the unbelievers were allied with Francis I against the Emperor and the Church. They have gone to ruin, a few still stand intact, and mine is one of the largest. How it came into my possession ten years ago, and why I spend a part of each year in it, are matters which do not concern this tale. The tower stands in one of the loneliest spots in Southern Italy, at the extremity of a curving rocky promontory, which forms a small but safe natural harbor at the southern extremity of the Gulf of Policastro, and just north of Cape Scalea, the birthplace of Judas Iscariot, according to the old local legend. The tower stands alone on this hooked spur of the rock, and there is not a house to be seen within three miles of it. When I go there I take a couple of sailors, one of whom is a fair cook, and when I am away it is in charge of a gnome-like little being who was once a miner and who attached himself to me long ago.

My friend, who sometimes visits me in my summer solitude, is an artist by profession, a Scandinavian by birth, and a cosmopolitan by force of circumstances. We had dined at sunset; the sunset glow had reddened and faded again, and the evening purple steeped the vast chain of the mountains that embrace the deep gulf to eastward and rear themselves higher and higher toward the south. It was hot, and we sat at the landward corner of the platform, waiting for the night breeze to come down from the lower hills. The color sank out of the air, there was a little interval of deep-grey twilight, and a lamp sent a yellow streak from the open door of the kitchen, where the men were getting their supper.

Then the moon rose suddenly above the crest of the promontory, flooding the platform and lighting up every little spur of rock and knoll of grass below us, down to the edge of the motionless water. My friend lighted his pipe and sat looking at a spot on the hillside. I knew that he was looking at it, and for a long time past I had wondered whether he would ever see anything there that would fix his attention. I knew that spot well. It was clear that he was interested at last, though it was a long time before he spoke. Like most painters, he trusts to his own eyesight, as a lion trusts his strength and a stag his speed, and he is always disturbed when he cannot reconcile what he sees with what he believes that he ought to see.

"It's strange," he said. "Do you see that little mound just on this side of the boulder?"

"Yes," I said, and I guessed what was coming.

"It looks like a grave," observed Holger.

"Very true. It does look like a grave."

"Yes," continued my friend, his eyes still fixed on the spot. "But the strange thing is that I see the body lying on the top of it. Of course," continued Holger, turning his head on one side as artists do, "it must be an effect of light. In the first place, it is not a grave at all. Secondly, if it were, the body would be inside and not outside. Therefore, it's an effect of the moonlight. Don't you see it?"

"Perfectly; I always see it on moonlight nights."

"It doesn't seem to interest you much," said Holger.

"On the contrary, it does interest me, though I am used to it. You're not so far wrong, either. The mound is really a grave."

"Nonsense!" cried Holger, incredulously. "I suppose you'll tell me what I see lying on it is really a corpse!"

"No," I answered, "it's not. I know, because I have taken the trouble to go down and see."

"Then what is it?" asked Holger.

"It's nothing."

"You mean that it's an effect of light, I suppose?"

"Perhaps it is. But the inexplicable part of the matter is that it makes no difference whether the moon is rising or setting, or waxing or waning. If there's any moonlight at all, from east or west or overhead, so long as it shines on the grave you can see the outline of the body on top."

Holger stirred up his pipe with the point of his knife, and then used his finger for a stopper. When the tobacco burned well he rose from his chair.

"If you don't mind," he said, "I'll go down and take a look at it."

He left me, crossed the roof, and disappeared down the dark steps. I did not move, but sat looking down until he came out of the tower below. I heard him humming an old Danish song as he crossed the open space in the bright moonlight, going straight to the mysterious mound. When he was ten paces from it, Holger stopped short, made two steps forward, and then three or four backward, and then stopped again. I know what that meant. He had reached the spot where the Thing ceased to be visible—where, as he would have said, the effect of light changed.

Then he went on till he reached the mound and stood upon it. I could see the Thing still, but it was no longer lying down; it was on its knees now, winding its white arms round Holger's body and looking up into his face. A cool breeze stirred my hair at that moment, as the night wind began to come down from the hills, but it felt like a breath from another world.

The Thing seemed to be trying to climb to its feet, helping itself up by Holger's body while he stood upright, quite unconscious of it and apparently looking toward the tower, which is very picturesque when the moonlight falls upon it on that side.

"Come along!" I shouted. "Don't stay there all night!"

It seemed to me that he moved reluctantly as he stepped from the mound, or else with difficulty. That was it. The Thing's arms were still round his waist, but its feet could not leave the grave. As he came slowly forward it was drawn and lengthened like a wreath of mist, thin and white, till I saw distinctly that Holger shook himself, as a man does who feels a chill. At the same instant a little wail of pain came to me on the breeze—it might have been the cry of the small owl that lives among the rocks—and the misty presence floated swiftly back from Holger's advancing figure and lay once more at its length upon the mound.

Again I felt the cool breeze in my hair, and this time an icy thrill of dread ran down my spine. I remembered very well that I had once gone down there alone in the moonlight; that presently, being near, I had seen nothing; that, like Holger, I had gone and had stood upon the mound; and I remembered how, when I came back, sure that there was nothing there, I had felt the sudden conviction that there was something after all if I would only look behind me. I remembered the strong temptation to look back, a temptation I had resisted as unworthy of a man of sense, until, to get rid of it, I had shaken myself just as Holger did.

And now I knew that those white, misty arms had been round me too; I knew it in a flash, and I shuddered as I remembered that I had heard the night owl then too. But it had not been the night owl. It was the cry of the Thing.

I refilled my pipe and poured out a cup of strong southern wine; in less than a minute Holger was seated beside me again.

"Of course there's nothing there," he said, "but it's creepy, all the same. Do you know, when I was coming back I was so sure that there was something behind me that I wanted to turn round and look? It was an effort not to."

He laughed a little, knocked the ashes out of his pipe, and poured himself out some wine. For a while neither of us spoke, and the moon rose higher, and we both looked at the Thing that lay on the mound.

"You might make a story about that," said Holger after a long time.

"There is one," I answered. "If you're not sleepy, I'll tell it to you."

"Go ahead," said Holger, who likes stories.

***

Old Alario was dying up there in the village behind the hill. You remember him, I have no doubt. They say that he made his money by selling sham jewelry in South America, and escaped with his gains when he was found out. Like all those fellows, if they bring anything back with them, he at once set to work to enlarge his house, and as there are no masons here, he sent all the way to Paola for two workmen. They were a rough-looking pair of scoundrels—a Neapolitan who had lost one eye and a Sicilian with an old scar half an inch deep across his left cheek. I often saw them, for on Sundays they used to come down here and fish off the rocks. When Alario caught the fever that killed him the masons were still at work. As he had agreed that part of their pay should be their board and lodging, he made them sleep in the house. His wife was dead, and he had an only son called Angelo, who was a much better sort than himself. Angelo was to marry the daughter of the richest man in the village, and, strange to say, though the marriage was arranged by their parents, the young people were said to be in love with each other.

For that matter, the whole village was in love with Angelo, and among the rest a wild, good-looking creature called Cristina, who was more like a gipsy than any girl I ever saw about here. She had very red lips and very black eyes, she was built like a greyhound, and had the tongue of the devil. But Angelo did not care a straw for her. He was rather a simple-minded fellow, quite different from his old scoundrel of a father, and under what I should call normal circumstances I really believe that he would never have looked at any girl except the nice plump little creature, with a fat dowry, whom his father meant him to marry. But things turned up which were neither normal nor natural.

On the other hand, a very handsome young shepherd from the hills above Maratea was in love with Cristina, who seems to have been quite indifferent to him. Cristina had no regular means of subsistence, but she was a good girl and willing to do any work or go on errands to any distance for the sake of a loaf of bread or a mess of beans, and permission to sleep under cover. She was especially glad when she could get something to do about the house of Angelo's father. There is no doctor in the village, and when the neighbors saw that old Alario was dying they sent Cristina to Scalea to fetch one. That was late in the afternoon, and if they had waited so long, it was because the dying miser refused to allow any such extravagance while he was able to speak. But while Cristina was gone matters grew rapidly worse, the priest was brought to the bedside, and when he had done what he could he gave it as his opinion to the bystanders that the old man was dead, and left the house.

You know these people. They have a physical horror of death. Until the priest spoke, the room had been full of people. The words were hardly out of his mouth before it was empty. It was night now. They hurried down the dark steps and out into the street.

Angelo, as I have said, was away, Cristina had not come back—the simple woman-servant who had nursed the sick man fled with the rest, and the body was left alone in the flickering light of the earthen oil lamp.

Five minutes later two men looked in cautiously and crept forward toward the bed. They were the one-eyed Neapolitan mason and his Sicilian companion. They knew what they wanted. In a moment they had dragged from under the bed a small but heavy iron-bound box, and long before any one thought of coming back to the dead man they had left the house and the village under cover of the darkness. It was easy enough, for Alario's house is the last toward the gorge which leads down here, and the thieves merely went out by the back door, got over the stone wall, and had nothing to risk after that except the possibility of meeting some belated countryman, which was very small indeed, since few of the people use that path. They had a mattock and shovel, and they made their way here without accident.

I am telling you this story as it must have happened, for, of course, there were no witnesses to this part of it. The men brought the box down by the gorge, intending to bury it until they should be able to come back and take it away in a boat. They must have been clever enough to guess that some of the money would be in paper notes, for they would otherwise have buried it on the beach in the wet sand, where it would have been much safer. But the paper would have rotted if they had been obliged to leave it there long, so they dug their hole down there, close to that boulder. Yes, just where the mound is now.

Cristina did not find the doctor in Scalea, for he had been sent for from a place up the valley, halfway to San Domenico. If she had found him, he would have come on his mule by the upper road, which is smoother but much longer. But Cristina took the short cut by the rocks, which passes about fifty feet above the mound, and goes round that corner. The men were digging when she passed, and she heard them at work. It would not have been like her to go by without finding out what the noise was, for she was never afraid of anything in her life, and, besides, the fishermen sometimes come ashore here at night to get a stone for an anchor or to gather sticks to make a little fire. The night was dark, and Cristina probably came close to the two men before she could see what they were doing. She knew them, of course, and they knew her, and understood instantly that they were in her power. There was only one thing to be done for their safety, and they did it. They knocked her on the head, they dug the hole deep, and they buried her quickly with the iron-bound chest. They must have understood that their only chance of escaping suspicion lay in getting back to the village before their absence was noticed, for they returned immediately, and were found half an hour later gossiping quietly with the man who was making Alario's coffin. He was a crony of theirs, and had been working at the repairs in the old man's house. So far as I have been able to make out, the only persons who were supposed to know where Alario kept his treasure were Angelo and the one woman-servant I have mentioned. Angelo was away; it was the woman who discovered the theft.

It is easy enough to understand why no one else knew where the money was. The old man kept his door locked and the key in his pocket when he was out, and did not let the woman enter to clean the place unless he was there himself. The whole village knew that he had money somewhere, however, and the masons had probably discovered the whereabouts of the chest by climbing in at the window in his absence. If the old man had not been delirious until he lost consciousness, he would have been in frightful agony of mind for his riches. The faithful woman-servant forgot their existence only for a few moments when she fled with the rest, overcome by the horror of death. Twenty minutes had not passed before she returned with the two hideous old hags who are always called in to prepare the dead for burial. Even then she had not at first the courage to go near the bed with them, but she made a pretence of dropping something, went down on her knees as if to find it, and looked under the bedstead. The walls of the room were newly whitewashed down to the floor, and she saw at a glance that the chest was gone. It had been there in the afternoon, it had therefore been stolen in the short interval since she had left the room.

There are no carabineers stationed in the village; there is not so much as a municipal watchman, for there is no municipality. There never was such a place, I believe. Scalea is supposed to look after it in some mysterious way, and it takes a couple of hours to get anybody from there. As the old woman had lived in the village all her life, it did not even occur to her to apply to any civil authority for help. She simply set up a howl and ran through the village in the dark, screaming out that her dead master's house had been robbed. Many of the people looked out, but at first no one seemed inclined to help her. Most of them, judging her by themselves, whispered to each other that she had probably stolen the money herself. The first man to move was the father of the girl whom Angelo was to marry; having collected his household, all of whom felt a personal interest in the wealth which was to have come into the family, he declared it to be his opinion that the chest had been stolen by the two journeyman masons who lodged in the house. He headed a search for them, which naturally began in Alario's house and ended in the carpenter's workshop, where the thieves were found discussing a measure of wine with the carpenter over the half-finished coffin, by the light of one earthen lamp filled with oil and tallow. The search party at once accused the delinquents of the crime, and threatened to lock them up in the cellar till the carabineers could be fetched from Scalea. The two men looked at each other for one moment, and then without the slightest hesitation they put out the single light, seized the unfinished coffin between them, and using it as a sort of battering ram, dashed upon their assailants in the dark. In a few moments they were beyond pursuit.

That is the end of the first part of the story. The treasure had disappeared, and as no trace of it could be found the people naturally supposed that the thieves had succeeded in carrying it off. The old man was buried, and when Angelo came back at last he had to borrow money to pay for the miserable funeral, and had some difficulty in doing so. He hardly needed to be told that in losing his inheritance he had lost his bride. In this part of the world marriages are made on strictly business principles, and if the promised cash is not forthcoming on the appointed day the bride or the bridegroom whose parents have failed to produce it may as well take themselves off, for there will be no wedding. Poor Angelo knew that well enough. His father had been possessed of hardly any land, and now that the hard cash which he had brought from South America was gone, there was nothing left but debts for the building materials that were to have been used for enlarging and improving the old house. Angelo was beggared, and the nice plump little creature who was to have been his turned up her nose at him in the most approved fashion. As for Cristina, it was several days before she was missed, for no one remembered that she had been sent to Scalea for the doctor, who had never come. She often disappeared in the same way for days together, when she could find a little work here and there at the distant farms among the hills. But when she did not come back at all, people began to wonder, and at last made up their minds that she had connived with the masons and had escaped with them.

***

I paused and emptied my glass.

"That sort of thing could not happen anywhere else," observed Holger, filling his everlasting pipe again. "It is wonderful what a natural charm there is about murder and sudden death in a romantic country like this. Deeds that would be simply brutal and disgusting anywhere else become dramatic and mysterious because this is Italy and we are living in a genuine tower of Charles V built against genuine Barbary pirates."

"There's something in that," I admitted. Holger is the most romantic man in the world inside of himself, but he always thinks it necessary to explain why he feels anything.

"I suppose they found the poor girl's body with the box," he said presently.

"As it seems to interest you," I answered, "I'll tell you the rest of the story."

The moon had risen high by this time; the outline of the Thing on the mound was clearer to our eyes than before.

***

The village very soon settled down to its small, dull life. No one missed old Alario, who had been away so much on his voyages to South America that he had never been a familiar figure in his native place. Angelo lived in the half-finished house, and because he had no money to pay the old woman-servant she would not stay with him, but once in a long time she would come and wash a shirt for him for old acquaintance's sake. Besides the house, he had inherited a small patch of ground at some distance from the village; he tried to cultivate it, but he had no heart in the work, for he knew he could never pay the taxes on it and on the house, which would certainly be confiscated by the Government, or seized for the debt of the building material, which the man who had supplied it refused to take back.

Angelo was very unhappy. So long as his father had been alive and rich, every girl in the village had been in love with him; but that was all changed now. It had been pleasant to be admired and courted, and invited to drink wine by fathers who had girls to marry. It was hard to be stared at coldly, and sometimes laughed at because he had been robbed of his inheritance. He cooked his miserable meals for himself, and from being sad became melancholy and morose.

At twilight, when the day's work was done, instead of hanging about in the open space before the church with young fellows of his own age, he took to wandering in lonely places on the outskirts of the village till it was quite dark. Then he slunk home and went to bed to save the expense of a light. But in those lonely twilight hours he began to have strange waking dreams. He was not always alone, for often when he sat on the stump of a tree, where the narrow path turns down the gorge, he was sure that a woman came up noiselessly over the rough stones, as if her feet were bare; and she stood under a clump of chestnut trees only half a dozen yards down the path, and beckoned to him without speaking.

Though she was in the shadow he knew that her lips were red, and that when they parted a little and smiled at him she showed two small sharp teeth. He knew this at first rather than saw it, and he knew that it was Cristina, and that she was dead. Yet he was not afraid; he only wondered whether it was a dream, for he thought that if he had been awake he should have been frightened.

Besides, the dead woman had red lips, and that could only happen in a dream. Whenever he went near the gorge after sunset she was already there waiting for him, or else she very soon appeared, and he began to be sure that she came a little nearer to him every day. At first he had only been sure of her blood-red mouth, but now each feature grew distinct, and the pale face looked at him with deep and hungry eyes.

It was the eyes that grew dim. Little by little he came to know that some day the dream would not end when he turned away to go home, but would lead him down the gorge out of which the vision rose. She was nearer now when she beckoned to him. Her cheeks were not livid like those of the dead, but pale with starvation, with the furious and unappeased physical hunger of her eyes that devoured him. They feasted on his soul and cast a spell over him, and at last they were close to his own and held him. He could not tell whether her breath was as hot as fire or as cold as ice; he could not tell whether her red lips burned his or froze them, or whether her five fingers on his wrists seared scorching scars or bit his flesh like frost; he could not tell whether he was awake or asleep, whether she was alive or dead, but he knew that she loved him, she alone of all creatures, earthly or unearthly, and her spell had power over him.

When the moon rose high that night the shadow of that Thing was not alone down there upon the mound.

Angelo awoke in the cool dawn, drenched with dew and chilled through flesh, and blood, and bone. He opened his eyes to the faint grey light, and saw the stars still shining overhead. He was very weak, and his heart was beating so slowly that he was almost like a man fainting. Slowly he turned his head on the mound, as on a pillow, but the other face was not there. Fear seized him suddenly, a fear unspeakable and unknown; he sprang to his feet and fled up the gorge, and he never looked behind him until he reached the door of the house on the outskirts of the village.

Drearily he went to his work that day, and wearily the hours dragged themselves after the sun, till at last he touched the sea and sank, and the great sharp hills above Maratea turned purple against the dove-colored eastern sky.

Angelo shouldered his heavy hoe and left the field. He felt less tired now than in the morning when he had begun to work, but he promised himself that he would go home without lingering by the gorge, and eat the best supper he could get himself, and sleep all night in his bed like a Christian man. Not again would he be tempted down the narrow way by a shadow with red lips and icy breath; not again would he dream that dream of terror and delight. He was near the village now; it was half an hour since the sun had set, and the cracked church bell sent little discordant echoes across the rocks and ravines to tell all good people that the day was done. Angelo stood still a moment where the path forked, where it led toward the village on the left, and down to the gorge on the right, where a clump of chestnut trees overhung the narrow way. He stood still a minute, lifting his battered hat from his head and gazing at the fast-fading sea westward, and his lips moved as he silently repeated the familiar evening prayer. His lips moved, but the words that followed them in his brain lost their meaning and turned into others, and ended in a name that he spoke aloud—Cristina! With the name, the tension of his will relaxed suddenly, reality went out and the dream took him again, and bore him on swiftly and surely like a man walking in his sleep, down, down, by the steep path in the gathering darkness. And as she glided beside him, Cristina whispered strange, sweet things in his ear, which somehow, if he had been awake, he knew that he could not quite have understood; but now they were the most wonderful words he had ever heard in his life. And she kissed him also, but not upon his mouth. He felt her sharp kisses upon his white throat, and he knew that her lips were red. So the wild dream sped on through twilight and darkness and moonrise, and all the glory of the summer's night. But in the chilly dawn he lay as one half dead upon the mound down there, recalling and not recalling, drained of his blood, yet strangely longing to give those red lips more. Then came the fear, the awful nameless panic, the mortal horror that guards the confines of the world we see not, neither know of as we know of other things, but which we feel when its icy chill freezes our bones and stirs our hair with the touch of a ghostly hand. Once more Angelo sprang from the mound and fled up the gorge in the breaking day, but his step was less sure this time, and he panted for breath as he ran; and when he came to the bright spring of water that rises halfway up the hillside, he dropped upon his knees and hands and plunged his whole face in and drank as he had never drunk before—for it was the thirst of the wounded man who has lain bleeding all night long upon the battle-field.

She had him fast now, and he could not escape her, but would come to her every evening at dusk until she had drained him of his last drop of blood. It was in vain that when the day was done he tried to take another turning and to go home by a path that did not lead near the gorge. It was in vain that he made promises to himself each morning at dawn when he climbed the lonely way up from the shore to the village. It was all in vain, for when the sun sank burning into the sea, and the coolness of the evening stole out as from a hiding-place to delight the weary world, his feet turned toward the old way, and she was waiting for him in the shadow under the chestnut trees; and then all happened as before, and she fell to kissing his white throat even as she flitted lightly down the way, winding one arm about him. And as his blood failed, she grew more hungry and more thirsty every day, and every day when he awoke in the early dawn it was harder to rouse himself to the effort of climbing the steep path to the village; and when he went to his work his feet dragged painfully, and there was hardly strength in his arms to wield the heavy hoe. He scarcely spoke to any one now, but the people said he was "consuming himself" for love of the girl he was to have married when he lost his inheritance; and they laughed heartily at the thought, for this is not a very romantic country. At this time, Antonio, the man who stays here to look after the tower, returned from a visit to his people, who live near Salerno. He had been away all the time since before Alario's death and knew nothing of what had happened. He has told me that he came back late in the afternoon and shut himself up in the tower to eat and sleep, for he was very tired. It was past midnight when he awoke, and when he looked out the waning moon was rising over the shoulder of the hill. He looked out toward the mound, and he saw something, and he did not sleep again that night.

When he went out again in the morning it was broad daylight, and there was nothing to be seen on the mound but loose stones and driven sand. Yet he did not go very near it; he went straight up the path to the village and directly to the house of the old priest.

"I have seen an evil thing this night," he said; "I have seen how the dead drink the blood of the living. And the blood is the life."

"Tell me what you have seen," said the priest in reply.

Antonio told him everything he had seen.

"You must bring your book and your holy water to-night," he added. "I will be here before sunset to go down with you, and if it pleases your reverence to sup with me while we wait, I will make ready."

"I will come," the priest answered, "for I have read in old books of these strange beings which are neither quick nor dead, and which lie ever fresh in their graves, stealing out in the dusk to taste life and blood."

Antonio cannot read, but he was glad to see that the priest understood the business; for, of course, the books must have instructed him as to the best means of quieting the half-living Thing for ever.

So Antonio went away to his work, which consists largely in sitting on the shady side of the tower, when he is not perched upon a rock with a fishing-line catching nothing. But on that day he went twice to look at the mound in the bright sunlight, and he searched round and round it for some hole through which the being might get in and out; but he found none. When the sun began to sink and the air was cooler in the shadows, he went up to fetch the old priest, carrying a little wicker basket with him; and in this they placed a bottle of holy water, and the basin, and sprinkler, and the stole which the priest would need; and they came down and waited in the door of the tower till it should be dark. But while the light still lingered very grey and faint, they saw something moving, just there, two figures, a man's that walked, and a woman's that flitted beside him, and while her head lay on his shoulder she kissed his throat. The priest has told me that, too, and that his teeth chattered and he grasped Antonio's arm. The vision passed and disappeared into the shadow. Then Antonio got the leathern flask of strong liquor, which he kept for great occasions, and poured such a draught as made the old man feel almost young again; and he got the lantern, and his pick and shovel, and gave

the priest his stole to put on and the holy water to carry, and they went
out together toward the spot where the work was to be done. Antonio
says that in spite of the rum his own knees shook together, and the priest
stumbled over his Latin. For when they were yet a few yards from the
mound the flickering light of the lantern fell upon Angelo's white face,
unconscious as if in sleep, and on his upturned throat, over which a very
thin red line of blood trickled down into his collar; and the flickering
light of the lantern played upon another face that looked up from the
feast—upon two deep, dead eyes that saw in spite of death—upon parted
lips redder than life itself—upon two gleaming teeth on which glistened
a rosy drop. Then the priest, good old man, shut his eyes tight and show-
ered holy water before him, and his cracked voice rose almost to a scream;
and then Antonio, who is no coward after all, raised his pick in one hand
and the lantern in the other, as he sprang forward, not knowing what
the end should be; and then he swears that he heard a woman's cry, and
the Thing was gone, and Angelo lay alone on the mound unconscious,
with the red line on his throat and the beads of deathly sweat on his
cold forehead. They lifted him, half-dead as he was, and laid him on the
ground close by; then Antonio went to work, and the priest helped him,
though he was old and could not do much; and they dug deep, and at
last Antonio, standing in the grave, stooped down with his lantern to see
what he might see.

His hair used to be dark brown, with grizzled streaks about the temples; in less than a month from that day he was as grey as a badger. He
was a miner when he was young, and most of these fellows have seen ugly
sights now and then, when accidents have happened, but he had never
seen what he saw that night—that Thing which is neither alive nor dead,
that Thing that will abide neither above ground nor in the grave. Antonio
had brought something with him which the priest had not noticed. He
had made it that afternoon—a sharp stake shaped from a piece of tough
old driftwood. He had it with him now, and he had his heavy pick, and
he had taken the lantern down into the grave. I don't think any power on
earth could make him speak of what happened then, and the old priest
was too frightened to look in. He says he heard Antonio breathing like
a wild beast, and moving as if he were fighting with something almost

as strong as himself; and he heard an evil sound also, with blows, as of something violently driven through flesh and bone; and then the most awful sound of all—a woman's shriek, the unearthly scream of a woman neither dead nor alive, but buried deep for many days. And he, the poor old priest, could only rock himself as he knelt there in the sand, crying aloud his prayers and exorcisms to drown these dreadful sounds. Then suddenly a small iron-bound chest was thrown up and rolled over against the old man's knee, and in a moment more Antonio was beside him, his face as white as tallow in the flickering light of the lantern, shoveling the sand and pebbles into the grave with furious haste, and looking over the edge till the pit was half full; and the priest said that there was much fresh blood on Antonio's hands and on his clothes.

I had come to the end of my story. Holger finished his wine and leaned back in his chair.

"So Angelo got his own again," he said. "Did he marry the prim and plump young person to whom he had been betrothed?"

"No, he had been badly frightened. He went to South America, and has not been heard of since."

"And that poor thing's body is there still, I suppose," said Holger. "Is it quite dead yet, I wonder?"

I wonder, too. But whether it be dead or alive, I should hardly care to see it, even in broad daylight. Antonio is as grey as a badger, and he has never been quite the same man since that night.

The Night Wire

By H. F. Arnold

"New York, September 30 CP FLASH

"Ambassador Holliwell died here today. The end came suddenly as the ambassador was alone in his study. . . . "

There is something ungodly about these night wire jobs. You sit up here on the top floor of a skyscraper and listen in to the whispers of a civilization. New York, London, Calcutta, Bombay, Singapore—they're your next-door neighbors after the streetlights go dim and the world has gone to sleep.

Alone in the quiet hours between two and four, the receiving operators doze over their sounders and the news comes in. Fires and disasters and suicides. Murders, crowds, catastrophes. Sometimes an earthquake with a casualty list as long as your arm. The night wire man takes it down almost in his sleep, picking it off on his typewriter with one finger.

Once in a long time you prick up your ears and listen. You've heard of some one you knew in Singapore, Halifax or Paris, long ago. Maybe they've been promoted, but more probably they've been murdered or drowned. Perhaps they just decided to quit and took some bizarre way out. Made it interesting enough to get in the news.

But that doesn't happen often. Most of the time you sit and doze and tap, tap on your typewriter and wish you were home in bed.

Sometimes, though, queer things happen. One did the other night, and I haven't got over it yet. I wish I could.

You see, I handle the night manager's desk in a western seaport town; what the name is, doesn't matter.

There is, or rather was, only one night operator on my staff, a fellow named John Morgan, about forty years of age, I should say, and a sober, hard-working sort.

He was one of the best operators I ever knew, what is known as a "double" man. That means he could handle two instruments at once and type the stories on different typewriters at the same time. He was one of the three men I ever knew who could do it consistently, hour after hour, and never make a mistake.

Generally, we used only one wire at night, but sometimes, when it was late and the news was coming fast, the Chicago and Denver stations would open a second wire, and then Morgan would do his stuff. He was a wizard, a mechanical automatic wizard which functioned marvelously but was without imagination.

On the night of the sixteenth he complained of feeling tired. It was the first and last time I had ever heard him say a word about himself, and I had known him for three years.

It was just three o'clock and we were running only one wire. I was nodding over the reports at my desk and not paying much attention to him, when he spoke.

"Jim," he said, "does it feel close in here to you?"

"Why, no, John," I answered, "but I'll open a window if you like."

"Never mind," he said. "I reckon I'm just a little tired."

That was all that was said, and I went on working. Every ten minutes or so I would walk over and take a pile of copy that had stacked up neatly beside the typewriter as the messages were printed out in triplicate.

It must have been twenty minutes after he spoke that I noticed he had opened up the other wire and was using both typewriters. I thought it was a little unusual, as there was nothing very "hot" coming in. On my next trip I picked up the copy from both machines and took it back to my desk to sort out the duplicates.

The first wire was running out the usual sort of stuff and I just looked over it hurriedly. Then I turned to the second pile of copy. I remembered it particularly because the story was from a town I had never heard of: "Xebico." Here is the dispatch. I saved a duplicate of it from our files:

"Xebico, Sept 16 CP BULLETIN

"The heaviest mist in the history of the city settled over the town at 4 o'clock yesterday afternoon. All traffic has stopped and the mist hangs like a pall over everything. Lights of ordinary intensity fail to pierce the fog, which is constantly growing heavier.

"Scientists here are unable to agree as to the cause, and the local weather bureau states that the like has never occurred before in the history of the city.

"At 7 P.M. last night the municipal authorities . . .

(more)

That was all there was. Nothing out of the ordinary at a bureau headquarters, but, as I say, I noticed the story because of the name of the town.

It must have been fifteen minutes later that I went over for another batch of copy. Morgan was slumped down in his chair and had switched his green electric light shade so that the gleam missed his eyes and hit only the top of the two typewriters.

Only the usual stuff was in the righthand pile, but the lefthand batch carried another story from Xebico. All press dispatches come in "takes," meaning that parts of many different stories are strung along together, perhaps with but a few paragraphs of each coming through at a time. This second story was marked "add fog." Here is the copy:

"At 7 P.M. the fog had increased noticeably. All lights were now invisible and the town was shrouded in pitch darkness.

"As a peculiarity of the phenomenon, the fog is accompanied by a sickly odor, comparable to nothing yet experienced here."

Below that in customary press fashion was the hour, 3:27, and the initials of the operator, JM.

There was only one other story in the pile from the second wire. Here it is:

"2nd add Xebico Fog.

"Accounts as to the origin of the mist differ greatly. Among the most unusual is that of the sexton of the local church, who groped his way to headquarters in a hysterical condition and declared that the fog originated in the village churchyard.

"'It was first visible as a soft gray blanket clinging to the earth above the graves,' he stated. 'Then it began to rise, higher and higher. A subterranean breeze seemed to blow it in billows, which split up and then joined together again.

"'Fog phantoms, writhing in anguish, twisted the mist into queer forms and figures. And then, in the very thick midst of the mass, something moved.

"'I turned and ran from the accursed spot. Behind me I heard screams coming from the houses bordering on the graveyard.'

"Although the sexton's story is generally discredited, a party has left to investigate. Immediately after telling his story, the sexton collapsed and is now in a local hospital, unconscious."

Queer story, wasn't it? Not that we aren't used to it, for a lot of unusual stories come in over the wire. But for some reason or other, perhaps because it was so quiet that night, the report of the fog made a great impression on me.

It was almost with dread that I went over to the waiting piles of copy. Morgan did not move, and the only sound in the room was the tap-tap of the sounders. It was ominous, nerve-racking.

There was another story from Xebico in the pile of copy. I seized on it anxiously.

"New Lead Xebico Fog CP

"The rescue party which went out at 11 P.M. to investigate a weird story of the origin of a fog which, since late yesterday, has shrouded the city in darkness has failed to return. Another and larger party has been dispatched.

"Meanwhile, the fog has, if possible, grown heavier. It seeps through the cracks in the doors and fills the atmosphere with a depressing odor of decay. It is oppressive, terrifying, bearing with it a subtle impression of things long dead.

"Residents of the city have left their homes and gathered in the local church, where the priests are holding services of prayer. The scene is beyond description. Grown folk and children are alike terrified and many are almost beside themselves with fear.

"Amid the whisps of vapor which partly veil the church auditorium, an old priest is praying for the welfare of his flock. They alternately wail and cross themselves.

"From the outskirts of the city may be heard cries of unknown voices. They echo through the fog in queer uncadenced minor keys. The sounds resemble nothing so much as wind whistling through a gigantic tunnel. But the night is calm and there is no wind. The second rescue party . . . (more)"

I am a calm man and never in a dozen years spent with the wires have I been known to become excited, but despite myself I rose from my chair and walked to the window.

Could I be mistaken, or far down in the canyons of the city beneath me did I see a faint trace of fog? Pshaw! It was all imagination.

In the pressroom the click of the sounders seemed to have raised the tempo of their tune. Morgan alone had not stirred from his chair. His head sunk between his shoulders, he tapped the dispatches out on the typewriters with one finger of each hand.

He looked asleep, but no; endlessly, efficiently, the two machines rattled off line after line, as relentlessly and effortlessly as death itself. There was something about the monotonous movement of the typewriter keys that fascinated me. I walked over and stood behind his chair, reading over his shoulder the type as it came into being, word by word.

Ah, here was another:

"Flash Xebico CP

"There will be no more bulletins from this office. The impossible has happened. No messages have come into this room for twenty minutes. We are cut off from the outside and even the streets below us.

"I will stay with the wire until the end.

"It is the end, indeed. Since 4 P.M. yesterday the fog has hung over the city. Following reports from the sexton of the local church, two rescue parties were sent out to investigate conditions on the outskirts of the city. Neither party has ever returned nor was any word received from them. It is quite certain now that they will never return.

"From my instrument I can gaze down on the city beneath me. From the position of this room on the thirteenth floor, nearly the entire city can be seen. Now I can see only a thick blanket of blackness where customarily are lights and life.

"I fear greatly that the wailing cries heard constantly from the outskirts of the city are the death cries of the inhabitants. They are constantly increasing in volume and are approaching the center of the city.

"The fog yet hangs over everything. If possible, it is even heavier than before, but the conditions have changed. Instead of an opaque, impenetrable wall of odorous vapor, there now swirls and writhes a shapeless mass in contortions of almost human agony. Now and again the mass parts and I catch a brief glimpse of the streets below.

"People are running to and fro, screaming in despair. A vast bedlam of sound flies up to my window, and above all is the immense whistling of unseen and unfelt winds.

"The fog has again swept over the city and the whistling is coming closer and closer.

"It is now directly beneath me.

"God! An instant ago the mist opened and I caught a glimpse of the streets below.

"The fog is not simply vapor—it lives! By the side of each moaning and weeping human is a companion figure, an aura of strange and vari-colored hues. How the shapes cling! Each to a living thing!

"The men and women are down. Flat on their faces. The fog figures caress them lovingly. They are kneeling beside them. They are—but I dare not tell it.

"The prone and writhing bodies have been stripped of their clothing. They are being consumed—piecemeal.

"A merciful wall of hot, steaming vapor has swept over the whole scene. I can see no more.

"Beneath me the wall of vapor is changing colors. It seems to be lighted by internal fires. No, it isn't. I have made a mistake. The colors are from above, reflections from the sky.

"Look up! Look up! The whole sky is in flames. Colors as yet unseen by man or demon. The flames are moving; they have started to intermix; the colors are rearranging themselves. They are so brilliant that my eyes burn, they are a long way off.

"Now they have begun to swirl, to circle in and out, twisting in intricate designs and patterns. The lights are racing each with each, a kaleidoscope of unearthly brilliance.

"I have made a discovery. There is nothing harmful in the lights. They radiate force and friendliness, almost cheeriness. But by their very strength, they hurt.

"As I look, they are swinging closer and closer, a million miles at each jump. Millions of miles with the speed of light. Aye, it is light of quintessence of all light. Beneath it the fog melts into a jeweled mist radiant, rainbow-colored of a thousand varied spectra.

"I can see the streets. Why, they are filled with people! The lights are coming closer. They are all around me. I am enveloped. I . . ."

The message stopped abruptly. The wire to Xebico was dead. Beneath my eyes in the narrow circle of light from under the green lamp-shade, the black printing no longer spun itself, letter by letter, across the page.

The room seemed filled with a solemn quiet, a silence vaguely impressive, powerful.

I looked down at Morgan. His hands had dropped nervelessly at his sides, while his body had hunched over peculiarly. I turned the lamp-shade back, throwing light squarely in his face. His eyes were staring, fixed.

Filled with a sudden foreboding, I stepped beside him and called Chicago on the wire. After a second the sounder clicked its answer.

Why? But there was something wrong. Chicago was reporting that Wire Two had not been used throughout the evening.

"Morgan!" I shouted. "Morgan! Wake up, it isn't true. Some one has been hoaxing us. Why . . ." In my eagerness I grasped him by the shoulder.

His body was quite cold. Morgan had been dead for hours. Could it be that his sensitized brain and automatic fingers had continued to record impressions even after the end?

I shall never know, for I shall never again handle the night shift. Search in a world atlas discloses no town of Xebico. Whatever it was that killed John Morgan will forever remain a mystery.

Timber

By John Galsworthy

Sir Arthur Hirries, Baronet of Hirriehugh, in a northern county, came to the decision to sell his timber in that state of mind— common during the War—which may be called patrio- profiteering. Like newspaper proprietors, writers on strategy, shipbuilders, owners of works, makers of arms and the rest of the working classes at large, his mood was: "Let me serve my country, and if thereby my profits are increased, let me put up with it, and invest in national bonds."

With an encumbered estate and some of the best coverts in that northern county, it had not become practical politics to sell his timber till the Government wanted it at all costs. To let his shooting had been more profitable, till now, when a patriotic action and a stroke of business had become synonymous. A man of sixty-five, but not yet grey, with a reddish tinge in his moustache, cheeks, lips, and eyelids, slightly knock-kneed, and with large, rather spreading feet, he moved in the best circles in a somewhat embarrassed manner. At the enhanced price, the timber at Hirriehugh would enfranchise him for the remainder of his days. He sold it therefore one day of April when the War news was bad, to a Government official on the spot. He sold it at half-past five in the afternoon, practically for cash down, and drank a stiff whisky and soda to wash away the taste of the transaction; for, though no sentimentalist, his great-great-grandfather had planted most of it, and his grandfather the rest. Royalty too had shot there in its time; and he himself (never much of a sportsman) had missed more birds in the rides and hollows of his fine coverts than he cared to remember. But the country was in need, and the price considerable. Bidding the Government official good-bye, he lighted a cigar, and went across the Park to take a farewell stroll among his timber.

He entered the home covert by a path leading through a group of pear trees just coming into bloom. Smoking cigars and drinking whisky in the afternoon in preference to tea, Sir Arthur Hirries had not much sense of natural beauty. But those pear trees impressed him, greenish white against blue sky and fleecy thick clouds which looked as if they had snow in them. They were deuced pretty, and promised a good year for fruit, if they escaped the late frosts, though it certainly looked like freezing to-night! He paused a moment at the wicket gate to glance back at them—like scantily-clothed maidens posing on the outskirts of his timber. Such, however, was not the vision of Sir Arthur Hirries, who was considering how he should invest the balance of the cash down after paying off his mortgages. National bonds—the country was in need!

Passing through the gate he entered the ride of the home covert. Variety lay like colour on his woods. They stretched for miles, and his ancestors had planted almost every kind of tree—beech, oak, birch, sycamore, ash, elm, hazel, holly, pine; a lime tree and a hornbeam here and there, and further in among the winding coverts, spinneys and belts of larch. The evening air was sharp, and sleet showers came whirling from those bright clouds; he walked briskly, drawing at his richly fragrant cigar, the whisky still warm within him. He walked thinking, with a gentle melancholy slowly turning a little sulky, that he would never again be pointing out with his shooting stick to such or such a guest where he was to stand to get the best birds over him.

The pheasants had been let down during the War, but he put up two or three old cocks who went clattering and whirring out to left and right; and rabbits crossed the rides quietly to and fro, within easy shot. He came to where Royalty had stood fifteen years ago during the last drive. He remembered Royalty saying: "Very pretty shooting at that last stand, Hirries; birds just about as high as I like them." The ground indeed rose rather steeply there, and the timber was oak and ash, with a few pines sprinkled into the bare greyish twiggery of the oaks, always costive in spring, and the just greening feather of the ashes.

'They'll be cutting those pines first,' he thought—strapping trees, straight as the lines of Euclid, and free of branches, save at their tops. In the brisk wind those tops swayed a little and gave forth soft complaint. 'Three times my age,' he thought; 'prime timber.'

The ride wound sharply and entered a belt of larch, whose steep rise entirely barred off the rather sinister sunset—a dark and wistful wood, delicate dun and grey, whose green shoots and crimson tips would have perfumed the evening coolness, but for the cigar smoke in his nostrils. 'They'll have this spinney for pit props.' he thought; and, taking a cross ride through it, he emerged in a heathery glen of birch trees. No forester, he wondered if they would make anything of those whitened, glistening shapes. His cigar had gone out now, and he leaned against one of the satin-smooth stems, under the lacery of twig and bud, sheltering the flame of a relighting match. A hare lopped away among the bilberry shoots; a jay, painted like a fan, squawked and flustered past him up the glen. Interested in birds, and wanting just one more jay to complete a fine stuffed group of them, Sir Arthur, though devoid of a gun, followed, to see where "the beggar's" nest was.

The glen dipped rapidly and the character of the timber changed, assuming greater girth and solidity. There was a lot of beech here—a bit he did not know, for though taken in by the beaters, no guns could be stationed there because of the lack of under-growth. The jay had vanished, and light had begun to fail. 'I must get back,' he thought, 'or I shall be late for dinner.' He debated for a moment whether to retrace his steps or to cut across the beeches and regain the home covert by a loop. The jay, reappearing to the left, decided him to cross the beech grove. He did so, and took a narrow ride up through a dark bit of mixed timber with heavy undergrowth. The ride, after favouring the left for a little, bent away to the right; Sir Arthur followed it hurriedly, conscious that twilight was gathering fast. It must bend again to the left in a minute! It did, and then to the right, and, the undergrowth remaining thick, he could only follow on, or else retrace his steps. He followed on, beginning to get hot in spite of a sleet shower falling through the dusk. He was not framed by Nature for swift travelling—his knees turning in and his toes turning out—but he went at a good bat, uncomfortably aware that the ride was still taking him away from home, and expecting it at any minute to turn left again. It did not, and hot, out of breath, a little bewildered, he stood still in three-quarter darkness, to listen. Not a sound save that of wind in the tops of the trees, and a faint creaking of timber, where two stems had grown athwart and were touching.

The path was a regular will-o'-the-wisp. He must make a bee line of it through the undergrowth into another ride! He had never before been amongst his timber in the dusk, and he found the shapes of the confounded trees more weird, and as if menacing, than he had ever dreamed of. He stumbled quickly on in and out of them among the undergrowth, without coming to a ride.

'Here I am stuck in this damned wood!' he thought. To call these formidably encircling shapes "a wood" gave him relief. After all, it was his wood, and nothing very untoward could happen to a man in his own wood, however dark it might get; he could not be more than a mile and a half at the outside from his dining-room! He looked at his watch, whose hands he could just see—nearly half-past seven! The sleet had become snow, but it hardly fell on him, so thick was the timber just here. But he had no overcoat, and suddenly he felt that first sickening little drop in his chest, which presages alarm. Nobody knew he was in this damned wood! And in a quarter of an hour it would be black as your hat! He *must* get on and out! The trees amongst which he was stumbling produced quite a sick feeling now in one who hitherto had never taken trees seriously.

What monstrous growths they were! The thought that seeds, tiny seeds or saplings, planted by his ancestors, could attain such huge impending and imprisoning bulk—ghostly great growths mounting up to heaven and shutting off this world, exasperated and unnerved him. He began to run, caught his foot in a root and fell flat on his face. The cursed trees seemed to have a down on him! Rubbing elbows and forehead with his snow-wetted hands, he leaned against a trunk to get his breath, and summon the sense of direction to his brain. Once as a young man he had been "bushed" at night in Vancouver Island; quite a scary business! But he had come out all right, though his camp had been the only civilised spot within a radius of twenty miles. And here he was, on his own estate, within a mile or two of home, getting into a funk. It was childish! And he laughed. The wind answered, sighing and threshing in the tree tops. There must be a regular blizzard blowing now, and, to judge by the cold, from the north—but whether north-east or north-west was the question. Besides, how keep definite direction without a compass, in the dark?

The timber, too, with its thick trunks, diverted the wind into keen, directionless draughts. He looked up, but could make nothing of the two or three stars that he could see. It was a mess! And he lighted a second cigar with some difficulty, for he had begun to shiver. The wind in this blasted wood cut through his Norfolk jacket and crawled about his body, which had become hot from his exertion, and now felt clammy and half-frozen. This would mean pneumonia, if he didn't look out! And, half feeling his way from trunk to trunk, he started on again, but for all he could tell he might be going round in a circle, might even be crossing rides without realising, and again that sickening drop occurred in his chest. He stood still and shouted. He had the feeling of shouting into walls of timber, dark and heavy, which threw the sound back at him.

'Curse you!' he thought; 'I wish I'd sold you six months ago!' The wind fleered and mowed in the tree tops; and he started off again at a run in that dark wilderness; till, hitting his head against a low branch, he fell stunned. He lay several minutes unconscious, came to himself deadly cold, and struggled up on to his feet.

'By Jove!' he thought, with a sort of stammer in his brain; 'this is a bad business! I may be out here all night!' For an unimaginative man, it was extraordinary what vivid images he had just then. He saw the face of the Government official who had bought his timber, and the slight grimace with which he had agreed to the price. He saw his butler, after the gong had gone, standing like a stuck pig by the sideboard, waiting for him to come down. What would they do when he didn't come? Would they have the sense to imagine that he might have lost his way in the coverts, and take lanterns and search for him? Far more likely they would think he had walked over to "Greenlands" or "Berrymoor," and stayed there to dinner. And, suddenly, he saw himself slowly freezing out here, in the snowy night, among this cursed timber. With a vigorous shake, he butted again into the darkness among the tree trunks. He was angry now—with himself, with the night, with the trees; so angry that he actually let out with his fist at a trunk against which he had stumbled, and scored his knuckles. It was humiliating; and Sir Arthur Hirries was not accustomed to humiliation. In anybody else's wood—yes; but to be lost like this in one's own coverts! Well, if he had to walk all night, he would get out! And he plunged on doggedly in the darkness.

He was fighting with his timber now, as if the thing were alive and each tree an enemy. In the interminable stumbling exertion of that groping progress his angry mood gave place to half-comatose philosophy. Trees! His great-great-grandfather had planted them! His own was the fifth man's life, but the trees were almost as young as ever; they made nothing of a man's life! He sniggered: And a man made nothing of theirs! Did they know they were going to be cut down? All the better if they did, and were sweating in their shoes. He pinched himself—his thoughts were becoming so queer! He remembered that once, when his liver was out of order, trees had seemed to him like solid, tall diseases—bulbous, scarred, cavernous, witch-armed, fungoid emanations of the earth. Well, so they were! And he was among them, on a snowy pitch-black night, engaged in this death-struggle!

The occurrence of the word death in his thoughts brought him up all standing. Why couldn't he concentrate his mind on getting out; why was he mooning about the life and nature of trees instead of trying to remember the conformation of his coverts, so as to re-kindle in himself some sense of general direction? He struck a number of matches to get a sight of his watch again. Great heaven! He had been walking nearly two hours since he last looked at it; and in what direction? They said a man in a fog went round and round because of some kink in his brain!

He began now to feel the trees, searching for a hollow trunk. A hollow would be some protection from the cold—his first conscious confession of exhaustion. He was not in training, and he was sixty-five. The thought: 'I can't keep this up much longer,' caused a second explosion of sullen anger. Damnation! Here he was—for all he could tell—standing where he had sat perhaps a dozen times on his spread shooting stick; watching sunlight on bare twigs, or the nose of his spaniel twitching beside him, listening to the tap of the beaters' sticks, and the shrill, drawn-out: "Marrk! Cock over!"

Would they let the dogs out, to pick up his tracks? No! ten to one they would assume he was staying the night at the Summertons,' or at Lady Mary's, as he had done before now, after dining there. And suddenly his strained heart leaped. He had struck a ride again! His mind slipped back into place like an elastic let-go, relaxed, quivering gratefully. He had only to follow this ride, and somewhere, somehow, he would come out. And be hanged if he would let them know what a fool he had made of himself! Right or left—which way? He turned so that the flying snow came on his back, hurrying forward between the denser darkness on either hand, where the timber stood in walls, moving his arms across and across his body, as if dragging a concertina to full stretch, to make sure that he was keeping in the patch.

He went what seemed an interminable way like this, till he was brought up all standing by trees, and could find no outlet, no continuation. Turning in his tracks, with the snow in his face now, he retraced his steps till once more he was brought up short by trees. He stood panting. It was ghastly—ghastly! And in a panic he dived this way and that to find the bend, the turning, the way on. The sleet stung his eyes, the wind fleered and whistled, the boughs sloughed and moaned. He struck matches, trying to shade them with his cold, wet hands, but one by one they went out, and still he found no turning. The ride must have a blind alley at either end, the turning be down the side somewhere! Hope revived in him. Never say die!

He began a second retracing of his steps, feeling the trunks along one side, to find a gap. His breath came with difficulty. What would old Brodley say if he could see him, soaked, frozen, tired to death, stumbling along in the darkness among this cursed timber—old Brodley who had told him his heart was in poor case! . . . A gap? Ah! No trunks—a ride at last! He turned, felt a sharp pain in his knee and pitched forward. He could not rise—the knee dislocated six years ago was out again. Sir Arthur Hirries clenched his teeth. Nothing more could happen to him! But after a minute—blank and bitter—he began to crawl along the new ride. Oddly he felt less discouraged and alarmed on hands and knee—for he could use but one. It was a relief to have his eyes fixed on the ground, not peering at the tree trunks; or perhaps there was less strain for the moment on his heart. He crawled, stopping every minute or so to renew his strength. He crawled mechanically, waiting for his, heart, his knee, his lungs to stop him.

The earth was snowed over, and he could feel its cold wetness as he scraped along. Good tracks to follow, if anybody struck them! But in this dark forest! In one of his halts, drying his hands as best he could, he struck a match, and sheltering it desperately, fumbled out his watch. Past ten o'clock! He wound the watch, and put it back against his heart. If only he could wind his heart! And squatting there he counted his matches—four! 'Well,' he thought grimly, 'I won't light them to show me my blasted trees. I've got a cigar left; I'll keep them for that.' And he crawled on again. He must keep going while he could!

He crawled till his heart and lungs and knee struck work; and, leaning his back against a tree, sat huddled together, so exhausted that he felt nothing save a sort of bitter heartache. He even dropped asleep, waking with a shudder, dragged from a dream armchair at the club into this cold, wet darkness and the blizzard moaning in the trees. He tried to crawl again, but could not, and for some minute stayed motionless, hugging his body with his arms. "Well," he thought dimly, "I have done it!" His mind was in such lethargy that he could not even pity himself. Then he remembered his cigar. He got it out, bit the end off, and began with infinite precautions to prepare for lighting it.

The first two matches went out. The third burned, and the cigar drew. He had one match left, in case he dozed and let the thing go out. Looking up through the blackness he could see a star. He fixed his eyes on it, and leaning against the trunk, drew the smoke down into lungs. With his arms crossed tightly on his breast he smoked very slowly. When it was finished—what? Cold, and the wind in the trees until the morning! Half-way through the cigar, he dozed off, slept a long time, and woke up so cold that he could barely summon vitality enough to strike his last match. By some miracle it burned, and he got his cigar to draw again. This time he smoked it nearly to its end, without mentality, almost without feeling, except the physical sense of bitter cold. Once with a sudden clearing of the brain, he thought faintly: "Thank God, I sold the——trees, and they'll all come down!" The thought drifted away in frozen incoherence, drifted out like his cigar smoke into the sleet; and with a faint grin on his lips he dozed off again. . . .

An underkeeper found him at ten o'clock next morning, blue from cold, under a tall elm tree, within a mile of his bed, one leg stretched out, the other hunched up toward his chest, with its foot dug into the undergrowth for warmth, his head huddled into the collar of his coat, his arms crossed on his breast. They said he must have been dead at least five hours. Along one side snow had drifted against him; but the trunk had saved his back and other side. Above him, the spindly top boughs of that tall tree were covered with green-gold clusters of tiny crinkled elm flowers, against a deep blue sky—gay as a song of perfect praise. The wind had dropped, and after the cold of the night the birds were singing their clearest in the sunshine.

They did not cut down the elm tree under which they found his body, with the rest of the sold timber, but put a little iron fence round it, and a little tablet on its trunk.

1920.

Carnivorine

By Lucy H. Hooper

WHEN I, ELLIS GRAHAM, BEING A MAN OF MIDDLE AGE, MEANS, AND leisure, determined upon starting, last autumn, for Rome, with a view to studying up the localities for my projected history of the Cenci family, I never expected assuredly that a momentous and important task, regarding other people's affairs and not my own, should be imposed upon me. Yet I could not well refuse the mission. I had known the Lambert family for many years, and had always cherished a warm friendship for Mr. and Mrs. Lambert—a friendship which, after the demise of the former, I had continued to his widow. And Julius, the elder son, had been quite a favorite of mine in his boyish days, though I could not altogether sympathize with his craze for scientific pursuits, and especially for botany. It must be confessed, however, that his researches into the formation and functions of the vegetable kingdom had led to some curious discoveries. But these discoveries had only served to arouse in his mind, as he grew to manhood, a wild ambition for further successes in the same line. I never exactly comprehended what course his investigations had taken, but I knew he was deeply interested in the Darwinian theories, and had set himself, in that connection, some inscrutable problem that he was trying to make out. He lived such a secluded life, shut up with his plants and his theories, that I had wholly lost sight of him for some years, though my visits to Mrs. Lambert were still continued.

I was a good deal surprised, however, on the eve of my departure for Europe, to receive from my old friend a few hurried lines, begging that I would call to see her before I left and fixing the very next evening for my visit. I responded to the appeal, and found the usually serene and dignified lady in a state of unwonted emotion.

"I have sent for you, dear Mr. Graham," she said, "to ask if you will undertake for me a very important mission. It is hardly right, I know, for me to make such a request of you, involving, as your consent will surely do, a good deal of trouble and the loss of a considerable portion of your time. But my peace of mind is at stake, and I do not know what else to do if you are not willing to help me."

"Anything that is in my power to execute, dear Mrs. Lambert, I will gladly undertake," I answered. And, indeed, I was so much moved by her distress and by noticing the traces left upon her still fair features by wearing anxiety, that I was ready to promise anything or to undertake anything in her behalf.

"I want you to find Julius for me."

"Julius? Is he absent from home? I did not even know that he had gone away."

"Yes; he sailed for Europe three years ago. You know, his uncle left him a handsome fortune a little before that time, and he went abroad—to pursue, as he stated, his scientific experiments. I know that he believed himself to be on the verge of a great discovery; but, of what nature that discovery was, he never would reveal, even to me. As you may remember, I have never sympathized with him in his studies, so I suppose he did not consider me worthy of his confidence. Perhaps I did wrong. Maybe, if I had interested myself more in his pursuits, he would not have left me as he has done. He told me, before he went away, that his experiments must be perfected in thorough seclusion, and that he never meant to relinquish them till he had arrived at some great result. We heard from him, afterward, at Paris, and, later on, at Milan; but he has not written to his brothers or to me for months."

"Have you no idea as to his whereabouts at present?"

"I have reason to think that he has taken up his abode somewhere in the neighborhood of Rome. He was seen there, two winters ago, by Alan

Spencer, the artist—who had quite a talk with him, but who could find out nothing from him respecting his residence or his pursuits."

"Did he seem well?"

"He looked tired and haggard, Mr. Spencer said, but was otherwise well. The reason for my anxiety is—is—well, I may as well confess it to you at once: I fear that there is some entanglement in the case—a passion for some woman, who may entrap Julius into matrimony."

"And have you any foundation for this dread?"

"Only this: he let fall something to Mr. Spencer about a personage called Carnivorine."

"What an extraordinary name! Did he give his friend any information concerning her?"

"No. He was singularly reticent on the subject, and seemed really distressed at having let even her name slip out unawares. He requested Mr. Spencer never to mention it; but Alan has always been on very intimate terms with Richard and Maude, and, seeing how uneasy we were at Julius's long silence, he did not hesitate, not having made any promise of secrecy, to tell us the little that he knew. So, when you reach Rome, if you will try to find our lost Julius for us, I shall be more indebted to you than I can well tell you."

I promised to do my best, and Mrs. Lambert, visibly relieved, added some details about her son's banker in Rome and also respecting the few persons that he knew in that city, and who might have learned something concerning him during the last few months. Also, she gave me the name and address of the herbalist before whose door—and, indeed, issuing from it—Alan Spencer had met Julius in such an unexpected fashion.

"You will write to me as soon as you have any news," she said, wistfully, to me, at parting. "And, above all, let me know everything you can find out about Carnivorine. Do not hesitate to tell me the worst—even if Julius has married this creature with the singular name."

I must confess that, when I first arrived in Rome, so many personal interests claimed me that I did not at once begin my search for Julius Lambert, as I had intended to do. There were so many of my old friends and old haunts to revisit, and such numbers of new and interesting statues in the studios of the Roman sculptors, both native and foreign, to go to see, and my negotiations with the artists who were to execute the illustrations for my history of the Cenci family took up so much time, that the weeks insensibly slipped away before I had taken any steps in the matter. I had had the time to receive more than one letter from Mrs. Lambert on the subject before I commenced my investigations. I must acknowledge that I had come to the conclusion that the mystery, on investigation, would prove to be no mystery at all, and that Julius would be discovered in one of the minor hotels in Rome—too busy, or perhaps too much in love, to write. But, when I did finally set out in search of him, I found myself baffled at the very outset by an impenetrable wall of mystery. Nobody had seen him, and nobody knew anything about him. He had drawn all his funds from the banker's on his first arrival in the city. He had been in Rome some two years before, and had bought a collection of the curious insect-eating plants of South America from the old herbalist at whose door Alan Spencer had met him. That was all. If the earth had opened beneath his feet and had swallowed him up, he could not have vanished more utterly from human ken. I sought for him in every direction. I employed the services of a private detective. I offered a reward for any news of him. All was of no use. I succeeded in learning that he had not left Rome—and that was all I could find out.

Some months had elapsed, and I had pretty much abandoned the search in despair, when one day the fancy took me to go on a ride on horseback over the Campagna. I had long cherished the desire to explore the less frequented and scarcely known districts of that vast region, haunted by malaria and tenanted only by a few fever-stricken shepherds, that lies outside the beaten track of tourists and travelers beyond the city walls. As may be imagined, I found my excursion rather dreary. I rode on and on, passing now a flock of sheep watched over by a brigand-looking guardian and a fierce rough dog that looked ready, at a word or a sign from his master, to tear down my horse and throttle its rider, and then some huge arch of a ruined aqueduct that in the days of classic Rome had been musical with laughing water. Sometimes I came upon the shattered fragments of an abandoned hovel, or met with a herd of the gray-coated long-horned oxen of the region, beautiful, placid-looking creatures, that gazed at me inquiringly out of their large soft eyes as I rode by, as though saying, What is this stranger doing in this home of solitude and ruin? Still, I was interested by the very novelty of the dreary region, and I rode on and on, till the sun began to sink toward the western horizon. I have always considered myself fever-proof, but, all the same, a ride after sunset over the Campagna is not the healthiest experiment in the world, so I wheeled my horse round and started to return to the city. And, as I did so, I became aware of the existence of a house at a very short distance. I might very well have passed it without noticing it, as it was so embowered in a mass of vegetation, vines, and bushes, as well as trees, that its shape and architecture were barely discernible. As I rode nearer, I saw that it was a modern villa of imposing dimensions, which had been suffered to fall into almost total ruin. Whether the freak of a speculator or the wild idea of some Campagna proprietor had caused the erection, in this lonely unhealthy place, of a costly country residence, there was no evidence to reveal. The grounds, once spacious and well laid out, were overrun with a thick undergrowth of plants and grasses. Here and there, a statue in white marble, streaked with damp and green with mold, showed under the shadow of the trees, and one, a graceful figure of a nymph, overthrown from its pedestal, lay prostrate amongst the rank grass. The facade of the house itself was adorned with moss-grown sculptures, and one of the pillars supporting the doorway had been broken away and its place was supplied by the trunk of a cypress. One-half of the building showed deserted and ruinous with its broken windows and decaying roof. But there were traces elsewhere of human habitation. The roof of the right wing had been mended, the windows were in good condition, and a gleam of firelight from the lower rooms gave a cheery aspect to that part of the edifice. And, oddly enough, in spite of the universal decay and dilapidation, there were traces not only of comfort, but of luxury, in one portion of the premises, which I noticed as I drew near. This was a large conservatory adjoining the inhabited portion of the house. It was in perfect order. Not a pane was missing in its glazed walls, through which I could discern the red glare of the stove-fires within, as well as the dull green of the foliage of the plants.

Both I and my horse were weary, so I decided that I would halt for an hour or so at this singular habitation, and try for a feed of oats for my horse, as well as for a flask of Chianti and a crust of bread for myself. I drew rein at the dilapidated doorway, and, just as I was about to announce my presence by a resounding knock from the butt-end of my riding-whip, the door was suddenly opened and a man came hurriedly forth. He started when he saw me, and was about to retreat into the house; but, by the red light of the waning sunset, I discerned his features and recognized him instantly. It was the man I had so long sought for and in vain—it was Julius Lambert.

"Julius!" I cried, as he was about to vanish through the door-way. "Julius Lambert! Is it thus that you treat an old friend who has come so far to visit you?"

He turned back at the sound of my voice. "So it is really you, Mr. Graham," he said, hesitatingly. "How in the world did you ever find me or the Villa Anzieri? Nobody has come near it or me either, for over two years past. But come in—my man shall take charge of your horse—and you can tell me something about home matters."

I willingly relinquished the charge of my wearied steed to the black-eyed, bronze-complexioned, picturesque-looking young fellow who came in answer to his master's call, and I followed Julius into the house. I could hardly believe my senses, or that I had found my missing friend at last. It had all happened so simply and yet so strangely. Meanwhile Julius, after he had gotten over the first shock of my intrusion, seemed really glad to see me. He piled fresh wood on the fire, and gave orders that dinner should be served as soon as possible, and plied me with questions respecting his mother and his brother and sisters. As for himself, I found him looking far from well. He was never very stout, but he had grown lean and emaciated, and the yellowish pallor of his face gave evidence of the effects that the malaria of the Campagna had on his system. Dinner was served at last—a very palatable stew flavored with red peppers and tomatoes, with the accompaniment of some fine oranges and grapes by way of dessert, and a flask or two of Chianti wine and one of the delicate Chita Lavinia. Throughout the re-past, I noticed with pain that Julius talked in a feverish incoherent way, pressing me to eat or to drink, and hurrying questions and remarks about home matters, half the time without waiting for an answer.

At last, pushing my plate aside, I remarked:

"Now, Julius, I have told you everything that you wished to know. It is my turn now to ask for a little information. What have you been doing all this long time in this solitude?"

He moved uneasily in his chair, and his wandering glance avoided mine.

"Nothing," he muttered—"I have done—I am doing—nothing."

"Nonsense! You cannot persuade me of the truth of that assertion, so ardent an experimentalist as you have always been, and so interested in the cause of science. Confess, now—have you not made, or are you not on the verge of perfecting, some great discovery?"

I had touched the right chord. His eyes flashed, and his whole countenance grew bright with animation.

"Yes!" he cried. "I have succeeded at last in my researches. For years I have tried to perfect a demonstration of the link between the vegetable and the animal kingdom. If you have come to scoff at my discoveries, go—go at once! Otherwise, follow me—and be prepared for full conviction as to the truth of what I have said."

He rose as he spoke, and, taking me by the hand, he led me to a door at the extremity of the large room in which we had dined. This door he unlocked with a key which he took from his pocket. Night had closed in, and he completed his preparations by lighting a great torch of pine-branches.

"Wait on the threshold, as you value your life," he said to me, impressively. Then he threw open the door.

It was the entrance to the conservatory. The first thing that struck me was a sort of faint rustling sound like that of a trailing garment or a sweeping bird's-wing. Then, by the light of the torch which Julius held on high, I discerned, in the centre of the room, a vast tub filled with masses of spongy moss, from which rose a strange plant—a hideous shapeless monster: a sort of vegetable hydra—or, rather, octopus—gigantic in size and repulsive in aspect and in coloring. So immense were its proportions, that it filled by itself the whole space of the conservatory. It consisted of a central bladder-shaped trunk or core, from which sprang countless branches—or, rather, arms—thick, leafless, of a livid green, and streaked with blotches of a dull-crimson. Each arm terminated in an oval protuberance which had a resemblance to the human eye. Julius took, from a basket that stood near the door, a great slice of raw meat, and, fastening it to the end of a stick, he advanced it, taking infinite precautions to keep well out of reach within the circle of outstretched branches. Then I saw these great tentacle-like arms fold around their prey, which they transmitted to the central core; and then, closing around it, I saw it no more. It was this slow motion of the branches that had caused the rustling sound which had amazed me on my first entrance.

So repulsive was the aspect of this enormous creature, half plant and half animal, that I was glad to beat a retreat to the dining-room. Julius followed, flushed and elated at the healthful aspect of his monstrous creation.

"The plant you have just seen," he said, "is a Drosera, which, by dint of careful selection and persevering attention, I have developed into this unheard-of size. I have studied the discoveries of Warming and of Darwin concerning those strange plants, the Drosera and the Dioncea—which, though still vegetables, feed on the insects that they kill. It has been my desire for years to perfect the missing link and to develop the animal side of these curious vegetable natures. It has always been my theory that the hydra, the dragon, and other monstrous forms of animal life really did exist, and that, in the evolution of ages and by reason of geological changes on the surface of the earth, these creatures, deprived of their accustomed forms of nourishment, degenerated into trees and plants and took root in the earth. Some of them still preserve their primitive forms, as witness the dragon-tree of Java. It has been my aim and endeavor to resuscitate the animal in the plant. Chance threw in my way a Drosera of great size. I have fed it on animal food for years, and developed it into something that is not yet a dragon or a hydra, but which is surely something more than a plant. Had you ventured within reach of its branches, the grasp of a boa would not have been more swift or more deadly."

"And what further do you propose doing with your dreadful plant?"

"My aim now is to give it locomotion—to see it detach itself from the soil and go forth in search of prey."

"How can you contemplate the possibility of letting loose such a monster on the world?"

"For science, there is no such thing as a monster. Moreover, are there not crocodiles and anacondas and tigers upon earth, to say nothing of the shark and the octopus? Beside these, my creation—my Carnivorine—is a harmless creature."

I started as I heard the name. So this, then, was the object of my poor friend's affections—this ghastly shape, not yet wholly animal, yet scarcely vegetable, with the form of a plant and the appetites of a beast of prey?

Just then, Pietro, the man-servant, came in to announce that my horse was at the door. It was a beautiful moonlight night, promising a pleasant ride to the city. I took my leave of Julius, therefore, with something of the feeling of relief of a man who awakes from sleep after having been oppressed by a terrible nightmare. But I did not depart without leaving my address, and I begged Julius to let me know if his strange discovery took any new developments in the near future.

Weeks passed away, and I had nearly forgotten all about Julius and Carnivorine, when one day I received a letter from him, written in a strain of great exultation and excitement. "Come to me, dear friend," he wrote; "come at once! The hour of the perfecting of my experiment is at hand. Already, amid the masses that surround Carnivorine, I discern the stirring and striving of the roots, that are acquiring powers of independent locomotion. In a few days, the problem will be solved. I want you to be present as a witness of the phenomenon. My ambition is satisfied at last—my name shall be inscribed on the list of the great discoverers of the world of science. Come to me, and be at my side in the moment of my triumph."

It was not without difficulty that I once more made my way to the Villa Anzieri. It was late in the afternoon when I drew rein at the dilapidated doorway that I remembered so well. I knocked loudly at the door, but there was no response to my call. Looking around, I saw that the whole place wore an inexplicable air of desertion. No firelight was visible at the windows, and the red glare of the stove-fire no longer shone behind the dim panes of the hot-house. Finally, in vague alarm, finding that my shouts and knocking produced no response, I tied my horse to one of the door-posts, and, singling out a window of the large room in which we had dined on the occasion of my former visit, I swung myself up to it by the help of a thick stem of ivy, and peered into the room. The sight that I beheld within froze my soul with horror.

At the end of the room, near the entrance to the conservatory, rose the hideous form of Carnivorine, no longer planted in a tub, but supported on what seemed, to me, a pair of paddle-like feet or paws like those of some misshapen antediluvian animal. The powerful branches—or, rather, tentacles—were upraised and closely folded around some central object. And at the summit of these livid green, closely-pressed, serpent-like stems appeared a ghastly object: it was a livid human head—the head of a corpse—and the pallid features were those of Julius Lambert!

With one stroke of my arm, I burst open the casement. I sprang into the room and hastened toward the dreadful object. The long arms quivered and began to unfold themselves. But, before the creature could put itself in motion, a shot from the revolver that I always carried during my Campagna wanderings pierced its central core. The tentacles fell apart, and the hideous plant sank prone upon the ground, bearing with it, in its fall, the crushed and lifeless form of Julius Lambert. A stream of reddish sap that looked like blood flowed from the shattered stem and mingled with the branches, stained as they were with a ruddier crimson—the life-blood of my unhappy friend.

I never discovered how or when the catastrophe took place. From the condition of the body, death must have taken place at least twenty-four hours before my arrival. The servants, brought face-to-face with such a shocking—and, to them, inexplicable—catastrophe, had fled from the house, taking with them whatever money or valuables they could lay their hands upon. I tried to trace them out, but in vain. As to the rest, it was all mere conjecture on my part. The uptorn earth and mosses in the tub in which Carnivorine had originally found an abode seemed to prove that a sudden development of the long-sought-for powers of locomotion in the creature had unexpectedly taken place, and that Julius had been seized either in the act of inspecting its condition or at the moment of offering it food. At all events, the vegetable-animal or animal-vegetable had made a solitary trial of its newly-formed powers, and had found a solitary prey when the bullet from my pistol put an end to its existence.

Among the papers left behind by Julius was a series of memoranda respecting the experiments he had tried and the processes he had used to bring his dread creation to full perfection. These I destroyed without hesitation. It would not have been well to have suffered the race of the vegetable octopus to be extended and propagated by curious scientists in the future. Then, lest a new growth should spring from the stem or branches of the accursed tree, I hewed them to pieces with my own hand and burned the fragments to ashes. The annihilation of my friend's discovery may be a loss to science, but humanity will only have cause to rejoice in the total destruction of Carnivorine.

The Ring of Thoth

By Arthur Conan Doyle

MR. JOHN VANSITTART SMITH, F.R.S., OF 147-A GOWER STREET, WAS a man whose energy of purpose and clearness of thought might have placed him in the very first rank of scientific observers. He was the victim, however, of a universal ambition which prompted him to aim at distinction in many subjects rather than preeminence in one.

In his early days he had shown an aptitude for zoology and for botany which caused his friends to look upon him as a second Darwin, but when a professorship was almost within his reach he had suddenly discontinued his studies and turned his whole attention to chemistry. Here his researches upon the spectra of the metals had won him his fellowship in the Royal Society; but again he played the coquette with his subject, and after a year's absence from the laboratory he joined the Oriental Society, and delivered a paper on the Hieroglyphic and Demotic inscriptions of El Kab, thus giving a crowning example both of the versatility and of the inconstancy of his talents.

The most fickle of wooers, however, is apt to be caught at last, and so it was with John Vansittart Smith. The more he burrowed his way into Egyptology the more impressed he became by the vast field which it opened to the inquirer, and by the extreme importance of a subject which promised to throw a light upon the first germs of human civilisation and the origin of the greater part of our arts and sciences. So struck was Mr. Smith that he straightway married an Egyptological young lady who had written upon the sixth dynasty, and having thus secured a sound base of operations he set himself to collect materials for a work which should unite the research of Lepsius and the ingenuity of Champollion. The preparation of this magnum opus entailed many hurried visits to the magnificent Egyptian collections of the Louvre, upon the last of which, no longer ago than the middle of last October, he became involved in a most strange and noteworthy adventure.

The trains had been slow and the Channel had been rough, so that the student arrived in Paris in a somewhat befogged and feverish condition. On reaching the Hotel de France, in the Rue Laffitte, he had thrown himself upon a sofa for a couple of hours, but finding that he was unable to sleep, he determined, in spite of his fatigue, to make his way to the Louvre, settle the point which he had come to decide, and take the evening train back to Dieppe. Having come to this conclusion, he donned his greatcoat, for it was a raw rainy day, and made his way across the Boulevard des Italiens and down the Avenue de l'Opera. Once in the Louvre he was on familiar ground, and he speedily made his way to the collection of papyri which it was his intention to consult.

The warmest admirers of John Vansittart Smith could hardly claim for him that he was a handsome man. His high-beaked nose and prominent chin had something of the same acute and incisive character which distinguished his intellect. He held his head in a birdlike fashion, and birdlike, too, was the pecking motion with which, in conversation, he threw out his objections and retorts. As he stood, with the high collar of his greatcoat raised to his ears, he might have seen from the reflection in the glass-case before him that his appearance was a singular one. Yet it came upon him as a sudden jar when an English voice behind him exclaimed in very audible tones, "What a queer-looking mortal!"

The student had a large amount of petty vanity in his composition which manifested itself by an ostentatious and overdone disregard of all personal considerations. He straightened his lips and looked rigidly at the roll of papyrus, while his heart filled with bitterness against the whole race of travelling Britons.

"Yes," said another voice, "he really is an extraordinary fellow."

"Do you know," said the first speaker, "one could almost believe that by the continual contemplation of mummies the chap has become half a mummy himself?"

"He has certainly an Egyptian cast of countenance," said the other.

John Vansittart Smith spun round upon his heel with the intention of shaming his countrymen by a corrosive remark or two. To his surprise and relief, the two young fellows who had been conversing had their shoulders turned towards him, and were gazing at one of the Louvre attendants who was polishing some brass-work at the other side of the room.

"Carter will be waiting for us at the Palais Royal," said one tourist to the other, glancing at his watch, and they clattered away, leaving the student to his labours.

"I wonder what these chatterers call an Egyptian cast of countenance," thought John Vansittart Smith, and he moved his position slightly in order to catch a glimpse of the man's face. He started as his eyes fell upon it. It was indeed the very face with which his studies had made him familiar. The regular statuesque features, broad brow, well-rounded chin, and dusky complexion were the exact counterpart of the innumerable statues, mummy-cases, and pictures which adorned the walls of the apartment. The thing was beyond all coincidence. The man must be an Egyptian. The national angularity of the shoulders and narrowness of the hips were alone sufficient to identify him.

John Vansittart Smith shuffled towards the attendant with some intention of addressing him. He was not light of touch in conversation, and found it difficult to strike the happy mean between the brusqueness of the superior and the geniality of the equal. As he came nearer, the man presented his side face to him, but kept his gaze still bent upon his work. Vansittart Smith, fixing his eyes upon the fellow's skin, was conscious of a sudden impression that there was something inhuman and preternatural about its appearance. Over the temple and cheek-bone it was as glazed and as shiny as varnished parchment. There was no suggestion of pores. One could not fancy a drop of moisture upon that arid surface. From brow to chin, however, it was cross-hatched by a million delicate wrinkles, which shot and interlaced as though Nature in some Maori mood had tried how wild and intricate a pattern she could devise.

"Ou est la collection de Memphis?" asked the student, with the awkward air of a man who is devising a question merely for the purpose of opening a conversation.

"C'est la," replied the man brusquely, nodding his head at the other side of the room.

"Vous etes un Egyptien, n'est-ce pas?" asked the Englishman.

The attendant looked up and turned his strange dark eyes upon his questioner. They were vitreous, with a misty dry shininess, such as Smith had never seen in a human head before. As he gazed into them he saw some strong emotion gather in their depths, which rose and deepened until it broke into a look of something akin both to horror and to hatred.

"Non, monsieur; je suis Francais." The man turned abruptly and bent low over his polishing. The student gazed at him for a moment in astonishment, and then turning to a chair in a retired corner behind one of the doors he proceeded to make notes of his researches among the papyri. His thoughts, however refused to return into their natural groove. They would run upon the enigmatical attendant with the sphinx-like face and the parchment skin.

"Where have I seen such eyes?" said Vansittart Smith to himself. "There is something saurian about them, something reptilian. There's the membrana nictitans of the snakes," he mused, bethinking himself of his zoological studies. "It gives a shiny effect. But there was something more here. There was a sense of power, of wisdom—so I read them—and of weariness, utter weariness, and ineffable despair. It may be all imagination, but I never had so strong an impression. By Jove, I must have another look at them!" He rose and paced round the Egyptian rooms, but the man who had excited his curiosity had disappeared.

The student sat down again in his quiet corner, and continued to work at his notes. He had gained the information which he required from the papyri, and it only remained to write it down while it was still fresh in his memory. For a time his pencil travelled rapidly over the paper, but soon the lines became less level, the words more blurred, and finally the pencil tinkled down upon the floor, and the head of the student dropped heavily forward upon his chest.

Tired out by his journey, he slept so soundly in his lonely post behind the door that neither the clanking civil guard, nor the footsteps of sight-seers, nor even the loud hoarse bell which gives the signal for closing, were sufficient to arouse him.

Twilight deepened into darkness, the bustle from the Rue de Rivoli waxed and then waned, distant Notre Dame clanged out the hour of midnight, and still the dark and lonely figure sat silently in the shadow. It was not until close upon one in the morning that, with a sudden gasp and an intaking of the breath, Vansittart Smith returned to conscious-ness. For a moment it flashed upon him that he had dropped asleep in his study-chair at home. The moon was shining fitfully through the unshut-tered window, however, and, as his eye ran along the lines of mummies and the endless array of polished cases, he remembered clearly where he was and how he came there. The student was not a nervous man. He possessed that love of a novel situation which is peculiar to his race. Stretching out his cramped limbs, he looked at his watch, and burst into a chuckle as he observed the hour. The episode would make an admirable anecdote to be introduced into his next paper as a relief to the graver and heavier speculations. He was a little cold, but wide awake and much refreshed. It was no wonder that the guardians had overlooked him, for the door threw its heavy black shadow right across him.

The complete silence was impressive. Neither outside nor inside was there a creak or a murmur. He was alone with the dead men of a dead civilisation. What though the outer city reeked of the garish nineteenth century! In all this chamber there was scarce an article, from the shriv-elled ear of wheat to the pigment-box of the painter, which had not held its own against four thousand years. Here was the flotsam and jetsam washed up by the great ocean of time from that far-off empire. From stately Thebes, from lordly Luxor, from the great temples of Heliopolis, from a hundred rifled tombs, these relics had been brought. The student glanced round at the long silent figures who flickered vaguely up through the gloom, at the busy toilers who were now so restful, and he fell into a reverent and thoughtful mood. An unwonted sense of his own youth and insignificance came over him. Leaning back in his chair, he gazed dreamily down the long vista of rooms, all silvery with the moonshine, which extend through the whole wing of the widespread building. His eyes fell upon the yellow glare of a distant lamp.

John Vansittart Smith sat up on his chair with his nerves all on edge. The light was advancing slowly towards him, pausing from time to time, and then coming jerkily onwards. The bearer moved noiselessly. In the utter silence there was no suspicion of the pat of a footfall. An idea of robbers entered the Englishman's head. He snuggled up further into the corner. The light was two rooms off. Now it was in the next chamber, and still there was no sound. With something approaching to a thrill of fear the student observed a face, floating in the air as it were, behind the flare of the lamp. The figure was wrapped in shadow, but the light fell full upon the strange eager face. There was no mistaking the metallic glistening eyes and the cadaverous skin. It was the attendant with whom he had conversed.

Vansittart Smith's first impulse was to come forward and address him. A few words of explanation would set the matter clear, and lead doubtless to his being conducted to some side door from which he might make his way to his hotel. As the man entered the chamber, however, there was something so stealthy in his movements, and so furtive in his expression, that the Englishman altered his intention. This was clearly no ordinary official walking the rounds. The fellow wore felt-soled slippers, stepped with a rising chest, and glanced quickly from left to right, while his hurried gasping breathing thrilled the flame of his lamp. Vansittart Smith crouched silently back into the corner and watched him keenly, convinced that his errand was one of secret and probably sinister import.

There was no hesitation in the other's movements. He stepped lightly and swiftly across to one of the great cases, and, drawing a key from his pocket, he unlocked it. From the upper shelf he pulled down a mummy, which he bore away with him, and laid it with much care and solicitude upon the ground. By it he placed his lamp, and then squatting down beside it in Eastern fashion he began with long quivering fingers to undo the cerecloths and bandages which girt it round. As the crackling rolls of linen peeled off one after the other, a strong aromatic odour filled the chamber, and fragments of scented wood and of spices pattered down upon the marble floor.

It was clear to John Vansittart Smith that this mummy had never been unswathed before. The operation interested him keenly. He thrilled all over with curiosity, and his birdlike head protruded further and further from behind the door. When, however, the last roll had been removed from the four-thousand-year-old head, it was all that he could do to stifle an outcry of amazement. First, a cascade of long, black, glossy tresses poured over the workman's hands and arms. A second turn of the bandage revealed a low, white forehead, with a pair of delicately arched eyebrows. A third uncovered a pair of bright, deeply fringed eyes, and a straight, well-cut nose, while a fourth and last showed a sweet, full, sensitive mouth, and a beautifully curved chin. The whole face was one of extraordinary loveliness, save for the one blemish that in the centre of the forehead there was a single irregular, coffee-coloured splotch. It was a triumph of the embalmer's art. Vansittart Smith's eyes grew larger and larger as he gazed upon it, and he chirruped in his throat with satisfaction.

Its effect upon the Egyptologist was as nothing, however, compared with that which it produced upon the strange attendant. He threw his hands up into the air, burst into a harsh clatter of words, and then, hurling himself down upon the ground beside the mummy, he threw his arms round her, and kissed her repeatedly upon the lips and brow. "Ma petite!" he groaned in French. "Ma pauvre petite!" His voice broke with emotion, and his innumerable wrinkles quivered and writhed, but the student observed in the lamplight that his shining eyes were still as dry and tearless as two beads of steel. For some minutes he lay, with a twitching face, crooning and moaning over the beautiful head. Then he broke into a sudden smile, said some words in an unknown tongue, and sprang to his feet with the vigorous air of one who has braced himself for an effort.

In the centre of the room there was a large circular case which contained, as the student had frequently remarked, a magnificent collection of early Egyptian rings and precious stones. To this the attendant strode, and, unlocking it, he threw it open. On the ledge at the side he placed his lamp, and beside it a small earthenware jar which he had drawn from his pocket. He then took a handful of rings from the case, and with a most serious and anxious face he proceeded to smear each in turn with some liquid substance from the earthen pot, holding them to the light as he did so. He was clearly disappointed with the first lot, for he threw them petulantly back into the case, and drew out some more. One of these, a massive ring with a large crystal set in it, he seized and eagerly tested with the contents of the jar. Instantly he uttered a cry of joy, and threw out his arms in a wild gesture which upset the pot and sent the liquid streaming across the floor to the very feet of the Englishman. The attendant drew a red handkerchief from his bosom, and, mopping up the mess, he followed it into the corner, where in a moment he found himself face to face with his observer.

"Excuse me," said John Vansittart Smith, with all imaginable politeness; "I have been unfortunate enough to fall asleep behind this door."

"And you have been watching me?" the other asked in English, with a most venomous look on his corpse-like face.

The student was a man of veracity. "I confess," said he, "that I have noticed your movements, and that they have aroused my curiosity and interest in the highest degree."

The man drew a long flamboyant-bladed knife from his bosom. "You have had a very narrow escape," he said; "had I seen you ten minutes ago, I should have driven this through your heart. As it is, if you touch me or interfere with me in any way you are a dead man."

"I have no wish to interfere with you," the student answered. "My presence here is entirely accidental. All I ask is that you will have the extreme kindness to show me out through some side door." He spoke with great suavity, for the man was still pressing the tip of his dagger against the palm of his left hand, as though to assure himself of its sharpness, while his face preserved its malignant expression.

"If I thought——" said he. "But no, perhaps it is as well. What is your name?"

The Englishman gave it.

"Vansittart Smith," the other repeated. "Are you the same Vansittart Smith who gave a paper in London upon El Kab? I saw a report of it. Your knowledge of the subject is contemptible."

"Sir!" cried the Egyptologist.

"Yet it is superior to that of many who make even greater pretensions. The whole keystone of our old life in Egypt was not the inscriptions or monuments of which you make so much, but was our hermetic philosophy and mystic knowledge, of which you say little or nothing."

"Our old life!" repeated the scholar, wide-eyed; and then suddenly, "Good God, look at the mummy's face!"

The strange man turned and flashed his light upon the dead woman, uttering a long doleful cry as he did so. The action of the air had already undone all the art of the embalmer. The skin had fallen away, the eyes had sunk inwards, the discoloured lips had writhed away from the yellow teeth, and the brown mark upon the forehead alone showed that it was indeed the same face which had shown such youth and beauty a few short minutes before.

The man flapped his hands together in grief and horror. Then mastering himself by a strong effort he turned his hard eyes once more upon the Englishman.

"It does not matter," he said, in a shaking voice. "It does not really matter. I came here to-night with the fixed determination to do something. It is now done. All else is as nothing. I have found my quest. The old curse is broken. I can rejoin her. What matter about her inanimate shell so long as her spirit is awaiting me at the other side of the veil!"

"These are wild words," said Vansittart Smith. He was becoming more and more convinced that he had to do with a madman.

"Time presses, and I must go," continued the other. "The moment is at hand for which I have waited this weary time. But I must show you out first. Come with me."

Taking up the lamp, he turned from the disordered chamber, and led the student swiftly through the long series of the Egyptian, Assyrian, and Persian apartments. At the end of the latter he pushed open a small door let into the wall and descended a winding stone stair. The Englishman felt the cold fresh air of the night upon his brow. There was a door opposite him which appeared to communicate with the street. To the right of this another door stood ajar, throwing a spurt of yellow light across the passage. "Come in here!" said the attendant shortly.

Vansittart Smith hesitated. He had hoped that he had come to the end of his adventure. Yet his curiosity was strong within him. He could not leave the matter unsolved, so he followed his strange companion into the lighted chamber.

It was a small room, such as is devoted to a concierge. A wood fire sparkled in the grate. At one side stood a truckle bed, and at the other a coarse wooden chair, with a round table in the centre, which bore the remains of a meal. As the visitor's eye glanced round he could not but remark with an ever-recurring thrill that all the small details of the room were of the most quaint design and antique workmanship. The candle-sticks, the vases upon the chimney-piece, the fire-irons, the ornaments upon the walls, were all such as he had been wont to associate with the remote past. The gnarled heavy-eyed man sat himself down upon the edge of the bed, and motioned his guest into the chair.

"There may be design in this," he said, still speaking excellent English. "It may be decreed that I should leave some account behind as a warning to all rash mortals who would set their wits up against workings of Nature. I leave it with you. Make such use as you will of it. I speak to you now with my feet upon the threshold of the other world.

"I am, as you surmised, an Egyptian—not one of the down-trodden race of slaves who now inhabit the Delta of the Nile, but a survivor of that fiercer and harder people who tamed the Hebrew, drove the Ethio-pian back into the southern deserts, and built those mighty works which have been the envy and the wonder of all after generations. It was in the reign of Tuthmosis, sixteen hundred years before the birth of Christ, that I first saw the light. You shrink away from me. Wait, and you will see that I am more to be pitied than to be feared.

"My name was Sosra. My father had been the chief priest of Osiris in the great temple of Abaris, which stood in those days upon the Bubastic branch of the Nile. I was brought up in the temple and was trained in all those mystic arts which are spoken of in your own Bible. I was an apt pupil. Before I was sixteen I had learned all which the wisest priest could teach me. From that time on I studied Nature's secrets for myself, and shared my knowledge with no man.

"Of all the questions which attracted me there were none over which I laboured so long as over those which concern themselves with the nature of life. I probed deeply into the vital principle. The aim of medicine had been to drive away disease when it appeared. It seemed to me that a method might be devised which should so fortify the body as to prevent weakness or death from ever taking hold of it. It is useless that I should recount my researches. You would scarce comprehend them if I did. They were carried out partly upon animals, partly upon slaves, and partly on myself. Suffice it that their result was to furnish me with a substance which, when injected into the blood, would endow the body with strength to resist the effects of time, of violence, or of disease. It would not indeed confer immortality, but its potency would endure for many thousands of years. I used it upon a cat, and afterwards drugged the creature with the most deadly poisons. That cat is alive in Lower Egypt at the present moment. There was nothing of mystery or magic in the matter. It was simply a chemical discovery, which may well be made again.

"Love of life runs high in the young. It seemed to me that I had broken away from all human care now that I had abolished pain and driven death to such a distance. With a light heart I poured the accursed stuff into my veins. Then I looked round for some one whom I could benefit. There was a young priest of Thoth, Parmes by name, who had won my goodwill by his earnest nature and his devotion to his studies. To him I whispered my secret, and at his request I injected him with my elixir. I should now, I reflected, never be without a companion of the same age as myself.

"After this grand discovery I relaxed my studies to some extent, but Parmes continued his with redoubled energy. Every day I could see him working with his flasks and his distiller in the Temple of Thoth, but he said little to me as to the result of his labours. For my own part, I used to walk through the city and look around me with exultation as I reflected that all this was destined to pass away, and that only I should remain. The people would bow to me as they passed me, for the fame of my knowledge had gone abroad.

"There was war at this time, and the Great King had sent down his soldiers to the eastern boundary to drive away the Hyksos. A Governor, too, was sent to Abaris, that he might hold it for the King. I had heard much of the beauty of the daughter of this Governor, but one day as I walked out with Parmes we met her, borne upon the shoulders of her slaves. I was struck with love as with lightning. My heart went out from me. I could have thrown myself beneath the feet of her bearers. This was my woman. Life without her was impossible. I swore by the head of Horus that she should be mine. I swore it to the Priest of Thoth. He turned away from me with a brow which was as black as midnight.

"There is no need to tell you of our wooing. She came to love me even as I loved her. I learned that Parmes had seen her before I did, and had shown her that he too loved her, but I could smile at his passion, for I knew that her heart was mine. The white plague had come upon the city and many were stricken, but I laid my hands upon the sick and nursed them without fear or scathe. She marvelled at my daring. Then I told her my secret, and begged her that she would let me use my art upon her.

"'Your flower shall then be unwithered, Atma,' I said. 'Other things may pass away, but you and I, and our great love for each other, shall outlive the tomb of King Chefru.'

"But she was full of timid, maidenly objections. 'Was it right?' she asked, 'was it not a thwarting of the will of the gods? If the great Osiris had wished that our years should be so long, would he not himself have brought it about?'

"With fond and loving words I overcame her doubts, and yet she hesitated. It was a great question, she said. She would think it over for this one night. In the morning I should know her resolution. Surely one night was not too much to ask. She wished to pray to Isis for help in her decision.

"With a sinking heart and a sad foreboding of evil I left her with her tirewomen. In the morning, when the early sacrifice was over, I hurried to her house. A frightened slave met me upon the steps. Her mistress was ill, she said, very ill. In a frenzy I broke my way through the attendants, and rushed through hall and corridor to my Atma's chamber. She lay upon her couch, her head high upon the pillow, with a pallid face and a glazed eye. On her forehead there blazed a single angry purple patch. I knew that hell-mark of old. It was the scar of the white plague, the sign-manual of death.

"Why should I speak of that terrible time? For months I was mad, fevered, delirious, and yet I could not die. Never did an Arab thirst after the sweet wells as I longed after death. Could poison or steel have shortened the thread of my existence, I should soon have rejoined my love in the land with the narrow portal. I tried, but it was of no avail. The accursed influence was too strong upon me. One night as I lay upon my couch, weak and weary, Parmes, the priest of Thoth, came to my chamber. He stood in the circle of the lamplight, and he looked down upon me with eyes which were bright with a mad joy.

"'Why did you let the maiden die?' he asked; 'why did you not strengthen her as you strengthened me?'

"'I was too late,' I answered. 'But I had forgot. You also loved her. You are my fellow in misfortune. Is it not terrible to think of the centuries which must pass ere we look upon her again? Fools, fools, that we were to take death to be our enemy!'

"'You may say that,' he cried with a wild laugh; 'the words come well from your lips. For me they have no meaning.'

"'What mean you?' I cried, raising myself upon my elbow. 'Surely, friend, this grief has turned your brain.' His face was aflame with joy, and he writhed and shook like one who hath a devil.

"'Do you know whither I go?' he asked.

"'Nay,' I answered, 'I cannot tell.'

"'I go to her,' said he. 'She lies embalmed in the further tomb by the double palm-tree beyond the city wall.'

"'Why do you go there?' I asked.

"'To die!' he shrieked, 'to die! I am not bound by earthen fetters.'

"'But the elixir is in your blood,' I cried.

"'I can defy it,' said he; 'I have found a stronger principle which will destroy it. It is working in my veins at this moment, and in an hour I shall be a dead man. I shall join her, and you shall remain behind.'

"As I looked upon him I could see that he spoke words of truth. The light in his eye told me that he was indeed beyond the power of the elixir.

"'You will teach me!' I cried.

"'Never!' he answered.

"'I implore you, by the wisdom of Thoth, by the majesty of Anubis!'

"'It is useless,' he said coldly.

"'Then I will find it out,' I cried.

"'You cannot,' he answered; 'it came to me by chance. There is one ingredient which you can never get. Save that which is in the ring of Thoth, none will ever more be made.

"'In the ring of Thoth!' I repeated; 'where then is the ring of Thoth?'

"'That also you shall never know,' he answered. 'You won her love. Who has won in the end? I leave you to your sordid earth life. My chains are broken. I must go!' He turned upon his heel and fled from the chamber. In the morning came the news that the Priest of Thoth was dead.

"My days after that were spent in study. I must find this subtle poison which was strong enough to undo the elixir. From early dawn to midnight I bent over the test-tube and the furnace. Above all, I collected the papyri and the chemical flasks of the Priest of Thoth. Alas! they taught me little. Here and there some hint or stray expression would raise hope in my bosom, but no good ever came of it. Still, month after month, I struggled on. When my heart grew faint I would make my way to the tomb by the palm-trees. There, standing by the dead casket from which the jewel had been rifled, I would feel her sweet presence, and would whisper to her that I would rejoin her if mortal wit could solve the riddle.

"Parmes had said that his discovery was connected with the ring of Thoth. I had some remembrance of the trinket. It was a large and weighty circlet, made, not of gold, but of a rarer and heavier metal brought from the mines of Mount Harbal. Platinum, you call it. The ring had, I remembered, a hollow crystal set in it, in which some few drops of liquid might be stored. Now, the secret of Parmes could not have to do with the metal alone, for there were many rings of that metal in the Temple. Was it not more likely that he had stored his precious poison within the cavity of the crystal? I had scarce come to this conclusion before, in hunting through his papers, I came upon one which told me that it was indeed so, and that there was still some of the liquid unused.

"But how to find the ring? It was not upon him when he was stripped for the embalmer. Of that I made sure. Neither was it among his private effects. In vain I searched every room that he had entered, every box, and vase, and chattel that he had owned. I sifted the very sand of the desert in the places where he had been wont to walk; but, do what I would, I could come upon no traces of the ring of Thoth. Yet it may be that my labours would have overcome all obstacles had it not been for a new and unlooked-for misfortune.

"A great war had been waged against the Hyksos, and the Captains of the Great King had been cut off in the desert, with all their bowmen and horsemen. The shepherd tribes were upon us like the locusts in a dry year. From the wilderness of Shur to the great bitter lake there was blood by day and fire by night. Abaris was the bulwark of Egypt, but we could not keep the savages back. The city fell. The Governor and the soldiers were put to the sword, and I, with many more, was led away into captivity.

"For years and years I tended cattle in the great plains by the Euphrates. My master died, and his son grew old, but I was still as far from death as ever. At last I escaped upon a swift camel, and made my way back to Egypt. The Hyksos had settled in the land which they had conquered, and their own King ruled over the country. Abaris had been torn down, the city had been burned, and of the great Temple there was nothing left save an unsightly mound. Everywhere the tombs had been rifled and the monuments destroyed. Of my Atma's grave no sign was left. It was buried in the sands of the desert, and the palm-trees which marked the spot had long disappeared. The papers of Parmes and the remains of the Temple of Thoth were either destroyed or scattered far and wide over the deserts of Syria. All search after them was vain.

"From that time I gave up all hope of ever finding the ring or discovering the subtle drug. I set myself to live as patiently as might be until the effect of the elixir should wear away. How can you understand how terrible a thing time is, you who have experience only of the narrow course which lies between the cradle and the grave! I know it to my cost, I who have floated down the whole stream of history. I was old when Ilium fell. I was very old when Herodotus came to Memphis. I was bowed down with years when the new gospel came upon earth. Yet you see me much as other men are, with the cursed elixir still sweetening my blood, and guarding me against that which I would court. Now at last, at last I have come to the end of it!

"I have travelled in all lands and I have dwelt with all nations. Every tongue is the same to me. I learned them all to help pass the weary time. I need not tell you how slowly they drifted by, the long dawn of modern civilisation, the dreary middle years, the dark times of barbarism. They are all behind me now, I have never looked with the eyes of love upon another woman. Atma knows that I have been constant to her.

"It was my custom to read all that the scholars had to say upon Ancient Egypt. I have been in many positions, sometimes affluent, sometimes poor, but I have always found enough to enable me to buy the journals which deal with such matters. Some nine months ago I was in San Francisco, when I read an account of some discoveries made in the neighbourhood of Abaris. My heart leapt into my mouth as I read it. It said that the excavator had busied himself in exploring some tombs recently unearthed. In one there had been found an unopened mummy with an inscription upon the outer case setting forth that it contained the body of the daughter of the Governor of the city in the days of Tuth-mosis. It added that on removing the outer case there had been exposed a large platinum ring set with a crystal, which had been laid upon the breast of the embalmed woman. This, then was where Parmes had hid the ring of Thoth. He might well say that it was safe, for no Egyptian would ever stain his soul by moving even the outer case of a buried friend.

"That very night I set off from San Francisco, and in a few weeks I found myself once more at Abaris, if a few sand-heaps and crumbling walls may retain the name of the great city. I hurried to the Frenchmen who were digging there and asked them for the ring. They replied that both the ring and the mummy had been sent to the Boulak Museum at Cairo. To Boulak I went, but only to be told that Mariette Bey had claimed them and had shipped them to the Louvre. I followed them, and there at last, in the Egyptian chamber, I came, after close upon four thousand years, upon the remains of my Atma, and upon the ring for which I had sought so long.

"But how was I to lay hands upon them? How was I to have them for my very own? It chanced that the office of attendant was vacant. I went to the Director. I convinced him that I knew much about Egypt. In my eagerness I said too much. He remarked that a Professor's chair would suit me better than a seat in the Conciergerie. I knew more, he said, than he did. It was only by blundering, and letting him think that he had over-estimated my knowledge, that I prevailed upon him to let me move the few effects which I have retained into this chamber. It is my first and my last night here.

"Such is my story, Mr. Vansittart Smith. I need not say more to a man of your perception. By a strange chance you have this night looked upon the face of the woman whom I loved in those far-off days. There were many rings with crystals in the case, and I had to test for the platinum to be sure of the one which I wanted. A glance at the crystal has shown me that the liquid is indeed within it, and that I shall at last be able to shake off that accursed health which has been worse to me than the foulest disease. I have nothing more to say to you. I have unburdened myself. You may tell my story or you may withhold it at your pleasure. The choice rests with you. I owe you some amends, for you have had a narrow escape of your life this night. I was a desperate man, and not to be baulked in my purpose. Had I seen you before the thing was done, I might have put it beyond your power to oppose me or to raise an alarm. This is the door. It leads into the Rue de Rivoli. Good night!"

The Englishman glanced back. For a moment the lean figure of Sosra the Egyptian stood framed in the narrow doorway. The next the door had slammed, and the heavy rasping of a bolt broke on the silent night.

It was on the second day after his return to London that Mr. John Vansittart Smith saw the following concise narrative in the Paris correspondence of the Times:—

"Curious Occurrence in the Louvre.—Yesterday morning a strange discovery was made in the principal Egyptian Chamber. The ouvriers who are employed to clean out the rooms in the morning found one of the attendants lying dead upon the floor with his arms round one of the mummies. So close was his embrace that it was only with the utmost difficulty that they were separated. One of the cases containing valuable rings had been opened and rifled. The authorities are of the opinion that the man was bearing away the mummy with some idea of selling it to a private collector, but that he was struck down in the very act by long-standing disease of the heart. It is said that he was a man of uncertain age and eccentric habits, without any living relations to mourn over his dramatic and untimely end."

The Canal

By Everil Worrell

PAST THE SLEEPING CITY THE RIVER SWEEPS; ALONG ITS LEFT BANK THE old canal creeps.

I did not intend that to be poetry, although the scene is poetic—somberly, gruesomely poetic, like the poems of Poe. Too well I know it—too often I have walked over the grass-grown path beside the reflections of black trees and tumble-down shacks and distant factory chimneys in the sluggish waters that moved so slowly, and ceased to move at all.

I shall be called mad, and I shall be a suicide. I shall take no pains to cover up my trail, or to hide the thing that I shall do. What will it matter, afterward, what they say of me? If they knew the truth—if they could vision, even dimly, the beings with whom I have consorted—if the faintest realization might be theirs of the thing I am becoming, and of the fate from which I am saving their city—then they would call me a great hero. But it does not matter what they call me, as I have said before. Let me write down the things I am about to write down, and let them be taken, as they will be taken, for the last ravings of a madman. The city will be in mourning for the thing I shall have done—but its mourning will be of no consequence beside that other fate from which I shall have saved it.

I have always had a taste for nocturnal prowling. We as a race have grown too intelligent to take seriously any of the old, instinctive fears that preserved us through preceding generations. Our sole remaining salvation, then, has come to be our tendency to travel in herds. We wander at night—but our objective is somewhere on the brightly lighted streets, or still somewhere where men do not go alone. When we travel far afield, it is in company. Few of my acquaintance, few in the whole city here, would care to ramble at midnight over the grass-grown path I have spoken of; not because they would fear to do so, but because such things are not being done.

Well, it is dangerous to differ individually from one's fellows. It is dangerous to wander from the beaten road. And the fears that guarded the race in the dawn of time and through the centuries were real fears, founded on reality.

A month ago, I was a stranger here. I had just taken my first position—I was graduated from college only three months before, in the spring. I was lonely, and likely to remain so for some time, for I have always been of a solitary nature, making friends slowly.

I had received one invitation out—to visit the camp of a fellow employee in the firm for which I worked, a camp which was located on the farther side of the wide river, the side across from the city and the canal, where the bank was high and steep and heavily wooded, and little tents blossomed all along the water's edge. At night these camps were a string of sparkling lights and tiny, leaping campfires, and the tinkle of music carried faintly far across the calmly flowing water. That far bank of the river was no place for an eccentric, solitary man to live. But the near bank, which would have been an eyesore to the campers had not the river been so wide—the near bank attracted me from my first glimpse of it.

We embarked in a motor-boat at some distance downstream, and swept up along the near bank, and then out and across the current. I turned my eyes backward. The murk of stagnant water that was the canal, the jumble of low buildings beyond it, the lonely, low-lying waste of the narrow strip of land between canal and river, the dark, scattered trees growing there—I intended to see more of these things.

That week-end bored me, but I repaid myself no later than Monday evening, the first evening when I was back in the city, alone and free. I ate a solitary dinner immediately after leaving the office. I went to my room and slept from 7 until nearly midnight. I wakened naturally, then, for my whole heart was set on exploring the alluring solitude I had discovered.

I dressed, slipped out of the house and into the street, started the motor in my roadster which I had left parked at the curb, and drove through the lighted streets.

I left behind that part of town which was thick with vehicles carrying people home from their evening engagements, and began to thread my way through darker and narrower streets. Once I had to back out of a cul-de-sac, and once I had to detour around a closed block. This part of town was not alluring, even to me. It was dismal without being solitary.

But when I had parked my car on a rough, cobbled street that ran directly down into the inky waters of the canal, and crossed a narrow bridge, I was repaid. A few minutes set my feet on the old tow-path where mules had drawn river-boats up and down only a year or so ago. Across the canal now, as I walked upstream at a swinging pace, the miserable shacks where miserable people lived seemed to march with me, and then fell behind. They looked like places in which murders might be committed, every one of them.

The bridge I had crossed was near the end of the city going north, as the canal marked its western extremity. Ten minutes of walking, and the dismal shacks were quite a distance behind, the river was farther away and the strip of waste land much wider and more wooded, and tall trees across the canal marched with me as the evil-looking houses had done before. Far and faint, the sound of a bell in the city reached my ears. It was midnight.

I stopped, enjoying the desolation around me. It had the savor I had expected and hoped for. I stood for some time looking up at the sky, watching the low drift of heavy clouds, which were visible in the dull reflected glow from distant lights in the heart of the city, so that they appeared to have a lurid phosphorescence of their own. The ground under my feet, on the contrary, was utterly devoid of light. I had felt my way carefully, knowing the edge of the canal partly by instinct, partly by the even more perfect blackness of the water in it, and even holding pretty well to the path, because it was perceptibly sunken below the ground beside it.

Now as I stood motionless in this spot, my eyes upcast, my mind adrift with strange fancies, suddenly my feelings of satisfaction and well-being gave way to something different. Fear was an emotion unknown to me—for those things which make men fear, I had always loved. A graveyard at night was to me a charming place for a stroll and meditation.

But now, the roots of my hair seemed to move upright on my head, and all along the length of my spine I was conscious of a prickling, tingling sensation—such as my forefathers may have felt in the jungle when the hair on their backs stood up the hair on my head was doing now. Also, I was afraid to move; and I knew that there were eyes upon me, and that that was why I was afraid to move. I was afraid of those eyes—afraid to see them, to look into them.

All this while, I stood perfectly still, my face uptilted toward the sky. But after a terrible mental effort, I mastered myself.

Slowly—slowly, with an attempt to propitiate the owner of the unseen eyes by my casual manner, I lowered my own. I looked straight ahead—at the softly swaying silhouette of the tree-tops across the canal as they moved gently in the cool night wind; at the mass of blackness that was those trees, and the opposite shore; at the shiny blackness, where the reflections of the clouds glinted vaguely and disappeared, that was the canal. And again I raised my eyes a little, for just across the canal where the shadows massed most heavily, there was that at which I must look more closely. And now, as I grew accustomed to the greater blackness and my pupils expanded, I dimly discerned the contours of an old boat or barge, half sunken in the water.

An old, abandoned canal-boat.

But was I dreaming, or was there a white-clad figure seated on the roof of the low cabin aft, a pale, heart-shaped face gleaming strangely at me from the darkness, the glow of two eyes seeming to light up the face, and to detach it from the darkness?

Surely, there could be no doubt as to the eyes. They shone as the eyes of animals shine in the dark—with a phosphorescent gleam, and a glimmer of red! Well, I had heard that some human eyes have that quality at night.

But what a place for a human being to be—a girl, too, I was sure. That daintily heart-shaped face was the face of a girl, surely—I was seeing it clearer and clearer, either because my eyes were growing more accustomed to peering into the deeper shadows, or because of that phosphorescence in the eyes that stared back at me.

I raised my voice softly, not to break too much the stillness of night.

"Hello! who's there? Are you lost, or marooned, and can I help?"

There was a little pause. I was conscious of a soft lapping at my feet. A stronger night wind had sprung up, was ruffling the dark waters. I had been over-warm, and where it struck me the perspiration turned cold on my body, so that I shivered uncontrollably.

"You can stay—and talk awhile, if you will. I am lonely, but not lost—I—I live here."

I could hardly believe my ears. The voice was little more than a whisper, but it had carried clearly—a girl's voice, sure enough. And she lived *there*—in an old, abandoned canal-boat, half submerged in the stagnant water.

"You are not *alone* there?"

"No, not alone. My father lives here with me, but he is deaf—and he sleeps soundly."

Did the night wind blow still colder, as though it came to us from some unseen, frozen sea—or was there something in her tone that chilled me, even as a strange attraction drew me toward her? I wanted to draw near to her, to see closely the pale, heart-shaped face, to lose myself in the bright eyes that I had seen shining in the darkness. I wanted—I wanted to hold her in my arms, to find her mouth with mine, to kiss it—

With a start, I realized the nature of my thoughts, and for an instant lost all thought in surprise. Never in my twenty-two years had I felt love before. My fancies had been otherwise directed—a moss-grown, fallen gravestone was a dearer thing to me to contemplate then the fairest face in all the world. Yet, surely, what I felt now was love!

I took a reckless step nearer the edge of the bank.

"Could I come over to you?" I begged. "It's warm, and I don't mind a wetting. It's late, I know—but I would give a great deal to sit beside you and talk, if only for a few minutes before I go back to town. It's a lonely place here for a girl like you to live—your father should not mind if you exchange a few words with someone occasionally."

Was it the unconventionality of my request that made her next words sound like a long-drawn shudder of protest? There was a strangeness in the tones of her voice that held me wondering, every time she spoke.

"No—no. Oh, no! *You must not swim across.*"

"Then—could I come tomorrow, or some day soon, in the daytime; and would you let me come on board then—or would you come on shore and talk to me, perhaps?"

"Not in the daytime—*never* in the daytime!"

Again the intensity of her low-toned negation held me spellbound.

It was not her sense of the impropriety of the hour, then, that had dictated her manner. For surely, any girl with the slightest sense of the fitness of things would rather have a tryst by daytime than after midnight—yet there was an inference in her last words that if I came again it should be at night.

Still feeling the spell that had enthralled me, as one does not forget the presence of a drug in the air that is stealing one's senses, even when those senses begin to wander and to busy themselves with other things, I yet spoke shortly.

"Why do you say, 'Never in the daytime'? Do you mean that I may come more than this once at night, though now you won't let me cross the canal to you at the expense of my own clothes, and you won't put down your plank or drawbridge or whatever you come on shore with, and talk to me here for only a moment? I'll come again, if you'll let me talk to you instead of calling across the water. I'll come again, anytime you will let me—day or night, I don't care. But I only ask you to explain. If I came in the daytime and met your father, wouldn't that be the best thing to do? Then we could be really acquainted—we could be friends."

"In the night time, my father sleeps. In the daytime, *I* sleep. How could I talk to you, or introduce you to my father then? If you came on board this boat in the daytime, you would find my father—and you would be sorry. As for me, I would be sleeping. I could never introduce you to my father, do you see?"

"You sleep soundly, you and your father." Again there was pique in my voice.

"Yes, we sleep soundly."

"And always at different times?"

"Always at different times. We are on guard—one of us is always on guard. We have been hardly used, down there in your city. And we have taken refuge here. And we are always—always—on guard."

The resentment vanished from my breast, and I felt my heart go out to her anew. She was so pale, so pitiful in the night. My eyes were learning better and better how to pierce the darkness, they were giving me a more definite picture of my companion—if I could think of her as a companion, between myself and whom stretched the black water.

The sadness of the lonely scene, the perfection of the solitude itself, these things contributed to her pitifulness. Then there was that strangeness of atmosphere of which, even yet, I had only partly taken note. There was the strange, shivering chill, which yet did not seem like the healthful chill of a cool evening. In fact, it did not prevent me from feeling the oppression of the night, which was unusually sultry. It was like a little breath of deadly cold that came and went, and yet did not alter the temperature of the air itself, as the small ripples on the surface of the water do not concern the water even a foot down.

And even that was not all. There was an unwholesome smell about the night—a dank, moldy smell that might have been the very breath of death and decay. Even I, the connoisseur in all things dismal and unwholesome, tried to keep my mind from dwelling overmuch upon that smell. What it must be to live breathing it constantly in, I could not think. But no doubt the girl and her father were used to it; and no doubt it came from the stagnant water of the canal and from the rotting wood of the old, half-sunken boat that was their refuge.

My heart throbbed with pity again. Their refuge—what a place! And my clearer vision of the girl showed me that she was pitifully thin, even though possessed of the strange face that drew me to her. Her clothes hung around her like old rags, but hers was no scarecrow aspect. Although little flesh clothed her bones, her very bones were beautiful. I was sure the little, pale, heart-shaped face would be more beautiful still, if I could only see it closely. I must see it closely—I must establish some claim to consideration as a friend of the strange, lonely crew of the half-sunken wreck.

"This is a poor place to call a refuge," I said finally. "One might have very little money, and yet do somewhat better. Perhaps I might help you—I am sure I could. If your ill-treatment in the city was because of poverty—I am not rich, but I could help that. I could help you a little with money—if you would let me—or, in any case, I could find a position for you. I'm sure I could do that."

The eyes that shone fitfully toward me like two small pools of water intermittently lit by a cloud-swept sky seemed to glow more brightly. She had been half crouching, half sitting on top of the cabin; now she leaped to her feet with one quick, sinuous, abrupt motion, and took a few rapid, restless steps to and fro before she answered.

When she spoke, her voice was little more than a whisper; yet surely rage was in its shrill sibilance.

"Fool! Do you think you would be helping me, to tie me to a desk, to shut me behind doors, away from freedom, away from the delight of doing my own will, of seeking my own way? Never, never would I let you do that. Rather this old boat, rather a deserted grave under the stars, for my home!"

A boundless surprize swept over me, and a positive feeling of kinship with this strange being, whose face I had hardly seen, possessed me. So I myself might have spoken—so I had often felt, though I had never dreamed of putting my thoughts so definitely, so forcibly. My regularized daytime life was a thing I thought little of; I really lived only in my nocturnal prowlings. Why, this girl was right! All of life should be free—and spent in places that interested and attracted.

How little, how little I knew, that night, that dread forces were tugging at my soul, were finding entrance to it and easy access through the morbid weakness of my nature! How little I knew at what a cost I deviated so radically from my kind, who herd in cities and love well-lit ways and the sight of man, and sweet and wholesome places to be solitary in, when the desire for solitude comes over them!

That night it seemed to me that there was but one important thing in life—to allay the angry passion my unfortunate words had aroused in the breast of my beloved, and to win from her some answering feeling.

"I understand—much better than you think," I whispered tremulously.

"What I want is to see you again, to come to know you. And to serve you in any way that I may. Surely, there must be something in which I can be of use to you. All you have to do from tonight on forever, is to command me. I swear it!"

"You swear *that*—you do swear it?"

Delighted at the eagerness of her words, I lifted my hand toward the dark heavens.

"I swear it. From this night on, forever—I swear it."

"Then listen. Tonight you may not come to me, nor I to you. I do not want you to board this boat, not tonight, not any night. And most of all, not any day. But do not look so sad. I will come to you. No, not tonight. Perhaps not for many nights—yet before very long. I will come to you there, on the bank of the canal, when the water in the canal ceases to flow."

I must have made a gesture of impatience, or of despair. It sounded like a way of saying "never"—for why should the water in the canal cease to flow? She read my thoughts in some way, for she answered them.

"You do not understand. I am speaking seriously—I am promising to meet you there on the bank, and soon. For the water within these banks is moving slower, always slower. Higher up, I have heard that the canal has been drained. Between these lower locks, the water still seeps in and drops slowly, slowly downstream. But there will come a night when it will be quite, quite stagnant—and on that night I will come to you. And when I come, I will ask of you a favor. And you will keep your oath."

It was all the assurance I could get that night. She had come back to the side of the cabin where she had sat crouched before, and she resumed again that posture and sat still and silent, watching me. Sometimes I could see her eyes upon me, and sometimes not. But I felt that their gaze was unwavering. The little cold breeze, which I had finally forgotten while I was talking with her, was blowing again, and the unwholesome smell of decay grew heavier before the dawn.

She would not speak again, nor answer me when I spoke to her, and I grew nervous, and strangely ill at ease.

At last I went away. And in the first faint light of dawn I slipped up the stairs of my rooming-house, and into my own room.

I was deadly tired at the office next day. And day after day slipped away and I grew more and more weary. For a man can not wake day and night without suffering, especially in hot weather, and that was what I was doing. I haunted the old tow-path and waited, night after night, on the bank opposite the sunken boat. Sometimes I saw my lady of the darkness, and sometimes not. When I saw her, she spoke little; but sometimes she sat there on the top of the cabin and let me watch her till the dawn, or until the strange uneasiness that was like fright drove me from her and back to my room, where I tossed restlessly in the heat and dreamed strange dreams, half waking, till the sun shone in on my forehead and I tumbled into my clothes and down to the office again.

Once I asked her why she had made the fanciful condition that she would not come ashore to meet me until the waters of the canal had ceased to run. (How eagerly I studied those waters; how I stole away at noontime more than once, not to approach the old boat, but to watch the almost imperceptible downward drift of bubbles, bits of straw, twigs, rubbish!)

My questioning displeased her, and I asked her that no more. It was enough that she chose to be whimsical. My part was to wait.

It was more than a week later that I questioned her again, this time on a different subject. And after that, I curbed my curiosity relentlessly.

"Never speak to me of things you do not understand about me. Never again, or I will not show myself to you again. And when I walk on the path yonder, it will not be with you."

I had asked her what form of persecution she and her father had suffered in the city, that had driven them out to this lonely place, and where in the city they had lived.

Frightened seriously lest I lose the ground I was sure I had gained with her, I was about to speak of something else. But before I could find the words, her low voice came to me again.

"It was horrible—horrible! Those little houses below the bridge, those houses along the canal—tell me, are they not worse than my boat? Life there was shut in, and furtive. I was not free as I am now—and the freedom I will soon have will make me forget the things I have not yet forgotten. The screaming, the reviling and cursing! Fear and flight! As you pass back by those houses, think how you would like to be shut in one of them, and in fear of your life! And then think of them no more—for I would forget them, and I will never speak of them again!"

I dared not answer her. I was surprized that she had vouchsafed me so much. But surely her words meant this—that before she had come to live on the decaying, water-rotted old boat, she had lived in one of those horrible houses I passed by on my way to her. Those houses, each of which looked like the predestined scene of a murder!

As I left her that night, I felt that I was very daring.

"One or two nights more and you will walk beside me," I called to her. "I have watched the water at noon, and it hardly moves at all. I threw a scrap of paper into the canal, and it whirled and swung a little where a thin skim of oil lay on the water down there—oil from the big, dirty city you are well out of. But though I watched and watched, I could not see it move downward at all. Perhaps tomorrow night, or the night after, you will walk on the bank with me. I hope it will be clear and moonlight; and I will be near enough to see you clearly—as well as you seem always to see me in darkness or moonlight, equally well. And perhaps I will kiss you—but not unless you let me."

And yet, the next day, for the first time, my thoughts were definitely troubled. I had been living in a dream—I began to speculate concerning the end of the path on which my feet were set.

I had conceived, from the first, such a horror of those old houses by the canal! They were well enough to walk past, nursing gruesome thoughts for a midnight treat. But, much as I loved all that was weird and eery about the girl I was wooing so strangely, it was a little too much for my fancy that she had come from them.

By this time, I had become decidedly unpopular in my place of business. Not that I had made enemies, but that my peculiar ways had caused too much adverse comment. It would have taken very little, I think, to have made the entire office force decide that I was mad. After the events of the next twenty-four hours, and after this letter is found and read, they will be sure that they knew it all along! At this time, however, they were punctiliously polite to me, and merely let me alone as much as possible—which suited me perfectly. I dragged wearily through day after day, exhausted for lack of sleep, conscious of their speculative glances, living only for the night to come.

But on this day, I approached the man who had invited me to the camp across the river, who had unknowingly shown me the way that led to my love.

"Have you ever noticed the row of tumble-down houses along the canal on the city side?" I asked him.

He gave me an odd look. I suppose he sensed the significance of my breaking silence after so long to speak of *them*—sensed that in some way I had a deep interest in them.

"You have odd tastes, Morton," he said after a moment. "I suppose you wander into strange places sometimes—I've heard you speak of an enthusiasm for graveyards at night. But my advice to you is to keep away from those houses. They're unsavory, and their reputation is unsavory. Positively, I think you'd be in danger of your life, if you go poking around there. They have been the scene of several murders, and a dope den or two has been cleaned out of them. Why in the world you should want to investigate them——"

"I don't expect to investigate them," I said testily. "I was merely interested in them—from the outside. To tell you the truth, I'd heard a story, a rumor—never mind where. But you say there have been murders there—I suppose this rumor I heard may have had to do with an attempted one. There was a girl who lived there with her father once—and they were set upon there, or something of the sort, and had to run away. Did you ever hear *that* story?"

Barrett gave me an odd look such as one gives in speaking of a past horror so dreadful that the mere speaking of it makes it live terribly again.

"What you say reminds me of a horrible thing that was said to have happened down there once," he said. "It was in all the papers. A little child disappeared in one of those houses—and a girl and her father were accused of having made away with it. They were accused—they were accused—oh, well, I don't like to talk about such things. It was too dreadful. The child's body was found—*part* of it was found. It was mutilated, and the people in the house seemed to believe it had been mutilated in order to conceal the manner of its death—there was an ugly wound in the throat, it finally came out, and it seemed as if the child might have been bled to death. It was found in the girl's room, hidden away. The old man and his daughter escaped, before the police were called. The countryside was scoured for them—the whole country was scoured, but they were never found. Why, you must have read it in the papers—several years ago."

I nodded, with a heavy heart. I *had* read it in the papers, I remembered now. And again, a terrible questioning came over me. Who was this girl, *what* was this girl, who seemed to have my heart in her keeping?

Why did not a merciful God let me die then?

Befogged with exhaustion, bemused in a dire enchantment, my mind was incapable of thought. And yet, some soul-process akin to that which saves the sleepwalker poised at perilous heights sounded its warning now.

My mind was filled with doleful images. There were women—I had heard and read—who slew to satisfy a blood-lust. There were ghosts, specters—call them what you will, their names have been legion in the dark pages of that lore which dates back to the infancy of the races of the earth—who retained even in death this blood-lust. Vampires—they had been called that. I had read of them. Corpses by day, spirits of evil by night, roaming abroad in their own forms or in the forms of bats or unclean beasts, killing body and soul of their victims—for whoever dies of the repeated "kiss" of the vampire, which leaves its mark on the throat and draws the blood from the body, becomes a vampire also—of such beings I had read.

And, horror of horrors! In that last cursed day at the office, I remembered reading of these vampires—these undead—that in their nocturnal flights they had one limitation—*they could not cross running water.*

That night I went my usual nightly way with tears of weakness on my face—for my weakness was supreme, and I recognized fully at last the misery of being the victim of an enchantment stronger than my feeble will. But I went.

I approached the neighborhood of the canal-boat as the distant city clock chimed the first stroke of 12. It was the dark of the moon and the sky was overcast. Heat-lightning flickered low in the sky, seeming to come from every point of the compass and circumscribe the horizon, as if unseen fires burned behind the rim of the world. By its fitful glimmer, I saw a new thing—between the old boat and the canal bank stretched a long, slim, solid-looking shadow—a plank had been let down! In that moment, I realized that I had been playing with powers of evil which had no intent now to let me go, which were indeed about to lay hold upon me with an inexorable grasp. Why had I come tonight? Why, but that the spell of the enchantment laid upon me was a thing more potent, and far more unbreakable, than any wholesome spell of love? The creature I sought out—oh, I remembered now, with the cold perspiration beading my brow, the lore hidden away between the covers of the dark old book which I had read so many years ago and half forgotten!—until dim memories of it stirred within me, this last day and night.

My lady of the night! No woman of wholesome flesh and blood and odd perverted tastes that matched my own, but one of the undead. In that moment, I knew it, and knew that the vampires of old legends polluted still, in these latter days, the fair surface of the earth.

And on the instant, behind me in the darkness there was the crackle of a twig, and something brushed against my arm!

This, then, was the fulfillment of my dream. I knew, without turning my head, that the pale, dainty face with its glowing eyes was near my own—that I had only to stretch out my arm to touch the slender grace of the girl I had so longed to draw near. I knew, and should have felt the rapture I had anticipated. Instead, the roots of my hair prickled coldly, unendurably, as they had on the night when I had first sighted the old boat. The miasmic odors of the night, heavy and oppressive with heat and unrelieved by a breath of air, all but overcame me, and I fought with myself to prevent my teeth clicking in my head. The little waves of coldness I had felt often in this spot were chasing over my body; yet they were not from any breeze; the leaves on the trees hung down motionless, as though they were actually wilting on their branches.

With an effort, I turned my head.

Two hands caught me around my neck. The pale face was so near, that I felt the warm breath from its nostrils fanning my cheek.

And, suddenly, all that was wholesome in my perverted nature rose uppermost. I longed for the touch of the red mouth, like a dark flower opening before me in the night. I longed for it—and yet more I dreaded it. I shrank back, catching in a powerful grip the fragile wrists of the hands that strove to hold me. I must not—I must not yield to the faintness that I felt stealing languorously over me.

I was facing down the path toward the city. A low rumble of thunder—the first—broke the torrid hush of the summer night. A glare of lightning seemed to tear the night asunder, to light up the whole universe. Overhead, the clouds were careening madly in fantastic shapes, driven by a wind that swept the upper heavens without as yet causing even a trembling in the air lower down. And far down the canal, that baleful glare seemed to play around and hover over the little row of shanties—murder-cursed, and haunted by the ghost of a dead child.

My gaze was fixed on them, while I held away from me the pallid face and fought off the embrace that sought to overcome my resisting will. And so a long moment passed. The glare faded out of the sky, and a greater darkness took the world. But there was a near, more menacing glare fastened upon my face—the glare of two eyes that watched mine, that had watched me as I, unthinking, stared down at the dark houses.

This girl—this woman who had come to me at my own importunate requests, did not love me, since I had shrunk from her. She did not love me; but it was not only that. She had watched me as I gazed down at the houses that held her dark past—and I was sure that she divined my thoughts. She knew my horror of those houses—she knew my new-born horror of *her*. And she hated me for it, hated me more malignantly than I had believed a human being could hate.

And at that point in my thoughts, I felt my skin prickle and my scalp rise again: could a *human being* cherish such hatred as I read, trembling more and more, in those glowing fires lit with what seemed to me more like the fires of hell than any light that ought to shine in a woman's eyes?

And through all this, not a word had passed between us!

So far I have written calmly. I wish that I could write on so, to the end. If I could do that there might be one or two of those who will regard this as the document of a maniac, who would believe the horrors of which I am about to write.

But I am only flesh and blood. At this point in the happenings of the awful night, my calmness deserted me—at this point I felt that I had been drawn into the midst of a horrible nightmare from which there was no escape, no waking! As I write, this feeling again overwhelms me, until I can hardly write at all—until, were it not for the thing which I must do, I would rush out into the street and run, screaming, until I was caught and dragged away, to be put behind strong iron bars. Perhaps I would feel safe there—perhaps!

I know that, terrified at the hate I saw confronting me in those redly gleaming eyes, I would have slunk away. The two thin hands that caught my arm again were strong enough to prevent that, however. I had been spared her kiss—I was not to escape from the oath I had taken to serve her.

"You promised—you swore," she hissed in my ear. "And tonight you are to keep your oath."

I felt my senses reel. My oath—yes, I had an oath to keep. I had lifted my hand toward the dark heavens, and sworn to serve her in any way she chose—freely, and of my own volition, I had sworn. I sought to evade her.

"Let me help you back to your boat," I begged. "You have no kindly feeling for me—and—you have seen it—I love you no longer. I will go back to the city—you can go back to your father, and forget that I broke your peace."

The laughter that greeted my speech I shall never forget—not in the depths under the scummy surface of the canal—not in the empty places between the worlds, where my tortured soul may wander.

"So you do not love me, and I hate you! Fool! Have I waited these weary months for the water to stop, only to go back now? After my father and I returned here and found the old boat rotting in the drained canal, and took refuge in it; when the water was turned into the canal while I slept, so that I could never escape until its flow should cease, *because of the thing that I am*—even then I dreamed of tonight.

"When the imprisonment we still shared ceased to matter to my father—come on board the deserted boat tomorrow, and see why, if you dare!—still I dreamed on, of tonight!

"I have been lonely, desolate, starving—now the whole world shall be mine! And by *your* help!"

I asked her, somehow, what she wanted of me, and a madness overcame me, so that I hardly heard her reply. Yet somehow, I knew that there was that on the opposite shore of the great river where the pleasure camps were, that she wanted to find. In the madness of my terror, she made me understand and obey her.

I must carry her in my arms across the long bridge over the river, deserted in the small hours of the night!

The way back to the city was long tonight—long. She walked behind me, and I turned my eyes neither to right nor left. Only as I passed the tumble-down houses, I saw their reflection in the canal and trembled so that I could have fallen to the ground, at the thoughts of the little child this woman had been accused of slaying there, and at the certainty I felt that she was reading my thoughts.

And now the horror that engulfed me darkened my brain.

I know that we set our feet upon the long, wide bridge that spanned the river. I know the storm broke there, so that I battled for my footing, almost for my life, it seemed, against the pelting deluge. And the horror I had invoked was in my arms, clinging to me, burying its head upon my shoulder. So increasingly dreadful had my pale-faced companion become to me, that I hardly thought of her now as a woman at all—only as a demon of the night.

The tempest raged still as she leaped down out of my arms on the other shore. And again I walked with her against my will, while the trees lashed their branches madly around me, showing the pale undersides of their leaves in the vivid frequent flashes that rent the heavens.

On and on we went, branches flying through the air and missing us by a miracle of ill fortune. Such as she and I are not slain by falling branches. The river was a welter of whitecaps, flattened down into strange shapes by the pounding rain. The clouds as we glimpsed them were like devils flying through the sky.

Past dark tent after dark tent we stole, and past a few where lights burned dimly behind their canvas walls. And at last we came to an old quarry. Into its artificial ravine she led me, and up to a crevice in the rock wall.

"Reach in your hand and pull out the loose stone you will feel," she whispered. "It closes an opening that leads into deep caverns. A human hand must remove that stone—your hand must move it!" Why did I struggle so to disobey her? Why did I fail? It was as though I *knew*—but my failure was foreordained—I had taken oath!

If you who read have believed that I have set down the truth thus far, the little that is left you will call the ravings of a madman overtaken by his madness. Yet these things happened.

I stretched out my arm, driven by a compulsion I could not resist. At arm's length in the niche in the rock, I felt something move—the loose rock, a long, narrow fragment, much larger than I had expected. Yet it moved easily, seeming to swing on a natural pivot. Outward it swung, toppling toward me—a moment more and there was a swift rush of the ponderous weight I had loosened. I leaped aside and went down, my forehead grazed by the rock.

For a brief moment I must have been unconscious. But only for a moment. My head a stabbing agony of pain, unreal lights flashing before my eyes, I yet knew the reality of the storm that beat me down as I struggled to my feet. I knew the reality of the dark, loathsome shapes that passed me in the dark, crawling out of the orifice in the rock and flapping through the wild night, along the way that led to the pleasure camps.

So the caverns I had laid open to the outer world were infested with bats. I had been inside unlit caverns, and had heard there the squeaking of the things, felt and heard the flapping of their wings—*but never in all my life before had I sees bats as large as men and women!*

Sick and dizzy from the blow on my head, and from disgust, I crept along the way they were going. If I touched one of them, I felt that I should die of horror.

Now, at last, the storm abated, and a heavy darkness made the whole world seem like the inside of a tomb.

Where the tents stood in a long row, the number of the monster bats seemed to diminish. It was as though—horrible thought!—they were creeping into the tents, with their slumbering occupants.

At last I came to a lighted tent, and paused, crouching so that the dim radiance that shone through the canvas did not touch me in the shadows. And there I waited, but not for long. There was a dark form silhouetted against the tent—a movement of the flap of the tent—a rustle and confusion, and the dark thing was again in silhouette—but with a difference in the quality of the shadow. The dark thing was *inside* the tent now, its bat wings extending across the entrance through which it had crept.

Fear held me spellbound. And as I looked the shadow changed again—imperceptibly, so that I could not have told *how* it changed.

But now it was not the shadow of a bat, but of a woman.

"The storm—the storm! I am lost, exhausted—I crept in here, to beg for refuge until the dawn!"

That low, thrilling, sibilant voice—too well I knew it!

Within the tent I heard a murmur of acquiescent voices. At last I began to understand. I knew the nature of the woman I had carried over the river in my arms, the woman who would not even cross the canal until the water should have ceased utterly to flow. I remembered books I had read—*Dracula*—other books, and stories. I knew they were true books and stories, now—I knew those horrors existed for me.

I had indeed kept my oath to the creature of darkness—I had brought her to her kind, under her guidance. I had let them loose in hordes upon the pleasure camps. The campers were doomed—and through them, others——

I forgot my fear. I rushed from my hiding-place up to the tent door, and there I screamed and called aloud.

"Don't take her in—don't let her stay—nor the others, that have crept into the other tents! Wake all the campers—they will sleep on to their destruction! Drive out the interlopers—drive them out quickly! *They are not human—no, and they are not bats.* Do you hear me?—do you understand?"

I was fairly howling, in a voice that was strange to me.

"She is a vampire—they are all vampires. *Vampires!*"

Inside the tent I heard a new voice. "What can be the matter with that poor man?" the voice said. It was a woman's, and gentle.

"Crazy—somebody out of his senses, dear," a man's voice answered. "Don't be frightened."

And then the voice I knew so well—so well: "I saw a falling rock strike a man on the head in the storm. He staggered away, but I suppose it crazed him."

I waited for no more. I ran away, madly, through the night and back across the bridge to the city.

Next day—today—I boarded the sunken canal-boat. It is the abode of death—no woman could have lived there—only such a one as *she*. The old man's corpse was there—he must have died long, long ago. The smell of death and of decay on the boat was dreadful.

Again, I felt that I understood. Back in those awful houses, she had committed the crime when first she became the thing she is. And he— her father—less sin-steeped, and less accursed, attempted to destroy the evidence of her crime, and fled with her, but died without becoming like her. She had said that one of those two was always on watch—did he indeed divide her vigil on the boat? What more fitting—the dead standing watch with the undead! And no wonder that she would not let me board the craft of death, even to carry her away.

And still I feel the old compulsion. I have been spared her kiss—but for a little while. Yet I will not let the power of my oath to her draw me back, till I enter the caverns with her and creep forth in the form of a bat to prey upon mankind. Before that can happen, I too will die.

Today in the city I heard that a horde of strange insects or small animals infested the pleasure camps last night. Some said, with horror-bated breath, that they perhaps were rats. None of them was seen; but in the morning nearly every camper had a strange, deep wound in his throat. I almost laughed aloud. They were so horrified at the idea of an army of rats, creeping into the tents and biting the sleeping occupants on their throats! If they had seen what I saw—if they knew that they are doomed to spread corruption——

So my own death will not be enough. Today I bought supplies for blasting. Tonight I will set my train of dynamite, from the hole I made in the cliff where the vampires creep in and out, along the row of tents, as far as the last one—then I shall light my fuse. It will be done before the dawn. Tomorrow, the city will mourn its dead and execrate my name. And then, at last, in the slime beneath the unmoving waters of the canal, I shall find peace! But perhaps it will not be peace—for I shall seek it midway between the old boat with its cargo of death and the row of dismal houses where a little child was done to death when first *she* became the thing she is. That is my expiation.

The Dead Smile

By F. Marion Crawford

Chapter I

Sir Hugh Ockram smiled as he sat by the open window of his study, in the late August afternoon. A curiously yellow cloud obscured the low sun, and the clear summer light turned lurid, as if it had been suddenly poisoned and polluted by the foul vapours of a plague. Sir Hugh's face seemed, at best, to be made of fine parchment drawn skin-tight over a wooden mask, in which two sunken eyes peered from far within. The eyes peered from under wrinkled lids, alive and watchful like toads in their holes, side by side and exactly alike. But as the light changed, a little yellow glare flashed in each. He smiled, stretching pale lips across discoloured teeth in an expression of profound self-satisfaction, blended with the most unforgiving hatred and contempt for the human doll.

Nurse Macdonald, who was a hundred years old, said that when Sir Hugh smiled he saw the faces of two women in hell—two dead women he had betrayed. The smile widened.

The hideous disease of which Sir Hugh was dying had touched his brain. His son stood beside him, tall, white and delicate as an angel in a primitive picture. And though there was deep distress in his violet eyes as he looked at his father's face, he felt the shadow of that sickening smile stealing across his own lips, parting and drawing them against his will. It was like a bad dream, for he tried not to smile and smiled the more.

Beside him—strangely like him in her wan, angelic beauty, with the same shadowy golden hair, the same sad violet eyes, the same luminously pale face—Evelyn Warburton rested one hand upon his arm. As she looked into her uncle's eyes, she could not turn her own away and she too knew that the deathly smile was hovering on her own red lips, drawing them tightly across her little teeth, while two bright tears ran down her cheeks to her mouth, and dropped from the upper to the lower lip. The smile was like the shadow of death and the seal of damnation upon her pure, young face.

"Of course," said Sir Hugh very slowly, still looking out at the trees, "if you have made your mind up to be married, I cannot hinder you, and I don't suppose you attach the smallest importance to my consent—"

"Father!" exclaimed Gabriel reproachfully.

"No. I do not deceive myself," continued the old man, smiling terribly. "You will marry when I am dead, though there is a very good reason why you had better not—why you had better not," he repeated very emphatically, and he slowly turned his toad eyes upon the lovers.

"What reason?" asked Evelyn in a frightened voice.

"Never mind the reason, my dear. You will marry just as if it did not exist." There was a long pause. "Two gone," he said, his voice lowering strangely, "and two more will be four all together forever and ever, burning, burning, burning bright."

At the last words his head sank slowly back, and the little glare of his toad eyes disappeared under the swollen lids. Sir Hugh had fallen asleep, as he often did in his illness, even while speaking.

Gabriel Ockram drew Evelyn away, and from the study they went out into the dim hall. Softly closing the door behind them, each audibly drew a breath, as though some sudden danger had been passed. As they laid their hands each in the other's, their strangely-like eyes met in a long look in which love and perfect understanding were darkened by the secret terror of an unknown thing. Their pale faces reflected each other's fear.

"It is his secret," said Evelyn at last. "He will never tell us what it is."

"If he dies with it," answered Gabriel, "let it be on his own head!"

"On his head!" echoed the dim hall. It was a strange echo. Some were frightened by it, for they said that if it were a real echo it should repeat everything and not give back a phrase here and there—now speaking, now silent. Nurse Macdonald said that the great hall would never echo a prayer when an Ockram was to die, though it would give back curses ten for one.

"On his head!" it repeated quite softly, and Evelyn started and looked round.

"It is only the echo," said Gabriel, leading her away.

They went out into the late afternoon light, and sat upon a stone seat behind the chapel, which had been built across the end of the east wing. It was very still. Not a breath stirred, and there was no sound near them. Only far off in the park a song-bird was whistling the high prelude to the evening chorus.

"It is very lonely here," said Evelyn, taking Gabriel's hand nervously and speaking as if she dreaded to disturb the silence. "If it were dark, I should be afraid."

"Of what? Of me?" Gabriel's sad eyes turned to her.

"Oh no! Never of you! But of the old Ockrams. They say they are just under our feet here in the north vault outside the chapel, all in their shrouds, with no coffins, as they used to bury them."

"As they always will. As they will bury my father, and me. They say an Ockram will not lie in a coffin."

"But it cannot be true. These are fairy tales, ghost stories!" Evelyn nestled nearer to her companion, grasping his hand more tightly as the sun began to go down.

"Of course. But there is the story of old Sir Vernon, who was beheaded for treason under James II. The family brought his body back from the scaffold in an iron coffin with heavy locks and put it in the north vault. But ever afterwards, whenever the vault was opened to bury another of the family, they found the coffin wide open, the body standing upright against the wall, and the head rolled away in a corner smiling at it."

"As Uncle Hugh smiles?" Evelyn shivered.

"Yes, I suppose so," answered Gabriel, thoughtfully. "Of course I never saw it, and the vault has not been opened for thirty years. None of us have died since then."

"And if . . . if Uncle Hugh dies, shall you . . . ?" Evelyn stopped. Her beautiful thin face was quite white.

"Yes. I shall see him laid there too, with his secret, whatever it is." Gabriel sighed and pressed the girl's little hand.

"I do not like to think of it," she said unsteadily. "O Gabriel, what can the secret be? He said we had better not marry. Not that he forbade it, but he said it so strangely, and he smiled. Ugh!" Her small white teeth chattered with fear, and she looked over her shoulder while drawing still closer to Gabriel. "And, somehow, I felt it in my own face."

"So did I," answered Gabriel in a low, nervous voice. "Nurse Macdonald—" He stopped abruptly.

"What? What did she say?"

"Oh, nothing. She has told me things. . . . They would frighten you, dear. Come, it is growing chilly." He rose, but Evelyn held his hand in both of hers, still sitting and looking up into his face.

"But we shall be married just the same—Gabriel! Say that we shall!"

"Of course, darling, of course. But while my father is so very ill, it is impossible—"

"O Gabriel, Gabriel, dear! I wish we were married now!" Evelyn cried in sudden distress. "I know that something will prevent it and keep us apart."

"Nothing shall!"

"Nothing?"

"Nothing human," said Gabriel Ockram, as she drew him down to her.

And their faces, that were so strangely alike, met and touched. Gabriel knew that the kiss had a marvelous savor of evil. Evelyn's lips were like the cool breath of a sweet and mortal fear that neither of them understood, for they were innocent and young. Yet she drew him to her by her lightest touch, as a sensitive plant shivers, waves its thin leaves, and bends and closes softly upon what it wants. He let himself be drawn to her willingly—as he would even if her touch had been deadly and poisonous—for he strangely loved that half voluptuous breath of fear, and he passionately desired the nameless evil something that lurked in her maiden lips.

"It is as if we loved in a strange dream," she said.

"I fear the waking," he murmured.

"We shall not wake, dear. When the dream is over it will have already turned into death, so softly that we shall not know it. But until then . . ."

She paused, her eyes seeking his, as their faces slowly came nearer. It was as if each had thoughts in their lips that foresaw and foreknew the other.

"Until then," she said again, very low, her mouth near to his.

"Dream—till then," he murmured.

Chapter II

Nurse MacDonald slept sitting all bent together in a great old leather arm chair with wings—many warm blankets wrapped about her, even in summer. She would rest her feet in a bag footstool lined with sheepskin while beside her, on a wooden table, there was a little lamp that burned at night, and an old silver cup, in which there was always something to drink.

Her face was very wrinkled, but the wrinkles were so small and fine and close together that they made shadows instead of lines. Two thin locks of hair, that were turning from white to a smoky yellow, fell over her temples from under her starched white cap. Every now and then she would wake from her slumber, her eyelids drawn up in tiny folds like little pink silk curtains, and her queer blue eyes would look straight ahead through doors and walls and worlds to a far place beyond. Then she'd sleep again with her hands one upon the other on the edge of the blanket, her thumbs grown longer than the fingers with age.

It was nearly one o'clock in the night, and the summer breeze was blowing the ivy branch against the panes of the window with a hushing caress. In the small room beyond, with the door ajar, the young maid who took care of Nurse Macdonald was fast asleep. All was very quiet. The old woman breathed regularly, and her drawn lips trembled each time the breath went out.

But outside the closed window there was a face. Violet eyes were looking steadily at the ancient sleeper. Strange, as there were eighty feet from the sill of the window to the foot of the tower. It was like the face of Evelyn Warburton, yet the cheeks were thinner than Evelyn's and as white as a gleam. The eyes stared and the lips were red with life. They were dead lips painted with new blood.

Slowly Nurse Macdonald's wrinkled eyelids folded back, and she looked straight at the face at the window.

"Is it time?" she asked in her little old, faraway voice.

While she looked the face at the window changed, the eyes opened wider and wider till the white glared all round the bright violet and the bloody lips opened over gleaming teeth. The shadowy golden hair surrounding the face rose and streamed against the window in the night breeze and in answer to Nurse Macdonald's question came a sound that froze the living flesh.

It was a low-moaning voice, one that rose suddenly, like the scream of storm. Then it went from a moan to a wail, from a wail to a howl, and from a howl to the shriek of the tortured dead. He who has heard it before knows, and he can bear witness that the cry of the banshee is an evil cry to hear alone in the deep night.

When it was over and the face was gone, Nurse Macdonald shook a little in her great chair. She looked at the black square of the window, but there was nothing more there, nothing but the night and the whispering ivy branch. She turned her head to the door that was ajar, and there stood the young maid in her white gown, her teeth chattering with fright.

"It is time, child," said Nurse Macdonald. "I must go to him, for it is the end."

She rose slowly, leaning her withered hands upon the arms of the chair as the girl brought her a woollen gown, a great mantle and her crutch-stick. But very often the girl looked at the window and was unjointed with fear, and often Nurse Macdonald shook her head and said words which the maid could not understand.

"It was like the face of Miss Evelyn," said the girl, trembling.

But the ancient woman looked up sharply and angrily. Her queer blue eyes glared. She held herself up by the arm of the great chair with her left hand, and lifted up her crutch-stick to strike the maid with all her might. But she did not.

"You are a good girl," she said, "but you are a fool. Pray for wit, child. Pray for wit—or else find service in a house other than Ockram Hall. Now bring the lamp and help me up."

Each step Nurse Macdonald took was a labour in itself, and as she moved, the maid's slippers clappered alongside. By the clacking noise the other servants knew that she was coming, very long before they saw her.

No one was sleeping now, and there were lights, and whisperings, and pale faces in the corridors near Sir Hugh's bedroom. Often someone would go in, and someone would come out, but every one made way for Nurse Macdonald, who had nursed Sir Hugh's father more than eighty years ago.

The light was soft and clear in the room. Gabriel Ockram stood by his father's bedside, and there knelt Evelyn Warburton—her hair lying like a golden shadow down her shoulder, and her hands clasped nervously together. Opposite Gabriel, a nurse was trying to make Sir Hugh drink, but he would not. His lips parted, but his teeth were set. He was very, very thin now, and as his eyes caught the light sideways, they were as yellow coals.

"Do not torment him," said Nurse Macdonald to the woman who held the cup. "Let me speak to him, for his hour is come."

"Let her speak to him," said Gabriel in a dull voice.

The ancient nurse leaned to the pillow and laid the feather-weight of her withered hand—that was like a grown moth—upon Sir Hugh's yellow fingers. Then she spoke to him earnestly, while only Gabriel and Evelyn were left in the room to hear.

"Hugh Ockram," she said, "this is the end of your life; and as I saw you born, and saw your father born before you, I come to see you die. Hugh Ockram, will you tell me the truth?"

The dying man recognized the little faraway voice he had known all his life and he very slowly turned his yellow face to Nurse Macdonald, but he said nothing. Then she spoke again.

"Hugh Ockram, you will never see the daylight again. Will you tell the truth?"

His toad like eyes were not yet dull. They fastened themselves on her face.

"What do you want of me?" he asked, each word sounding more hollow than the last. "I have no secrets. I have lived a good life."

Nurse Macdonald laughed—a tiny, cracked laugh that made her old head bob and tremble a little, as if her neck were on a steel spring. But Sir Hugh's eyes grew red, and his pale lips began to twist.

"Let me die in peace," he said slowly.

But Nurse Macdonald shook her head, and her brown, mothlike hand left his and fluttered to his forehead.

"By the mother that bore you and died of grief for the sins you did, tell me the truth!"

Sir Hugh's lips tightened on his discoloured teeth.

"Not on earth," he answered slowly.

"By the wife who bore your son and died heartbroken, tell me the truth!"

"Neither to you in life, nor to her in eternal death."

His lips writhed, as if the words were coals between them, and a great drop of sweat rolled across the parchment of his forehead. Gabriel Ockram bit his hand as he watched his father die. But Nurse Macdonald spoke a third time.

"By the woman whom you betrayed, and who waits for you this night, Hugh Ockram, tell me the truth!"

"It is too late. Let me die in peace."

His writhing lips began to smile across his yellow teeth, and his toad-like eyes glowed like evil jewels in his head.

"There is time," said the ancient woman. "Tell me the name of Evelyn Warburton's father. Then I will let you die in peace."

Evelyn started. She stared at Nurse Macdonald, and then at her uncle.

"The name of Evelyn's father?" he repeated slowly, while the awful smile spread upon his dying face.

The light was growing strangely dim in the great room. As Evelyn looked on, Nurse Macdonald's crooked shadow on the wall grew gigantic. Sir Hugh's breath was becoming thick, rattling in his throat, as death crept in like a snake and choked it back. Evelyn prayed aloud, high and clear.

Then something rapped at the window, and she felt her hair rise upon her head. She looked around in spite of herself. And when she saw her own white face looking in at the window, her own eyes staring at her through the glass—wide and fearful—her own hair streaming against the pane, and her own lips dashed with blood, she rose slowly from the floor and stood rigid for one moment before she screamed once and fell straight back into Gabriel's arms. But the shriek that answered hers was the fear-shriek of a tormented corpse out of which the soul cannot pass for shame of deadly sins.

Sir Hugh Ockram sat upright in his deathbed, and saw and cried aloud:

"Evelyn!" His harsh voice broke and rattled in his chest as he sank down. But still Nurse Macdonald tortured him, for there was a little life left in him still.

"You have seen the mother as she waits for you, Hugh Ockram. Who was this girl Evelyn's father? What was his name?"

For the last time the dreadful smile came upon the twisted lips, very slowly, very surely now. The toad eyes glared red and the parchment face glowed a little in the flickering light; for the last time words came.

"They know it in hell."

Then the glowing eyes went out quickly. The yellow face turned waxen pale, and a great shiver ran through the thin body as Hugh Ockram died.

But in death he still smiled, for he knew his secret and kept it still. He would take it with him to the other side, to lie with him forever in the north vault of the chapel where the Ockrams lie uncoffined in their shrouds—all but one. Though he was dead, he smiled, for he had kept his treasure of evil truth to the end. There was none left to tell the name he had spoken, but there was all the evil he had not undone left to bear fruit.

As they watched—Nurse Macdonald and Gabriel, who held the still unconscious Evelyn in his arms while he looked at the father—they felt the dead smile crawling along their own lips. Then they shivered a little as they both looked at Evelyn as she lay with her head on Gabriel's shoulder, for though she was very beautiful, the same sickening smile was twisting her young mouth too, and it was like the foreshadowing of a great evil that they could not understand.

By and by they carried Evelyn out, and when she opened her eyes the smile was gone. From far away in the great house the sound of weeping and crooning came up the stairs and echoed along the dismal corridors as the women had begun to mourn the dead master in the Irish fashion. The hall had echoes of its own all that night, like the far-off wail of the banshee among forest trees.

When the time was come they took Sir Hugh in his winding-sheet on a trestle bier and bore him to the chapel, through the iron door and down the long descent to the north vault lit with tapers, to lay him by his father. The two men went in first to prepare the place, and came back staggering like drunken men, their faces white.

But Gabriel Ockram was not afraid, for he knew. When he went in, alone, he saw the body of Sir Vernon Ockram leaning upright against the stone wall. Its head lay on the ground nearby with the face turned up. The dried leather lips smiled horribly at the dried-up corpse, while the iron coffin, lined with black velvet, stood open on the floor.

Gabriel took the body in his hands—for it was very light, being quite dried by the air of the vault—and those who peeped in the door saw him lay it in the coffin again. They heard it rustle a little, as it touched the sides and the bottom, like a bundle of reeds. He also placed the head upon the shoulders and shut down the lid, which fell to with the snap of its rusty spring.

After that they laid Sir Hugh beside his father, on the trestle bier on which they had brought him, and they went back to the chapel. But when they looked into one another's faces, master and men, they were all smiling with the dead smile of the corpse they had left in the vault. They could not bear to look at one another again until it had faded away.

Chapter III

Gabriel Ockram became Sir Gabriel, inheriting the baronetcy with the half-ruined fortune left by his father, and Evelyn Warburton continued to live at Ockram Hall, in the south room that had been hers ever since she could remember. She could not go away, for there were no relatives to whom she could have gone, and besides, there seemed to be no reason why she should not stay. The world would never trouble itself to care what the Ockrams did on their Irish estates. It was long since the Ockrams had asked anything of the world.

So Sir Gabriel took his father's place at the dark old table in the dining room, and Evelyn sat opposite to him—until such time as their mourning should be over—and they might be married at last. Meanwhile, their lives went on as before—since Sir Hugh had been a hopeless invalid during the last year of his life, and they had seen him but once a day for a little while—spending most of their time together in a strangely perfect companionship.

Though the late summer saddened into autumn, and autumn darkened into winter, and storm followed storm, and rain poured on rain through the short days and the long nights, Ockram Hall seemed less gloomy since Sir Hugh had been laid in the north vault beside his father.

At Christmastide Evelyn decked the great hall with holly and green boughs. Huge fires blazed on every hearth. The tenants were all bid to come to a New Year's dinner at which they ate and drank well, while Sir Gabriel sat at the head of the table. Evelyn came in when the port wine was brought and the most respected of the tenants made a speech to her health.

When the speechmaker said it had been a long time since there had been a Lady Ockram, Sir Gabriel shaded his eyes with his hand and looked down at the table; a faint color came into Evelyn's transparent cheeks. And, said the gray-haired farmer, it was longer still since there had been a Lady Ockram so fair as the next was to be, and he drank to the health of Evelyn Warburton.

Then the tenants all stood up and shouted for her. Sir Gabriel stood up likewise, beside Evelyn. But when the men gave the last and loudest cheer of all, there was a voice not theirs, above them all, higher, fiercer, louder—an unearthly scream—shrieking for the bride of Ockram Hall. It was so loud that the holly and the green boughs over the great chimney shook and waved as if a cool breeze were blowing over them.

The men turned very pale. Many of them set down their glasses, but others let them fall upon the floor. Looking into one another's faces, they saw that they were all smiling strangely—a dead smile—like dead Sir Hugh's.

The fear of death was suddenly upon them all, so that they fled in a panic, falling over one another like wild beasts in the burning forest when the thick smoke runs along before the flame. Tables were overturned, drinking glasses and bottles were broken in heaps, and dark red wine crawled like blood upon the polished floor.

Sir Gabriel and Evelyn were left standing alone at the head of the table before the wreck of their feast, not daring to turn to look at one another, for each knew that the other smiled. But Gabriel's right arm held her and his left hand clasped her tight as they stared before them. But for the shadows of her hair, one might not have told their two faces apart.

They listened long, but the cry came not again, and eventually the dead smile faded from their lips as each remembered that Sir Hugh Ockram lay in the north vault smiling in his winding sheet, in the dark, because he had died with his secret.

So ended the tenants' New Year's dinner. But from that time on, Sir Gabriel grew more and more silent and his face grew even paler and thinner than before. Often, without warning and without words, he would rise from his seat as if something moved him against his will. He would go out into the rain or the sunshine to the north side of the chapel, sit on the stone bench and stare at the ground as if he could see through it, through the vault below, and through the white winding sheet in the dark, to the dead smile that would not die.

Always when he went out in that way Evelyn would come out presently and sit beside him. Once, as in the past, their beautiful faces came suddenly near; their lids drooped, and their red lips were almost joined together. But as their eyes met, they grew wide and wild, so that the white showed in a ring all round the deep violet. Their teeth chattered and their hands were like the hands of corpses, for fear of what was under their feet, and of what they knew but could not see.

Once, Evelyn found Sir Gabriel in the chapel alone, standing before the iron door that led down to the place of death with the key to the door in his hand, but he had not put it into the lock. Evelyn drew him away, shivering, for she had also been driven—in waking dreams—to see that terrible thing again, and to find out whether it had changed since it had been laid there.

"I'm going mad," said Sir Gabriel, covering his eyes with his hand as he went with her. "I see it in my sleep. I see it when I am awake. It draws me to it, day and night and unless I see it I shall die!"

"I know," answered Evelyn, "I know. It is as if threads were spun from it like a spider's, drawing us down to it." She was silent for a moment and then she started violently and grasped his arm with a man's strength, and almost screamed the words she spoke. "But we must not go there!" she cried. "We must not go!"

Sir Gabriel's eyes were half shut, and he was not moved by the agony of her face.

"I shall die, unless I see it again," he said, in a quiet voice not like his own. And all that day and that evening he scarcely spoke, thinking of it, always thinking, while Evelyn Warburton quivered from head to foot with a terror she had never known.

One grey winter morning, she went alone to Nurse Macdonald's room in the tower, and sat down beside the great leather easy chair, laying her thin white hand upon the withered fingers.

"Nurse," she said, "what was it that Uncle Hugh should have told you, that night before he died? It must have been an awful secret—and yet, though you asked him, I feel somehow that you know it, and that you know why he used to smile so dreadfully."

The old woman's head moved slowly from side to side.

"I only guess. . . . I shall never know," she answered slowly in her cracked little voice.

"But what do you guess? Who am I? Why did you ask who my father was? You know I am Colonel Warburton's daughter, and my mother was Lady Ockram's sister, so that Gabriel and I are cousins. My father was killed in Afghanistan. What secret can there be?"

"I do not know. I can only guess."

"Guess what?" asked Evelyn imploringly, pressing the soft withered hands, as she leaned forward. But Nurse Macdonald's wrinkled lids dropped suddenly over her queer blue eyes, and her lips shook a little with her breath, as if she were asleep.

Evelyn waited. By the fire the Irish maid was knitting fast. Her needles clicked like three or four clocks ticking against each other. But the real clock on the wall solemnly ticked alone, checking off the seconds of the woman who was a hundred years old, and had not many days left. Outside the ivy branch beat the window in the wintry blast, as it had beaten against the glass a hundred years ago.

Then as Evelyn sat there she felt again the waking of a horrible desire—the sickening wish to go down, down to the thing in the north vault, and to open the winding-sheet, and see whether it had changed; and she held Nurse Macdonald's hands as if to keep herself in her place and fight against the appalling attraction of the evil dead.

But the old cat that kept Nurse Macdonald's feet warm, lying always on the footstool, got up and stretched itself, and looked up into Evelyn's eyes, while its back arched, and its tail thickened and bristled, and its ugly pink lips drew back in a devilish grin, showing its sharp teeth. Evelyn stared at it, half fascinated by its ugliness. Then the creature suddenly put out one paw with all its claws spread, and spat at the girl. All at once the grinning cat was like the smiling corpse far down below. Evelyn shivered down to her small feet, and covered her face with her free hand, lest Nurse Macdonald should wake and see the dead smile there, for she could feel it.

The old woman had already opened her eyes again, and she touched her cat with the end of her crutch-stick, whereupon its back went down and its tail shrunk, and it sidled back to its place on the footstool. But its yellow eyes looked up sideways at Evelyn, between the slits of its lids.

"What is it that you guess, nurse?" asked the young girl again.

"A bad thing, a wicked thing. But I dare not tell you, lest it might not be true, and the very thought should blast your life. For if I guess right, he meant that you should not know, and that you two should marry and pay for his old sin with your souls."

"He used to tell us that we ought not to marry."

"Yes—he told you that, perhaps. But it was as if a man put poisoned meat before a starving beast, and said 'do not eat,' but never raised his hand to take the meat away. And if he told you that you should not marry, it was because he hoped you would; for of all men living or dead, Hugh Ockram was the falsest man that ever told a cowardly lie, and the crudest that ever hurt a weak woman, and the worst that ever loved a sin."

"But Gabriel and I love each other," said Evelyn very sadly.

Nurse Macdonald's old eyes looked far away, at sights seen long ago, and that rose in the grey winter air amid the mists of an ancient youth.

"If you love, you can die together," she said, very slowly. "Why should you live, if it is true? I am a hundred years old. What has life given me? The beginning is fire; the end is a heap of ashes; and between the end and the beginning lies all the pain of the world. Let me sleep, since I cannot die."

Then the old woman's eyes closed again, and her head sank a little lower upon her breast.

So Evelyn went away and left her asleep, with the cat asleep on the footstool. The young girl tried to forget Nurse Macdonald's words, but she could not, for she heard them over and over again in the wind, and behind her on the stairs. And as she grew sick with fear of the frightful unknown evil to which her soul was bound, she felt a bodily something pressing her, pushing her, forcing her on from the other side. She felt threads that drew her mysteriously, and when she shut her eyes, she saw in the chapel behind the altar, the low iron door through which she must pass to go to the thing.

As she lay awake at night, she drew the sheet over her face, lest she should see shadows on the wall beckoning to her. The sound of her own warm breath made whisperings in her ears, while she held the mattress with her hands, to keep from getting up and going to the chapel. It would have been easier if there had not been a way thither through the library, by a door which was never locked. It would be fearfully easy to take her candle and go softly through the sleeping house. The key of the vault lay under the altar behind a stone that turned. She knew that little secret. She could go alone and see.

But when she thought of it, she felt her hair rise on her head. She shivered so that the bed shook, then the horror went through her in a cold thrill that was agony again, like a myriad of icy needles boring into her nerves.

CHAPTER IV

The old clock in Nurse Macdonald's tower struck midnight. From her room she could hear the creaking chains, and weights in their box in the corner of the staircase, and the jarring of the rusty lever that lifted the hammer. She had heard it all her life. It struck eleven strokes clearly, and then came the twelfth with a dull half stroke, as though the hammer were too weary to go on and had fallen asleep against the bell.

The old cat got up from the footstool and stretched itself. Nurse Macdonald opened her ancient eyes and looked slowly round the room by the dim light of the night lamp. She touched the cat with her crutch-stick, and it lay down upon her feet. She drank a few drops from her cup and went to sleep again.

But downstairs Sir Gabriel sat straight up as the clock struck, for he had dreamed a fearful dream of horror, and his heart stood still. He awoke at its stopping and it beat again furiously with his breath, like a wild thing set free. No Ockram had ever known fear waking, but sometimes it came to Sir Gabriel in his sleep.

He pressed his hands to his temples as he sat up in bed. His hands were icy cold, but his head was hot. The dream faded far and in its place there came the master thought that racked his life. With the thought also came the sick twisting of his lips in the dark that would have been a smile. Far off, Evelyn Warburton dreamed that the dead smile was on her mouth, and awoke—starting with a little moan—her face in her hands, shivering.

But Sir Gabriel struck a light and got up and began to walk up and down his great room. It was midnight and he had barely slept an hour, and in the north of Ireland the winter nights are long.

"I shall go mad," he said to himself, holding his forehead. He knew that it was true. For weeks and months the possession of the thing had grown upon him like a disease, till he could think of nothing without thinking first of that. And now all at once it outgrew his strength, and he knew that he must be its instrument or lose his mind. He knew that he must do the deed he hated and feared, if he could fear anything, or that something would snap in his brain and divide him from life while he was yet alive. He took the candlestick in his hand, the old-fashioned heavy candlestick that had always been used by the head of the house. He did not think of dressing, but went as he was—in his silk night clothes and his slippers—and opened the door.

Everything was very still in the great old house. He shut the door behind him and walked noiselessly on the carpet through the long corridor. A cool breeze blew over his shoulder and blew the flame of his candle straight out. Instinctively he stopped and looked round, but all was still, and the upright flame burned steadily. He walked on, and instantly a strong draught was behind him, almost extinguishing the light. It seemed to blow him on his way, ceasing whenever he turned, coming again when he went on—invisible, icy.

Down the great staircase to the echoing hall he went, seeing nothing but the flaring flame of the candle standing away from him over the guttering wax. The cold wind blew over his shoulder and through his hair. On he passed through the open door into the library dark with old books and carved bookcases. On he went through the door with shelves and the imitated backs of books painted on it, which shut itself after him with a soft click.

He entered the low-arched passage, and though the door was shut behind him and fitted tightly in its frame, still the cold breeze blew the flame forward as he walked. He was not afraid; but his face was very pale and his eyes were wide and bright, seeing already in the dark air the picture of the thing beyond. But in the chapel he stood still, his hand on the little turning stone tablet in the back of the stone altar. On the tablet were engraved the words: *Clavis sepulchri Clarissimorum Dominorum De Ockram* ("the key to the vault of the most illustrious lords of Ockram").

Sir Gabriel paused and listened. He fancied that he heard a sound far off in the great house where all had been so still, but it did not come again. Yet he waited at the last, and looked at the low iron door. Beyond it, down the long descent, lay his father uncoffined, six months dead, corrupt, terrible in his clinging shroud. The strangely preserving air of the vault could not yet have done its work completely. But on the thing's ghastly features, with their half-dried, open eyes, there would still be the frightful smile with which the man had died—the smile that haunted.

As the thought crossed Sir Gabriel's mind, he felt his lips writhing, and he struck his own mouth in wrath with the back of his hand so fiercely that a drop of blood ran down his chin, and another, and more, falling back in the gloom upon the chapel pavement. But still his bruised lips twisted themselves. He turned the tablet by the simple secret. It needed no safer fastening, for had each Ockram been coffined in pure gold, and had the door been open wide, there was not a man in Tyrone brave enough to go down to that place, save Gabriel Ockram himself, with his angel's face, his thin, white hands, and his sad unflinching eyes. He took the great old key and set it into the lock of the iron door. The heavy, rattling noise echoed down the descent beyond like footsteps, as if a watcher had stood behind the iron and were running away within, with heavy dead feet. And though he was standing still, the cool wind was from behind him, and blew the flame of the candle against the iron panel. He turned the key.

Sir Gabriel saw that his candle was short. There were new ones on the altar, with long candlesticks, so he lit one and left his own burning on the floor. As he set it down on the pavement his lip began to bleed again, and another drop fell upon the stones.

He drew the iron door open and pushed it back against the chapel wall, so that it should not shut of itself, while he was within; and the horrible draught of the sepulchre came up out of the depths in his face, foul and dark. He went in, but though the fetid air met him, yet the flame of the tall candle was blown straight from him against the wind while he walked down the easy incline with steady steps, his loose slippers slapping the pavement as he trod.

He shaded the candle with his hand, and his fingers seemed to be made of wax and blood as the light shone through them. And in spite of him the unearthly draught forced the flame forward, till it was blue over the black wick, and it seemed as if it must go out. But he went straight on, with shining eyes.

The downward passage was wide, and he could not always see the walls by the struggling light, but he knew when he was in the place of death by the larger, drearier echo of his steps in the greater space, and by the sensation of a distant blank wall. He stood still, almost enclosing the flame of the candle in the hollow of his hand. He could see a little, for his eyes were growing used to the gloom. Shadowy forms were outlined in the dimness, where the biers of the Ockrams stood crowded together, side by side, each with its straight, shrouded corpse, strangely preserved by the dry air, like the empty shell that the locust sheds in summer. And a few steps before him he saw clearly the dark shape of headless Sir Vernon's iron coffin, and he knew that nearest to it lay the thing he sought.

He was as brave as any of those dead men had been. They were his fathers, and he knew that sooner or later he should lie there himself, beside Sir Hugh, slowly drying to a parchment shell. But as yet, he was still alive. He closed his eyes a moment as three great drops stood on his forehead.

Then he looked again, and by the whiteness of the winding sheet he knew his father's corpse, for all the others were brown with age; and, moreover, the flame of the candle was blown toward it. He made four steps till he reached it, and suddenly the light burned straight and high, shedding a dazzling yellow glare upon the fine linen that was all white, save over the face, and where the joined hands were laid on the breast. And at those places ugly stains had spread, darkened with outlines of the features and of the tight clasped fingers. There was a frightful stench of drying death.

As Sir Gabriel looked down, something stirred behind him, softly at first, then more noisily, and something fell to the stone floor with a dull thud and rolled up to his feet. He started back and saw a withered head lying almost face upward on the pavement, grinning at him. He felt the cold sweat standing on his face, and his heart beat painfully.

For the first time in all his life that evil thing which men call fear was getting hold of him, checking his heart-strings as a cruel driver checks a quivering horse, clawing at his backbone with icy hands, lifting his hair with freezing breath, climbing up and gathering in his midriff with leaden weight.

Yet he bit his lip and bent down, holding the candle in one hand, to lift the shroud back from the head of the corpse with the other. Slowly he lifted it. It clove to the half-dried skin of the face, and his hand shook as if someone had struck him on the elbow, but half in fear and half in anger at himself, he pulled it, so that it came away with a little ripping sound. He caught his breath as he held it, not yet throwing it back, and not yet looking. The horror was working in him and he felt that old Vernon Ockram was standing up in his iron coffin, headless, yet watching him with the stump of his severed neck.

While he held his breath he felt the dead smile twisting his lips. In sudden wrath at his own misery, he tossed the death-stained linen backward, and looked at last. He ground his teeth lest he should shriek aloud. There it was, the thing that haunted him, that haunted Evelyn Warburton, that was like a blight on all that came near him.

The dead face was blotched with dark stains, and the thin, grey hair was matted about the discoloured forehead. The sunken lids were half open, and the candlelight gleamed on something foul where the toad eyes had lived.

But yet the dead thing smiled, as it had smiled in life. The ghastly lips were parted and drawn wide and tight upon the wolfish teeth, cursing still, and still defying hell to do its worst—defying, cursing, and always and forever smiling alone in the dark.

Sir Gabriel opened the sheet where the hands were. The blackened, withered fingers were closed upon something stained and mottled. Shivering from head to foot, but fighting like a man in agony for his life, he tried to take the package from the dead man's hold. But as he pulled at it the clawlike fingers seemed to close more tightly. When he pulled harder the shrunken hands and arms rose from the corpse with a horrible look of life following his motion—then as he wrenched the sealed packet loose at last, the hands fell back into their place still folded.

He set down the candle on the edge of the bier to break the seals from the stout paper. Kneeling on one knee, to get a better light, he read what was within, written long ago in Sir Hugh's queer hand. He was no longer afraid.

He read how Sir Hugh had written it all down that it might perchance be a witness of evil and of his hatred. He had written how he had loved Evelyn Warburton, his wife's sister; and how his wife had died of a broken heart with his curse upon her. He wrote how Warburton and he had fought side by side in Afghanistan, and Warburton had fallen; but

Ockram had brought his comrade's wife back a full year later, and little Evelyn, her child, had been born in Ockram Hall. And he wrote how he had wearied of the mother, and she had died like her sister with his curse on her; and how Evelyn had been brought up as his niece, and how he had trusted that his son Gabriel and his daughter, innocent and unknowing, might love and marry, and the souls of the women he had betrayed might suffer yet another anguish before eternity was out. And, last of all, he hoped that some day, when nothing could be undone, the two might find his writing and live on, as man and wife, not daring to tell the truth for their children's sake and the world's word.

This he read, kneeling beside the corpse in the north vault, by the light of the altar candle. He had read it all and then he thanked God aloud that he had found the secret in time. When he finally rose to his feet and looked down at the dead face it had changed. The smile was gone from it. The jaw had fallen a little and the tired, dead lips were relaxed. And then there was a breath behind him and close to him, not cold like that which had blown the flame of the candle as he came, but warm and human. He turned suddenly.

There she stood, all in white, with her shadowy golden hair. She had risen from her bed and had followed him noiselessly. When she found him reading, she read over his shoulder.

He started violently when he saw her, for his nerves were unstrung. Then he cried out her name in that still place of death:

"Evelyn!"

"My brother!" she answered softly and tenderly, putting out both hands to meet his.

The Monkey's Paw

By W. W. Jacobs

PART I

Without, the night was cold and wet, but in the small parlour of Laburnum villa the blinds were drawn and the fire burned brightly. Father and son were at chess; the former, who possessed ideas about the game involving radical chances, putting his king into such sharp and unnecessary perils that it even provoked comment from the white-haired old lady knitting placidly by the fire.

"Hark at the wind," said Mr. White, who, having seen a fatal mistake after it was too late, was amiably desirous of preventing his son from seeing it.

"I'm listening," said the latter grimly surveying the board as he stretched out his hand. "Check."

"I should hardly think that he's come tonight," said his father, with his hand poised over the board.

"Mate," replied the son.

"That's the worst of living so far out," balled Mr. White with sudden and unlooked-for violence; "Of all the beastly, slushy, out of the way places to live in, this is the worst. Path's a bog, and the road's a torrent. I don't know what people are thinking about. I suppose because only two houses in the road are let, they think it doesn't matter."

"Never mind, dear," said his wife soothingly; "perhaps you'll win the next one."

Mr. White looked up sharply, just in time to intercept a knowing glance between mother and son. the words died away on his lips, and he hid a guilty grin in his thin grey beard.

"There he is," said Herbert White as the gate banged to loudly and heavy footsteps came toward the door.

The old man rose with hospitable haste and opening the door, was heard condoling with the new arrival. The new arrival also condoled with himself, so that Mrs. White said, "Tut, tut!" and coughed gently as her husband entered the room followed by a tall, burly man, beady of eye and rubicund of visage.

"Sergeant-Major Morris," he said, introducing him.

The Sergeant-Major took hands and taking the proffered seat by the fire, watched contentedly as his host got out whiskey and tumblers and stood a small copper kettle on the fire.

At the third glass his eyes got brighter, and he began to talk, the little family circle regarding with eager interest this visitor from distant parts, as he squared his broad shoulders in the chair and spoke of wild scenes and doughty deeds; of wars and plagues and strange peoples.

"Twenty-one years of it," said Mr. White, nodding at his wife and son. "When he went away he was a slip of a youth in the warehouse. Now look at him."

"He don't look to have taken much harm." said Mrs. White politely.

"I'd like to go to India myself," said the old man, "just to look around a bit, you know."

"Better where you are," said the Sergeant-Major, shaking his head. He put down the empty glass and sighing softly, shook it again.

"I should like to see those old temples and fakirs and jugglers," said the old man. "what was that that you started telling me the other day about a monkey's paw or something, Morris?"

"Nothing," said the soldier hastily. "Leastways, nothing worth hearing."

"Monkey's paw?" said Mrs. White curiously.

"Well, it's just a bit of what you might call magic, perhaps," said the Sergeant-Major off-handedly.

His three listeners leaned forward eagerly. The visitor absent-mindedly put his empty glass to his lips and then set it down again. His host filled it for him again.

"To look at," said the Sergeant-Major, fumbling in his pocket, "it's just an ordinary little paw, dried to a mummy."

He took something out of his pocket and proffered it. Mrs. White drew back with a grimace, but her son, taking it, examined it curiously.

"And what is there special about it?" inquired Mr. White as he took it from his son, and having examined it, placed it upon the table.

"It had a spell put on it by an old Fakir," said the Sergeant-Major, "a very holy man. He wanted to show that fate ruled people's lives, and that those who interfered with it did so to their sorrow. He put a spell on it so that three separate men could each have three wishes from it."

His manners were so impressive that his hearers were conscious that their light laughter had jarred somewhat.

"Well, why don't you have three, sir?" said Herbert White cleverly.

The soldier regarded him the way that middle age is wont to regard presumptuous youth. "I have," he said quietly, and his blotchy face whitened.

"And did you really have the three wishes granted?" asked Mrs. White.

"I did," said the sergeant-major, and his glass tapped against his strong teeth.

"And has anybody else wished?" persisted the old lady.

"The first man had his three wishes. Yes," was the reply, "I don't know what the first two were, but the third was for death. That's how I got the paw."

His tones were so grave that a hush fell upon the group.

"If you've had your three wishes it's no good to you now then Morris," said the old man at last. "What do you keep it for?"

The soldier shook his head. "Fancy I suppose," he said slowly." I did have some idea of selling it, but I don't think I will. It has caused me enough mischief already. Besides, people won't buy. They think it's a fairy tale, some of them; and those who do think anything of it want to try it first and pay me afterward."

"If you could have another three wishes," said the old man, eyeing him keenly, "would you have them?"

"I don't know," said the other. "I don't know."

He took the paw, and dangling it between his forefinger and thumb, suddenly threw it upon the fire. White, with a slight cry, stooped down and snatched it off.

"Better let it burn," said the soldier solemnly.

"If you don't want it Morris," said the other, "give it to me."

"I won't," said his friend doggedly. "I threw it on the fire. If you keep it, don't blame me for what happens. Pitch it on the fire like a sensible man."

The other shook his head and examined his possession closely. "How do you do it?" he inquired.

"Hold it up in your right hand, and wish aloud," said the Sergeant-Major, "But I warn you of the consequences."

"Sounds like the 'Arabian Nights,'" said Mrs. White, as she rose and began to set the supper. "Don't you think you might wish for four pairs of hands for me."

Her husband drew the talisman from his pocket, and all three burst into laughter as the Sergeant-Major, with a look of alarm on his face, caught him by the arm.

"If you must wish," he said gruffly, "Wish for something sensible."

Mr. White dropped it back in his pocket, and placing chairs, motioned his friend to the table. In the business of supper the talisman was partly forgotten, and afterward the three sat listening in an enthralled fashion to a second installment of the soldier's adventures in India.

"If the tale about the monkey's paw is not more truthful than those he has been telling us," said Herbert, as the door closed behind their guest, just in time to catch the last train, "we shan't make much out of it."

"Did you give anything for it, father?" inquired Mrs. White, regarding her husband closely.

"A trifle," said he, colouring slightly, "He didn't want it, but I made him take it. And he pressed me again to throw it away."

"Likely," said Herbert, with pretended horror. "Why, we're going to be rich, and famous, and happy. Wish to be an emperor, father, to begin with; then you can't be henpecked."

He darted around the table, pursued by the maligned Mrs. White armed with an antimacassar.

Mr. White took the paw from his pocket and eyed it dubiously. "I don't know what to wish for, and that's a fact," he said slowly. "It seems to me I've got all I want."

"If you only cleared the house, you'd be quite happy, wouldn't you!" said Herbert, with his hand on his shoulder. "Well, wish for two hundred pounds, then; that'll just do it."

His father, smiling shamefacedly at his own credulity, held up the talisman, as his son, with a solemn face, somewhat marred by a wink at his mother, sat down and struck a few impressive chords.

"I wish for two hundred pounds," said the old man distinctly.

A fine crash from the piano greeted his words, interrupted by a shuddering cry from the old man. His wife and son ran toward him.

"It moved," he cried, with a glance of disgust at the object as it lay on the floor. "As I wished, it twisted in my hand like a snake."

"Well, I don't see the money," said his son, as he picked it up and placed it on the table, "and I bet I never shall."

"It must have been your fancy, father," said his wife, regarding him anxiously.

He shook his head. "Never mind, though; there's no harm done, but it gave me a shock all the same."

They sat down by the fire again while the two men finished their pipes. Outside, the wind was higher than ever, and the old man started nervously at the sound of a door banging upstairs. A silence unusual and depressing settled on all three, which lasted until the old couple rose to retire for the rest of the night.

"I expect you'll find the cash tied up in a big bag in the middle of your bed," said Herbert, as he bade them good night, "and something horrible squatting on top of your wardrobe watching you as you pocket your ill-gotten gains."

He sat alone in the darkness, gazing at the dying fire, and seeing faces in it. The last was so horrible and so simian that he gazed at it in amazement. It got so vivid that, with a little uneasy laugh, he felt on the table for a glass containing a little water to throw over it. His hand grasped the monkey's paw, and with a little shiver he wiped his hand on his coat and went up to bed.

PART II

In the brightness of the wintry sun next morning as it streamed over the breakfast table he laughed at his fears. There was an air of prosaic wholesomeness about the room which it had lacked on the previous night, and the dirty, shriveled little paw was pitched on the side-board with a carelessness which betokened no great belief in its virtues.

"I suppose all old soldiers are the same," said Mrs. White. "The idea of our listening to such nonsense! How could wishes be granted in these days? And if they could, how could two hundred pounds hurt you, father?"

"Might drop on his head from the sky," said the frivolous Herbert.

"Morris said the things happened so naturally," said his father, "that you might if you so wished attribute it to coincidence."

"Well don't break into the money before I come back," said Herbert as he rose from the table. "I'm afraid it'll turn you into a mean, avaricious man, and we shall have to disown you."

His mother laughed, and following him to the door, watched him down the road; and returning to the breakfast table, was very happy at the expense of her husband's credulity. All of which did not prevent her from scurrying to the door at the postman's knock, nor prevent her from referring somewhat shortly to retired Sergeant-Majors of bibulous habits when she found that the post brought a tailor's bill.

"Herbert will have some more of his funny remarks, I expect, when he comes home," she said as they sat at dinner.

"I dare say," said Mr. White, pouring himself out some beer; "but for all that, the thing moved in my hand; that I'll swear to."

"You thought it did," said the old lady soothingly.

"I say it did," replied the other. "There was no thought about it; I had just—What's the matter?"

His wife made no reply. She was watching the mysterious movements of a man outside, who, peering in an undecided fashion at the house, appeared to be trying to make up his mind to enter. In mental connection with the two hundred pounds, she noticed that the stranger was well dressed, and wore a silk hat of glossy newness. Three times he paused at the gate, and then walked on again. The fourth time he stood with his hand upon it, and then with sudden resolution flung it open and walked up the path. Mrs. White at the same moment placed her hands behind her, and hurriedly unfastening the strings of her apron, put that useful article of apparel beneath the cushion of her chair.

She brought the stranger, who seemed ill at ease, into the room. He gazed at her furtively, and listened in a preoccupied fashion as the old lady apologized for the appearance of the room, and her husband's coat, a garment which he usually reserved for the garden. She then waited as patiently as her sex would permit for him to broach his business, but he was at first strangely silent.

"I—was asked to call," he said at last, and stooped and picked a piece of cotton from his trousers. "I come from 'Maw and Meggins.'"

The old lady started. "Is anything the matter?" she asked breathlessly. "Has anything happened to Herbert? What is it? What is it?"

Her husband interposed. "There there mother," he said hastily. "Sit down, and don't jump to conclusions. You've not brought bad news, I'm sure sir," and eyed the other wistfully.

"I'm sorry—" began the visitor.

"Is he hurt?" demanded the mother wildly.

The visitor bowed in assent. "Badly hurt," he said quietly, "but he is not in any pain."

"Oh thank God!" said the old woman, clasping her hands. "Thank God for that! Thank—"

She broke off as the sinister meaning of the assurance dawned on her and she saw the awful confirmation of her fears in the others averted face. She caught her breath, and turning to her slower-witted husband, laid her trembling hand on his. There was a long silence.

"He was caught in the machinery," said the visitor at length in a low voice.

"Caught in the machinery," repeated Mr. White, in a dazed fashion, "yes."

He sat staring out the window, and taking his wife's hand between his own, pressed it as he had been wont to do in their old courting days nearly forty years before.

"He was the only one left to us," he said, turning gently to the visitor. "It is hard."

The other coughed, and rising, walked slowly to the window. "The firm wishes me to convey their sincere sympathy with you in your great loss," he said, without looking round. "I beg that you will understand I am only their servant and merely obeying orders."

There was no reply; the old woman's face was white, her eyes staring, and her breath inaudible; on the husband's face was a look such as his friend the sergeant might have carried into his first action.

"I was to say that Maw and Meggins disclaim all responsibility," continued the other. "They admit no liability at all, but in consideration of your son's services, they wish to present you with a certain sum as compensation."

Mr. White dropped his wife's hand, and rising to his feet, gazed with a look of horror at his visitor. His dry lips shaped the words, "How much?"

"Two hundred pounds," was the answer.

Unconscious of his wife's shriek, the old man smiled faintly, put out his hands like a sightless man, and dropped, a senseless heap, to the floor.

Part III

In the huge new cemetery, some two miles distant, the old people buried their dead, and came back to the house steeped in shadows and silence. It was all over so quickly that at first they could hardly realize it, and remained in a state of expectation as though of something else to happen—something else which was to lighten this load, too heavy for old hearts to bear.

But the days passed, and expectations gave way to resignation—the hopeless resignation of the old, sometimes mis-called apathy. Sometimes they hardly exchanged a word, for now they had nothing to talk about, and their days were long to weariness.

It was about a week after that the old man, waking suddenly in the night, stretched out his hand and found himself alone. The room was in darkness, and the sound of subdued weeping came from the window. He raised himself in bed and listened.

"Come back," he said tenderly. "You will be cold."

"It is colder for my son," said the old woman, and wept afresh.

The sounds of her sobs died away on his ears. The bed was warm, and his eyes heavy with sleep. He dozed fitfully, and then slept until a sudden wild cry from his wife awoke him with a start.

"*The paw!*" she cried wildly. "The monkey's paw!"

He started up in alarm. "Where? Where is it? What's the matter?"

She came stumbling across the room toward him. "I want it," she said quietly. "You've not destroyed it?"

"It's in the parlour, on the bracket," he replied, marveling. "Why?"

She cried and laughed together, and bending over, kissed his cheek.

"I only just thought of it," she said hysterically. "Why didn't I think of it before? Why didn't you think of it?"

"Think of what?" he questioned.

"The other two wishes," she replied rapidly. "We've only had one."

"Was not that enough?" he demanded fiercely.

"No," she cried triumphantly; "We'll have one more. Go down and get it quickly, and wish our boy alive again."

The man sat in bed and flung the bedclothes from his quaking limbs. "Good God, you are mad!" he cried aghast.

"Get it," she panted; "get it quickly, and wish—Oh my boy, my boy!"

Her husband struck a match and lit the candle. "Get back to bed," he said unsteadily. "You don't know what you are saying."

"We had the first wish granted," said the old woman, feverishly; "why not the second?"

"A coincidence," stammered the old man.

"Go get it and wish," cried his wife, quivering with excitement.

The old man turned and regarded her, and his voice shook. "He has been dead ten days, and besides he—I would not tell you else, but—I could only recognize him by his clothing. If he was too terrible for you to see then, how now?"

"Bring him back," cried the old woman, and dragged him towards the door. "Do you think I fear the child I have nursed?"

He went down in the darkness, and felt his way to the parlour, and then to the mantelpiece. The talisman was in its place, and a horrible fear that the unspoken wish might bring his mutilated son before him ere he could escape from the room seized up on him, and he caught his breath as he found that he had lost the direction of the door. His brow cold with sweat, he felt his way round the table, and groped along the wall until he found himself in the small passage with the unwholesome thing in his hand.

Even his wife's face seemed changed as he entered the room. It was white and expectant, and to his fears seemed to have an unnatural look upon it. He was afraid of her.

"WISH!" she cried in a strong voice.

"It is foolish and wicked," he faltered.

"WISH!" repeated his wife.

He raised his hand. "I wish my son alive again."

The talisman fell to the floor, and he regarded it fearfully. Then he sank trembling into a chair as the old woman, with burning eyes, walked to the window and raised the blind.

He sat until he was chilled with the cold, glancing occasionally at the figure of the old woman peering through the window. The candle-end, which had burned below the rim of the china candlestick, was throwing pulsating shadows on the ceiling and walls, until with a flicker larger than the rest, it expired. The old man, with an unspeakable sense of relief at the failure of the talisman, crept back to his bed, and a minute afterward the old woman came silently and apathetically beside him.

Neither spoke, but sat silently listening to the ticking of the clock. A stair creaked, and a squeaky mouse scurried noisily through the wall. The darkness was oppressive, and after lying for some time screwing up his courage, he took the box of matches, and striking one, went downstairs for a candle.

At the foot of the stairs the match went out, and he paused to strike another; and at the same moment a knock came so quiet and stealthy as to be scarcely audible, sounded on the front door.

The matches fell from his hand and spilled in the passage. He stood motionless, his breath suspended until the knock was repeated. Then he turned and fled swiftly back to his room, and closed the door behind him. A third knock sounded through the house.

"WHAT'S THAT?" cried the old woman, starting up.

"A rat," said the old man in shaking tones—"a rat. It passed me on the stairs."

His wife sat up in bed listening. A loud knock resounded through the house.

"It's Herbert!"

She ran to the door, but her husband was before her, and catching her by the arm, held her tightly.

"What are you going to do?" he whispered hoarsely.

"It's my boy; it's Herbert!" she cried, struggling mechanically. "I forgot it was two miles away. What are you holding me for? Let go. I must open the door."

"For God's sake don't let it in," cried the old man, trembling.

"You're afraid of your own son," she cried struggling. "Let me go. I'm coming, Herbert; I'm coming."

There was another knock, and another. The old woman with a sudden wrench broke free and ran from the room. Her husband followed to the landing, and called after her appealingly as she hurried downstairs. He heard the chain rattle back and the bolt drawn slowly and stiffly from the socket. Then the old woman's voice, strained and panting.

"The bolt," she cried loudly. "Come down. I can't reach it."

But her husband was on his hands and knees groping wildly on the floor in search of the paw. If only he could find it before the thing outside got in. A perfect fusillade of knocks reverberated through the house, and he heard the scraping of a chair as his wife put it down in the passage against the door. He heard the creaking of the bolt as it came slowly back, and at the same moment he found the monkey's paw, and frantically breathed his third and last wish.

The knocking ceased suddenly, although the echoes of it were still in the house. He heard the chair drawn back, and the door opened. A cold wind rushed up the staircase, and a long loud wail of disappointment and misery from his wife gave him the courage to run down to her side, and then to the gate beyond. The street lamp flickering opposite shone on a quiet and deserted road.

The Dream-Gown of the Japanese Ambassador

By Brander Matthews

I

After arranging the Egyptian and Mexican pottery so as to contrast agreeably with the Dutch and the German beer-mugs on the top of the bookcase that ran along one wall of the sitting-room, Cosmo Waynflete went back into the bedroom and took from a half-empty trunk the little cardboard boxes in which he kept the collection of playing-cards, and of all manner of outlandish equivalents for these simple instruments of fortune, picked up here and there during his two or three years of dilettante travelling in strange countries. At the same time he brought out a Japanese crystal ball, which he stood upon its silver tripod, placing it on a little table in one of the windows on each side of the fireplace; and there the rays of the westering sun lighted it up at once into translucent loveliness.

The returned wanderer looked out of the window and saw on one side the graceful and vigorous tower of the Madison Square Garden, with its Diana turning in the December wind, while in the other direction he could look down on the frozen paths of Union Square, only a block distant, but as far below him almost as though he were gazing down from a balloon. Then he stepped back into the sitting-room itself, and noted the comfortable furniture and wood-fire crackling in friendly fashion on the hearth, and his own personal belongings, scattered here and there as though they were settling themselves for a stay. Having arrived from Europe only that morning, he could not but hold himself lucky to have found these rooms taken for him by the old friend to whom he had announced his return, and with whom he was to eat his Christmas dinner that evening. He had not been on shore more than six or seven hours, and yet the most of his odds and ends were unpacked and already in place as though they belonged in this new abode. It was true that he had toiled unceasingly to accomplish this, and as he stood there in his shirt-sleeves, admiring the results of his labors, he was conscious also that his muscles were fatigued, and that the easy-chair before the fire opened its arms temptingly.

He went again into the bedroom, and took from one of his many trunks a long, loose garment of pale-gray silk. Apparently this beautiful robe was intended to serve as a dressing-gown, and as such Cosmo Waynflete utilized it immediately. The ample folds fell softly about him, and the rich silk itself seemed to be soothing to his limbs, so delicate was its fibre and so carefully had it been woven. Around the full skirt there was embroidery of threads of gold, and again on the open and flowing sleeves. With the skilful freedom of Japanese art the pattern of this decoration seemed to suggest the shrubbery about a spring, for there were strange plants with huge leaves broadly outlined by the golden threads, and in the midst of them water was seen bubbling from the earth and lapping gently over the edge of the fountain. As the returned wanderer thrust his arms into the dressing-gown with its symbolic embroidery on the skirt and sleeves, he remembered distinctly the dismal day when he had bought it in a little curiosity-shop in Nuremberg; and as he fastened across his chest one by one the loops of silken cord to the three coins which served as buttons down the front of the robe, he recalled also the time and the place where he had picked up each of these pieces of gold and silver, one after another. The first of them was a Persian daric, which he had purchased from a dealer on the Grand Canal in Venice; and the second was a Spanish peso struck under Philip II at Potosi, which he had found in a stall on the embankment of the Quay Voltaire, in Paris; and the third was a York shilling, which he had bought from the man who had turned it up in ploughing a field that sloped to the Hudson near Sleepy Hollow.

Having thus wrapped himself in this unusual dressing-gown with its unexpected buttons of gold and silver, Cosmo Waynflete went back into the front room. He dropped into the arm-chair before the fire. It was with a smile of physical satisfaction that he stretched out his feet to the hickory blaze.

The afternoon was drawing on, and in New York the sun sets early on Christmas day. The red rays shot into the window almost horizontally, and they filled the crystal globe with a curious light. Cosmo Waynflete lay back in his easy-chair, with his Japanese robe about him, and gazed intently at the beautiful ball which seemed like a bubble of air and water. His mind went back to the afternoon in April, two years before, when he had found that crystal sphere in a Japanese shop within sight of the incomparable Fugiyama.

II

As he peered into its transparent depths, with his vision focused upon the spot of light where the rays of the setting sun touched it into flame, he was but little surprised to discover that he could make out tiny figures in the crystal. For the moment this strange thing seemed to him perfectly natural. And the movements of these little men and women interested him so much that he watched them as they went to and fro, sweeping a roadway with large brooms. Thus it happened that the fixity of his gaze was intensified. And so it was that in a few minutes he saw with no astonishment that he was one of the group himself, he himself in the rich and stately attire of a samurai. From the instant that Cosmo Waynflete discovered himself among the people whom he saw moving before him, as his eyes were fastened on the illuminated dot in the transparent ball, he ceased to see them as little figures, and he accepted them as of the full stature of man. This increase in their size was no more a source of wonderment to him than it had been to discern himself in the midst of them. He accepted both of these marvellous things without question—indeed, with no thought at all that they were in any way peculiar or abnormal. Not only this, but thereafter he seemed to have transferred his personality to the Cosmo Waynflete who was a Japanese samurai and to have abandoned entirely the Cosmo Waynflete who was an American traveller, and who had just returned to New York that Christmas morning. So completely did the Japanese identity dominate that the existence of the American identity was wholly unknown to him. It was as though the American had gone to sleep in New York at the end of the nineteenth century, and had waked a Japanese in Nippon in the beginning of the eighteenth century.

With his sword by his side—a Murimasa blade, likely to bring bad luck to the wearer sooner or later—he had walked from his own house in the quarter of Kioto which is called Yamashina to the quarter which is called Yoshiwara, a place of ill repute, where dwell women of evil life, and where roysterers and drunkards come by night. He knew that the sacred duty of avenging his master's death had led him to cast off his faithful wife so that he might pretend to riot in debauchery at the Three Sea-Shores. The fame of his shameful doings had spread abroad, and it must soon come to the ears of the man whom he wished to take unawares. Now he was lying prone in the street, seemingly sunk in a drunken slumber, so that men might see him and carry the news to the treacherous assassin of his beloved master. As he lay there that afternoon, he revolved in his mind the devices he should use to make away with his enemy when the hour might be ripe at last for the accomplishment of his holy revenge. To himself he called the roll of his fellow-ronins, now biding their time, as he was, and ready always to obey his orders and to follow his lead to the death, when at last the sun should rise on the day of vengeance.

So he gave no heed to the scoffs and the jeers of those who passed along the street, laughing him to scorn as they beheld him lying there in a stupor from excessive drink at that inordinate hour of the day. And among those who came by at last was a man from Satsuma, who was moved to voice the reproaches of all that saw this sorry sight.

"Is not this Oishi Kuranosuke," said the man from Satsuma, "who was a councillor of Asano Takumi no Kami, and who, not having the heart to avenge his lord, gives himself up to women and wine? See how he lies drunk in the public street! Faithless beast! Fool and craven! Unworthy of the name of a samurai!"

And with that the man from Satsuma trod on him as he lay there, and spat upon him, and went away indignantly. The spies of Kotsuke no Suke heard what the man from Satsuma had said, and they saw how he had spurned the prostrate samurai with his foot; and they went their way to report to their master that he need no longer have any fear of the councillors of Asano Takumi no Kami. All this the man, lying prone in the dust of the street, noted; and it made his heart glad, for then he made sure that the day was soon coming when he could do his duty at last and take vengeance for the death of his master.

III

He lay there longer than he knew, and the twilight settled down at last, and the evening stars came out. And then, after a while, and by imperceptible degrees, Cosmo Waynflete became conscious that the scene had changed and that he had changed with it. He was no longer in Japan, but in Persia. He was no longer lying like a drunkard in the street of a city, but slumbering like a weary soldier in a little oasis by the side of a spring in the midst of a sandy desert. He was asleep, and his faithful horse was unbridled that it might crop the grass at will.

The air was hot and thick, and the leaves of the slim tree above him were never stirred by a wandering wind. Yet now and again there came from the darkness a faintly fetid odor. The evening wore on and still he slept, until at length in the silence of the night a strange huge creature wormed its way steadily out of its lair amid the trees, and drew near the sleeping man to devour him fiercely. But the horse neighed vehemently and beat the ground with his hoofs and waked his master. Then the hideous monster vanished; and the man, aroused from his sleep, saw nothing, although the evil smell still lingered in the sultry atmosphere. He lay down again once more, thinking that for once his steed had given a false alarm. Again the grisly dragon drew nigh, and again the courser notified its rider, and again the man could make out nothing in the darkness of the night; and again he was wellnigh stifled by the foul emanation that trailed in the wake of the misbegotten creature. He rebuked his horse and laid him down once more.

A third time the dreadful beast approached, and a third time the faithful charger awoke its angry master. But there came the breath of a gentle breeze, so that the man did not fear to fill his lungs; and there was a vague light in the heavens now, so that he could dimly discern his mighty enemy; and at once he girded himself for the fight. The scaly monster came full at him with dripping fangs, its mighty body thrusting forward its huge and hideous head. The man met the attack without fear and smote the beast full on the crest, but the blow rebounded from its coat of mail.

Then the faithful horse sprang forward and bit the dreadful creature full upon the neck and tore away the scales, so that its master's sword could pierce the armored hide. So the man was able to dissever the ghastly head and thus to slay the monstrous dragon. The blackness of night wrapped him about once more as he fell on his knees and gave thanks for his victory; and the wind died away again.

IV

Only a few minutes later, so it seemed to him, Cosmo Waynflete became doubtfully aware of another change of time and place—of another transformation of his own being. He knew himself to be alone once more, and even without his trusty charger. Again he found himself groping in the dark. But in a little while there was a faint radiance of light, and at last the moon came out behind a tower. Then he saw that he was not by the roadside in Japan or in the desert of Persia, but now in some unknown city of Southern Europe, where the architecture was hispano-moresque. By the silver rays of the moon he was able to make out the beautiful design damascened upon the blade of the sword which he held now in his hand ready drawn for self-defence.

Then he heard hurried footfalls down the empty street, and a man rushed around the corner pursued by two others, who had also weapons in their hands. For a moment Cosmo Waynflete was a Spaniard, and to him it was a point of honor to aid the weaker party. He cried to the fugitive to pluck up heart and to withstand the enemy stoutly. But the hunted man fled on, and after him went one of the pursuers, a tall, thin fellow, with a long black cloak streaming behind him as he ran.

The other of the two, a handsome lad with fair hair, came to a halt and crossed swords with Cosmo, and soon showed himself to be skilled in the art of fence. So violent was the young fellow's attack that in the ardor of self-defence Cosmo ran the boy through the body before he had time to hold his hand or even to reflect.

The lad toppled over sideways. "Oh, my mother!" he cried, and in a second he was dead. While Cosmo bent over the body, hasty footsteps again echoed along the silent thoroughfare. Cosmo peered around the corner, and by the struggling moonbeams he could see that it was the tall, thin fellow in the black cloak, who was returning with half a score of retainers, all armed, and some of them bearing torches.

Cosmo turned and fled swiftly, but being a stranger in the city he soon lost himself in its tortuous streets. Seeing a light in a window and observing a vine that trailed from the balcony before it, he climbed up boldly, and found himself face to face with a gray-haired lady, whose visage was beautiful and kindly and noble. In a few words he told her his plight and besought sanctuary. She listened to him in silence, with exceeding courtesy of manner, as though she were weighing his words before making up her mind. She raised the lamp on her table and let its beams fall on his lineaments. And still she made no answer to his appeal.

Then came a glare of torches in the street below and a knocking at the door. Then at last the old lady came to a resolution; she lifted the tapestry at the head of her bed and told him to bestow himself there. No sooner was he hidden than the tall, thin man in the long black cloak entered hastily. He greeted the elderly lady as his aunt, and he told her that her son had been set upon by a stranger in the street and had been slain. She gave a great cry and never took her eyes from his face. Then he said that a servant had seen an unknown man climb to the balcony of her house. What if it were the assassin of her son? The blood left her face and she clutched at the table behind her, as she gave orders to have the house searched.

When the room was empty at last she went to the head of the bed and bade the man concealed there to come forth and begone, but to cover his face, that she might not be forced to know him again. So saying, she dropped on her knees before a crucifix, while he slipped out of the window again and down to the deserted street.

He sped to the corner and turned it undiscovered, and breathed a sigh of relief and of regret. He kept on steadily, gliding stealthily along in the shadows, until he found himself at the city gate as the bell of the cathedral tolled the hour of midnight.

V

How it was that he passed through the gate he could not declare with precision, for seemingly a mist had settled about him. Yet a few minutes later he saw that in some fashion he must have got beyond the walls of the town, for he recognized the open country all around. And, oddly enough, he now discovered himself to be astride a bony steed. He could not say what manner of horse it was he was riding, but he felt sure that it was not the faithful charger that had saved his life in Persia, once upon a time, in days long gone by, as it seemed to him then. He was not in Persia now—of that he was certain, nor in Japan, nor in the Iberian peninsula. Where he was he did not know.

In the dead hush of midnight he could hear the barking of a dog on the opposite shore of a dusky and indistinct waste of waters that spread itself far below him. The night grew darker and darker, the stars seemed to sink deeper in the sky, and driving clouds occasionally hid them from his sight. He had never felt so lonely and dismal. In the centre of the road stood an enormous tulip-tree; its limbs were gnarled and fantastic, large enough to form trunks for ordinary trees, twisting down almost to the earth, and rising again into the air. As he approached this fearful tree he thought he saw something white hanging in the midst of it, but on looking more narrowly he perceived it was a place where it had been scathed by lightning and the white wood laid bare. About two hundred yards from the tree a small brook crossed the road; and as he drew near he beheld—on the margin of this brook, and in the dark shadow of the grove—he beheld something huge, misshapen, black, and towering. It stirred not, but seemed gathered up in the gloom like some gigantic monster ready to spring upon the traveller.

He demanded, in stammering accents, "Who are you?" He received no reply. He repeated his demand in a still more agitated voice. Still there was no answer. And then the shadowy object of alarm put itself in motion, and with a scramble and a bound stood in the middle of the road. He appeared to be a horseman of large dimensions and mounted on a black horse of powerful frame. Having no relish for this strange midnight companion, Cosmo Waynflete urged on his steed in hopes of leaving the apparition behind; but the stranger quickened his horse also to an equal pace. And when the first horseman pulled up, thinking to lag behind, the second did likewise. There was something in the moody and dogged silence of this pertinacious companion that was mysterious and appalling. It was soon fearfully accounted for. On mounting a rising ground which brought the figure of his fellow-traveller against the sky, gigantic in height and muffled in a cloak, he was horror-struck to discover the stranger was headless!—but his horror was still more increased in observing that the head which should have rested on the shoulders was carried before the body on the pommel of the saddle.

The terror of Cosmo Waynflete rose to desperation, and he spurred his steed suddenly in the hope of giving his weird companion the slip. But the headless horseman started full jump with him. His own horse, as though possessed by a demon, plunged headlong down the hill. He could hear, however, the black steed panting and blowing close behind him; he even fancied that he felt the hot breath of the pursuer. When he ventured at last to cast a look behind, he saw the goblin rising in the stirrups, and in the very act of hurling at him the grisly head. He fell out of the saddle to the ground; and the black steed and the goblin rider passed by him like a whirlwind.

VI

How long he lay there by the roadside, stunned and motionless, he could not guess; but when he came to himself at last the sun was already high in the heavens. He discovered himself to be reclining on the tall grass of a pleasant graveyard which surrounded a tiny country church in the outskirts of a pretty little village. It was in the early summer, and the foliage was green above him as the boughs swayed gently to and fro in the morning breeze. The birds were singing gayly as they flitted about over his head. The bees hummed along from flower to flower. At last, so it seemed to him, he had come into a land of peace and quiet, where there was rest and comfort and where no man need go in fear of his life. It was a country where vengeance was not a duty and where midnight combats were not a custom. He found himself smiling as he thought that a grisly dragon and a goblin rider would be equally out of place in this laughing landscape.

Then the bell in the steeple of the little church began to ring merrily, and he rose to his feet in expectation. All of a sudden the knowledge came to him why it was that they were ringing. He wondered then why the coming of the bride was thus delayed. He knew himself to be a lover, with life opening brightly before him; and the world seemed to him sweeter than ever before and more beautiful.

Then at last the girl whom he loved with his whole heart and who had promised to marry him appeared in the distance, and he thought he had never seen her look more lovely. As he beheld his bridal party approaching, he slipped into the church to await her at the altar. The sunshine fell full upon the portal and made a halo about the girl's head as she crossed the threshold.

But even when the bride stood by his side and the clergyman had begun the solemn service of the church the bells kept on, and soon their chiming became a clangor, louder and sharper and more insistent.

VII

So clamorous and so persistent was the ringing that Cosmo Waynflete was roused at last. He found himself suddenly standing on his feet, with his hand clutching the back of the chair in which he had been sitting before the fire when the rays of the setting sun had set long ago. The room was dark, for it was lighted now only by the embers of the burnt-out fire; and the electric bell was ringing steadily, as though the man outside the door had resolved to waken the seven sleepers.

Then Cosmo Waynflete was wide-awake again; and he knew where he was once more—not in Japan, not in Persia, not in Lisbon, not in

Sleepy Hollow, but here in New York, in his own room, before his own fire. He opened the door at once and admitted his friend, Paul Stuyvesant.

"It isn't dinner-time, is it?" he asked. "I'm not late, am I? The fact is, I've been asleep."

"It is so good of you to confess that," his friend answered, laughing; "although the length of time you kept me waiting and ringing might have led me to suspect it. No, you are not late and it is not dinner-time. I've come around to have another little chat with you before dinner, that's all."

"Take this chair, old man," said Cosmo, as he threw another hickory-stick on the fire. Then he lighted the gas and sat down by the side of his friend.

"This chair is comfortable, for a fact," Stuyvesant declared, stretching himself out luxuriously. "No wonder you went to sleep. What did you dream of?—strange places you had seen in your travels or the homely scenes of your native land?"

Waynflete looked at his friend for a moment without answering the question. He was startled as he recalled the extraordinary series of adventures which had fallen to his lot since he had fixed his gaze on the crystal ball. It seemed to him as though he had been whirled through space and through time.

"I suppose every man is always the hero of his own dreams," he began, doubtfully.

"Of course," his friend returned; "in sleep our natural and healthy egotism is absolutely unrestrained. It doesn't make any matter where the scene is laid or whether the play is a comedy or a tragedy, the dreamer has always the centre of the stage, with the calcium light turned full on him."

"That's just it," Waynflete went on; "this dream of mine makes me feel as if I were an actor, and as if I had been playing many parts, one after the other, in the swiftest succession. They are not familiar to me, and yet I confess to a vague feeling of unoriginality. It is as though I were a plagiarist of adventure—if that be a possible supposition. I have just gone through these startling situations myself, and yet I'm sure that they have all of them happened before—although, perhaps, not to any one man. Indeed, no one man could have had all these adventures of mine, because I see now that I have been whisked through the centuries and across the hemispheres with a suddenness possible only in dreams. Yet all my experiences seem somehow second-hand, and not really my own."

"Picked up here and there—like your bric-à-brac?" suggested Stuyvesant. "But what are these alluring adventures of yours that stretched through the ages and across the continents?"

Then, knowing how fond his friend was of solving mysteries and how proud he was of his skill in this art, Cosmo Waynflete narrated his dream as it has been set down in these pages.

When he had made an end, Paul Stuyvesant's first remark was: "I'm sorry I happened along just then and waked you up before you had time to get married."

His second remark followed half a minute later.

"I see how it was," he said; "you were sitting in this chair and looking at that crystal ball, which focussed the level rays of the setting sun, I suppose? Then it is plain enough—you hypnotized yourself!"

"I have heard that such a thing is possible," responded Cosmo.

"Possible?" Stuyvesant returned, "it is certain! But what is more curious is the new way in which you combined your self-hypnotism with crystal-gazing. You have heard of scrying, I suppose?"

"You mean the practice of looking into a drop of water or a crystal ball or anything of that sort," said Cosmo, "and of seeing things in it—of seeing people moving about?"

"That's just what I do mean," his friend returned. "And that's just what you have been doing. You fixed your gaze on the ball, and so hypnotized yourself; and then, in the intensity of your vision, you were able to see figures in the crystal—with one of which visualized emanations you immediately identified yourself. That's easy enough, I think. But I don't see what suggested to you your separate experiences. I recognize them, of course——"

"You recognize them?" cried Waynflete, in wonder.

"I can tell you where you borrowed every one of your adventures," Stuyvesant replied, "But what I'd like to know now is what suggested to you just those particular characters and situations, and not any of the many others also stored away in your subconsciousness."

So saying, he began to look about the room.

"My subconsciousness?" repeated Waynflete. "Have I ever been a samurai in my subconsciousness?"

Paul Stuyvesant looked at Cosmo Waynflete for nearly a minute without reply. Then all the answer he made was to say: "That's a queer dressing-gown you have on."

"It is time I took it off," said the other, as he twisted himself out of its clinging folds. "It is a beautiful specimen of weaving, isn't it? I call it the dream-gown of the Japanese ambassador, for although I bought it in a curiosity-shop in Nuremberg, it was once, I really believe, the slumber-robe of an Oriental envoy."

Stuyvesant took the silken garment from his friend's hand.

"Why did the Japanese ambassador sell you his dream-gown in a Nuremberg curiosity-shop?" he asked.

"He didn't," Waynflete explained. "I never saw the ambassador, and neither did the old German lady who kept the shop. She told me she bought it from a Japanese acrobat who was out of an engagement and desperately hard up. But she told me also that the acrobat had told her that the garment had belonged to an ambassador who had given it to him as a reward of his skill, and that he never would have parted with it if he had not been dead-broke."

Stuyvesant held the robe up to the light and inspected the embroidery on the skirt of it.

"Yes," he said, at last, "this would account for it, I suppose. This bit here was probably meant to suggest 'the well where the head was washed,'—see?"

"I see that those lines may be meant to represent the outline of a spring of water, but I don't see what that has to do with my dream," Waynflete answered.

"Don't you?" Stuyvesant returned. "Then I'll show you. You had on this silk garment embroidered here with an outline of the well in which was washed the head of Kotsuke no Suke, the man whom the Forty-Seven Ronins killed. You know the story?"

"I read it in Japan, but——" began Cosmo.

"You had that story stored away in your subconsciousness," interrupted his friend. "And when you hypnotized yourself by peering into the crystal ball, this embroidery it was which suggested to you to see yourself as the hero of the tale—Oishi Kuranosuke, the chief of the Forty-Seven Ronins, the faithful follower who avenged his master by pretending to be vicious and dissipated—just like Brutus and Lorenzaccio—until the enemy was off his guard and open to attack."

"I think I do recall the tale of the Forty-Seven Ronins, but only very vaguely," said the hero of the dream. "For all I know I may have had the adventure of Oishi Kuranosuke laid on the shelf somewhere in my subconsciousness, as you want me to believe. But how about my Persian dragon and my Iberian noblewoman?"

Paul Stuyvesant was examining the dream-gown of the Japanese ambassador with minute care. Suddenly he said, "Oh!" and then he looked up at Cosmo Waynflete and asked: "What are those buttons? They seem to be old coins."

"They are old coins," the other answered; "it was a fancy of mine to utilize them on that Japanese dressing-gown. They are all different, you see. The first is——"

"Persian, isn't it?" interrupted Stuyvesant.

"Yes," Waynflete explained, "it is a Persian daric. And the second is a Spanish peso made at Potosi under Philip II for use in America. And the third is a York shilling, one of the coins in circulation here in New York at the time of the Revolution—I got that one, in fact, from the farmer who ploughed it up in a field at Tarrytown, near Sunnyside."

"Then there are three of your adventures accounted for, Cosmo, and easily enough," Paul commented, with obvious satisfaction at his own explanation. "Just as the embroidery on the silk here suggested to you—after you had hypnotized yourself—that you were the chief of the Forty-Seven Ronins, so this first coin here in turn suggested to you that you were Rustem, the hero of the 'Epic of Kings.' You have read the 'Shah-Nameh'?"

"I remember Firdausi's poem after a fashion only," Cosmo answered. "Was not Rustem a Persian Hercules, so to speak?"

"That's it precisely," the other responded, "and he had seven labors to perform; and you dreamed the third of them, the slaying of the grisly dragon. For my own part, I think I should have preferred the fourth of them, the meeting with the lovely enchantress; but that's neither here nor there."

"It seems to me I do recollect something about that fight of Rustem and the strange beast. The faithful horse's name was Rakush, wasn't it?" asked Waynflete.

"If you can recollect the 'Shah-Nameh,'" Stuyvesant pursued, "no doubt you can recall also Beaumont and Fletcher's 'Custom of the Country'? That's where you got the midnight duel in Lisbon and the magnanimous mother, you know."

"No, I didn't know," the other declared.

"Well, you did, for all that," Paul went on. "The situation is taken from one in a drama of Calderon's, and it was much strengthened in the taking. You may not now remember having read the play, but the incident must have been familiar to you, or else your subconsciousness couldn't have yielded it up to you so readily at the suggestion of the Spanish coin, could it?"

"I did read a lot of Elizabethan drama in my senior year at college," admitted Cosmo, "and this piece of Beaumont and Fletcher's may have been one of those I read; but I totally fail to recall now what it was all about."

"You won't have the cheek to declare that you don't remember the 'Legend of Sleepy Hollow,' will you?" asked Stuyvesant. "Very obviously it was the adventure of Ichabod Crane and the Headless Horseman that the York shilling suggested to you."

"I'll admit that I do recollect Irving's story now," the other confessed.

"So the embroidery on the dream-gown gives the first of your strange situations; and the three others were suggested by the coins you have been using as buttons," said Paul Stuyvesant. "There is only one thing now that puzzles me: that is the country church and the noon wedding and the beautiful bride."

And with that he turned over the folds of the silken garment that hung over his arm.

Cosmo Waynflete hesitated a moment and a blush mantled his cheek. Then he looked his friend in the face and said: "I think I can account for my dreaming about her—I can account for that easily enough."

"So can I," said Paul Stuyvesant, as he held up the photograph of a lovely American girl that he had just found in the pocket of the dream-gown of the Japanese ambassador.

(1896.)

The Cremation of Sam McGee

By Robert W. Service

There are strange things done in the midnight sun

By the men who moil for gold;

The Arctic trails have their secret tales

That would make your blood run cold;

The Northern Lights have seen queer sights,

But the queerest they ever did see

Was that night on the marge of Lake Lebarge

I cremated Sam McGee.

Now Sam McGee was from Tennessee, where the cotton blooms and blows.

Why he left his home in the South to roam 'round the Pole, God only knows.

He was always cold, but the land of gold seemed to hold him like a spell;

Though he'd often say in his homely way that "he'd sooner live in hell."

On a Christmas Day we were mushing our way over the Dawson trail.

Talk of your cold! through the parka's fold it stabbed like a driven nail.

If our eyes we'd close, then the lashes froze till sometimes we couldn't see;

It wasn't much fun, but the only one to whimper was Sam McGee.

And that very night, as we lay packed tight in our robes beneath the snow,

And the dogs were fed, and the stars o'erhead were dancing heel and toe,

He turned to me, and "Cap," says he, "I'll cash in this trip, I guess;

And if I do, I'm asking that you won't refuse my last request."

Well, he seemed so low that I couldn't say no; then he says with a sort of moan:

"It's the cursèd cold, and it's got right hold till I'm chilled clean through to the bone.

Yet 'tain't being dead—it's my awful dread of the icy grave that pains;

So I want you to swear that, foul or fair, you'll cremate my last remains."

A pal's last need is a thing to heed, so I swore I would not fail;

And we started on at the streak of dawn; but God! he looked ghastly pale.

He crouched on the sleigh, and he raved all day of his home in Tennessee;

And before nightfall a corpse was all that was left of Sam McGee.

There wasn't a breath in that land of death, and I hurried, horror-driven,

With a corpse half hid that I couldn't get rid, because of a promise given;

It was lashed to the sleigh, and it seemed to say: "You may tax your brawn and brains,

But you promised true, and it's up to you to cremate those last remains."

Now a promise made is a debt unpaid, and the trail has its own stern code.

In the days to come, though my lips were dumb, in my heart how I cursed that load.

In the long, long night, by the lone firelight, while the huskies, round in a ring,

Howled out their woes to the homeless snows—O God! how I loathed the thing.

And every day that quiet clay seemed to heavy and heavier grow;

And on I went, though the dogs were spent and the grub was getting low;

The trail was bad, and I felt half mad, but I swore I would not give in;

And I'd often sing to the hateful thing, and it hearkened with a grin.

Till I came to the marge of Lake Lebarge, and a derelict there lay;

It was jammed in the ice, but I saw in a trice it was called the "Alice May."

And I looked at it, and I thought a bit, and I looked at my frozen chum;

Then "Here," said I, with a sudden cry, "is my cre-ma-tor-eum."

Some planks I tore from the cabin floor, and I lit the boiler fire;

Some coal I found that was lying around, and I heaped the fuel higher;

The flames just soared, and the furnace roared—such a blaze you seldom see;

And I burrowed a hole in the glowing coal, and I stuffed in Sam McGee.

Then I made a hike, for I didn't like to hear him sizzle so;

And the heavens scowled, and the huskies howled, and the wind began to blow.

It was icy cold, but the hot sweat rolled down my cheeks, and I don't know why;

And the greasy smoke in an inky cloak went streaking down the sky.

I do not know how long in the snow I wrestled with grisly fear;

But the stars came out and they danced about ere again I ventured near;

I was sick with dread, but I bravely said: "I'll just take a peep inside.

I guess he's cooked, and it's time I looked"; . . . then the door I opened wide.

And there sat Sam, looking cool and calm, in the heart of the furnace roar;

And he wore a smile you could see a mile, and he said: "Please close that door.

It's fine in here, but I greatly fear you'll let in the cold and storm—

Since I left Plumtree, down in Tennessee, it's the first time I've been warm."

There are strange things done in the midnight sun

By the men who moil for gold;

The Arctic trails have their secret tales

That would make your blood run cold;

The Northern Lights have seen queer sights,

But the queerest they ever did see

Was that night on the marge of Lake Lebarge

I cremated Sam McGee.

The Thing in the Forest

By Bernard Capes

INTO THE SNOW-LOCKED FORESTS OF UPPER HUNGARY STEAL WOLVES in winter; but there is a footfall worse than theirs to knock upon the heart of the lonely traveller.

One December evening Elspet, the young, newly-wedded wife of the woodman Stefan, came hurrying over the lower slopes of the White Mountains from the town where she had been all day marketing. She carried a basket with provisions on her arm; her plump cheeks were like a couple of cold apples; her breath spoke short, but more from nervousness than exhaustion. It was nearing dusk, and she was glad to see the little lonely church in the hollow below, the hub, as it were, of many radiating paths through the trees, one of which was the road to her own warm cottage yet a half-mile away.

She paused a moment at the foot of the slope, undecided about entering the little chill, silent building and making her plea for protection to the great battered stone image of Our Lady of Succour which stood within by the confessional box; but the stillness and the growing darkness decided her, and she went on. A spark of fire glowing through the presbytery window seemed to repel rather than attract her, and she was glad when the convolutions of the path hid it from her sight. Being new to the district, she had seen very little of Father Ruhl as yet, and somehow the penetrating knowledge and burning eyes of the pastor made her feel uncomfortable.

The soft drift, the lane of tall, motionless pines, stretched on in a quiet like death. Somewhere the sun, like a dead fire, had fallen into opalescent embers faintly luminous: they were enough only to touch the shadows with a ghastlier pallor. It was so still that the light crunch in the snow of the girl's own footfalls trod on her heart like a desecration.

Suddenly there was something near her that had not been before. It had come like a shadow, without more sound or warning. It was here—there,—behind her. She turned, in mortal panic, and saw a wolf. With a strangled cry and trembling limbs she strove to hurry on her way; and always she knew, though there was no whisper of pursuit, that the gliding shadow followed in her wake. Desperate in her terror, she stopped once more and faced it.

A wolf!—was it a wolf? O who could doubt it! Yet the wild expression in those famished eyes, so lost, so pitiful, so mingled of insatiable hunger and human need! Condemned, for its unspeakable sins, to take this form with sunset, and so howl and snuffle about the doors of men until the blessed day released it. A werewolf—not a wolf.

That terrific realisation of the truth smote the girl as with a knife out of darkness: for an instant she came near fainting. And then a low moan broke into her heart and flooded it with pity. So lost, so infinitely hopeless. And so pitiful—yes, in spite of all, so pitiful. It had sinned, beyond any sinning that her innocence knew or her experience could gauge; but she was a woman, very blest, very happy, in her store of comforts and her surety of love. She knew that it was forbidden to succour these damned and nameless outcasts, to help or sympathise with them in any way. But—

There was good store of meat in her basket, and who need ever know or tell? With shaking hands she found and threw a sop to the desolate brute—then, turning, sped upon her way.

But at home her secret sin stood up before her, and, interposing between her husband and herself, threw its shadow upon both their faces. What had she dared—what done? By her own act forfeited her birthright of innocence; by her own act placed herself in the power of the evil to which she had ministered. All that night she lay in shame and horror, and all the next day, until Stefan had come about his dinner and gone again, she moved in a dumb agony. Then, driven unendurably by the memory of his troubled, bewildered face, as twilight threatened she put on her cloak and went down to the little church in the hollow to confess her sin.

"Mother, forgive, and save me," she whispered, as she passed the statue.

After ringing the bell for the confessor, she had not knelt long at the confessional box in the dim chapel, cold and empty as a waiting vault, when the chancel rail clicked, and the footsteps of Father Ruhl were heard rustling over the stones. He came, he took his seat behind the grating; and, with many sighs and falterings, Elspet avowed her guilt. And as, with bowed head, she ended, a strange sound answered her—it was like a little laugh, and yet not so much like a laugh as a snarl. With a shock as of death she raised her face. It was Father Ruhl who sat there—and yet it was not Father Ruhl. In that time of twilight his face was already changing, narrowing, becoming wolfish—the eyes rounded and the jaw slavered. She gasped, and shrunk back; and at that, barking and snapping at the grating, with a wicked look he dropped—and she heard him coming. Sheer horror lent her wings. With a scream she sprang to her feet and fled. Her cloak caught in something—there was a wrench and crash and, like a flood, oblivion overswept her.

It was the old deaf and near senile sacristan who found them lying there, the woman unhurt but insensible, the priest crushed out of life by the fall of the ancient statue, long tottering to its collapse.

She recovered, for her part: for his, no one knows where he lies buried. But there were dark stories of a baying pack that night, and of an empty, bloodstained pavement when they came to seek it for the body.